INTO THE NIGHT

*Also by Suzanne Brockmann
in Large Print:*

The Admiral's Bride
Prince Joe
The Defiant Hero
Over the Edge

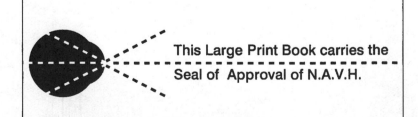

This Large Print Book carries the
Seal of Approval of N.A.V.H.

INTO THE NIGHT

SUZANNE BROCKMANN

Thorndike Press • Waterville, Maine

Published in 2003 by arrangement with The Ballantine Publishing Group, a division of Random House, Inc.

Thorndike Press Large Print Core Series.

The tree indicium is a trademark of Thorndike Press.

The text of this Large Print edition is unabridged.
Other aspects of the book may vary from the original edition.

Set in 16 pt. Plantin by Christina S. Huff.

Printed in the United States on permanent paper.

Library of Congress Cataloging-in-Publication Data

Brockmann, Suzanne.
    Into the night / Suzanne Brockmann.
        p. cm.
    ISBN 0-7862-5149-2 (lg. print : hc : alk. paper)
        1. United States. Navy. SEALs — Fiction.   2. Presidents —
United States — Fiction.   3. Terrorism — Prevention —
Fiction.   4. Presidents — Staff — Fiction.   5. California —
Fiction.   6. Large type books.   I. Title.
PS3552.R61455I58 2003
    813′.54—dc21   2002043023

For the brave men and women who fought for freedom during the Second World War, and for the brave men and women in the U.S. Armed Forces who continue that fight today. My most sincere and humble thanks. Let freedom ring!

ACKNOWLEDGMENTS

Thank you to Kathy Lague, Goddess of Knowledge, for emergency research help. Your assistance was hugely appreciated.

Thanks to my first draft readers: Deede Bergeron, Lee Brockmann, Patricia MacMahon, and Joan Kuhlman, all of whom bravely volunteered to throw themselves on the first draft of this book and read it (sometimes even twice!) from beginning to end in a very short amount of time.

Warmest thanks to my editor, Shauna Summers, and to my agents, Steve Axelrod and Damaris Rowland. Without you, this book would not have been possible.

And thanks, of course, always and forever, to Ed, who gets to live through and clean up after the birth of each book. I love you!

Any mistakes I've made or liberties I've taken are completely my own.

PROLOGUE

Afghanistan
Operation Enduring Freedom

Lieutenant junior grade Michael Muldoon held up his hand and signaled for his squad to stop.

Dark took on an entirely new meaning on a moonless night in a desolate country too poor and too war-torn for electricity. He sensed more than saw his men behind him, hugging the cold, rocky ground as intimately as he was.

He moved his hand again. *Listen.*

The sky overhead was worthy of a beach blanket and a bottle of wine, the Milky Way thick with the billions of stars he didn't have a prayer of seeing from his city apartment a half a world away.

It was breathtakingly beautiful, but Muldoon had no time to give it more than a cursory glance as he focused all of his attention on the distant hum.

Of a generator.

Hoo-yah.

It was always reassuring to know that they were, in fact, in the right place.

The coordinates marking the main entrance of the cave on their map were correct — a map that was one of the somewhat dubious bonuses that came from the United States having helped build these allegedly indestructible compounds many years and several different political regimes ago. Not only did the SEALs have maps and specifications, but those maps were proving to be accurate.

His men knew what they had to do, and when Muldoon gave the signal they went silently to work.

Their job tonight was to verify that the two known entrances to this cave were still where the map said they'd be — to verify coordinates for the "bunker buster" missiles that were scheduled to be launched from a Navy sub in less than two hours. The SEALs were to add additional explosives to various vulnerable points to give those bombs even bigger teeth.

The mission was to seal this cave so that no one could get out, but more importantly so that no one could get in.

Cosmo Richter had gotten right down to the bottom line during their briefing when he'd asked in his no-frills, telegram manner of speech, "Osama inside?"

They'd all looked up from the maps. It was the question of the hour.

Muldoon hated to disappoint them, but his answer had been no. Not according to NavIntel. However, this cave was being held by Taliban fighters with al-Qaeda ties. And the U.S. goal was to cross this compound off the list of potential safe havens bin Laden could come to to hide.

It was an important mission.

It just wasn't the one they particularly wanted.

He knew what his men were feeling. Each and every one of them — himself included — wanted to be part of the op that took down the terrorist leader. They all wanted to go *mano a mano* with the man, like some hokey Hollywood movie, and blow that bastard off the face of the earth.

But the real world wasn't anything like Hollywood. Victory wasn't won by being Rambo. It came from being a team player.

So tonight they'd tuck their anger back inside and follow their orders. They'd help clean up this little piece of enemy-held territory. They'd do their job, and they'd do it well. And when the word came down that bin Laden was no longer a threat to the United States, they would get together and have a beer and silently acknowledge the part they'd played in his demise. No discussions, no bragging, no news broadcasts, and most importantly, no feelings of inadequacy because none of them was the one who pulled the trigger.

Muldoon used infrared glasses to watch the two heat blobs that were the al-Qaeda guards as Gillman and Cosmo rigged enough explosives to take off the top of the mountain. There was no doubt in his mind that, before the sun rose, this cave was going to be history.

The only slightly snarky moment came when one of the guards — the bigger one, about Muldoon's own height and weight — left his post to take a leak, heading right for where Cosmo was hidden.

Their orders tonight included a warning not to let the enemy know that they were on the ground. The fact that they were going after this specific target would be concealed by carpet bombing in the area scheduled to begin at 0353.

The intent was to make it look as if the cave had been taken out by a couple of lucky hits from a random air strike, rather than as a result of Spec Op ground forces. The terrorists didn't have any patrols venturing far outside of their cave entrances, and the U.S. commanders didn't want to give them a reason to start.

Muldoon's team had to be covert.

Right now that guard was answering the call of nature literally feet from Cosmo's hiding place.

But it was Cosmo, the King of Invisible, so Muldoon didn't worry. He just watched as the SEAL blended even more completely into the night. The guard could've peed right on his head, and Cosmo wouldn't have moved an inch.

Finally, after an interminable amount of time — what had that guy been drinking? — the guard went back to his post and to stomping his feet to keep them warm.

The rest of the op went like a dream. The second entrance was just where they'd expected it to be. Natural fissures and cracks used for venting the cave were marked. No other entrances were found.

This was going to work. They were going to help put this cave permanently out of business.

At just before 0300, with nothing left to do save get their butts back down the mountain — Wild-Card approached.

Even in silence, the chief had a ferocity that made Muldoon want to smile. He was glad — not for the first time that night and probably not for the last — that he'd chosen WildCard Karmody for this op.

But one look at WildCard's face, and he knew there was trouble.

Problem? he signaled.

WildCard responded with an obscene gesture that more than conveyed his opinion that not only was this a problem, it was a big problem.

Muldoon jerked his head, and the chief followed him back away from the guards.

WildCard cut to the chase. "Silverman reports heavy movement coming up the trail. About thirty tangos. ETA at the cave about forty minutes."

"Okay." That was not anywhere near the complete reaming Muldoon had imagined. "We'll take a different route down." It would take a little longer because these hills were littered with land mines, but it was certainly doable in the time they had left.

"We could," WildCard agreed. "But they've got a prisoner — looks like that stupidass French reporter, that photojournalist who went missing from Kandahar last night."

Oh, man, *that* hurt. Dream op to nightmare, in two small words. *Prisoner* and *reporter*. Muldoon gritted his teeth and considered his options.

"Holy fuck," WildCard said. "When I tell you that a stupidass French photog is going to turn this perfect op into a total clusterfuck, what you say, sir, is *Oh, holy fuck.* If this isn't the time to use your full adult vocabulary, Lieutenant, I honestly don't know what is."

"Not helping," Muldoon said shortly.

"The guy's an asshole for putting himself in harm's way in the first place," WildCard pointed out.

11

Thirty terrorists, eight SEALs. The odds were in their favor. They could set up an ambush and take them out, no sweat. The problem would be keeping the prisoner alive while the bullets flew.

Oh, yeah, and maintaining their covert status.

Covert meant K-Bar knives instead of assault weapons.

But it was hard to be effective in a group ambush when using only knives. Of course, they could take the terrorists out quietly, one at a time, but at some point one of them would notice their forces dwindling and shots would be fired.

"Actually, the guy's just an asshole, period. Look at what he chooses to do for a living." WildCard believed there was a separate level of hell reserved especially for reporters and news photographers. His wife was Savannah von Hopf, a fact that never failed to amuse Muldoon, particularly when the foulmouthed chief went on a rant. Along with the Kennedys and the Rockefellers, the von Hopfs were the closest thing America had to royalty. They were frequently targeted by paparazzi, hence the Card's strong negative opinion of the press.

"What we should do," WildCard continued, "is go invisible while they pass us on the trail. Our mission is not to rescue some dickhead reporter and risk letting the entire al-Qaeda network know we were out here tonight. Am I right?"

He was right. And yet . . .

"We let them get into that cave, that reporter's not coming out." Muldoon told his chief the obvious. "Not ever."

WildCard was silent then, no doubt thinking

what a hideous way that would be to die, even for a reporter. Buried alive with a mob of angry terrorists . . .

"Get me Jenk," Muldoon ordered. Mark Jenkins had the radio. It was time to break silence and talk to some of the pilots of those F-18s that were constantly patrolling at high altitudes with full payloads. "Get Izzy and Cosmo. Send Gillman and Lopez down the trail. I want to know the location of every rock, every outcropping, and particularly every open area. There was one spot we passed coming up where there wasn't much cover, where the trail opened up. Find out how far the tangos are from there."

"Aye, aye, sir." WildCard didn't have far to go before dispensing Muldoon's orders, sending Lopez to fetch Jenk. He was back in a matter of seconds, with Izzy and Cosmo in tow. "I assume this means you have a plan to fuck these fuckers first."

That was one way of putting it. "Yeah."

"Knew you would, sir," Cosmo said.

"Do we have enough explosives left to rig something that'll sound like a land mine going off?" Muldoon asked.

"Piece of cake." WildCard was absolute.

"Do it, Chief." Muldoon turned to Cosmo and Izzy. "I need some clothes. One of those guards was about my size."

"About my size, too," Izzy said. "Back in California, the senior chief ordered me to remind you, with utmost respect, to delegate, Lieutenant. So I'm reminding you, sir. With utmost —"

"Yeah, and how's your French?" Muldoon

13

asked, already knowing the answer. Izzy spoke fluent street Spanish. He knew only enough French to order a meal, provided the restaurant had big golden arches. "Use your utmost respect to get me the clothes, Zanella. I'll be down the trail."

0329.

Muldoon could hear the terrorists approaching, moving slowly but steadily up toward the cave. They were quiet, not talking at all as they climbed through the night, but he still could hear the crunch of the cold earth beneath all those feet.

Silverman had told him that the prisoner — the French journalist — was wearing a burqa, the traditional Afghan woman's robe and hooded veil.

It was an effective means of transporting captives since it concealed them completely from public view.

Jenk was crouched beside him, plugged into the radio. He gave Muldoon an affirmative, then held two fingers to his watch. The first wave of bombs from the F-18s would hit their targets, with the utmost precision, in two minutes.

Seconds ticked by as the tangos slowly got closer, as somewhere overhead those smart bombs were cutting their way through the night sky. Muldoon breathed with the knowledge that the coordinates they'd given the Navy pilots were accurate. Those bombs were going to hit so close the SEALs were going to feel the ground shake and be able to warm their fingers from the heat.

But if those coordinates were off . . .

14

Yes, of course there was a chance of human error. Yes, it was possible that the air strike Muldoon had ordered Jenk to call in would land directly on top of his team.

But until that happened, he wasn't going to waste his time worrying about it.

And then there they were, rounding the corner and coming into view.

Their point men, three of them, came first, leading the way and checking for booby traps — much in the same way the SEALs had come up the trail mere hours earlier.

They weren't too far ahead of the main group, which was a motley-looking, straggling bunch. They were walking wounded, retreating to safety from the intense pockets of fighting in Kandahar. Some weren't even walking. There were at least four stretchers being carried, one of which held a boy who couldn't have been more than thirteen years old.

Who, like the rest of them, was carrying a personal arsenal of weapons and ammunition.

These were terrorists. All of them. They weren't poor little tired, hungry, and forlorn terrorists, as much as they currently looked the part. They were terrorists, plain and simple. They were the enemy, and a deadly enemy — period, the end.

They had pledged to die defending Osama bin Laden. They trained their boys to hate and kill, and enslaved their girls by forbidding their education. They supported a killer who fought his war against unarmed men, against women and children.

In theory, thirty terrorists weren't a whole heck

of a lot of terrorists. But when they were all crowding one small trail, thirty was plenty.

Muldoon searched for a burqa-clad figure — the reporter — and found him shuffling along in the center of the group, surrounded by dozens of men.

Figures he'd be there. If Muldoon were transporting a prisoner, he'd keep him secured and surrounded by his men, too.

The good news was that the reporter was slight of stature. He'd be easy to handle in the event he wasn't into following orders spoken in rusty French.

As Muldoon watched, he saw that the reporter was guarded in particular by two men, both of whom spent more time eyeing each other mistrustfully than watching their prisoner. And that was more good news.

Jenk, who was crouched beside him, silently tapped his watch.

Here it came. Any second now. Either he'd killed his men or . . .

Boom!

They were all still alive, thank you, God. The first bomb had hit exactly where Muldoon had asked for it to hit, just to the west of the trail. It was followed immediately by a second in the same vicinity, and he allowed himself to exhale.

As for the tangos, so much for maintaining silence. All thirty began talking at once as they picked themselves up and dusted themselves off.

Muldoon watched the crowd, trying to pick out the group's leader.

Was it ZZ Top over there, with the beard down to his waist? Or was it Young and Angry, with the

16

big arm gestures and the long coat that billowed as he walked? He must've practiced in front of a mirror for hours to get it to do that.

With only a few short months of Pashtu and Dari under his belt — courtesy of Potential Enemy Languages 101, a required class for all SEALs heading into the area — Muldoon could pick out only a word here and there in the din. Still, it was obvious from the gestures and body language that ZZ wanted to take cover, while Angry wanted to push on to the cave at a stepped-up pace.

Jenk tapped his watch again, signaling thirty seconds. Oh, good. Time to find out if this next set of coordinates was as accurate as the first.

Don't. Think. About. That. He knew better than to waste his time worrying about things that were out of his control.

The trail opened up into a clearing just ahead, and for one last time, Muldoon mentally traced the route he was going to take as he focused his attention on the burqa-clad reporter.

The two guards, Itchy and Scratchy, had taken different sides in the run-or-hide debate.

As Muldoon watched, Itchy gestured almost in unison with Angry, toward the mountains to the west, where the first two bombs had fallen. He could imagine what they were saying. "What, are you nuts? Not only are they shelling to the west, but it's a total minefield out there. We should head for the cave. We'll be safer there."

Scratchy and ZZ both gestured to the east. "We'll never make it that far. We should go this way. We can take cover in the valleys and —"

Boom!

17

The third bomb — special ordered by Muldoon — hit smack where he'd wanted it to, off to the east, followed by another slightly to the south.

Everyone dropped to the ground again, like some kind of funky dance.

And, as Muldoon had hoped, the decision and gestures became unanimous. They'd head to the safety of the cave. At a dead run. Last one in was a rotten egg.

Two more bombs hit on either side of the trail. Yes, that's right. This was a full-scale attack. Run, you terrorist scum. Run for your lives.

But they were bottlenecked until they reached that clearing ahead. They pushed and jostled and jockeyed for position, no love lost between ZZ's and Angry's men. It was just the kind of ugly chaos he'd been hoping for.

With one last nod at Jenk, Muldoon slipped out from his hiding place and into the severely distracted crowd.

He had his weapon held at ready as he kept the woolen scarf wrapped securely around most of his lower face. It wasn't a good idea to go for a walk in a crowd of Taliban-supporting terrorists with a clean-shaven chin, but there weren't a whole lot of options here.

Muldoon shouldered his way through the crowd toward the prisoner, who was having a hard time keeping up while he had what virtually amounted to a bag over his head. Itchy and Scratchy had begun pushing the guy, united at last in their attempt to make him move faster. It was inevitable, but still, the timing was perfect — the reporter tripped over his long robe and fell smack on his

18

burqa-covered face right at Muldoon's feet.

It was a gift from heaven, and he didn't hesitate. He hoisted the squirming reporter up and over his shoulder as Itchy and Scratchy shouted at him.

"Don't fight me," he muttered in French into the burqa's heavy folds. "I'm here to help you."

The struggling didn't stop, so Muldoon just gripped the reporter more tightly and focused on the shouting. The two guards might have been speaking a dialect he didn't know, or maybe they were simply talking too fast. Either way, he didn't catch a single word.

When in doubt, shout back. And shout louder.

"Go," he screamed at them in Pashtu. "Run. Now!"

But it wasn't until he started to run, too, that the shouters turned the volume down a notch. Although Scratchy, to his right, had a glare that was filled with suspicion.

The good news was that the Frenchman couldn't have weighed more than 120 pounds. It would have been laughably easy to carry him if he weren't trying his best to get away. Something solid kept jamming painfully into Muldoon's back, just hard enough to keep him thoroughly pissed off. It seemed improbable that the terrorists had let this guy keep his camera, but he couldn't figure out what else it might be.

"Stop," he finally ordered in French. The promise of help hadn't worked, so he tried the alternative. "Stop fighting, or I'll kill you right now."

The reporter's immediate surrender was a relief, especially since the scarf around Muldoon's very American chin was starting to come undone.

He tightened it back up and then there he was, in the clearing that he'd noticed when his team had first crept up the trail. But he was there earlier than he'd anticipated. And the next bomb — the most important one of them all; please God, don't let it kill his men — hadn't yet struck its target.

So he tripped and went down onto one knee, much harder than he'd intended. He landed right on a rock, right on what must've been his knee's freaking funny bone. Oh, shit, it hurt like hell, with waves of pain that rolled through him, really ringing his chimes. Still, it did the trick of slowing him down.

The reporter started struggling again, making it that much harder for him to get back to his feet.

Scratchy was tugging at him, shouting again. Itchy was long gone.

Muldoon didn't need to make a show of pulling himself painfully up and then —

Ka-boom!

It was the bomb that he'd been waiting for, and it hit so close the concussion knocked him back on his butt. And probably onto that same freaking rock that his knee had connected with. *Son* of a *bitch.*

It rained dust and debris and, still clutching the reporter, he scrambled to his feet and ran for cover.

Due west.

Scratchy was shouting yet again, and this time Muldoon caught the words he'd hoped to hear.

Land mines.

But he didn't slow as another bomb hit, again shaking the ground. He vaulted over an outcropping of rocks — and almost directly into Cosmo's and Silverman's open arms.

They half carried, half dragged both him and the reporter to safety behind yet another ridge of rock, while somewhere nearby WildCard thumbed a switch.

Boom!

It sounded convincingly like a weight-triggered land mine, but it was quickly drowned out by the din of more bombs falling.

Scratchy apparently had some amount of common sense, because he raced after the last of his al-Qaeda buddies.

There was no time for Muldoon's knee to still hurt like hell, but it did. God, it felt like it was the size of a watermelon, like it was starting to swell. But that was absurd. A banged funny bone didn't swell. You hit it, you writhe with pain and you scream for two or three minutes, and then life goes on. But try as he might, he couldn't seem to get past the writhing part.

He pulled himself to his feet, ridding himself of the extra clothes, refusing to consider the possibility that he'd actually injured himself in that fake fall. So what if it hurt? So what if it swelled? He was a SEAL. He'd worked through pain plenty of times before.

"Get that thing off of him," he ordered Silverman, who was untying the burqa-covered reporter.

"Sir!" It was Jenk, with the radio. "It's 0337, and the F-18s are still on course. The helo's picking us up four clicks down the trail, but we've got to hustle to get there before the real bombs start falling."

"Let's go," Muldoon ordered.

"Whoa," Silverman said. "The French guy's a girl."

"Americans," the reporter spat in heavily accented English. She was indeed a woman. "I should have known."

"Are you all right, ma'am?" Muldoon asked her.

Her hair was dyed a ridiculously fake-looking shade of black, and the glare she gave him was venomous. "Do you know how long it took me to arrange an interview with Abdul Mullah Zeeshan? And you have to go and rescue me. Thanks a lot, Captain, but no thanks. I'm going to that cave."

It would have been funny, the way she started marching back toward the trail, if only they hadn't been on such a tight deadline. If only his knee hadn't felt as if it were about to explode, and the only thing keeping it in one piece was his now too tight pants. If only it wasn't hurting so much that a river of cold sweat poured down his back with every other step he took.

"In about fifteen minutes, that cave is going to be destroyed," Muldoon told the young woman.

"Bullshit," she countered, with the kind of withering glance that only European women could deliver with such authority. "Your own government has issued statements admitting that these caves are bombproof."

"They were lying," he said. "It's called misinformation. They wanted Osama to feel nice and safe right where he was."

She said something in French filled with accusations, and turned and ran. Up the trail. Toward the cave.

22

And wasn't *that* just what he needed?

She was small and fast, but Muldoon had her tackled in fewer than five steps. His knee was on fire, but he managed to land on his left side, keeping his leg from connecting with the ground as he took her down. It hurt, but it was nothing like it could've been — until, as she flailed harder, trying to get free, she managed to kick him.

Whammo.

Right in the knee.

"Shit!" It was remarkable. Part of him watched from above, disassociated and completely dispassionate, as he damn near retched from the pain.

Don't let her get away!

He held her tightly, even managing to cover her as one of the last of the bombs that he'd ordered exploded, spraying them with more dirt. She was screaming about something, but he couldn't understand. She might as well have been speaking Martian. All he could do was cover her mouth, hope she didn't bite him too hard, and hang the hell on.

And then WildCard was there, thank you, glorious God, keeping the reporter from sprinting farther up the mountainside.

"Gag and carry her if you have to." Muldoon managed to form words into a direct order to the chief.

"I've got her, sir."

"Breathe," Izzy told him. "Just breathe and you'll be all right, Lieutenant. I promise, it'll get better soon."

Zanella thought he'd gotten whacked in the balls. Muldoon had to laugh. If only . . .

"You okay, sir?" Lopez hovered above him anxiously.

"Yes." Muldoon pushed himself up onto his elbows, up so that he was sitting, up all the way to his feet. *Shit, shit, shit, shit.* "Yes, I am." He said it again, mostly to convince himself that it was true.

"Sir," Jenk said. Tick tock.

"Let's run," Muldoon ordered them, ordered himself. "Come on, let's move out of here. *Now.*"

He could do this. Down the trail, one step at a time. Eventually he'd reach the helo and someone would give him some ice and the pain would start to recede.

"Can you really run, Mike?" WildCard was back beside him then, slowing to Muldoon's pace. It was probably the first time in his life he'd lowered his voice to be discreet.

"Yes." Muldoon didn't want to talk, not to WildCard, not to anyone. He needed all of his energy focused on moving forward. But he was in command. He couldn't just disappear. "Where's —"

"I passed her off to Cosmo," the chief told him, anticipating his question. "I thought maybe after she realizes we really did save her life, she'll be eternally grateful and he'll finally get laid."

Muldoon had to laugh. "You're a good chief."

"You bet your ass I am. I take care of my men." He looped Muldoon's arm around his shoulders. "It's the right leg, right, sir?"

"I'm okay." Muldoon wanted to pull away, but the truth was that putting some of his weight onto WildCard let him move faster. And the faster he

24

could move, the faster his team would get to safety. A SEAL team was only as fast as its slowest member — which right now was him. Which pissed him off, royally.

"You're not okay. You said *shit*," WildCard pointed out. "Nearly two years in Team Sixteen, and you finally said a four-letter word. In fact, I think it was 'shit, shit, shit, shit.' A quadruple. So what is it? Ankle?"

"Knee."

"Twist it?"

"No. I don't know. I landed on it, and . . . I'll be fine."

"Fucking hurts like a bitch, huh?"

"I'm okay," Muldoon said again. "Let's kick it faster."

"Aye, aye, sir."

WildCard somehow knew to be silent then. And the night became a blur of bombs still falling, of Jenk's reports every thirty seconds of how much time they had left, of his and the chief's ragged breathing, of red-hot, searing pain.

He heard the helo before he saw it, and then there it was — one of the most beautiful sights he'd ever seen.

Muldoon counted heads as his men climbed aboard, then the pilot swooped up and into the sky and got them the hell out of there.

The pain caught up with him as Lopez cut open his pants to look at the watermelon that had once been his knee. He puked quietly into one of the helo crewmember's helmets until, much to his intense embarrassment, his world tunneled, and he fainted.

He woke up groggy and disoriented as the helo landed. WildCard was there, and Muldoon grabbed his sleeve.

"Everyone okay?"

"Yes, sir. We're safely back on the carrier, Lieutenant. Mission accomplished."

"Good." His head felt so heavy, but his knee didn't hurt anymore, thank goodness. He tried to sit up, but WildCard and then Lopez was there, holding him down.

"Hey, hey, Mikey, where do you think you're going, man?"

"I'm okay," Muldoon said.

"He's fucking trying to walk off the helo," WildCard said over his head to Lopez.

"Sir, I don't know for sure," Jay Lopez told him, "not until we get you into X ray, but I think you probably fractured your patella."

"Fractured . . . what?"

"Remember the time Captain Muldoon ran down a mountain in Afghanistan with a broken kneecap?" WildCard said.

His words didn't make sense. "Meant to tell that reporter — I'm not a captain."

"Lieutenant, I gave you something for the pain," Lopez said, speaking slowly and clearly, "because you broke your kneecap."

"And then ran a few miles," WildCard added.

No way.

"But I'm okay," Muldoon said as the ship's hospital corpsmen carried his stretcher off the Seahawk. There were intravenous tubes attached to the back of his hand. It was surreal.

"No, really, you guys, I'm okay."

"That you are, Lieutenant," WildCard said.

His men watched as he was carried past. As usual, Cosmo said it best, giving him the Navy SEAL equivalent of a full salute. "Hoo-yah, sir. Glad you're on our side."

ONE

Months later

In the space of forty-five minutes, White House public relations assistant Joan DaCosta had been demoted from an admiral all the way to a lieutenant, junior grade.

She tried not to take it personally, or as a quantitative measure of her perceived importance here on the base, but rather as a crash course in U.S. Navy rankings.

Interestingly, not only did the face time get shorter and shorter with each step she was pushed down the chain of command, but the men inside the gleaming white uniforms got younger and more handsome.

Not that the admiral wasn't worthy of his own page in a hunk-of-the month calendar with his thick salt-and-pepper hair and that solid mix of both laughter and worry lines around his eyes. Since he was the Commander of Naval Special Warfare Command — or CDRNAVSPECWARCOM in Navyspeak — Joan would have been concerned if he *hadn't* had a worry line or two.

He'd greeted her upon her arrival in Coronado, and she'd instantly relaxed. She'd met Admiral Morton "Call me Chip" Crowley several times before on her own turf, back in Washington, D.C. He was that rare type of person who actually listened while others spoke.

But her sigh of relief proved to be a little premature when Crowley gently and almost apologetically passed her off to Rear Admiral Larry Tucker, the base commander.

Tucker was a bona fide dumbass, and she knew it even before he opened his mouth. In her job, she'd met enough self-important dumbasses to accurately ID them at first glance. And Tucker, with his too-handsome face and his impeccably combed hair — each strand inventoried and strategically placed to hide the fact that it was thinning — was a textbook case.

He was also a slimeball. He held her hand much too long after their handshake, his gaze lingering on her breasts, with a smile that said, "We both know you want me, because I am, after all, Mr. Wonderful."

Ick. He was wearing a wedding ring, which was a great big double ick.

Joan wanted to wash her hand as he bombastically reassured her that he would personally take charge of security on the base for the President and his daughter's upcoming visit.

She didn't know whether to be ecstatic or horrified at that news. Did it mean Tucker would be too busy Being Important to deal with the day-to-day details, i.e., all those little things on her agenda? Or did it mean that he'd be getting out his Krazy Glue and permanently bonding himself to her side?

The glue stayed in his desk, thank God. And she was far too relieved to be insulted when Tucker clearly got a rush of superiority as he lobbed her in the direction of one significantly lower ranking Lieutenant Commander Tom Paoletti, who was merely the commanding officer of SEAL Team Sixteen.

Merely.

Team Sixteen was the group of SEALs the President had specifically requested meeting during his upcoming visit. Team Sixteen was the group of SEALs with the incredible record of outstanding bravery and efficiency and ingenuity and stamina — all those things that made a huge difference when fighting a war against terrorism.

The rear admiral went off to be superior somewhere else as Paoletti ushered Joan into his office with a brief handshake.

And, oh my God. Wasn't he delicious? He was a Man, with a capital M and no hint of smarm about him. The broad chest, the jawline, the glint of intelligence in his hazel eyes . . .

Joan managed to keep herself from checking out his butt in those cute, pristine white uniform pants they all wore. She'd hated it when Tucker had done it to her, and she was determined not to disrespect Paoletti in the exact same way.

But, oh dearie, dearie me.

The commanding officer of Team Sixteen was about her age, maybe a few years older. His hair — or lack of it — was doing that Bruce Willis thing, and he took it just like Bruce. Like a real man, he was just going to let it disappear without a fuss. It so obviously didn't matter to him. And why should it? With a body like his . . .

She forced herself to focus on his face. On his hands. No wedding ring.

Stop it, Joan!

He was talking in a smoky voice about how honored the team was to be chosen to receive a presidential citation. "I understand the President's wish to visit the men on the base here in Coronado. And my team and I, of course, will be willing to give him a complete tour, if he should, in fact, decide to come —"

Joan cut him off. "Excuse me, Commander, I guess you haven't heard, but the visit is on the official schedule, and has been for quite some time. As far as I know, President Bryant will be here only for the morning, to present the citation and observe a demonstration, but his daughter will be arriving in a few days. And she'll definitely be taking a tour."

The muscle jumped in his jaw as he looked at his watch. He was not a happy camper. Joan wasn't sure why, although she suspected she knew. President Bryant's daughter Brooke, from his first marriage, was known throughout the world as "the wild child" despite the fact that she was pushing forty.

It was Joan's job to provide public relations opportunities in which Brooke would be unable to embarrass either herself or her father as she "helped" with his reelection campaign.

Brooke Bryant was actually quite a nice person. But she'd had terrible luck as far as news photographers went. Whenever she made a mistake, someone had always been there to record it for posterity and throw it onto the front page of *USA Today.*

And okay, admittedly Brooke had made her share of mistakes. She was notorious for falling in love with total shitheads and then acting stupid after finding out just how much of a shithead her latest boyfriend truly was. And since the shithead index in Washington, D.C., was pretty high, she'd had plenty of opportunities to expand her resume of mistakes.

Lieutenant Commander Paoletti was probably imagining the embarrassment of having pictures of Brooke falling off some Navy pier plastered on the front page of every major news publication and all over the Internet.

"This is something we'll need more time to discuss," Paoletti told her. "I'm really sorry, I wish I could talk right now, but I have another meeting I have to get to. I've made arrangements for you to tour the base this afternoon — in about ten minutes, actually, if that's okay with you."

"That's fine."

"We'll connect later," he told her. "If not today, then tomorrow or the next day. I'm going to leave you now in the very capable hands of Lieutenant Casper Jacquette, my XO."

"I'm free for dinner." Joan followed the commander out of his office. *Connect* was such an interesting word choice for him to have used. She was a firm believer in the "you cannot win if you do not play" adage, and she'd always had a real thing for Bruce Willis. "If that's convenient."

"Oh," he said, scratching his chin. "No. Thank you. Tonight's not good for me. I've already got plans to meet my fiancée."

Aha. Information received. And so gracefully and

painlessly delivered, too. "Completely understood." Joan smiled to make sure he understood,
too, so that there'd be no awkwardness or embarrassment. "You can't blame me for trying, Commander."

"Thank you," he said easily. "My ego thanks
you, too." His smile was a killer. Whoever this
fiancée was, she was one lucky babe. And probably
in a real rush to get a wedding band on Paoletti's
ring finger. "You're welcome to join us. I'm sure
Kelly wouldn't mind."

"Unless it's really urgent that we talk tonight,
I'll pass," Joan told him. "I'm still on D.C. time. I
should really use this evening to de–jet lag." She
was going to be in town for about four weeks,
taking a vacation after Brooke's visit. Normally
she'd just try to stay on East Coast time, but if
she spent anything more than a few days out of
her usual time zone, her body naturally adjusted.
She might as well try to get it over with all at
once.

"Maybe we can all do lunch later this week," he
said. "I happen to know that Kelly really would
like to meet you. *The West Wing* is her favorite TV
show."

Joan laughed. "Tell her that working there is
great, but not as great as it would be if Josh Lyman
really were in the next office over."

Commander Paoletti laughed, too, as he led her
into another room. He had a terrific laugh. What a
shame. But no real surprise. The smart, handsome, honorable, gracious, nice ones were always
already taken.

It was just as well. The dead last thing she

needed was to get involved with a Navy SEAL that she was working with. Talk about idiotic choices.

No, even if there were no fiancée, Tom Paoletti and his liquid eyes and sexy laugh and fantasy body were best placed in the look-but-don't-touch category.

And, since it was really just eye candy that she wanted, Paoletti's XO — whatever XO meant — was top shelf and a fine replacement.

Lieutenant Jacquette was a strikingly handsome and enormous African-American man — not so much tall as he was broad. And it wasn't the fat kind of broad, either. No, he was just plain huge, with the kind of shoulders that looked wide enough to carry the weight of the entire world, if need be.

His office was smaller than the lieutenant commander's, but they didn't stay there long after Paoletti excused himself with one last smile.

Jacquette led her back into the hall, down the stairs, and out into the brilliance of the afternoon as he repeated everything that Paoletti had told her.

His cell rang, and as he grimly excused himself and took the call, Joan had enough time both to find her sunglasses and to search through the long list of Navy abbreviations that Meredith had put into her file before she'd left her office last night.

XO . . . XO . . .

Executive officer. Second in command. Aha. This Lieutenant Jacquette was Navy SEAL Team Sixteen's Mr. Spock.

Thank God for all those *Star Trek* reruns she'd

watched in fifth grade, or she'd be completely in the dark.

"If there's anything you need while you're here," Jacquette told her with an appropriately Vulcan-like intensity, "come see me. Oh, good, here's Muldoon."

Joan looked up, and there, indeed, was Muldoon. Silhouetted by the sparkling backdrop of sunlight dancing on the ocean, this Muldoon couldn't have made a more dramatic appearance if he'd tried.

He was all broad shoulders and wide chest and long legs, packaged neatly into that same gleaming white uniform.

From a distance, he looked like a Lieutenant Commander Paoletti clone, with the same man-sized, extra-ripped build.

"Joan DaCosta — Lieutenant junior grade Michael Muldoon," Jacquette intoned.

The choir of angels missed their cue as Muldoon came close enough for her to see his face. But, hot damn, a face like that demanded a full forte *gloria in excelsis deo.*

Yes, as fit the pattern, Lieutenant junior grade — which made him sound as if he were a Daisy Scout compared to the non-junior lieutenants — Michael Muldoon was more picture-perfect handsome than both Jacquette and Paoletti combined. Of course, he was also only about twenty years old.

If the trend continued, within the next three minutes she was going to be handed off to a ten-year-old ensign, and then to that toddler seaman recruit she'd seen scrubbing the floor when she'd first arrived on the naval base.

"Lieutenant Muldoon is going to be your SEAL

35

liaison for the duration of your visit," Jacquette informed her.

It really was remarkable. The guy was right out of central casting. *Hello, Gertrude? Yeah, we need a Navy SEAL hero type over on lot twenty-four this afternoon. Make sure he stands well over six feet tall, is built like a Greek god, has neon blue eyes, golden brown hair, and a face more handsome than Brad Pitt's, will ya?*

"Ma'am."

And he should definitely be ridiculously young, so as to make me feel as old as possible by actually addressing me as ma'am.

Shit. When had she become a *ma'am?* Thirty-two didn't honestly qualify as *ma'am*-dom, did it?

"Lieutenant Muldoon will give you today's tour," Jacquette said. "And he'll accompany you whenever you're here on base. Please try to stay with him at all times."

Oh-ho. Lieutenant Junior was her baby-sitter. Wasn't *that* annoying news?

And although he gave no outward sign — Junior was either unswervingly polite or brain dead — Joan had to believe that this was not an assignment that he'd requested. No, this was one he'd gotten stuck with, poor thing. He was doomed to be as miserable as she was.

"That's not just for your own personal safety," Jacquette continued, "but also for security reasons, of course. Again, if you need anything . . ."

Enough games. The U.S. Navy might not take this PR opportunity for Brooke Bryant seriously, but she sure as hell did. "I need full access to this base, Lieutenant," Joan told him.

He pretended not to understand. "Then I'll let you and Lieutenant Muldoon get to it," the XO said smoothly. "Enjoy your tour."

"Sir, I have full security clearance," she said.

But he was already taking another call on his cell — or at least pretending to take one — ending their conversation by turning his broad back and walking away.

And then there she was. All alone with Junior.

"Do you want fries with that?" Mary Lou Starrett asked.

The skinny sailor with a bad case of acne hardly looked at her once, let alone twice. "Just a vanilla shake."

"Small or large?" There was a time — not so long ago — when this kid wouldn't have been able to take his eyes off of her. And she, well, she wouldn't've given an enlisted loser like him the time of day.

"Large. And I'm in a real rush, so if you don't mind . . . ?" He finally looked at her, and it was with "Come on, you moron" in his eyes.

Mary Lou took a chicken sandwich from the warming bin, squishing a big hole in the bun with her thumb as she put it into the paper sack. It wasn't as satisfying as spitting into his shake, but it would have to do.

She took his money and gave him his change, and he grabbed his food and left. And the lunchtime rush at the Navy base's McDonald's was officially over.

Her husband, Lieutenant Sam Starrett of U.S. Navy SEAL Team Sixteen, hadn't come in with the rest of the crowd. Even though he knew she was working today. Even though he knew this was one of the three weekdays she dropped their daughter, Haley, at Mrs. Ustenski's day care center and actually got her ass out of the house . . .

Her twenty pounds overweight, size humongous, never-gonna-wear-a-thong-again big-ass ass.

It had been thirteen months since Haley was born. And it had been longer than that since she and Sam had had sex. Real sex. Not this do-it-in-the-dark-with-any-random-blow-up-doll-available-type sex they'd had very infrequently since then.

Mary Lou slowly organized the stack of paper cups alongside the soda machine, knowing if she didn't look busy, Aaron the asshole manager would find something for her to do.

Maybe if she lost this weight, Sam would look at her again as if she were a woman, instead of a sack of potatoes. Maybe when she finally stopped breast-feeding. Everyone said that breast-feeding made you lose weight, but maybe she was some kind of freak of nature. Maybe after she weaned Haley, she'd get thinner. And maybe then Sam would want her.

He stayed up late, watching TV in the living room, waiting until after she was asleep to come to bed. Or so he thought. She was usually awake, lying there wishing that he would reach for her, but knowing that he wouldn't.

If she wanted some, she had to make it very obvious. And even then, there had been times when he shut her down. Which eventually became so mortifying, she'd flat out stopped trying.

But maybe if she lost this weight . . .

Desperate, Mary Lou had tried over the past few months to make Sam happy by making his home beautiful. She cleaned the shit out of it every single day.

She tried to please him in other ways, too. By being agreeable. By holding her tongue and avoiding arguments at all costs.

She might not be the thinnest wife in the world, but she was working hard to be the least troublesome.

For instance, Sam had made a stink about her visiting the Team Sixteen building on the base. Apparently — even though the other SEALs' wives came to visit frequently — Sam didn't want Mary Lou to visit him at work. So she'd made sure she didn't bother him there, unless it was important or unless he was being deployed. Then, of course, all bets were off.

Their marriage wasn't perfect, but what marriage was? And he didn't *have* to marry her. Some guys wouldn't have, despite the fact that she'd been pregnant.

No, he'd married her because on some level, deep down, he loved her. And now she finally had someone — not just *some*one, a Navy SEAL — to take care of her. They had a daughter together, and a house and two cars — although hers was pretty much a rolling piece of crap.

Sooner or later, she'd lose the weight and make Sam happy again. He'd admit that he loved her, and maybe then the rest of her life would turn around, too. She'd finally be accepted by the other wives of the SEALs in Team Sixteen.

They were polite to her, sure. But she couldn't call a single one of them *friend*.

It wasn't fair — the wives' club was supposed to be part of the package, one of the perks of marrying an officer in the U.S. Navy SEALs. Her life was supposed to be glorious now, filled with wonderful girlfriends with sweet little babies like her own Haley, with Sam hurrying home to her every night after his training missions here in Coronado.

He was supposed to look at her with the same keen hunger in his blue eyes that had made her weak in the knees when she'd first laid eyes on him in the Ladybug Lounge nearly two years ago. He was supposed to make jokes and then they would laugh the way they'd laughed back then.

Of course, back then they'd both been drunk off their asses pretty much all the time they were together. They'd make plans to meet at the bar, and she'd arrive early and get warmed up. He'd come in, pound down a few, and then they'd stagger back to her place and get naked and laugh some more.

'Course back then she usually ended up drinking until she puked or passed out.

But she'd grown up with a drunk for a mother. And she was good and goddamn sure that wasn't going to be the case for her little Haley.

"Mary Lou!"

Shit. Aaron was going to ask her to clean the fry machine. She just knew it.

But, "Counter," he said instead. She had customers. Glory be to God. She turned with relief at the reprieve and froze.

It was Alyssa Locke. Standing in front of Mary

40

Lou's counter, intently gazing up at the menu as if it had radically changed in the past few years. Her FBI partner was with her. Jules Something. Sam had told her he was actually gay.

He was even prettier than Alyssa, and that was saying something, because Alyssa Locke was beautiful.

She was slender, with slim hips and thighs. Of course, her breasts were barely there. Mary Lou probably wore a larger bra size at age eleven.

Her dark hair was cut boyishly short, accenting her exotic green eyes, her mocha-colored skin, her high cheekbones, and her full lips. Making her look extremely non-boyish.

They hadn't noticed her, hadn't recognized her. Please God, don't let them recognize her.

"What was it I swore I'd never order again?" Alyssa asked her partner, her eyes still firmly on the menu.

"That was at the other place," he said. "Burger Hell."

"Are you sure?"

"Yeah. What's today's special?" Jules asked, giving Mary Lou a wink.

Didn't it figure? The one man who flirted with her today was gay.

Mary Lou didn't pretend to laugh at his joke. She couldn't. She couldn't so much as smile.

She just stared at the cash register as she took their order, praying they wouldn't recognize her, praying they would just take their lunch and leave.

"My turn to pay," Alyssa said to Jules in a husky voice that didn't have a trace of the deep south's honey and syrup. Everything about her was all business. Efficient and precise. Except for that lush mouth.

As Mary Lou watched, she opened her fanny pack and got out her wallet.

And it was then, while Mary Lou was giving her change, that Alyssa's gaze flickered down to her name badge.

And then up directly into Mary Lou's eyes.

And there it was. Recognition. Realization of who was waiting on her dawned in Alyssa's eyes. And Mary Lou couldn't hide the fact that she knew damn well who Alyssa was, either.

For about seven seconds, no one spoke. Mary Lou actually dared to hope that Alyssa would turn away, pretend that flash of recognition had never happened. After all, there had to be at least several thousand women named Mary Lou in San Diego.

But no. Alyssa had to open her perfect mouth. "I didn't realize you worked here."

No shit, Sherlock. Mary Lou didn't doubt for one second that Alyssa wanted to avoid her as much as she wanted to avoid seeing Alyssa. If Alyssa had known, she wouldn't have come within two miles of this place.

"Yeah," Mary Lou said instead. "I've been here for about three months now." And just so that Alyssa wouldn't think she had to work, that somehow Sam wasn't providing for her, she added, "Three four-hour shifts a week. Just enough to get out of the house for a while. See a few people who don't have diaper rash for a change."

Jules was looking back and forth between Alyssa and Mary Lou as if he were mystified.

42

"This is Lieutenant Starrett's wife," Alyssa told him.

He instantly became expressionless and bland. "Oh, right. Of course. Mary Lou. We met at your house about six months ago."

Yes, they did. Right before Sam left for Indonesia. Mary Lou certainly remembered. It was right before Alyssa Locke left for Indonesia, too.

Are you in town to fuck my husband? The words were on the tip of her tongue, but she choked them back. She didn't have to ask. She already knew. Sam still mumbled Alyssa's name in his sleep.

He swore — repeatedly — that he hadn't been with her since he and Mary Lou got married, that whatever had been between him and Alyssa was over and done with, a thing of the past. But it had been well over a year since Sam and Mary Lou got married. There was no way he'd still be dreaming about Alyssa if he wasn't still seeing her.

No way.

Sam wasn't the kind of man to go for months on end without sex. And he sure as hell wasn't getting any from Mary Lou.

Jealousy clogged her throat and angry tears threatened to escape.

"It's nice seeing you," Alyssa said insincerely.

Mary Lou just stood there as they took their food and pushed through the doors, out into the heat of the sunny afternoon.

"Earth to Mary Lou!"

She turned to find Aaron the asshole standing right next to her. "Where the heck did *you* go?" he asked, laughing as if he'd made a huge joke.

43

"Standing there, spacing out, like someone came and vacuumed out your brain."

It took everything in her to keep from slapping him, simply for being a fool.

"Your husband called a while ago," Aaron told her. "It was before you got here. I forgot to tell you. He said he'd try to make it in during lunch."

Well, he hadn't. And Mary Lou didn't know whether to be upset about that or relieved. The only thing worse than seeing Alyssa would have been seeing Alyssa and Sam in the same room.

"He said to say he's going out with the team tonight," Aaron continued. "He won't be back until tomorrow, probably in the evening."

Of course Sam wouldn't make it home tonight. That was no real surprise.

Alyssa Locke was in town.

Mary Lou took off her hat. She had to get out of there.

Now.

"Where are you going?" Aaron asked.

"I told Matt last time I was in," Mary Lou lied. "I have to leave early today. Haley's baby-sitter has a doctor's appointment. I would've tried to get a replacement, but Matt said it was okay —"

"Go," Aaron said. "See you next week."

Mary Lou went.

TWO

"I work for the President," Joan told the junior lieutenant named Muldoon as they stood outside the Team Sixteen building on the U.S. Naval Base. "In the White House. I probably have a higher security clearance than you do."

He nodded expressionlessly. "Yes, ma'am."

Ma'am. Ouch.

On closer examination, it was clear that Junior was older than twenty. He was easily twenty-one.

"I'm not very happy about this," she told him.

"I'm sorry about that, ma'am."

"Yeah, I can tell — you're really weeping."

He glanced at her. "We're encouraged not to cry in public, ma'am. Ruins the warrior image."

Joan laughed. Well, what do you know? Perfect Boy had a sense of humor. Yet he still didn't even crack a smile.

"Shall we start the tour, ma'am?"

"Yeah, sure. Why the heck not?"

"You've seen the SpecWar and the Team Sixteen buildings," he said as he started to walk, slipping right into tour guide mode, automaton style. "Why don't we start with the BUD/S area? This is the grinder — it's called that for obvious reasons. It's where most of the physical training or PT starts.

45

BUD/S stands for Basic Underwater Demolition/SEALs — it's the intensive training we all go through. It's the toughest training program in the entire U.S. military. SEAL candidates enter in classes of about a hundred and forty men, most of whom don't complete the program. They ring out — quit. When all is said and done, most graduating classes have only about twenty percent of the men they started with still standing."

On the flight from D.C., Joan had read about BUD/S in a packet of info Meredith had dug up. It included something called Hell Week, which was five days of grueling physical activity in which the SEAL candidates got only a few hours of sleep in very short bursts. Junior wasn't kidding when he called the program tough. It was very impressive, but . . .

"You're one of the ones who made it through, huh?"

She'd gotten the impression that only the toughest and meanest actually went on to become SEALs. And while Junior was handsome and gleaming, he seemed neither of those other things. If he heard the skepticism in her voice, his mild glance in her direction was the only sign he gave that it bothered him. "Yes, ma'am."

"Congratulations."

"It was quite some time ago, but thank you, ma'am."

Ma'am, ma'am, ma'am. *Grrr*. Was it possible that he was saying it now because he knew that it bugged her?

He led her through a gate. "Since most SEAL operations involve water, a great deal of our

46

training takes place in the ocean or here in the pool."

"Where are you from?" she interrupted, wanting this tour to be given by the real, living person inside that sparkling uniform — the guy who got a bad case of gas when he ate beans with his burritos — rather than this information-spouting, picture-perfect Navy robot.

"Ohio, Maine, and Florida."

"Is that supposed to be multiple choice, or is the answer all of the above?"

A smile. Alleluia. Although it was painfully polite. "All of the above."

"Was your father in the military, too?"

"No, ma'am. He was a college professor," Junior told her. "He taught physics."

"Yikes. No wonder you ran off and joined the Navy."

Nothing. No real reaction to the fact that she'd just made a joke other than another polite smile.

It was a lame joke, sure, but still . . . Joan resisted the urge to take the kid's pulse. Maybe that joke he'd made about crying hadn't really been a joke. Maybe he'd been serious.

"Here we have a class going through drown-proofing," Muldoon said, and she focused on the enormous pool in front of them.

And on the fact that — "Holy shit!" — a young man, clad only in bathing trunks, was being thrown into the deep end with his hands tied behind his back. *What* are they *doing?*"

The pool was filled with similarly tied young men. Others stood along the side, patiently waiting their turn to be bound and thrown into the water.

Still other men, wearing T-shirts, floppy hats, and boots with their swim shorts, either tied up the younger men or prowled the edge of the pool, watching the ones in the water.

"*This* is training?" Joan asked Muldoon. "Training for what? Capture by an evil overlord?"

Junior's smile seemed far more real this time, but she might've been imagining that.

"SEALs have to be completely comfortable in the water," he told her. "These men are learning what it feels like to be in the water under, shall we say, less than perfect circumstances."

"Shall we say . . . ? I'd say, yeah, Junior, this is a teeny bit less than perfect."

He cleared his throat. "To successfully complete this exercise, they need to sink to the bottom, then use their feet to push off to get back to the surface. Once there, they can take a breath, then hold it as they again sink to the bottom, exhale on their way back up, take another breath . . . It's not that hard to do once you get into the rhythm — you can keep it going for hours as long as you don't panic."

Hours. Holy cow. "You really did this?"

He actually gazed at her for several long seconds before answering this time. "I am a SEAL, ma'am. I've really gone through BUD/S. I've done it all. And then some. Ma'am."

Well, well. A trace of an edge was in his voice. A spark of life. Maybe there was a real boy hidden inside this perfect, wooden one after all. And it was true. She'd guessed correctly. He *was* attempting to *ma'am* her to death.

"Will you please call me Joan or even Ms.

48

DaCosta — instead of ma'am?" she asked. "Every time you call me that, I feel as if I should rush out and buy a cane and support hose."

Junior didn't actually laugh, but he did manage another more genuine-seeming smile. "That would be a complete waste of money. In my opinion." His smile faded, and he fixed his gaze on a distant point. "Respectfully, of course. Ms. DaCosta."

Hello. A Navy SEAL who actually blushed? Yes, color was rising from the collar of his uniform and tingeing his perfect, smoothly shaven cheeks.

Was this not turning into one of the weirdest days of her life?

Obviously Junior here wanted to make sure that she knew he wasn't hitting on her or being inappropriate in any way. Or maybe he thought that her mention of support hose was her way of hitting on him, rather than another of her pathetic attempts to be funny and to get him to relax already. Maybe he'd somehow found out that she'd asked his CO to dinner and expected her to do the same with him. But unless Paoletti had intercepted him and told him . . . No, she just didn't see that happening. Still . . . Eek.

"So. This is called drownproofing," she said briskly, feeling her own face start to heat at the idea that he might think that *she* thought . . . Jesus God, he had to be ten years her junior. He couldn't possibly think she would . . . *Did* he . . . ? Unless he thought she was the female equivalent of Rear Admiral Tucker — hitting on everyone in range, provided he had a penis.

Maybe if she kept the conversation moving neither one of them would feel the urge to curl up and die. "God. Talk about extreme."

"This is one of the easier exercises," Muldoon informed her. "Believe me, this isn't extreme."

"Well, it's very . . . visually extreme," Joan said. Enough of this embarrassment already. Just *talk* to the kid. "One of the things I'm doing here is scouting locations for photo ops for the President's daughter's visit. The White House and the Navy want to turn this event into good PR for everyone. And a picture really is worth a thousand words, particularly when it's on the front page of *USA Today*. So what do you think? Should we recommend tying up Brooke Bryant and tossing her into the pool with these boys while the press is allowed to snap away?"

Laughter. Finally. It was only a chuckle, but hey, it counted. Muldoon the junior lieutenant actually had dimples, God bless him. He finally met her gaze again. "We?"

"Don't want your name on *that* report, huh?"

"No, thank you." He laughed again. "I'm just the liaison. I'd like to keep it that way. At least as far as the White House is concerned."

Coming from anyone else, that might've been a subtle come on. But from Junior . . . Joan simply could not think of it that way.

"How long have you been in the Navy?" she asked, using all of her so-called people skills to try to keep him from retreating back into the impersonal tour guide. Engage them in conversation about themselves, listen when they answer, smile and maintain eye contact, keep body language open and friendly. But not sexual. It was a fine line,

50

but one she'd walked many times before. It was one of her strengths — her ability to be "one of the boys."

God, she hoped he didn't think the support hose comment was her way of hitting on him, because that really was the last thing she'd been thinking.

"I joined while I was in college," he told her, relaxing another minute fraction of a smidgen. "I've been in eight years now, and I've been a SEAL for four of them."

She tried to do the math. "That would make you, what? Twenty-four?"

"Twenty-six," he corrected her.

So, okay, she wasn't all that much older than he was. At least not chronologically. And he'd crossed that do-not-touch, twenty-five-years-old-or-under-is-verboten barrier that automatically went up whenever a woman turned thirty.

"Well, I'm *almost* twenty-six," he admitted, as if God would strike him with a lightning bolt if he were caught lying. Who was this guy?

Joan laughed. At him and at herself. What did it really matter how old he was? This wasn't a date. And she wasn't looking for trouble.

"There was a time I always rounded up, too," she told him. "Amazing how age-ist people can be, huh? But it works on both ends of the spectrum, especially for women. Someone once told me that in my business, as a woman, you want to be perpetually thirty-five. Not too old and not too young. You know what I said when I heard that?"

"No. What?"

"I said, Screw that. I'm great now — I'm going

51

to be off the charts when I turn forty. At fifty, honey, I may be older, but I certainly won't be too old, and as for you, at that point, you're not going to be able to afford to hire me. And when I finally turn seventy — look out."

He was smiling at her, and it was a big, fat, genuine smile that actually touched his eyes. Attaboy, Muldoon. Way to be a human being.

"Don't play the game by their rules," she told him, because, damn, he actually seemed to be listening to what she had to say. "So come on, Grasshopper. Give me the rest of the official tour, and then we can fight to the death about the parts of the base you've been told not to let me see, okay?"

She was leaving work early. What was *that* about?

One thing Husaam Abdul-Fataah had learned about Mary Lou Starrett was that she lived her life like clockwork.

Three days a week she dropped the kid at day care in the morning, then drove her rattletrap of a car over to the Coronado Naval Base, past the guards at the gate, and down the road to the McDonald's, where she parked in the shade alongside the Dumpster. She worked a four-hour shift, and she always arrived twenty to thirty minutes early and sat with a cup of coffee, her nose in whatever book she was currently reading.

Five minutes before her shift started, she'd take her book bag back out to her car and stash it in the front seat. A trip to the ladies' room followed, and then four relentless hours of her beauty queen false smile and "Do you want fries with that?"

About a half hour in, the smile would start to

wilt. And by the time the shift was over, she made a beeline out of there.

She got back into her car, drove back to San Diego, picked up the kid at day care.

And that was when she got wild and crazy. Every two to three days she went to the library with the baby in a stroller. She read like a maniac — taking out an armload of books at a time. Once or twice a week, she stopped at the grocery store on her way back to the little house she shared with a husband who frequently wasn't home.

The kid probably napped every day from around 2:30 to 3:30, because Mary Lou always made sure they were home during that time. Occasionally she went out into the yard, carrying a book and some kind of radio receiver — probably something that allowed her to listen for the kid. And about once or twice a week, somewhat randomly, she went over to the little house right next door, where some kind of a shut-in lived.

She never stayed for long.

Her evenings were as organized as her days. She had an Alcoholics Anonymous meeting to attend in various churches in the city, one for every night of the week. She'd wait until the last minute for her husband to come home. Sometimes he made it before she had to go. Sometimes she planned in advance and took the kid back to the sitter. But sometimes she'd pack up the baby and, loading her into the car with ill-concealed exasperation, she'd simply take her along.

The husband barely ever looked at her, hardly did much more than go to work or sleep in front of the TV.

Husaam couldn't have asked for it to be any easier.

When he'd first arrived in San Diego, he'd hung out in the local bars and restaurants, the places where the Navy personnel came to drink and gossip.

The SEALs were a closemouthed bunch, but they were a hot topic of conversation. And not just them, but their wives and girlfriends were often discussed to death by the folks in the regular Navy.

Because of that, he knew all kinds of things about them all — most of which were probably wild rumors. But even the wildest of rumors tended to contain at least a grain of truth.

He'd heard that Meg Nilsson met her current husband while she was still married to her first.

That one he figured was probably true.

Teri and Stan Wolchonok had a hot tub in their backyard, and an invitation to their house would result in everyone getting naked.

He wasn't so sure about that.

Mary Lou Starrett was a bimbo SEAL groupie who had purposely gotten pregnant to trap Sam into marrying her.

A definite possibility.

Mark Jenkins was dating a kindergarten teacher from Escondido who had breast implants.

Only Jenkins and the teacher knew for sure.

Mike Muldoon was so good-looking and nice, he had to be gay.

Sounded like good, old-fashioned envy to him, but not impossible.

Jay Lopez's brother had overdosed on heroin, which had made Jay take a vow of celibacy, and

Cosmo Richter had been recruited by the SEALs from his cell in the lifers wing on Rikers Island.

Yeah, right.

Last but not least, rumor had it that Team Sixteen's commanding officer Tom Paoletti had lost interest in his live-in girlfriend, Dr. Kelly Ashton. He kept postponing their wedding date. Rumor was they were fighting pretty much constantly. A day didn't go by in which Kelly didn't drive out to the base to check up on Tom and to exchange heated words.

That situation sounded perfect for what he wanted to do, and he'd targeted Kelly Ashton first, for a number of reasons. But the rumors and gossip about her fading relationship with Paoletti were backward and upside down.

He hadn't followed her for more than thirty-six hours before she met Paoletti at a dinner party at the posh Hotel del Coronado. Minutes after she arrived, she slipped out of the dining room.

And as Husaam had watched, Paoletti followed her. Right into a hotel utility closet.

Husaam had strolled past the closed door and well, well, well. There was definitely not an argument going on inside.

A little more investigation revealed that Kelly was the one who kept pushing back their wedding date. She had cold feet. But that's about all she had that was cold.

Regretfully, he'd crossed her off his list, and started following Mary Lou Starrett instead.

Who lived her boring little life with mind-numbing predictability. Which he couldn't really complain about, seeing how it — as well as the broken lock on the trunk of her car — made things much easier for him.

But right now, something most definitely was up.

It was 1:37. It was twenty-three whole minutes before Mary Lou's shift ended, and she was already in her car and pulling out of the naval base.

It was pure chance that brought him here early. Normally he wouldn't have bothered to come before 2:00 P.M. on the dot.

Mary Lou would take the long way back to the mainland so she wouldn't have to pay the toll. He knew that about her, too.

He went in the opposite direction, determined to get to San Diego before she did.

Because today was the day, after following her for weeks, that he was finally going to make contact.

Vincent DaCosta was jealous of a man who'd been dead for more than sixty years.

James Fletcher.

Vince thought of him as Jim or Jimmy, even though Charlie had never called him anything but James. Of course, sometimes, like right now, Vince thought of him as *that son of a bitch*. Which was, he knew, entirely unfair.

That son of a bitch had died December 7, 1941 — a day that had very definitely managed to live in infamy for at least these past sixty-something years. That son of a bitch had left behind a beautiful young wife who had loved him dearly.

Even after nearly eighty years of living, Vince knew few things absolutely for sure. But one of those things he knew in his heart was that if he had been at Pearl Harbor and mortally wounded from shrapnel from a Japanese bomb, he would have fought death tooth and claw to keep from leaving behind a world that had sweet Charlie Fletcher living in it.

She was sitting, right now, on a chair in a living room–like set in this TV studio, her knees primly together, her back straight as a board. She'd been sitting just like that, at her secretary's desk in the senator's office in Washington, D.C., the first day Vince laid eyes on her.

Another thing Vince knew after all those years, well over fifty of 'em spent married to sweet Charlie, was that in truth he had no goddamned right to be jealous of Jim Fletcher.

Fletcher'd had Charlie for one year.

Vince had had her for a lifetime.

"He truly was a remarkable man," Charlie was saying now to young Tim Bradley, the host of this show being made for the History Channel, as the studio cameras rolled.

December was approaching and the anniversary of the Japanese attack was rolling around again. Since most of the men who'd actually been at Pearl Harbor during the battle were finding it more and more difficult to walk and talk, folks like Bradley were interested in interviewing the people who'd known the heroes of that fateful day.

And Medal of Honor winner Lieutenant James T. Fletcher had been one hell of a hero, there was no denying that.

The man had thrown himself on top of an admiral, saving the officer's life, shielding him from

57

shrapnel that would have torn him apart. And then when other men — medics — tried to keep Fletcher from bleeding to death, he'd refused to go to the hospital. Instead he'd led those very men — untrained, untried men — to an antiaircraft gun. With Fletcher's lead, they got it up and firing. Took out a fair number of Japanese planes. Enough to make a significant difference to save God knows how many American lives.

But it had not been without a price.

Vince watched the TV monitor, watched Charlie as she spoke in her usual no-nonsense manner to Tim Bradley.

"The sacrifice he made — that all the young men who fought and died to defend our country made — is awe inspiring." She smiled so sadly, so like she'd smiled in the early days of their friendship, that it nearly broke Vince's heart. "Of course, at the time, I was not inspired. I was devastated. I loved him, and he was dead."

"What did you think when you heard the news that your husband was being given a posthumous Medal of Honor?" Bradley asked.

"*First* husband," Vince muttered a correction. What was he? Chopped liver? It was weird, hearing Charlie talk about Fletcher again. During all these years they'd been married, neither of them ever mentioned him.

But maybe that had been a mistake. Maybe she'd needed to talk about the guy.

Look at the way she'd jumped at being interviewed when the producer of this show had called.

She'd loved him, she said, and he was dead.

On the video monitor, Charlie shifted her weight

and crossed her legs. At eighty-three, she still had a great pair of legs. She looked like she belonged on that TV screen. Like a movie star. But then again, Vince had always thought that. Right from day one. The woman was gorgeous. She still was.

"What did I think? I thought, '*Posthumous* — what an awful word.' "

"And when you heard the stories of his bravery at Pearl Harbor . . . ?"

"I thought, 'Why did you do that? James, you stupid ass.' "

Bradley gave a burst of laughter, and Charlie made a face. "I'm sorry," she said. "I probably can't say that on television, can I? But you did ask."

"It's okay," Bradley assured her. "It's fine."

"I was twenty-two when he died," she told him. "I didn't read the reports and records of what happened until years later. I couldn't stand to. My mother-in-law — his mother — somehow managed to read them. She told me what James had done."

She laughed softly, sadly, her eyes out of focus, remembering.

Vince remembered, too. He remembered how wounded she'd been when he'd almost literally fallen into her and Edna Fletcher's lives. Jim had been dead for nearly two years, and Charlie was still raw from it.

"I'd asked her to come and stay with me in Washington when the news of the attack on Pearl Harbor was first announced. We knew James was stationed in Hawaii, we knew the attack was horrendous, that lots of our boys had died, but that's all we knew. So I called Mother Fletcher and asked her to come. I pretended it was so I could comfort her in case we got bad news, but the truth was she came and she comforted me. Can you imagine getting a telegram telling you that your only child is dead?"

"No, ma'am."

"Well, she lived it. We lived it. Lots of mothers and wives did after December seventh. Edna Fletcher was a Gold Star Mother after the Japanese bombed Pearl Harbor. And at twenty-two, I was a war widow. And yes, we were presented with James's Medal of Honor shortly after that. But it was cold comfort, sir. I know from shows like this one that James will be forever remembered and revered as a hero. That's as it should be. But I hope he'll also be remembered as a greatly loved husband and son. That's how I remember him."

"Thank you so much for taking the time to talk to us, Mrs. Fletcher," Bradley said.

Mrs. Fletcher.

For the first few weeks after they'd met in the senator's office, Vince had called her that.

"Is the senator in, Mrs. Fletcher?"

"He is, Private DaCosta, but I'm afraid —"

"Vince."

"— his schedule is completely full again today."

"I'll wait."

She was sympathetic but firm. "He can't see you today."

"I'll wait. Maybe something will open up."

"Private —"

"My name is Vince."

She gave him that look. Exasperated and disap-

60

proving and yet laced with something else. Some-thing that made him more determined than ever to stay. "Go home, Private DaCosta. Leave me your phone number, and I'll call you if something opens up and —"

"I'll wait, thanks. Mrs. Fletcher."

"It's Mrs. DaCosta now," Charlie told the inter-viewer.

"Of course," he said. "You were twenty-two when he died."

"Life goes on."

"It does," Bradley agreed. "You do the best you can with the hand you've been dealt."

And fate had dealt her Vince DaCosta. No doubt about that. He'd made it impossible for her to shut herself away from life, to spend the rest of her days as Jim Fletcher's grieving widow.

Or had he? Hearing her talk about her first hus-band now gave him pause.

All these years, and he'd never dared to sit down with her, to look into her eyes, and to ask her, "Do you still miss him?"

He'd never dared, because deep inside, he was afraid that the answer was yes.

So he'd worked his butt off to be the best damn second choice she'd ever had. He'd made her smile, he'd made her laugh, he'd given her a home and a family. He'd loved her completely, unequivocally, unconditionally.

But he'd never given her a chance to put Fletcher properly and permanently to rest.

"Vince."

He looked up to find Charlie off the set and halfway to the door to the parking lot, looking back at him with that same exasperated look that he'd come to know so well.

"I said, we're done," she told him. "We can go now."

"Sorry," he said, digging into his pocket for the car keys.

"You didn't hear me," she said.

Not this again. She thought he needed a hearing aid, of all the ridiculous ideas. It was true he had to turn up the TV a little bit louder when the ball game was on, but that was just part of turning eighty. Hearing aids were expensive, and they had better things to do with their hard-earned money. "I wasn't listening. I was woolgathering." He held the door for her. Changed the subject. "You were great."

She looked anxious. "You think? I wasn't sure what they wanted, and then . . . Did you hear me say ass?"

"Loud and clear."

"Oh, dear. That'll make it into the program, guaranteed. Did Joanie call?"

Vince checked the messages on his cell phone for any sign that his granddaughter had phoned. "No, but remember she said she probably wouldn't have time to get in touch until tomorrow."

"I know. I'm just anxious to see her."

"She also said she'll be in town for about four weeks. We'll get a chance to spend some time with her."

"I'm afraid that she doesn't realize just how bad Donny's gotten," Charlie said as Vince unlocked their car from twenty feet away.

Best invention since the PC, this keyless entry. Vince loved technology. Couldn't wait to see what they'd come up with next.

"She knows, Charles. She talks to him on the phone." Vince opened the car door for her.

"That's not the same as visiting."

"Well, she's here, she'll visit. And maybe she'll get him to stop being such an ass and start taking his meds again." He made sure her coat wouldn't get caught before he shut the car door, then went around to the other side.

"It's all your fault, you know," Charlie said with a laugh as Vince got behind the wheel. Her smile still killed him. "Before I met you, I wouldn't have dreamed of uttering the word *ass* in public, let alone on national television." She paused. "Think they'll use that part of the tape?"

He looked at her over the top of his sunglasses. More than fifty years of marriage, and he really didn't have to say anything. She knew darn well what he was thinking. And he could predict exactly what she'd say next.

"Well, too bad," she said. "It was the truth. They asked, and I answered."

He started the car. "Well, good."

"I'm not worrying about it," she said, a slight frown furrowing her brow.

This was the moment right here where it absolutely wouldn't do either of them any good if he laughed. Even a smile could be dangerous and could segue into either "Vince, Don't Laugh, This Is a Serious Thing," or "I Know You Think Otherwise, Vincent, but I Am Not Really Worrying When I Bring Up a Subject and Talk about It to Death."

They'd been having variations of those two conversations on a pretty regular basis for nearly six decades.

Neither was even remotely possible for him to win.

Which was all right with Vince, because his goal with Charlie was not — and had never been — to win. It was part of her nature to worry things to death. He knew that about her before he'd asked her to marry him.

For some reason she seemed to believe that worrying was a bad thing, and she was therefore determined to try as often as possible to convince both of them that she honestly wasn't worrying.

It hadn't taken Vince more than a decade to figure out that the trick was to let her go ahead and talk a subject to death if she wanted. Because the real trouble came when she held her worries inside.

He'd learned to be subtle in his attempts to soothe her fears and always to agree completely when she said she wasn't worrying.

But it was hard, at times, not to laugh.

This time, however, all he had to do was think about everything that Charlie had been hiding inside all these long years.

Did she ever think *what if?* What if Jim Fletcher hadn't died that day? What if he'd survived the war? Did she ever wonder how different — how much better — her life would have been?

He glanced at her as he pulled out of the studio parking lot. "That must've been hard. Talking about it like that."

"I'm glad he'll be remembered," she said.

"He has been," Vince said quietly. Every day for nearly sixty years. Every day since Vince found out that the impossibly efficient and improbably young Mrs. Fletcher, who was a secretary in Senator Howard's office, had been widowed by the war.

Every night, too. Yes, Vince had certainly remembered when he'd slipped into bed beside Jim Fletcher's wife. He'd remembered every night that he hadn't been with Charlie, too — when he'd been training to return to the war, back when he'd fought for his country, back when there was a very real chance that he wouldn't come home, either. Oh, he'd thought about Fletcher just as much on those nights, too.

Yeah, it was obvious to Vince now that between him and Charlie, Lt. James Fletcher had been anything but forgotten.

THREE

"Are you crazy?"

Muldoon laughed. "No, sir. She wanted a demonstration of the obstacle course, so I thought we could give her something that would really make an impact."

Lt. Sam Starrett used a finger to pull down one slat in the office blinds to get a better look at Joan, who was waiting outside, lifting her face to the warmth of the sun. "That's not her, is it?"

"Yes, sir."

"Jesus, Muldoon . . ."

Muldoon couldn't keep himself from bristling. "I beg your pardon, Lieutenant. What is *that* supposed to mean?"

"Nothing," Sam said hastily. "I didn't mean . . . No offense, Mike. She's very attractive, if you go for, you know, that type, which I should have remembered that you do." He shook his head. "I'm sorry, but I just thought, from what you were asking . . . I mean, I thought she'd be a total babe. You know, in a more entirely obvious way. I mean, I'm sure she's . . ." He laughed ruefully, rolling his eyes and settling back into his chair. "Look, go and do whatever you want to do. Just try not to kill her, okay? The White House might get pissed." He

66

consulted a roster on his desk. "Use Jenk, Gilligan, and Cosmo. They're all yours for the next few hours. If you kill her, hide the body." He turned back to his paperwork.

Muldoon had the permission he needed, and Sam had virtually dismissed him, but he couldn't manage to turn and walk out the door.

"You need something more?" Sam asked, eyeing him warily from his seat behind his desk.

"Believe it or not, Lieutenant, there are men who walk this earth who actually think about things other than when is the next time they're going to get laid."

Sam put down his pen and sighed. "Well, all right then, Mr. Pure as the Driven Snow. If by saying that, you're attempting to convince me that you fall into that somewhat dubious category, then tell me why the hell you're trying so hard to impress her."

It was a good question. Why *was* he trying so hard to impress Joan DaCosta?

Was it because she'd so clearly doubted the fact that he was a SEAL? Was it because she was exactly his so-called type — a strong, take charge, outgoing, opinionated woman — and yet, after spending several hours together, she hadn't given him even the slightest indication that she was interested in taking him back to her hotel room and keeping him up all night?

Sam was watching him, and now he laughed softly. "Wouldn't it just be easier to ask her to dinner?"

Now what was Muldoon supposed to say? That *she* was supposed to ask *him?* That that's how it had always worked in the past? The woman — usually someone more mature, who knew exactly what she wanted and liked — would approach him.

Because somewhere down the line, God had played a practical joke and given the fat kid a makeover — a trim, muscular body and a face that women seemed to like to look at from an intimate perch atop him.

They sought *him* out.

All he had to say was *yes* or *no*.

When it came to Joan DaCosta, his answer was yes all the way. He liked her. She was funny and smart with a vivacious, expressive face, sparkling eyes, and a generous, full, sexy mouth that was quick to curve into a smile. She was tall, with long legs and a curvy body that a guy wouldn't be afraid would snap like a twig if she wanted sex that was even the least little bit rough.

He would bet big money that she liked sex that was physical, sex that was filled with laughter and an incredible amount of honest passion. As opposed to some women who wanted their sexual encounters to mimic the still-life mood of a perfume commercial.

Muldoon could imagine them both tearing off their clothes and going at it the second he locked her hotel room door behind them.

Except they were almost done for the day and Joan hadn't raised the question. She hadn't given him one even slightly heated look. She hadn't dropped even the tiniest hint that told him he was, indeed, going to end up anywhere near her hotel room.

Wow, he was pathetic. He really had come into Sam's office to set up this demonstration of the BUD/S obstacle course because he wanted to impress her, because he hoped that if he did impress her, maybe he'd get laid.

What a loser.

"I just want her to take me a little more seriously," he told Sam now. It wasn't a complete lie. "I'm supposed to keep her fully occupied for the next few days and evenings, too, and . . ."

Sam leaned forward, his eyes narrowing. "You were actually *ordered* to —"

"No! Sir. No. Wow, that came out wrong. Commander Paoletti assigned me to stay with her, to keep her far away from the areas where the team is prepping for the upcoming op, and to try to talk her out of this entire presidential visit that's being planned. It's just kind of hard to do any of that when she thinks of me as *Junior*." She'd called him that a few times today, which had stung. "I just . . . want her to see what I'm capable of." And if she suddenly saw him as someone worthy of spending the night with in the process, well, wouldn't that be a shame.

"Okay," Sam said with a shrug. "Go show her." He sat up. "What time is it?" he asked, spinning in his seat to check the clock on his computer. "Oh, *fuck!* I am *so* screwed."

"Anything I can help with?" Muldoon asked.

"How's the work on that time machine coming?" Sam asked. "Unless you're ready to test it, there's nothing you or anyone else can do to save my balls." He shook his head in disgust. "Shit. Mary Lou was working today, and this morning she was dropping all these hints about me stopping in for lunch. I even called and said I was coming. But now her shift ends in five minutes and I'm so fucking cooked because I'm already not coming home this evening because of that night exercise. I can't believe I fucked this up. I could've canceled out all the shit I'm going to get about tonight's training with very little effort."

There was a knock, and WildCard Karmody stuck his head in the door. "Sorry to bother you, Sam — hey, Mikey! How's the knee, my man?"

"Just about up to speed again," Muldoon told the irreverent chief. "Thanks."

WildCard looked at Sam. "I just ran into Alyssa Locke and Jules Cassidy in the parking lot. They say they're going to be in town for a while, that Max and some of the other FBI agents were coming in tonight. Do you know anything about that?"

"Fuck no!" If it was possible, Sam had gotten even more tense. "I had absolutely no fucking idea."

No one had ever told Muldoon directly, but he'd overheard some conversations and he'd been able to figure out most of it. Sam Starrett had been seeing FBI agent Alyssa Locke — and Muldoon didn't know exactly what had gone down between them, but he gathered it was on the verge of being pretty serious — when Sam had found out that his former girlfriend Mary Lou was four months pregnant. He'd ended his relationship with Alyssa and married Mary Lou.

At least Muldoon had assumed that since Sam was married he wasn't seeing Alyssa anymore. And

70

Sam's next words to WildCard seemed to confirm that.

"Find out whatever you can," he ordered the chief. "How long they're going to be here. Where they're staying. Whether Max Bhagat's team is going to be with us every step of the way during prep for this new operation, you know — Black Lagoon."

WildCard nodded. "In other words, do you need to twist your ankle to avoid seeing her or do you need to break your leg? I'm on it, boss."

Sam turned to him. "Muldoon, get out of here. Go get laid."

WildCard waited for him, then closed Sam's office door behind them both. "How come I get *Find out whatever you can,* and you get *Go get laid?* It's one of those officer versus enlisted things again, isn't it? I knew I should have reconsidered Officers Candidate School back when I was in college."

"Anything I can do to help Sam?" Muldoon asked.

The chief instantly sobered up. "How much do you know, sir?"

"Enough. You know, just from putting two and two together."

"Don't talk about it with anyone else," Wild-Card warned him.

"You know I wouldn't."

"Yeah, I do know that, Mikey. I just had to say the words." WildCard sighed. "The bitch of it is there's really nothing any of us can do, except maybe run interference. Sam told me that Alyssa's with Max Bhagat these days, and he won't admit it, but it kills him to see them together. Jesus, it kills

71

him just to see *her,* period. He pretends it doesn't, but I know him pretty well."

"I'm here to help, if you need me," Muldoon told the chief. "Just call."

"Thank you, sir," WildCard said, as he took a corner and went down another hallway, going in the opposite direction from the door that led outside. "Now obey your orders from Lieutenant Starrett and go get laid. Make us proud."

"You know, Chief, I can explain about that," Muldoon called after him.

"I'd rather you didn't," WildCard called back. "I'm sure it's not even one millionth as good as what I'm imagining. Enjoy your afternoon, sir."

Lieutenant Muldoon, Junior, came out of the building dressed in shorts and a chest-hugging T-shirt.

"We're good to go," he said to Joan as she fumbled to put her sunglasses back on. "Jenk, Cosmo, and Gilligan will meet us over at the obstacle course."

The cargo shorts with slouchy socks and ankle-high boots was a look that most of the men she knew back in D.C. wouldn't have been able to pull off. But it seemed to be one of the basic uniforms here in SEAL Central, and they all — Muldoon especially — made it look like the height of men's fashion. Brooke was really going to love this visit.

"Gilligan?" she asked. "Without the Skipper?"

He shook his head and sighed. "You don't want to know how many times I've heard that exact same joke. It's always the Skipper. No one ever asks about the Professor or Ginger."

72

"Damn," she said. "Guilty of being trite. Is there anything worse?"

"Actually, I can think of one or two things." He said it with a grin, but a strange truth struck her for the first time. This man — with all of his well-toned muscles — had surely spent quite a bit of time over the past months putting himself into jeopardy, hunting down members of al-Qaeda.

He was wearing an intricate brace on his knee — probably the result of being injured, possibly even shot, in the line of duty. It was a sobering thought.

"Yeah, it couldn't really be worse than going to Afghanistan, could it?" she asked.

He gazed directly into her eyes and suddenly looked ten years older and capable of just about anything, despite the dreamboat, beefcake, boytoy packaging. "Is this conversation on the record or off the record?"

All that intensity aimed directly at her made her voice come out sounding a little breathless. A little embarrassingly like Marilyn Monroe. "I'm not a reporter." Happy Birthday, Mr. President.

Thankfully, he didn't seem to notice.

"You know what I mean. You're a PR person," he said. "You help make news for the White House. But me, I'm not news. Not in any way, shape, or form. None of us in Team Sixteen is. Where we've been, what we've been doing — if you want to know that so you can try to generate a news story, forget it. Let's talk about the weather instead. But if this is Joan asking Mike, if it's off the record . . ."

"It is," Joan said. Was she being completely honest? She wasn't sure. She hadn't had a conversation in years that was completely off the record, that she hadn't listened to with one ear tuned in to the fact that she might learn something she could later use to her — and to the President's — advantage.

"Okay." Muldoon nodded, seemingly satisfied, but the intensity in his eyes didn't fade. "Even off the record, I can't tell you much," he said. "But I'll tell you one thing. Being there isn't even half as hard as *not* being there. I'm an officer — I understand completely that there are reasons we need to come back to the base, reasons for us to be rotated out. We need to keep up with our training. Shooting skills deteriorate pretty quickly out in the real world. Which makes sense because we're a covert unit. Do you follow? We're not going out there to fire our weapons — we only do that when there's no other option. So we need to come home — or at least to a secure location — and train to retain the skills we need to be invincible when we are out there.

"But every one of us, Joan, every single man, is sitting here waiting for a chance to go back into action and do what we do best. Which is to protect our country from people who take their my-way-or-the-highway views of religion and politics to such an extreme that they'll intentionally target and kill innocent civilians. We're dying to get back out there to protect you and all your family and friends and coworkers — even the obnoxious guy who lives in the apartment upstairs and plays the greatest hits from the disco era at high volume all night long. We want to protect you from the people who proclaim that all Americans, including

74

the tiniest newborn infants, are their sworn enemies and deserving of death.

"They want to kill American civilians? Well, all right. But they're going to have to go through us —" He actually thumped his chest. "— first."

It was fascinating. Joan was completely enthralled. It was like realizing that Bambi had a full set of fangs and claws — and the burning desire to go one-on-one with Godzilla.

And the steely determination to win.

He was standing there, looking at her with all that fire in his eyes, and she wasn't quite sure what to do, what to say.

"Thank you," she told him. "That was . . . important for me to hear. Important for *every*one to hear, I think."

He laughed then as they started walking, transforming back into Muldoon, Junior. Although now that she knew it was back there, it was impossible to look at him and not see a glimmer of Muldoon, SuperSEAL, champion of the innocent.

"No, I will not repeat it at a ceremony during the President's visit, thank you very much."

Joan laughed, too. "I didn't ask that."

"Yeah, but you were going to. Admit it."

Muldoon was smiling at her, and she smiled back at him, suddenly aware of how pleasant this was, how pleasant a day it had been. Once she'd coaxed the real Lieutenant Muldoon into emerging from behind his spit-and-polish facade, she'd begun enjoying herself thoroughly. He truly was a lovely young man both inside and out, particularly with the sunlight making his golden brown hair glisten.

"So tell me the truth, as long as we're still off the record," she said. "Is this guy's name really Gilligan?"

"Nope. Gillman. Petty Officer Dan Gillman. Gilligan's just a nickname," he explained. "Nearly everyone's got one. Mark Jenkins is Jenk, for obvious reasons. Lieutenant Jacquette is Jazz — the reasons aren't so obvious, but he's not the warm and fuzzy kind of XO that you can sit and have a beer with and shoot the breeze, so I'm afraid I can't explain."

"What's yours?" she asked.

"I don't have one," he obviously lied. But then he immediately backpedaled. "I mean, yeah. I had a nickname during BUD/S, sure, but it didn't stick. Thank God."

"So what was it?"

"Nah, it's best left buried. Believe me."

"Oh, come on. I can keep a secret."

"I'm sure you can. But it took me a long time to live it down, so, sorry, I'm not telling," he said.

It would take her about five minutes alone with a few of his teammates to find out what Muldoon's nickname had been. But Joan didn't tell him that. She just pretended to let it drop.

"Let's see, other nicknames . . ." he said. "Sam Starrett — you haven't met him yet, but you will. His name isn't really Sam, it's Roger. *Sam* has something to do with him being from Texas. I don't even know what Cosmo Richter's real first name is. I mean, jeez, maybe it's Cosmo. He doesn't like to talk about himself very much."

He wasn't the only one. "His name is probably Leslie or Jean," Joan said. "Something a little too

76

androgynous for a big, bad Navy SEAL."

"Maybe, but I don't think so. He doesn't seem the type to worry much about something as inconsequential as his given name. And no one in their right mind would dare tease him about anything. He could be named Elizabeth, and no one would snicker when he walked into the room. He's one of those really quiet, really intense guys who just kind of stays in the background until you need someone's neck broken." He smiled tightly. "And he'll even do that without making a sound."

Yikes. "Gee, I can't wait to meet them. When you describe them like that . . . You know, maybe I'll pass on this part of the tour."

Muldoon laughed. "Hey, it's me you have to worry about. I'm in command. No one's neck gets broken unless I say so."

"Well, that's comforting. I think. How old did you say you were?"

"Old enough. Hang on a sec . . ."

As Joan watched, Muldoon bent over and made an adjustment to the brace he was wearing on his right knee.

Men should definitely wear shorts all the time. In fact, when Joan went back to the hotel tonight, she was going to sign on to the Internet with her laptop and start circulating a petition to bring the kilt back into fashion.

Muldoon's thighs were actually bigger than hers. Only his were solid. As he straightened up, Joan pretended to be looking at his intricate brace instead of his tanned legs with their springy, sun-bleached hair and powerful muscles.

"Bad knee?" she asked as they started walking again.

"Recent injury," he told her. "No big deal. It's fine now. But my doctor is a captain who goes for a run past the obstacle course every day about this time."

"I take it this means you're participating in the demonstration."

Muldoon smiled. "I am. And you are, too."

Joan laughed. "Yeah, right. In this skirt and heels. Can't you see me crawling on my elbows through the mud? 'Don't wait up, boys — I'm right behind you! I just gotta get my ass untangled from this barbed wire.' "

"That's not how it's going to work. *I'm* going to be right behind *you*."

Joan laughed again, but then stopped. Holy shit. The SuperSEAL was serious about this. She stopped walking.

"We won't do the whole course." He stopped, too.

"Well, gee," she said, "why ever not?"

"For one thing, you haven't had any training, and parts of the course are —"

"That *was* sarcasm dripping from my voice," Joan interrupted him. "I don't do obstacle courses, regardless of what I'm wearing. Yoo-hoo. Hello! I'm the kid who flunked gym. I sometimes do aerobics and yoga, sure, but that's nothing like real life — it's always in a carefully unrealistic, hermetically sealed health club environment, complete with air conditioning. The only time I run is when I'm out of chocolate and the store's closing in fifteen minutes. If I get within ten yards of that course, I'm going to wind up in the hospital, in traction."

"I won't let you get hurt," he told her quietly but very absolutely.

It was an amazing moment, and Joan let it hang there for several long seconds, just letting herself look at him, experience him, breathe him in. Lieutenant junior grade Michael Muldoon was like a living Norman Rockwell painting — sharp and sweet and patriotic and brave and honest and clean.

And he wouldn't let her get hurt.

Not ever? she wanted to ask him. Wouldn't that be nice? He could follow her around for the rest of her life — her own personal Navy SEAL guardian angel, keeping her from harm.

"Do you have a girlfriend?" she heard herself ask instead, and was instantly horrified at herself. What did she care beyond basic curiosity? And how could she have possibly thought to ask that now? It was like meeting Jesus and wondering aloud if he suffered from athlete's foot. Completely irrelevant and disrespectful to the moment.

"No," he said.

"That's too bad." She tried to look sympathetic, but she had to paste the expression on her face. She wasn't sure what she was feeling, but sympathy sure as hell wasn't part of it.

"Yeah, I guess." He just stood there, gazing at her as if he expected her to say something else.

So she said, "Well." And she forced a smile. She was about to turn away, to start walking toward the obstacle course again, to shake off the absurd notion that this odd connection she was feeling toward this kid — this little boy — was anything more than the friendship that she'd worked hard to achieve this afternoon, when he cleared his throat.

"Do you have, um, plans for dinner tonight?"

Oh, my God, was he actually asking her out?

Or was he just doing his job and checking to see that she wasn't at loose ends her first night in town?

"Actually, yes. I'm going to get room service and go to bed early. I'm still on D.C. time."

"Oh," he said. "Great."

"You know that old jet lag saying: East to west, get some rest. West to east, party beast. The party beasting will have to wait until I get back home."

Muldoon laughed. "I've never heard that one before."

Yeah, Junior, because you're so freaking *young.* Britney Spears was practically his peer. Wasn't *that* a frightening thought?

"I've been thinking about it," she told him, "and I'm pretty sure I just want to watch this demonstration. I can do without the firsthand experience."

"How about we just take you over the cargo net?" he asked.

"That really tall thing with the ropes?" Joan laughed. Dream on, Junior. "Why don't you just take me to the moon?"

He was quiet for a moment, but then cleared his throat again. "Look. Here's the deal. You can watch us do this stuff. It's impressive, it requires us to be in top physical condition, but so what."

"Yeah," Joan said. "So what. That's what I've been saying this entire tour whenever you tell me about stuff like BUD/S training's surf torture and carrying telephone poles around twenty-four/seven, and going through Hell Week with only a few hours of sleep. So what if you've got to be able to do forty-two push-ups in two minutes and fifty sit-ups in another two minutes and you've got to run one and a half miles in what? Eleven and a half minutes? Wearing your uniform and boots, no less — and that's just to get into the SEAL program. Never mind what you have to be able to do when you've finished the training. Yeah. So what. Right."

"Wow, you remembered all that? That's impressive."

She laughed in complete disgust. "Yes, I'm very clever, thanks. But as for what you can do, well, *so what.*"

He was laughing, too. "That's not what I meant."

"Well, what did you mean? Come on, 'splain it to me, Junior. I'm listening."

He stopped smiling, stopped walking. In fact, he moved in front of her, blocking her way, all but blocking the sun. "First, the name is *Mike,*" he said in a voice that allowed absolutely no argument. "The rank is *lieutenant,* ma'am. You can call me that, too. But there's nothing about me — whatsoever — that's junior, so do not call me that again."

Whoa. He was actually angry. It was a little bit scary.

"I'm sorry," Joan said. "Really. I didn't mean to. It slipped out."

"Stop thinking about me that way and there'll be nothing to slip."

"I *am* sorry. It's just you . . . well, it's not that you

remind me of my little brother, because I never had a little brother. I had — have — an older brother and he's pretty close to certifiable and you really don't remind me of him at all." Great, now she was babbling. "But I always wanted a little brother and I think I've always imagined that he'd be a lot like you. Kind of . . . perfect and sweet, you know?"

Muldoon laughed, turned away, turned back, scratching his head. "Well, that's great." He started to say something else, stopped, laughed again in what sounded like disgust.

Note to self: Avoid calling a Navy SEAL *sweet*. Even if he is.

"So what *did* you mean when you said 'so what'?" she asked, trying to distract him from the fact that she'd managed to get him both angry and disgusted with her all in the space of a few seconds.

He looked at her, and she couldn't for the life of her read his expression.

But he finally said, "I meant, so what because of course we can run the O course in record time. We've been trained for it. And that's great, but it's no longer a big deal when we do it. But, see, at times our job involves going into places that are heavily guarded or hard to get to, and rescuing hostages. We bring those people out and get them to safety. Most of the time the hostages that we rescue are people who *haven't* trained on the O course for hours. Some of them don't ever run unless the store's closing and they're out of chocolate."

Joan nodded. "Point and match awarded to Lieutenant Muldoon."

"I want to show you the way a team of SEALs can deal with the additional challenge of an inexperienced, untrained individual."

Ah. "Like me."

"Exactly like you," he agreed.

They were at the obstacle course now, and Joan pointed to the thing he'd referred to as the cargo net — a frame upon which a series of ropes were strung, going both vertically and horizontally, indeed like a giant net. It had to be at least fifty feet high. "And you think you can actually get me up and over that thing. Safely."

"I don't just think it. I know we can."

Joan looked at the rigging, looked back at Muldoon, and laughed. If they could get her over that, they could get Brooke Bryant over it, no problem. And wouldn't *that* be a photo op? "Okay, SuperSEAL," she said. "Let's see you do it."

FOUR

"I'm not here right now," Rene's answering machine drawled. "But I surely do want to talk to you. Leave a message at the beep, sugar, and I'll call you back."

"Rene, it's Mary Lou. Call me as soon as you get this. *Please*. I need to talk to you."

Lord Jesus, no one was home. No one? Yeah, right. It wasn't as if she had dozens of friends to call for a shoulder to cry on. Her sister Janine and her AA sponsor Rene were it. End of the very short list.

Mary Lou had called her day care lady first thing when she'd walked in the door, asking if it was okay that she didn't pick Haley up right at 2:15, the way she usually did.

Mrs. Ustenski had reassured her that Haley was making tired sounds, and that she could just as easily get in her nap here as at home. It was no problem.

So here Mary Lou was. Alone in her kitchen, stinking like a french fry.

And wanting a drink so badly that her hair was damn near standing on end.

She could do it. With Haley safe at Mrs. U.'s, she could drive down to the Ladybug Lounge. She

84

could walk inside and instantly be surrounded by the dark coolness. She'd take a deep breath of that sweet, stale, spilled beer smell and . . .

Mary Lou grabbed the phone and dialed Rene's number again. Again, her answering machine clicked on. She hung up the phone and pushed her way outside.

Rene and Janine *weren't* the only people on her list of friends. That list also included crazy Donny, who lived next door.

He was home. He was *always* home. Crazy people tended not to get out much, as a rule.

She crossed the lawn to his house. Rang the bell and knocked. Called out to him right through the door. "Donny, it's me. Mary Lou. Can I come in? Open up, hon."

She rang the bell again and again, until the curtain moved and he peered out at her. Checking, no doubt, to make sure she wasn't an alien, come to suck out his brains.

"What do you want?" he asked from behind the safety of his door. He had about forty dead bolts on the damn thing. It took five minutes for him to open them all. If there was ever a fire, he'd never make it out alive.

"May I please come in?" Mary Lou called back to him.

Sam called Donny "the Nutjob" and rolled his eyes whenever Mary Lou brought the man some cookies or a casserole. It wasn't that he feared for Mary Lou's safety as she went inside the house of a man who was mentally ill. No, Sam's objections had to do with the fact that Mary Lou had managed to make Donny think of her as a friend. And because of that, the one time Donny had actually left his house in the entire time they'd lived here had been to insert a series of reflectors on metal sticks in a circular pattern on the Starretts' front lawn.

He'd told them — completely seriously — that it was to keep the alien ships from using their yard as a landing pad.

Sam wasn't openly rude to Donny's face, but he was never more than coolly polite, either, even when Donny made it clear that he thought Sam was just one step down from God, simply because he was a U.S. Navy SEAL. Sam chided Mary Lou for encouraging "the little freak" — a cruel name that would have badly hurt Donny's feelings if he'd heard it, which he hadn't, thank God for small favors.

"I can't open the door," Donny called back to her now. "It's too dangerous today."

She could see that he'd wrapped a hat with aluminum foil again and was wearing it pulled way down over his ears — to keep the aliens from being able to read his thoughts.

The hat came out of the front closet when he was having a particularly bad day.

"I need to talk to you," she said. She was going to explode if he didn't open this door. "Please, Donny. I'm always there for you when you need me. You know it. You call me, and I come over. So let me in, okay?"

"I can't do that today."

"Yes, you can. Just unlock the door. Or — open the window. I'll come in through the window, so quick that the aliens won't be able to come in with me."

Donny backed away from the door. "That's what you'd say if you were an alien." He started to mutter and mumble to himself, chanting God knows what — maybe incantations designed to keep the aliens at bay. Once he started doing that, there was no hope of having a regular conversation with him.

And Mary Lou's desperation and despair exploded in a burst of temper. "Oh, for Christ's sake! I'm not an alien, you fucking freak!"

As soon as the words left her lips, she felt instantly like shit on a stick. There was nothing Donny hated more than being called a freak. Except maybe having aliens really come down from Pluto and suck out his brains. And she wasn't even sure about that.

"Donny!" she called, ringing his doorbell again. "I'm sorry! I didn't mean it!"

He didn't answer. She listened hard, but now there was only silence from inside the house.

Mary Lou slumped down on the front steps to Donny's house, aware that she'd just shortened her list of friends by a full third. No wonder Sam hated her and sought comfort in the arms of another woman. No wonder Meg Nilsson and the other SEAL wives wanted nothing to do with her. No wonder she hadn't been able to make a single friend among the women and girls who worked at McDonald's.

She was a terrible person.

She started to cry.

She'd been holding it in since she was face-to-face with Alyssa at Mickey D's, but now it escaped, and she sobbed like a four-year-old with a skinned knee.

She was a terrible, *lonely* person.

She might as well go and get drunk. She might as well drink until she couldn't stand up, until she couldn't think, until she couldn't breathe anymore.

If it wasn't for Haley, she'd do it.

Of course if it wasn't for Haley, Mary Lou wouldn't be sitting right here. If it wasn't for Haley, she wouldn't be married to Sam.

Oh, Lord, all she'd ever wanted was to be married to someone like Sam Starrett and to live in a cute little house just like the one that she lived in.

Except here she was. On the surface, she had everything she'd ever wanted. But although Sam was her husband, he didn't love her. And although she finally had the house, it wasn't a real home.

God, it sucked.

And she wanted a drink as badly as she'd ever wanted anything in her life.

She pushed her giant ass up and off Donny's concrete steps. She crossed his lawn and found herself standing out on her driveway.

Where her car was parked.

The car that she could climb into and use to drive herself to the Ladybug Lounge. It would be that easy.

Her keys were in her pocket. She took them out.

And threw them. As hard and as far as she could. All the way across her yard and into the yard of the neighbor on the other side of her house from Donny's. Into the carefully tended, thick patch of flowers and bushes next to the Robinsons' screened porch.

And then she sat down, right there in her driveway, and cried some more.

★ ★ ★

Wednesday, January 6, 1944.

It was a day that would change her life forever, but Charlotte Fletcher had been completely unaware of that at the time.

She'd written in her diary, "Ate lunch at my desk again today, and still haven't managed to keep up with the typing. Stayed late, but Mrs. P. finally chased me out at 7:10. I don't know why. I feel as if I'm helping the war effort while I'm there, and I've nothing to go home to. Mother F. was at her quilting circle at the church when I came in. This apartment that once held James's and my laughter is as silent and empty as I feel inside. And S. has brought yet another soldier home from the U.S.O. These walls and floors are paper thin. Or maybe the problem is mine. I find it impossible not to listen. Mother F. simply turns on the radio to mask the nightly noise, but I can't. Or maybe it's that I won't. It seems the perfect accompaniment to my misery as I lie alone and sleepless in this bed of mine that's far too cold."

That had been an added burden to her during the two years since James had been killed — the fact that she missed the physical intimacy of their marriage so very sharply. It seemed petty and selfish, but she ached for more than just his smile and his arms around her. She missed his kisses, his touch, the way he'd quickly set her on fire.

Her loneliness was made worse by the upstairs tenant, Sally Slaggerty. Sally the Slut, Charlotte called her in her less kind moments. She'd moved into the apartment upstairs two months ago and seemed determined to have intimate relations with every member of the armed forces who passed through Washington, D.C.

Charlotte again read the entry for January the sixth. "Ate lunch at my desk again today . . ." Nope, no mention at all of Vince, who'd come into the senator's office even earlier than she had that morning.

He'd been sitting there, in one of the straight-backed chairs that lined the outer office, waiting for a chance to talk to the senator, when she'd arrived at quarter to seven.

She might not have even noticed him were it not for the fact that he sat directly across from her desk. Whenever she looked up from her typing, there he was. Sometimes watching her, sometimes with his eyes shut.

He kept himself wrapped in a Navy overcoat. Only occasionally did she get a glimpse of the rumpled Marine uniform he wore beneath it.

He was painfully young — Charlotte guessed nineteen at the most. He was quite handsome despite the fact that his face was thin and his cheeks hollow. His eyes and hair were both dark. He looked as Italian-American as his name — Vincent DaCosta.

By ten A.M., Charlotte asked Mrs. Pierce in a low voice why the Marine had been kept waiting for so long.

Mrs. P. told her, also speaking quietly, that he hadn't an appointment. He'd been waiting outside the office door this morning when she'd unlocked it. Mrs. P. had informed him that the senator had no extra time today, but he asked if he might wait, on the chance that something might open up.

Charlotte ate her sandwich furtively at her desk, during one of the times he had his eyes closed. She knew that he must be hungry, but didn't know how to share lunch with such a handsome young man without seeming inappropriately forward.

At two P.M., when it became clear that the day was becoming more snarled rather than less, Charlotte went out from behind her desk and over to the Marine.

He got to his feet immediately, and she realized that he must've been injured recently, because, although he tried to hide it, she could see that it caused him pain just to stand.

"You're wasting your time today," she told him, quickly perching on the edge of the chair next to his, so that he could return to his seat as well. She didn't have time herself to be anything but direct. "I'm sorry, but Senator Howard will be going from one scheduled meeting to the next all afternoon. I think it would be wise for you to make an appointment."

"The next available appointment isn't for three weeks," the young man countered. He sat, but not before his face had turned another shade of pale. "I need to see him now."

"I'm sorry, but —"

"Look, all I want is his ear for five short minutes."

"You and his wife," Charlotte said dryly. "Get in line."

The Marine didn't laugh. "It's very important," he said.

He may have been young and only an enlisted private in the Marines, but there was something

91

about his dark eyes in that lean, pale face that was disconcerting.

"Everything that goes on in this office is very important," Charlotte informed him, retreating back behind her desk.

"May I wait here anyway, Miss . . . ?" he asked.

"Missus," she corrected him. "Fletcher. And yes, you may. It's still a free country, Private."

He smiled and it transformed his face, turning him from merely handsome into truly beautiful. "Yes, ma'am. I do believe that's what we're fighting for."

Joan liked both Jenk and Gilligan immediately.

Jenk was the shorter of the two. In fact, with his slight stature, his freckled face, and his cheerful smile, he looked to be even younger than Muldoon. More like a high school freshman than a Navy SEAL.

Gilligan was taller, with dark hair and an interesting, angular nose that kept his face from being overly pretty.

They were both friendly and relaxed, and she didn't have to work overtime to make them laugh.

The SEAL nicknamed Cosmo was a different story. He not only was older than the other men, but he didn't say a word as she shook his hand in greeting. And although he kept his distance, running up and down the ropes as he rigged some kind of harness thingy to the top of the cargo net's frame, she got the sense that he was listening to everything that was being said.

It was entirely possible that he even smiled once or twice. But it was hard to tell, especially since he wore sunglasses and she couldn't see his eyes.

They were all extremely physically fit. There was no doubt about it — Brooke would enjoy this type of hands-on demonstration very much indeed. And the news photographers would be in heaven.

And — alleluia — there would finally be a positive news story and photo featuring Brooke Bryant on the front page of every paper across the country.

Muldoon took charge immediately, making sure they were ready to go. He gave orders effortlessly, without apology, maintaining his status of leader while at the same time managing to be a working part of the tight-knit unit.

It was more than obvious that the other men — including Cosmo-the-silent-but-deadly, or maybe especially Cosmo — completely respected him.

Joan couldn't help but be impressed.

Which, she suspected, was one of the reasons Muldoon had set up this little demonstration. Although she wasn't quite sure if his intention had been for her to be impressed by him, or by the Navy SEALs.

It was her guess that those two things were one and the same. Muldoon was the Navy SEALs, and the SEALs were made up of men like Muldoon.

Yeah, she was impressed all the way to her toes, and the demonstration hadn't even officially started yet.

"Here's the scenario," Muldoon told them after double-checking to make sure the harness was secure. "We've been sent in to rescue Joan DaCosta, a thirty-year-old American woman in good health who works, let's say, at the U.S. embassy in Manila."

"Thirty-two," Joan interjected. "Almost thirty-three."

Muldoon chose to ignore her. "She's been grabbed and taken hostage by Abu Sayyat, a terrorist group linked to al-Qaeda in the Philippines. We've pinpointed her location — she's on a remote island. We've gone in and eliminated the terrorists who were holding her and —"

"Eliminated," Joan interrupted. "Why don't you military guys just say what you really mean — *killed?*"

"Because what we really mean is *eliminated,*" Muldoon told her evenly. "Targets are eliminated and terrorists are targets."

His eyes were a truly remarkable shade of blue. Cosmo was still wearing his sunglasses, so she couldn't see his eyes, but Gilligan's were a deep, soft brown, and also very pretty. Jenk's were on the blue side of hazel.

They were all looking at her, and Joan looked back at them, one by one, suddenly aware that all of these men — and maybe particularly scary Cosmo — had eliminated many terrorist targets. It was part of their job description.

She looked into Muldoon's eyes again, trying to see regret or even remorse at having taken human lives.

It wasn't there. She only saw . . . patience and maybe a hint of warm amusement. He liked her. She knew that. But it wasn't going to ruin his day if she disapproved of this aspect of his job. He didn't need her approval — he was that sure of himself.

It was a tremendously attractive thing — that

much self-confidence. Joan quickly looked away from him, afraid of what he might see in her own eyes.

"I'm sorry," she said. "Please go on."

"We've eliminated —" His gaze flickered back to her for a second. "— the tangos in the immediate area, but Intel has made us aware that the entire island is crawling with potential hostiles. World War Three will break out if they realize we're in the area, so we can't bring a helo— helicopter —" He looked at her again as he translated. "— for extraction. Extraction means leaving an operation —"

"And insertion means arriving. You told me that before," she said. "It's proven to be an effective tool for me in my job if I actually listen to the people from whom I'm getting information. Go on, please."

"Our safest, fastest route off the island is to proceed with stealth down to the harbor and swim," he continued. "Out in the harbor is a French freighter about to leave port. They know we're coming, and have rigging similar to our cargo net here secured along the starboard side of the vessel — the side facing away from town. We can climb on board without drawing any attention to ourselves. Any questions?"

"What do you do with a plan like that when your former hostage informs you that she can't swim?" Joan asked.

"As long as Lieutenant Muldoon's with you, you don't need to know how to swim," Jenk told her with a grin. "You just need to know how to hold on."

"Yeah, but what if she's really freaked out by

deep water, like really can't handle it, can't even go out on a boat?" she asked.

"Are you really?" Muldoon asked.

"No. I love boats. My only fear relating to the ocean is being forced to wear a bikini in public. I'm much more the tank suit type." She liked to swim — although calling it swimming was an exaggeration. She was an excellent doggy paddler, despite the fact that she hated getting water in her ears. She was prone to sinus infections. "I'm just saying *what if*."

"There's a good chance that information about any severe phobias would be included in the personnel records made available after the hostage went missing," he told her. "Although, you never know." He turned to Jenk. "You have Joan's file?"

She turned to Jenk, too. Joan's what?

The shorter SEAL was already holding something out toward Muldoon. A file. Her file. Holy shit. What exactly was in there?

"This is your file," Muldoon told her. "It contains information about you — next-of-kin type stuff, as well as standard info like all the places you've ever lived, colleges you attended, you know. Any known medical conditions. There's also a list of basic physical characteristics along with several photos — because hostages are not always alert and able to identify themselves. And occasionally they've been beaten to the point that the photos really don't help, hence the list of identifying marks." He smiled. "You know that tattoo you got about five years ago . . . ?"

"Oh, shit!" Joan snatched the file from his hands. "Let me see that."

Not only were there several extremely hideous pictures of her in there — out of three, only one of them wasn't awful — but there was indeed a brief list of physical characteristics, including her double piercings in each ear, and yes, the small rose tattoo she'd gotten just below her left hip.

She flipped through the rest of the papers.

"God, how embarrassing. My tattoo's in my file, yet there's nothing here at all about my skill as a public relations person and a writer. Isn't *that* telling about our society?"

Jenk pointed helpfully to the page that held a summary of her college transcript. "They list your SAT scores. Which were almost as high as mine."

Muldoon gave him one look and Jenk pulled his hand back as quickly as if he'd gotten smacked.

"This isn't that sort of file," Muldoon told her. "This is basic and limited information that will help us ID you and therefore be able to get you to safety. If there was more time to prepare, we'd receive more information about you." He smiled. "Maybe even a writing sample. But for right now, this file has one of the things we need most. Your measurements."

"Excuse me?" Was he kidding? Joan couldn't tell because he was smiling. If he was, it was a bad joke. But he looked pointedly behind her, and she turned.

"Your new wardrobe," Muldoon said.

Jenk was now holding up a pair of ankle-high boots. And Gilligan held what looked like a green-and-brown camouflage jumpsuit. Jungle print, she remembered it was called.

"When we kick down the doors and rescue you,"

Muldoon told her, suddenly serious, "we come in prepared for you to be in any condition. You might be beaten so badly that you can't walk. If that's the case, we'll stabilize you and carry you out. You might be naked and handcuffed in the corner of the room. We'll get you unlocked and cover you up. You might — and we always hope this is the case — you might be physically unharmed but wearing a skirt and high heels, like you are right now. I don't know about you, but personally, I've never been able to run well in heels."

"Me, neither," Cosmo said, perfectly deadpan.

Joan took the jumpsuit from Gilligan. "Is there somewhere I can go to put this on?"

"Chances are you wouldn't have time to be modest," Gilligan told her apologetically. "You'd either change right there or just pull this on over your clothes."

"If those are my choices, I'll take option two." She kicked off her shoes and stepped into the pants.

"It'll work better if you hike up your skirt," Muldoon suggested, and for a second she thought he might actually reach in and help.

But she turned her back on him — on all of them.

"I'm going to be really hot in this," she realized. And doubly uncomfortable with her skirt bunched up around her ass.

"There'll be less of a chance of rope burns," Gilligan said.

Joan reached behind her, unfastened her skirt, and, zipping the jumpsuit up in the front, squeezed her skirt over her head. She tossed it onto a nearby bench and kicked her shoes over there as well as she slipped her arms into the jumpsuit and zipped it the rest of the way up.

The boots they'd brought for her were a little big, but then again, she was wearing pantyhose instead of socks. Transformation complete.

And then they were all heading to the cargo net.

"You ready to try this?" Muldoon asked her.

"Don't I look ready?" Actually, in this loose-fitting jumpsuit, she probably looked like a camouflaged marshmallow. When they did this with Brooke, she'd have to make sure to get clothes that fit. The camouflage pattern was nice, though — it would make for a good photo.

But then Joan looked up. And up. And all those little details didn't matter right now.

Standing next to this thing, she knew this was completely insane. The framework holding the ropes seemed to stretch upward for a long, long way.

"You want me to hose you down?" Jenk asked helpfully. "To make the scenario more realistic? Because supposedly you just had a nice long swim out into the harbor."

Was he serious? God, he was.

"Thanks, but no thanks," Joan said. She tried to sound casual. "Hey, uh, Mike? Is this really safe?"

"Yeah. Doubly so because you'll be wearing this." Muldoon fastened the harness around her. It went between her legs and up around her waist and around her torso and over her shoulders. It was attached to a blue mountain-climbing rope that went all the way up to some kind of device attached to the top of the frame.

99

God damn, this thing was big. She stared up at it, unable to look away. Muldoon really expected her to climb all the way up there? And down the other side . . . ?

"So if you do slip — but you won't, I won't let you — the harness'll catch you. What you need to remember is, if that happens, protect your head. You listening to me, Joan? Look at me, okay?"

He pulled her chin down so that she was looking into his eyes.

"You with me?" he asked.

Huh? Oh. "Yeah."

"If you slip, protect your head. The harness will keep you from falling far, but you'll swing. You'll just bounce off the ropes, but it's not impossible for you to hit the frame. Which is solid wood. Which you don't want your head to connect with. You got that?"

Joan nodded.

He tightened the harness around her waist. "So what do you do if you slip?"

"Protect my head. I was listening."

"Good." It was an odd sensation to have him snapping and buckling her in. It was very safe-feeling — not unlike being five years old and bundled up by her mother before she went outside and played in the snow.

She half expected him to kiss her on the nose when he finished.

Instead he just smiled. "Don't look so worried. I'm going to be with you every step of the way. And Jenk and Cosmo will be right behind us and beside us. Gillman will be up top, making sure the harness system works. Okay?"

"Okay." She forced herself to smile.

"There we go. That's more like it. This is going to be fun."

Joan laughed. "No, no, no. Fun is getting invited to a dinner party and finding out you're seated next to Colin Firth. Fun is having the First Lady invite you to lunch in Paris. Fun is not climbing four million feet into the air and four million feet back down."

"To each his own," he said easily. "I wouldn't have the slightest clue what to say to the First Lady. Or Colin Firth."

"You just ask about their day. Everyone likes to talk about themselves," Joan said. "It's easy."

"Yeah, well, I happen to think this is easier. As you climb, it's going to feel kind of soft. Springy. The ropes give. And they'll tighten and bounce when Cosmo and Jenk climb onto the rigging, too. Hold on as tightly as you can. And when you take a step, if you feel at all like you're slipping, try to catch the heel of your boot on the rope — it'll make you feel more secure." He turned her to face the ropes. "Start by climbing on."

"Now?"

He laughed. "As opposed to next Friday? Yes, now. Don't think about it, Joan. Just do it."

She did it. Both hands and then her feet. Yikes, it was definitely wiggly underfoot. And her own body weight pulled her backward, gravity tugging her toward the ground. This was going to be much more difficult than climbing a wooden ladder.

"There you go. Hold on tightly," he ordered. And then the ropes squirmed even more as he climbed on, too.

And Muldoon really did climb on — right on top of her.

He surrounded her, his hands and feet on either side of hers, his chest against her back. He was actually touching her, as if they were lovers spooning together.

"This is how we're going to do it," he said, his voice in her ear. "Me right here with you. All the way up to the top. When you move, I move. If you need to stop and take a break, you can lean back against me. I'll hold on to you and make sure you don't fall."

He was extremely solid against her back, a very male wall of hard muscles.

Oh, my.

"You okay?" he asked.

"Fine," she managed. Her heart was already pounding, and she was only a foot or so off the ground. "Except I don't seem to want to let go of these ropes, so climbing's going to be a little difficult."

"Start with your left foot." His breath was warm against her ear, and he pushed his leg up underneath her left thigh, actually lifting her foot off the ropes.

She had no choice but to find the next rung in this giant rope ladder.

"Good. Then your right hand." He helped her with that as well, prying her fingers from the rope and guiding her up a square. "Excellent. Now your right foot. And left hand."

And there she was.

Climbing.

Well, actually, it was more like she was sitting on

his lap, and he was climbing, but at least he no longer had to pry her hands from the ropes as they moved.

"You're doing great," he said into her ear. "Just don't look down."

Of course she immediately looked down and it was all over. She froze. "Oh, shit." It hadn't taken them long to get way, way off the ground. And yet they were still only halfway to the top.

"Oops," Muldoon said. "My bad. Sorry. I shouldn't have told you not to look down, because then you're going to look down, right? Human nature."

"Oh, shit," she said again.

"Do you have trouble with heights?" he asked. "It's nothing to be ashamed of. A lot of people do."

"I do," Jenk chimed in, hanging like a monkey by only one arm from the net, just slightly above them.

He was making the entire thing shake, and Joan heard herself squeak with alarm. God, how embarrassing to actually *squeak*.

"Go all the way up to the top," Muldoon ordered Jenkins. "Cosmo, too. Get off the net. Let's make this thing as stable as possible."

Joan closed her eyes as the two other men quickly climbed up the rigging, as the net bounced and shook. But then, thankfully, it stopped.

"I'm not afraid of heights," she told Muldoon. "At least I didn't think I was. But, oh, God, I guess I am."

"Take a break, okay?" he told her. "Lean back against me and concentrate on breathing. I've got you." Somehow he managed to put his arm around her waist, to secure her more tightly against him, even as he held on to the ropes. "Is that better?"

If she didn't know better, if she hadn't already firmly established the fact that they were friends and nothing more than friends, she would have thought he'd told her not to look down on purpose, purely for a chance to get his arms around her.

God, he had big arms. One of them was wrapped tightly around her so she could feel firsthand just how strong he was. His other arm, she could see. It was right next to her cheek, muscles standing out as he held them both in place.

"You're not wearing a harness," she realized, suddenly dizzier than ever. "Oh, God! Oh, Mike! This was a really bad idea. I want to get down. I want us both to go back down to the ground, okay?"

"Shhh," he said. "Joan, come on, breathe. I'm up here all the time. Remember what I told you? For me, it's no big deal."

"Yeah, but you're not usually up here with me. I'm a total klutz. I'm going to knock you off of this thing, I know it. In case you haven't noticed, I need to lose about twenty pounds. I'm not some delicate lightweight."

"Well, actually," he said into her ear, as calmly as if they were having a conversation back on the ground, "I *have* noticed. Kind of hard not to, considering our physical proximity and, well, you want to know the truth, I don't think you need to lose anything. You feel pretty perfect to me."

FIVE

Muldoon held on to the ropes as Joan didn't say anything. As she *still* didn't say anything. As she continued not to say anything.

Oh, man, he'd never done this before. He'd never had to, never wanted to. And now he knew why. Facing potential rejection like this was no fun.

Especially when she smelled so damn good and fit so well in his arms. Man, this woman was incredibly sexy and she apparently didn't even know it. Her skin was beautiful, smooth and soft on her cheeks, but crinkling slightly around her eyes. He loved laughter lines on women. From now on it was going to be the first thing he looked for when he checked out a woman. He'd wasted far too much time on far too serious women who wouldn't laugh even if they were dating Adam Sandler. Yeah, he was forever done with women who didn't have a solid sense of humor.

He was done with women who didn't fill his arms, too. No more bony, half-starving, pencil-thin women who wanted him to escort them to dinner — which was ridiculous because once they got to the restaurant, they barely dented a salad.

No more blondes, either. He liked hair like

Joan's — thick and dark with a hint of red highlights. Chestnut, he thought it was called. Yeah. And he liked brown eyes, too. Just like hers.

Right now her brown eyes were closed. But then she opened them and glanced back over her shoulder at him. And then, finally, she spoke. "Are you fricking *hitting* on me, Muldoon, sixty feet off the ground?"

"Thirty-five feet," he corrected her. "And no," he lied, because she didn't look particularly happy at the idea. "I'm not. I'm . . . You said you weren't a lightweight, like there was something wrong with that. And I just thought you should know that a lot of guys don't like women who look like they'll blow away in a strong breeze. A lot of guys like women who actually look like women, and have, like, women's bodies, and well, I'm one of those guys, and I happen to think that you've got, you know, a really fabulous body. So don't go ruining it by losing twenty pounds and turning into a walking skeleton, okay?"

He'd surprised her. He'd surprised himself as well. Despite his initial lie, he'd never been so completely honest with a woman before — at least not about what turned him on.

A great smile, laughter lines, lots of curves, and legs just like Joan DaCosta's.

"Well," she said rather faintly. "Thank you. That's . . . the most compelling argument for not skipping dessert that I've heard in a long time."

She glanced at him again, smiled weakly, then looked away.

Ah, come on, Joan. Say it. This was where she was supposed to take his incredibly unsubtle cue

106

and invite him to her hotel room to share some of that dessert. And breakfast, too.

She cleared her throat. Here it came . . .

"You're a very nice young man," she said.

Ah, jeez. That was even worse than being called Junior. He knew from experience that calling someone — or being called — *nice* promised a relationship filled with exactly zero sex.

Yes, buried inside of her innocuous-sounding vague words of dubious praise was his answer. The No Sex Tonight buzzer sounded with seeming finality. He wasn't going anywhere near her hotel room any time in the near future. *Nice young man* was a full one-eighty degrees from *steamin' hot stud muffin*.

There was no doubt about it. She thought he was too young for her.

"But I really do want to get down now," she added.

"I'm not going to let you fall," Muldoon said for what seemed like the four thousandth time in the past fifteen minutes, working hard not to let his frustration sound in his voice. But he knew that she wasn't really listening, that she didn't really trust him. How could she? He was obviously too young to be trusted.

"I'm not afraid of *me* falling," she said. "I'm afraid of *you* — Hey, you're not listening to me, Michael. Let me try to make this really simple. *I'm* wearing a harness. I will not hit the ground if I slip. But if I somehow make *you* slip, and I know that I will, it'll be Splatsville."

"No, it won't."

"Oh, yes, it will."

"No," he said, resisting the urge to shake her. "It won't. You're the one who's not listening to me." Muldoon knew what he had to do. "Will you be okay if I move away from you? I want to show you something, but I won't leave you if it's not okay with you."

She craned her neck to look at him over her shoulder. "What are you going to do?"

"Are you going to be okay?" he asked.

"Yes, but —"

"Yes is all I need to hear," he interrupted.

"But —"

"Shhh. I want you to hold on really tight, because the net's going to bounce. Put your arms all the way through and loop the ropes with your elbows. Yeah, like that. Good. You feel secure?"

He'd gotten her attention now, that was for sure. Her eyes were wide as she turned to look at him. "What are you going to —"

He didn't wait for her to finish. He went up, fast, almost all the way to the top of the obstacle. He could see her face, looking up at him. Good.

Okay, Joan. Watch this.

Muldoon let himself drop. Fast. With his legs free. From Joan's point of view it would look as if he were falling. And maybe, technically, he was. But it was a controlled fall. One that he could stop anytime.

And he did stop, directly beside Joan.

The ropes strained and groaned under his weight, and she bounced pretty hard, but she didn't lose her grip.

He'd timed it perfectly, executed it beautifully — and she had her eyes tightly closed.

"Oh, my God," she was saying. "Oh, my God, oh, my God!"

"You want me to do that again?" he asked. "And this time you can keep your eyes open so you can watch?"

Joan opened eyes that were filled with anger. "You childish bastard! You could have told me what you were going to do!"

Whoa. She was really pissed.

"This is supposed to be a demonstration, so —"

"This was a mistake. A big mistake. So if you're done showing off, dickhead, I want to get down."

"Oh, come on, you're not really going to quit on me, are you?"

"I Want To Get Down," she enunciated. "Why am I waiting for you? I don't need you to help me." She started toward the ground.

Muldoon followed alongside of her. "Joan —"

"Stop making it bounce!" she ordered. "Just stay where you are. I can get to the bottom by myself."

And she did.

But as soon as she hit the ground and started unfastening the harness, Muldoon went after her.

"I didn't expect you to be the type to quit and run away," he said. That was probably not the smartest thing to say given Joan's emotional state.

She looked about to boil over. "I didn't expect *you* to be a *dickhead*."

She got the last of the harness off of her and stormed to the bench, snatching her skirt, her shoes, and that oversized purse thing she carried around with her, before heading toward the gate and the parking lot.

Muldoon looked back at the cargo net. Jenk and

Gillman were already on their way back to the ground. Cosmo was still perched up at the very top, like some kind of weird giant bird, basking in the afternoon sunshine.

"Stow the harness and rope," he ordered them, before dashing after Joan.

"Come on, wait a sec," he said, catching up to her, catching her arm in the parking lot.

But she yanked herself free and kept walking. "You scared me to death! You should have told me you could do that circus trick stuff right from the start! But no. You had to show off."

"I told you the O course was no big deal to any of us," he protested as she stopped in front of a rental car and fished in her bag for the keys. "I spent not an insignificant amount of time today talking to you about insertion techniques like HALO jumps out of airplanes and fast-roping down from helicopters. Didn't it occur to you that if we can do that, then something like the cargo net on the O course might not be such a challenge?"

"No." Joan unlocked the car door and threw her stuff into the backseat.

"Well, then, okay, I'm sorry."

She laughed as she climbed in behind the wheel, but it wasn't because she thought he was funny. "You're only sorry now?"

"No, that's not what I —"

"I think it would be a good idea if I were assigned a different liaison." She wouldn't look him in the eyes.

Oh, man. "Look, Joan, I don't think —"

"I'll call Lieutenant Commander Paoletti's office in the morning." She closed the door and started the car.

"Joan —"

But she kept the window up as she put the car into reverse, pulled out of the parking spot, and drove away.

"Shit!"

Muldoon turned to stomp back toward the O course and found Sam Starrett a few feet away from him, getting something out of the back of his pickup truck.

"Looks like that didn't go too well," Sam commented.

"Yeah, well, it would have gone really great — if my goal was to have her call me a dickhead and drive off without me."

Sam had the decency not to laugh in his face as he hefted his seabag onto his shoulder and crossed around the back of his truck so he could talk to Muldoon without shouting. "Sometimes you can measure how much a woman likes you by how mad you can make her."

Muldoon snorted.

"I know it sounds crazy," Sam said. "But it's true. And it's something I learned a little too late. Don't make the same mistakes I did. This White House lady might be in the exactly perfect emotional place right now for you to call her up and apologize profusely. I mean, really crawl. Admit to anything and everything. Tell her she was a hundred percent right. Women really like to be right. And then ask her to dinner."

"Yeah, I don't know about that." It was kind of hard to take romantic advice from a man who was miserable in his marriage and still carrying a torch for someone else. And the cowboy Texas drawl didn't help his credibility as Dear Abby, either.

"Suit yourself," the lieutenant said with a shrug. "But if I were you, I'd ask her to dinner before it's too late."

"I did," Muldoon told him. "She said no. She said she was tired."

"Tired isn't no. Tired is tired. Ask her again, for Christ's sake. Ask her to lunch if you don't want to ask her to dinner again. Ask her to have a drink. Ask her out on your boat. Don't just sit around with your thumb up your butt. Ask her fucking something. Or else she's right. You are a dickhead."

"Gee, thanks, Lieutenant."

"Anytime."

Mary Lou couldn't find her car keys. She was going to have to go pick up Haley in about half an hour, and she couldn't do it without her keys.

To make matters worse, it wasn't going to be too long before it got dark, and once it did, then she'd *really* have trouble finding them.

She was on her hands and knees in the Robinsons' garden, praying that any spiders and snakes she encountered would be of the nontoxic variety. She tried not to start crying again as she searched mostly by feel among the thick pink and yellow flowers.

"May I help you?" a musically accented voice asked.

Oh, Lord.

She couldn't bring herself to turn and look up

112

into the face of the man standing beside her. The leather sandals and long, almost elegant dark-skinned toes were all she could bear to focus on.

It was the Robinsons' yard guy. She'd seen him in the neighborhood often enough over the past month or so — a tall, reed-thin, dark-haired, dark-skinned, foreign-looking man. He came every week to cut the Robinsons' lawn and tend their flower beds — one of which she was currently kneeling in, trying desperately not to crush. He was relatively new, but he kept the Robinsons' yard looking so good he'd already landed contracts with some of the other neighbors as well.

Despite the fact that he looked as if he might spend his free time organizing an al-Qaeda terrorist cell.

"I, uh, lost my car keys," she said. Mercy, what a stupid, foolish thing to have to admit. As if she'd been doing cartwheels here in this flower bed and they'd fallen out of her pocket.

"I threw them over here," she went ahead and admitted, wiping her sweaty forehead with the back of her hand, "so I wouldn't be tempted to drive to the Ladybug Lounge and get shit-faced drunk, all right? So, no, unless you have X-ray vision and can see where my keys landed, you probably can't help me. But thank you so very much for asking."

The sandals walked away, thank God for small favors.

But then the sandals came back. And she saw that the yard guy was carrying one of those metal detectors that people used on the beach to find lost jewelry and coins. "Please, allow me."

113

Mary Lou extracted herself from the garden, moving back to sit on the lawn. As she brushed dirt from her knees, he turned on the doohickey, and about four seconds later, he turned it back off, then reached carefully down among the pink flowers and pulled out her keys.

Thank God.

Instead of handing them to her, he sat down, cross-legged, beside her.

"Are you absolutely sure you want these back?" he said in a slightly British English-as-a-second-language accent.

With him sitting next to her, Mary Lou could look at him — really look at his face and into his eyes. When he'd first started working next door, she'd complained to her sister about it. It wasn't that she was prejudiced against foreigners. She was the first to admit he made the Robinsons' yard look great. But really, after 9/11, who wanted strange Arabs prowling around their neighborhood?

He was older than she'd thought from watching him from her kitchen window as he'd worked next door. Up close, she could see lines around his eyes and mouth. He wore a full beard that, although it was neatly trimmed, made his already dark face seem even darker.

From a distance, he'd always appeared to be scowling, but she saw now that that wasn't true. His craggy features and thick eyebrows only made it seem as if he were perpetually angry. In fact, up close, she saw that his default expression was a gentle smile.

And right now she saw nothing but kindness in his dark brown eyes.

He held her keys loosely in his big, work-hardened hand. She could have reached out, taken them, thanked him, and walked away and that would have been that.

But then he said, "I've seen you at some of the local meetings. I also go almost every night."

The lawn guy went to Alcoholics Anonymous, too. She stared at him.

"You're often there with your baby," he continued. "She is so beautiful, always smiling. You must be so very proud."

"I am," Mary Lou said.

He nodded. "I don't think you really want to go to the Ladybug Lounge today, do you?"

She started to cry. It was absurd — she was sure she'd cried herself out, over on her driveway and then inside the house as well. She'd sat in her kitchen, expressing her breast milk like some kind of human cow as she'd cried and cried and cried. But here she was, melting down again, and there was nothing she could do to stop it.

The lawn guy just sat there. He didn't reach for her, but he didn't run away, either. He just sat quietly beside her and let her cry.

"I'm sorry," she finally managed to say.

"Your sponsor is not home to talk to?"

"No."

He nodded. "Too bad. But that was very good thinking," he told her. "Throwing away your keys. Very smart."

Mary Lou looked up at him, wiping her eyes. "You think so?"

He gave her an even wider but no less gentle smile. "I know it to be so. You're here and you're still sober, and maybe that very bad moment has passed."

She wasn't so sure about that. This entire night was going to suck — picturing Sam with Alyssa . . . Oh, Lord, don't think about that.

"How long have you been sober?" she asked him. "I mean, if you don't mind my asking."

"Just over four years."

"Wow."

"And you?"

"Eighteen months," she told him.

He gave her another of those smiles. "That's excellent."

"Not as good as you. Dear Lord, four years . . ."

Out on the street, a car slowly drove past. It wasn't one of the neighbors — at least not one she recognized. What they would think, seeing them sitting here like this, she couldn't imagine.

"The trick lies in not thinking about it as one large block of time," he told her. "It's impossible for anyone to not drink for four whole years. But to choose not to drink for today? That's still difficult, but not quite as impossible. I should have answered your question by saying I have chosen to be sober today for four years' worth of days in a row."

"I thought Arabs weren't allowed to drink," Mary Lou said.

"*Muslims* have laws in which drinking alcohol is forbidden, yes," he corrected her. "But many still do. Christians aren't supposed to take the Lord's name in vain, is that not true? Jews shouldn't eat ham or pork. And Catholics have certain rules about procreation that they tend to ignore. Just as with every religion, there are those Muslims who follow the exact rule of the law, and those who practice less strenuously — to varying degrees. I myself grew up in a household where my parents and their friends chose to embrace the ways of the West and to serve and drink alcohol. And yet we observed Ramadan and practiced our faith in other ways."

"Where are you from?" she asked.

He smiled. "Anaheim."

"I meant —"

"Saudi Arabia," he said. "My parents had an opportunity to leave when I was sixteen. We moved first to Beverly Hills, and then to Anaheim." He smiled at her again. "Where are you from?"

Nowhere. "We moved around a lot when I was a kid," she told him. "Alabama, Arkansas, Louisiana. If the town had a bar, we lived there. See, I'm a second-generation drunk. I come by it naturally."

"But you don't drag your daughter from town to town, bar to bar," he pointed out.

"Yeah, I just want to."

"But you don't," he said again, in his gentle voice.

Mary Lou hugged her knees tightly to her chest. "My husband's girlfriend's in town. I'm pretty sure he's going to see her tonight."

The lawn guy was silent, and Mary Lou glanced at him. He was watching her, his expression finally somber, his eyes sad. "And this is why you wish to punish yourself . . . ?"

"No," she said. "This is why I wish to get shit-faced drunk — so I don't have to think about him fucking her."

He blinked at her foul language, but that was the extent of his reaction. He was just too goddamn relentlessly serene, and for a moment, Mary Lou hated him for that. She hated everything, everyone.

Except Haley.

"Maybe you need to ask yourself why you stay with him when his actions make you want to drink," he said.

"I love him," Mary Lou said, but the words sounded hollow to her.

"Ah. Maybe you should confront him, then, tell him you don't want him to see this woman anymore."

"I have." She couldn't believe she was telling the Robinsons' lawn guy some of her deepest, most miserable, most pathetic secrets. "He just denies it. He says he hasn't seen her since we got married."

"Maybe he is telling the truth."

"She's in town. I saw her. And he called to say he wouldn't be home tonight. I don't need to be a rocket scientist to figure that one out."

He was silent then.

"Just so you know, I wasn't looking for the keys so I could go drink," she told him. "I wanted to find them before it gets dark because I need them. But I wasn't going to the Ladybug, I swear. I was going to take a shower, and then go pick up my daughter from day care. That's why I need the keys. To fetch her back home."

"And maybe tonight you'll use those keys to drive yourself to an AA meeting?" he asked.

She nodded. "Definitely."

"That's very good."

"You wouldn't happen to know any that last all night, would you?"

He sat for a moment, just looking at her with those dark as midnight, bottomless-pit eyes, as if he were trying to make up his mind. He finally reached into his pocket, took out a worn leather wallet, and pulled out a slightly bent business card.

"This is my home phone number," he told her as he handed it to her with her keys. "I'm at home every night after nine-thirty. If you need someone to talk to, even if it's late . . ."

YARD WORK, the plain white card said in a simple font. IHBRAHAM RAHMAN. It was followed by his phone number.

"I'm not sure —" Mary Lou stopped. *If my husband would approve,* was what she'd been about to say. But that was a lie. Sam wouldn't give a shit if she took this man's card and called him up every night of the week.

"Thank you," she said instead.

SIX

There was a telephone in the bathroom, so Joan didn't have to get out of the tub when it rang. She knew who was calling, though, because she'd already received her nightly update from her boss, Myra, who was acting as Brooke Bryant's current "handler."

Brooke's visit to Houston was going as well as could be expected — whatever that meant. There was something going on that Joan hadn't been told. Which made her job just that much harder to do.

Myra reported that they'd be in San Diego on schedule. "Oh, and find Brooke an escort for the admiral's party — the one being held at the hotel," she'd commanded. "Find her someone loaded with medals. A captain or a commodore or —"

"Or a Navy SEAL?" Joan had asked.

"Yes! Even better, make him a war hero."

"I think they probably all are at this point," Joan had told her.

She now waited three rings before she picked up the phone. "Hello."

"Hi, Joan, it's Mike. Muldoon," he added, as if she got dozens of phone calls all of the time from dozens of different Mikes.

She'd been expecting his call. A man didn't work

his ass off to become a Navy SEAL by lying down and accepting failure. Even if said failure was as insignificant as an inability to be an acceptable liaison to the White House public relations assistant in charge of publicity ops for the president's unconventional daughter.

"Okay, Muldoon. Let's hear it," she said. "Make it good, expend a little emotional energy, maybe even shed a few tears, and I won't call your CO in the morning."

He laughed with what sounded a lot like relief. Had he really been worried? "Thank you."

"Don't thank me yet, Junior. You've got at least fourteen hoops to leap through before you can start thanking me." She stuck her toe up to the faucet to catch a drip, waiting to see how *Junior* would go over this time around.

He didn't even acknowledge it. "I *am* sorry," he said. "It wasn't my intention this afternoon to frighten you."

"Oh, boo, hiss," Joan said. "You sound completely insincere. Try again. Maybe with a little wobble in your voice. 'Oh, Joan,' " she demonstrated. " 'Please, *please* forgive me for being such an incredible, unbelievable asshole today. If you don't forgive me, why, I'm going to crumple into a little heap right here in the lobby of the Team Sixteen building and cry my little heart out.' "

He laughed. "I can't say that because I happen to be calling you from home. But I am really sorry," he said. He didn't sound quite as young over the phone. "You were right — you were absolutely right. I was showing off. I wanted to impress you. I wanted to, um . . ."

Joan waited, dying to hear this, remembering his voice in her ear. *You feel pretty perfect to me.* He hadn't sounded too young then, either.

He took a deep breath. "Well, I wanted to —"

But then she didn't want to hear it. She couldn't stand to hear it. There was no way on God's green earth she could have a clandestine fling with a twenty-five-year-old Navy SEAL — even after her job here was over and she officially went on vacation. She couldn't do it. She would look too pathetic. Because it *was* too pathetic.

Sure, she would enjoy it immensely while it was happening, but she'd look back upon it with great embarrassment. After it was over, it would become a total cringe-fest. Especially since said twenty-five-year-old Navy SEAL had been specifically assigned to keep her entertained. She would forever wonder if she had been just a job or a true adventure.

And so would the rest of the world.

So instead of hearing what exactly he wanted, she cut him off. "You know, I've been thinking about why I freaked out this afternoon, and the truth is, I wouldn't have been so upset if I didn't like you so much. If I didn't already really value your *friendship*," she clarified quickly. "I wasn't lying when I said that it felt like you were my long lost little brother. You're a great kid, Mike," she enunciated carefully, heavy on the K and D so he'd be sure to understand, "and I want very much for us to continue to be friends."

Silence. Joan closed her eyes tightly, praying that he wouldn't push the issue. Praying that maybe she had been wrong about the news flash he'd sent her up on that cargo net. She was sure that he had been hitting on her, despite his denial. He couldn't have sent a more clear message if he'd used semaphore flags.

But, please God, maybe she was wrong.

He finally spoke. "Then you'll meet me for lunch tomorrow? I'm going to be busy right up until about 1130, but what do you say we meet at Bellitani's at noon? It's an Italian place right on the water here in Coronado."

Lunch was good. Lunch was decidedly the most nonromantic meal of the day. Joan turned on the water, letting more hot into the tub as she refused to be disappointed.

Well, okay. Honesty time. A very tiny part of her was disappointed. But it was the same small part that had been disappointed that time she went to Niagara Falls and didn't give in to the urge to jump over the fence and into the water churning below.

"Great," she said. "I'll see you tomorrow."

"Great," Muldoon echoed. "Oh, and Joan?"

"Yeah?"

"Next time you call me Junior, I'm telling Mom."

"That was Joanie on the phone, calling from Coronado —" Vince stopped short at the door to their bedroom.

Charlie was fast asleep, curled up on their bed, surrounded by a packet of old letters tied up with ribbon and a small pile of cloth-covered books.

Letters from James.

And her journals.

The first time he'd seen that notebook with the

roses on the cover was decades ago, as she hurriedly cleared her things from her bedroom to make room for him there.

That was after he'd done a nosedive onto the Persian rug that covered the worn floorboards of Senator Howard's office. It had been day four of waiting for five short minutes of the man's nonexistent time.

Vince had protested as stridently as possible as Charlotte brought him home with her in a taxi, which perhaps wasn't very strident considering he was shaking with fever and unable to stand on his own two feet. Aside from going to a hospital, the last thing he'd wanted to do was to remove her from her own bedroom, in her own home.

"Our spare room is very small," she informed him as she helped him slowly climb the steps to the front porch of her apartment. It was a two- or three-family house — he couldn't tell how many apartments it held just by looking — and although the entire place needed paint, it was neat as a pin. "We can't possibly take care of you in there — not much fits besides the bed."

The spare room was sized to hold a baby's cradle, he'd later found out. It was a room Charlie and her husband James had never gotten around to using, thinking they had all the time in the world to start a family.

"Mother!" she shouted as she maneuvered him around the screen and pushed open the door to the house. He looked up to see a gold star hanging in the front window. Someone in this house had lost a son in the war. "Edna! I need help!"

A woman came out of the kitchen, wiping her

124

hands on a towel. "Oh, dear Lord!" She rushed toward them.

"I just need to sleep," Vince said, as Charlotte and her mother-in-law half carried, half pushed him up the stairs of their house. "I don't want to trouble you any further. Please, you've already been more than kind bringing me here."

"He flat out refused to go to a hospital," Charlotte told her mother-in-law. "I didn't know what else to do."

"He's barely a child," Mother Fletcher said. She was a large-boned, gray-haired woman with a booming voice that reminded Vince of the nuns in his grammar school.

"I'm twenty-one," he felt compelled to say. "Old enough to —"

"Old enough to go to war and get shot, apparently," Charlotte finished for him tartly. "Like most of the young men in America today. In here. In my room, Mother."

It was two against one, and together they efficiently removed his overcoat and gently pushed him into Charlotte's bed.

God, the sheets smelled just like her. He just wanted to close his eyes and sleep forever, with Charlotte Fletcher's sweet perfume giving him beautiful dreams.

"That uniform's got to come off," Mother Fletcher told Charlotte in that voice that would have been perfect for the stage. Now, however, it only managed to drill its way deep inside his throbbing head. "Where are your injuries, young man?"

His right leg and his hip, in places that were private. There was no way he was going to let either of them see the bandages, let alone his wounds. "Just gotta sleep," he said, as the room swam. And both Charlotte's and the elder Mrs. Fletcher's faces — one young and one old, but both lined with worry — swirled and faded.

Vince came to as naked as the day he was born and only slightly more lucid. Lucid enough, though, to realize that he was partially covered by a sheet, but, God, only partially.

Mother Fletcher was wiping his forehead with a cool cloth, and Charlotte — oh, shit! She was rebandaging his thigh. Jesus, it hurt. But the pain was nothing compared to the sheer embarrassment.

"He needs a doctor," Charlotte said. "He needs penicillin."

"I'll call Dr. Barnes." Mother Fletcher disappeared. Leaving him alone in the bed of the woman of his dreams — who literally had to move his balls aside to bandage his leg.

"No," he said. "No doctor."

Charlotte looked up at him, startled. Her eyes were so blue. "You're awake."

"Can't go to the hospital. They'll send me away from Washington. I . . . need my clothes. Where are my clothes?" He tried to pull his legs away from her while still keeping that sheet covering him. He tried to sit up, but she pushed him back down, pinning his shoulders.

"Your uniform needs a good washing," she told him sternly. "What have you been doing, sleeping in it?"

Yes.

"You're burning with fever." Her hands were so

126

cool against his face, he just wanted to close his eyes and drift away again. But he couldn't.

"I can't go to the hospital. I need to talk to Senator Howard." He focused on her very blue eyes. Despite her efficient demeanor and her seeming inability to smile, she'd been the kindest person in the senator's office. In all the days he'd spent in the waiting room, she'd made a point to greet him each day by name — Private DaCosta, never Vince — and to talk to him. She'd even brought him lunch. Not that he'd had much of an appetite. He'd been fighting this damned fever even then.

He reached for her hands. "Promise — you won't let the doctor send me to the hospital."

"If I do, will you promise to lie still? And to let Mother and me take care of you properly? Those wounds of yours need rebandaging every day."

God, how mortifying. If he stayed here, then every day she would have to . . . He closed his eyes. "Can't let you . . . do that. That's . . . more than you counted on when you brought me here."

"There's very little I count on these days, Private. We're at war. It helps to have no set expectations." She moved back down to his leg. "This must hurt you very much. It's mostly healed, but it's definitely infected. I'll try to be quick."

Pain seared. "Oh, God!"

"Where did this happen?" she asked. "Where were you wounded?"

"Tarawa," he ground out. She was trying to distract him, and he answered her. Let her think that it helped. "Gilbert Islands. South Pacific."

"I know all about Tarawa," she said darkly. "The

127

Japanese fortifications were so much stronger than anyone expected. The casualty lists were beyond heartbreaking. It must've been awful."

Vince made a noise that he hoped sounded like agreement.

"Thank God you made it back home. Your mother must be so relieved. Which reminds me. You must let me ring your family. I'm sure they're worried about you."

"Mother died . . . I was nine," he managed.

"I'm terribly sorry."

"Pop's with my sister — I sent a postcard . . . a couple days ago. No phone. Oh, Jesus, oh, Christ!"

"I'm so, so sorry." Her voice shook, but she quickly regained control. "Part of the old bandage was stuck. It's off now. The worst is done. I promise."

He was crying. God, what a baby. He tried to wipe his eyes, wipe his face, but his goddamn eyes just kept on tearing. The intense pain had subsided, but the accompanying waves of nausea continued.

Charlotte pretended not to notice his tears, the same way she pretended not to notice that she was bandaging him mere inches from his family jewels. Every now and then she tugged the sheet back to cover him more completely, but he got the sense that was more for his sake than for hers.

God, he was completely mortified. And yet things were about to get even worse.

"Sorry." He tried to sit up again. "I'm sorry, but I'm going to be sick —"

She was ready for him. She had a basin in front of him in a split second, and a strong arm around him, holding him up as he lost what little food he'd forced at noontime.

"I'm sorry," he gasped.

"It's all right," she said soothingly, cooling his face with a damp cloth. "Stop apologizing, Private. You're ill. You didn't become ill on purpose, although remind me later to scold you more thoroughly for not taking better care of yourself this past week."

His stomach felt better emptied, but his head was drumming with a new intensity. Vince sank back onto Charlotte's sweetly scented pillows as Edna Fletcher bustled back into the room.

"The doctor's on his way. I had to call the Wendts and then the Fishers to find him, but he should be here in moments." She vanished with the basin as Charlotte put the cool cloth back on his head.

He fought to keep his eyes open, to look up at her. "Please . . ."

"No hospital," she said. "I know. But our deal is off if the infection doesn't start improving by tomorrow." She put her fingers on his lips. "No, don't argue. Don't bother wasting your breath. I don't know what kind of quest you're on — I'm sure it's very noble — but I will not stand by and help you let the enemy take another American life. Far too many young men have already been cut down and I will not let you die, too."

God, she was magnificent.

And it was then that he knew he could never tell her the truth about Tarawa. She'd already lost too much in this war. The truth about what had happened would be too terrible for her to hear.

No, he had to figure out another way to get her onto his side, to convince her to let him speak to the senator.

And, while he was at it . . . "Marry me," he whispered.

She gave him that exasperated look that he'd already come to know so well. "Don't be an idiot."

Mother Fletcher came into the room. "The doctor's here."

Charlotte pushed his hair back from his forehead. "Don't worry," she said to Vince in a low voice. "I'll stay and hold your hand while he examines your leg."

She then turned to greet the man.

Vince took it as a very good sign that she hadn't actually said no.

Mary Lou stared at the rows of movie tapes in the video section of the library, wishing they had a section labeled "Movies Guaranteed to Distract You When Your Husband Steps Out."

Haley was in the stroller, happily kicking her feet and chewing on the Clifford the Big Red Dog board book Mary Lou had bought her at Target last week. She'd had a long nap at Mrs. U.'s, and, with the help of a Tupperware container of Cheerios, would be happy as pumpkin pie for most of the AA meeting at the Catholic church.

Mary Lou finally settled on *Saving Private Ryan*. She'd never managed to see that one — not being particularly interested in gory battle scenes from World War One or Two or whatever it was. But just a few days ago she'd heard Sam telling his friend Nils that he'd loved it. Maybe if she watched it and they talked about it, he'd realize how serious she was about making their marriage work. Maybe he'd see just how hard she was willing to try.

He'd come home tomorrow, and she wouldn't say a thing about Alyssa. She'd keep her mouth shut this time, no matter how hard it was. She'd make sure the house was extra clean, all his laundry done. She and Haley would both get dressed up, and they'd make something special for dinner.

But what?

She didn't even really know what her husband liked to eat. He shoveled it all in with the same grim lack of enthusiasm. He always thanked her for cooking and politely said it tasted good. But he said the exact same thing on the nights she opened a can of corned beef hash and fried up a couple of eggs on top of it.

Okay, so she'd ask him about his favorite food. She'd call him at work — not to check to see where he was, not to see if he was even there, but simply to see what he'd like to have for dinner tomorrow night.

And if he wasn't there, she wouldn't freak. She'd just leave a very calm message, asking him to call her when he got the chance.

And then, when he came home, they'd have that dinner and discuss how much they both enjoyed watching *Saving Private Ryan*.

Even if she hated the battle scenes as much as she suspected she would.

"Hey, aren't *you* the sweetest little thing?"

The man in front of them in the library's checkout line had, like most people on this planet, fallen instantly in love with Haley.

131

She grinned up at him, all curly golden hair and big blue eyes and soft, chubby cheeks that were just perfect for smooching.

He looked at Mary Lou then, giving her the same warm smile that most people usually reserved for her daughter these days. "How old is she?"

"Thirteen months," she told him.

He looked like Heath Ledger's older, sexier brother — chiseled jawline, amazing cheekbones, light blond hair and all. As she smiled back at him, she was glad she'd taken the time to brush her hair before leaving the house.

"That's a great age," he said in a voice that reminded her of Jack Nicholson. It was a jarring combination with that face and hair.

"Yes, it is," she said.

"She's beautiful. She takes after her mother."

He was spreading on the bullshit a little thick, but Mary Lou gave him another smile.

The sensation of a pair of male eyes on her, actually looking at her as if she were a desirable woman, was nice. She smiled again, determined to enjoy it while it lasted. There was no harm in that. Any second now he would turn back to the counter, check out his book, and walk out of her life.

"Are you really going to read *all* of those?" he asked, gesturing with his chin to the stack of books she was carrying. Struggling to carry. He noticed, and moved toward her. "Let me get them for you."

"Oh, that's okay. I'm going to have to carry them to my car and . . ."

But he took them anyway. He got close enough to brush her arm with his fingers, close enough for

Mary Lou to catch a whiff of his cologne. Oh, baby, he smelled terrific. Sam never wore cologne. She'd bought him a bottle back when they were first married and it was still in the medicine cabinet in the bathroom, unopened.

"Thank you," she said, as the blond man put her books and the movie on the counter. "And yes. I'll probably be done reading those day after tomorrow."

"No kidding." And now he was looking at her as if she were some kind of genius. God, why couldn't everybody be this nice? Why couldn't Sam look at her like that? "That's impressive."

"I like to read."

"Obviously. That's wonderful."

It was his turn at the counter. He turned away, but only for a moment, only to give the librarian his book and his card.

"I'm just getting a travel guide," he told Mary Lou. "I'm going out to New York City and I've never been, so . . ."

New York! "I've always wanted to go there."

"Sir." The librarian was holding out his book and card.

"Thanks," he said, stepping out of Mary Lou's way as he slipped his library card back into his wallet, and his wallet back into his pants.

He was wearing a business suit with a red-and-blue tie atop a crisp white shirt. He'd loosened his tie though, and unfastened the top button of his shirt. Some men looked sloppy when they did that. He wasn't one of them.

"I hope you have a nice trip," she told him as the librarian checked out her stack of books.

He smiled at her. "Thanks, but I'm not leaving for another few weeks." He reached down and gently squeezed Haley's foot. "Be good for your mommy, sweetheart. But I'm sure you are, aren't you? Aren't you? Yeah, I bet you are." He looked up at Mary Lou. "Need some help carrying that entire shelf of the library out to your car?"

She laughed. "No. Thank you. I wouldn't dream of imposing."

He gently shook Haley's foot, making her smile. "Your mommy thinks that spending a little more time with two gorgeous women would *impose* on me. She's crazy, isn't she?"

Haley laughed out loud. Baby laughter was such a pure, clean sound. Even the grumpy librarian smiled.

And the man looked up at Mary Lou again. He was smiling, but she could see pain in his eyes. "Your husband is a lucky guy. My wife filed for divorce and moved to New York, taking my two-year-old son with her." He straightened up. "I haven't seen him in three months and it's killing me. I used to put him to bed every night, tell him a story, take him to the park every Sunday afternoon after church . . ." He shook his head. "I even miss changing his diapers. Believe me when I say it's really no imposition if I help you carry a couple of books to your car."

It was unreal. Who in their right mind would walk away from a man like this? An attentive, handsome man who obviously loved children? Whoever his ex-wife was, she was completely addled.

He was determined to help, scooping up her

books before Mary Lou could take them herself.

"Thank you," she said.

He followed her outside and over to her car. "It's unlocked," she told him, and he put the books on the floor of the front passenger's side while she strapped Haley into her car seat.

When she straightened up, he was attempting to fold her stroller. And getting it completely wrong.

"Sorry," he said, with a laugh. "The one we had was a different model."

She closed it with a snap. "It couldn't have been that different."

"My wife was into things from Europe. If it didn't cost a thousand dollars, it wasn't good enough for Ethan. That's my son."

"That's a nice name." Mary Lou tossed the stroller into the trunk.

Because the trunk was broken — anyone could open it by sticking their finger in the hole where the lock used to be — she had to lean on the lid a certain way to get it to latch.

Lately it had been popping open by itself. She'd come out of work just this past week to find it not quite closed. It was annoying, but not worth the money to get it fixed.

She took out her keys and turned to the blond man. "Well."

"Well," he said.

"Thank you."

"You're welcome." But still he didn't move.

She jingled her keys. "I have a meeting to get to."

"Ah," he said. "Of course. Okay. It was nice meeting you, Mrs. . . . ?"

"Starrett," she said. "Mary Lou Starrett. And that's my Haley in the car."

He held out his hand and she took it and they shook. He had hands that were a lot like Sam's. Long, masculine fingers, slightly work roughened, with a warm, firm grip.

"Bob Schwegel. Insurance sales." If he'd been wearing a hat, he would have tipped it. "Enjoy your evening, Mrs. Starrett. You've certainly brightened up mine."

And with that he walked away, blond hair gleaming.

Mary Lou got into the car and looked at Haley in the rearview mirror. "He wants to sell us life insurance, Hale," she said, forcing herself to laugh because she would not cry in front of her baby girl. "Suddenly it all makes sense, doesn't it?"

"We're calling it Operation Black Lagoon," SEAL Team Sixteen's commanding officer, Tom Paoletti, told them from his perch on the desk at the front of the room. "We're currently scheduled to go wheels up in about fourteen days."

"Fourteen days? Four-fucking-teen days?"

"You got a problem with that, Mr. Collins?" Lt. Jazz Jacquette had been sitting next to the CO, but when Joel Collins couldn't keep his mouth shut, he slid down off the desk.

Muldoon was leaning against the side wall with WildCard Karmody and Sam Starrett.

Ensign Collins — also known as TNG, or the new guy — stood up, shoulders back, head high, looking for all the world like Davy to Jacquette's Godzilla. "Yes, sir, I do. And so does every other

136

man in this room. We want to get back out there now, not in two weeks. Sir."

"The new guy pisses and moans more than you do," Sam muttered to WildCard in a voice meant to be overheard.

Everyone in the room laughed. Including the CO.

"I hear you, Mr. Collins," Paoletti said. "But we've got this little thing called a presidential citation to accept — trust me, we can't just call up the White House and say, 'Sorry, Allen, we don't want your medal.'

"Now, with that said, you should know that we're doing the best we can to try to convince the visiting White House staffer that a presidential dog and pony show here on the base isn't a wise move right now, considering potential terrorist threats." Paoletti looked at Muldoon. "How's that going, Lieutenant?"

"I'll be having lunch with Joan — uh, Ms. DaCosta — tomorrow. We'll be talking about that specifically."

"Good work," Sam murmured.

"Thanks," Muldoon murmured back.

"Joan, huh?" Izzy speculated. "I'd like to be assigned to have lunch with someone named Joan. Although, wait — you say she's from the White House? I think I'll pass."

"I've met her," Cosmo spoke up. Cosmo, who never said a word in these briefings. "She's all right. She looks you in the eye when she speaks to you."

"Well, then she can't be from the White House," Izzy countered.

"I've met her, too," Jenk said. "And I'm in love. Hey, Lieutenant, can I come to lunch with you?"

"Let's keep this on track," Jacquette intoned. "We've got a long night ahead of us. Sit down, Collins."

Collins sat as Jacquette turned back to the commander.

"We're going out tonight to do the first in a series of night dives," Paoletti told them. "There's a certain cave in an as-yet-undisclosed location that's a big favorite of a high level al-Qaeda leader due to its proximity to an underground source of fresh water. A lot of fresh water. As in an entire lake's worth.

"We've found what we think is an access route into that cave, via that underground lake. At least one seven-man team is going to swim in and get a read on how many al-Qaeda fighters are inside this cave. If the numbers are small enough, they'll rise out of the lake like creatures from the Black Lagoon — hence the op's name — and secure the cave from the inside out. If the numbers are too large, they'll stay invisible and plant explosives."

"In addition to night dives, we're going to be spending a serious chunk of prep time over the next fourteen days spelunking," Jacquette added.

"As well as practicing everyone's favorite: close quarters combat," Paoletti said. "Are there any questions?"

WildCard raised his hand. "I ran into a couple of members of Max Bhagat's FBI counterterrorist team in the parking lot today. I've heard a lot of conflicting rumors about this that maybe you can clear up, sir. Is the Bureau going to play a major part in Black Lagoon?"

"Not that I've been told," Paoletti said. "Although maybe we should ask that question of Max Bhagat himself."

He nodded at Jenkins, who left his seat to go open the door at the back of the room.

Standing next to Muldoon, Sam got very tense as, one step behind Max, FBI agent Alyssa Locke walked in.

SEVEN

Sam had fully intended to crash after the dive in the BOQ — the Bachelor Officers Quarters — on the base instead of going home.

But he changed his plans when Jules Cassidy intercepted him on his way out the door. It was right after the meeting in which Max Bhagat — who was sleeping with Alyssa — had informed them that the FBI had a source claiming San Diego was a viable target for an impending terrorist attack. That source had indicated a threat to the area's airports.

This type of threat had been going on pretty much nonstop since 9/11, and no one in Team Sixteen was particularly perturbed. Security at the Coronado Naval Base would be moved up a notch, which meant it would take them all a little bit longer to get through the gates when they arrived in the morning as the vehicles of any strangers coming onto the base were subjected to random searches.

Max — who was sleeping with Alyssa — had asked them all to be aware of and report any suspicious behavior, and to remind their families to do the same.

The good news was that the FBI wasn't playing any part in Operation Black Lagoon.

The bad news was that Max, Alyssa, her partner

140

Jules, and a support team would be spending the next few weeks in the area, although not on the base, per se.

It was good they wouldn't be hanging around, since Sam would prefer sticking needles in his eye to seeing Max and Alyssa together, day in and day out.

Jesus, she'd looked good with her hair cut short like that.

Jules was a different story. Jules was an okay guy and Sam didn't mind him hanging around. Over the years, he'd even managed to become one of Sam's closest friends.

Which added an interesting twist to the entire surreal situation, considering that Jules was flamboyantly homosexual.

And Sam wasn't.

Jules had approached him after that meeting with a smile that couldn't hide the worry in his eyes. "I know you're in a hurry, Sam, but I thought you should know that Alyssa and I ran into your wife today at the McDonald's here on base."

Oh, fuck. "Well, that'll teach me to think 'It can't get much worse.' Thanks for the warning."

"It's been a while — I've been meaning to call you, but . . ." Jules walked with him toward the boats that would take the SEALs to the dive's location. "Are things okay with you?"

"Oh, yeah," Sam said. "Everything is fucking wonderful. And now when I go home, I'm going to get four straight days of accusations on top of 'But why do you have to leave? Why can't you stay home this time and let someone else go?' That'll be loads of fun."

"I'm sorry we went in there," Jules said.

"Yeah, fuck sorry — you didn't know. You just wanted a burger."

"Actually, it was a chicken sandwich, but, yeah. We went in for lunch, not to add to your personal hell."

There was silence then as Mike Muldoon moved into earshot. But as he glanced from Sam to Jules, he broke into a trot, quickly passing them and giving them a chance to continue talking privately.

"Be still my heart," Jules said, gazing after him. "I don't suppose Michael Muldoon has come out of the closet yet."

Sam rolled his eyes. Jules knew damn well that Muldoon wasn't gay. He was only doing this to annoy him. Or maybe distract him from his shitty home life. "Even if he was gay, I thought you and Adam were, you know . . ." Living together. Jesus, he couldn't believe he was friends with a guy who was romantically involved with someone named Adam.

"Adam packed up and moved out. He went to L.A."

Ouch. "Sorry."

"Yeah." Jules's smile was forced. "Well, life goes on, doesn't it?"

"Yeah," Sam agreed. "It sure as fuck does." But, Christ, wasn't anyone happy anymore?

Max. Max Bhagat was happy. He *had* to be happy, with Alyssa Locke in his life, the lucky son of a bitch. Sam had found himself watching the man tonight, thinking that for someone who shared a bed with Alyssa, he sure as hell didn't manage to look blissfully content.

He and Jules walked in silence for a bit, and then Sam said it. He swore to himself that he wouldn't, but he couldn't keep his stupid mouth closed.

"How is she?"

As soon as he said it, he didn't want to know. He couldn't bear to know. But now he couldn't seem to get his mouth open to say, *Ignore that. Ignore me.*

Jules, of course, knew he was talking about Alyssa. "She's all right. She's been spending a lot of time with her sister and her niece, which is always good for her. That little kid is amazing. Lanora. I've met her a few times. She's good medicine. So that's good. And well, I'm sure you've heard that careerwise, Alyssa's doing great —"

"Yeah, way to go. Sleeping with the boss'll really make those promotions happen."

"What's that earthy expression you always use?" Jules said. "Oh, yeah. *Fuck you.* Fuck you, Sam. You dumped her and married someone else. Remember? Does that ring any bells for you?"

Sam hated arguing with Jules because the little fucker had all the answers. He was always right. But this time Sam had access to insider information. "Yeah, well, Alyssa was never serious about me anyway, so —"

"Oh, you have no clue what she went through —"

"I was just a transition out of her private ice age." Alyssa had told him herself that she'd never intended her relationship with Sam to be anything but temporary. "She probably had her fucking eye on Bhagat the entire time. Why just have an affair when you can have an affair and a promotion, too?" God, Sam sounded like the pathetic loser that he was, but he couldn't stop himself.

Jules stepped directly in front of Sam, getting right in his face, despite the fact that the fruitcake was seriously vertically challenged. "*Double* fuck you! You have no right to whine or complain or belittle the emotional support she's found from a solid, stand-up guy who's been nothing but good to her. Whenever she spends time with Max, I applaud. And you should, too, you dumb shit! If you really care about her, you should be happy for her."

"Are you happy for Adam?" Sam countered.

"I'll be happy if he falls into the La Brea tar pits with his new pretentious friend Branford," Jules said tightly, "but that's hardly the same situation. This was *your* choice."

"I had no fucking choice." Sam brushed past him. "I got Mary Lou pregnant."

Jules caught his arm. "You and Mary Lou had already split up, what, four months earlier? That's a long time, Sam. Why didn't she tell you about the baby back when there were other options? Why did she wait so long to let you know?"

"She tried," Sam said. "All right? She didn't manage to connect with me. I was the one who didn't take her phone calls — I never called her back. And then I was out of the country . . ." And then he was with Alyssa, thinking that the rest of his life was going to be one golden, glowing, good time.

But Mary Lou's sister called Johnny Nilsson's wife, Meg, who called Johnny, who called Sam. And the shit hit the fan.

"Mary Lou didn't manage to connect with you because she didn't want any options other than the one she got." Jules could be a regular pit bull when

144

he was feeling self-righteous. "Marriage to a Navy SEAL. Congratulations. The bride may kiss her grand prize. The groom wins a chance to be completely miserable for the rest of his life. And the baby grows up with this really warped sense of family and —"

"Stop," Sam ordered. "Maybe you don't understand this, Cassidy, because you live your life however the fuck you want to, but I got Mary Lou pregnant, and I had to deal with it. I had to do the right thing."

His words echoed in his head as he crept into his house at 0400, as he found Mary Lou asleep in the living room, curled up on the sofa, in front of the TV.

Shit.

Her makeup was smudged around her eyes and running down her face in big black streaks — obvious evidence that she'd been crying.

Maybe from watching one of those weepy romantic movies she liked so much.

But probably not.

On the TV screen, Tom Hanks, dressed in WWII combat gear, died. *Saving Private Ryan*. It was a long movie, but still, she must've started it well after midnight. Well after she usually was in bed.

Unless she was up, crying over something Sam had done, or something Sam had failed to do, or something she was afraid he might go and do.

Jesus save him, what a god-awful way for both of them to live their lives.

He'd wanted to do the right thing, but it was entirely possible he'd done the exact opposite for everyone involved.

Except maybe Max Bhagat, who was sleeping with Alyssa.

Sam wanted to cry, too. But, Jesus, he'd shed enough tears in the past few years to float a battleship. It didn't do a damn bit of good. In fact, it only made him feel worse.

The remote was on the floor in front of the couch. Sam picked it up and turned off the TV.

Which woke up Mary Lou. She was groggy at first. "Sam?" With her thick southern accent, she could make his name sound as if it had two syllables.

"Yeah, it's me. Sorry. I didn't mean to wake you."

She sat up, got her bearings. "What time is it?"

"A little after four."

She was wearing a pair of thin cotton pajamas that did little to contain the bounty of her bosom. He'd read that somewhere. He couldn't remember exactly where or what. But the phrase came to mind immediately whenever he looked at Mary Lou.

She had a body that didn't quit. After her pregnancy she thought of herself as fat, but Sam had seen her naked and the more appropriate word was *lush*.

With just a little bit of sweet talk, a few hints, and some extra warmth in his smile, he could have her. Whenever he wanted.

Trouble was, he didn't want her.

He knew she was working hard to try to make him happy. In every possible way. Even right now, after she'd spent the night crying over him. If he so much as told her that she smelled good, she'd be on her back, waiting for him.

And, Jesus, that was weird. Like, instead of a wife, he had a concubine. Her selflessness — and he didn't mean that in any positive sense of the word — was getting kind of freaky.

She did something of the same thing when it came to her so-called domestic duties. She cooked and cleaned and did his laundry with a devotion that was a little frightening. If he so much as mentioned that the kitchen floor needed sweeping, she not only had the broom in her hands, but the mop and bucket out as well.

As if maybe keeping the house clean enough would magically make him happy.

Mary Lou opened her mouth to speak, and he braced himself. Because as compliant as she was these days about everything else, the line was drawn when it came to Alyssa Locke.

And no matter how often Sam assured her that he hadn't slept with Alyssa since they were married, Mary Lou didn't buy it.

But this time she only said, "You're home earlier than I expected."

"Yeah." Unwilling to wait for her to bring up the subject, Sam threw it out on the table. "I spoke to Jules today. He told me he and Alyssa bumped into you at work."

"Yes." Mary Lou stood up. "They both looked . . . fit. It was . . . nice to see them."

What the hell . . . ? Sam stared as Mary Lou headed toward the bedroom.

"I'd appreciate it if you took a shower before coming to bed" was all she said before she vanished down the hall.

His first thought was that she finally believed

147

him. That everything Sam had told her about Alyssa hooking up with Max had been verified through the local grapevine and that Mary Lou now knew the truth — that his affair with Alyssa really was a thing of the distant past.

But he knew that wasn't a possibility. Because who would've told her that about Alyssa? Who would've dared bring Alyssa up in a conversation?

No one, unless Nutjob Don next door had received the info via an alien radio signal picked up by his fillings . . .

Sam looked at the video box for *Saving Private Ryan* that was lying on the coffee table. Mary Lou hadn't been watching that movie because she'd wanted to. She didn't like war movies. She didn't like anything that didn't have a happy-ever-after ending.

But just last week Sam had casually mentioned how much he'd enjoyed that film.

It was all just more goddamn selflessness, both her watching this movie tonight and her walking away from a potential fight about Alyssa.

She was trying to make herself as easy as possible to live with.

Because on some level she knew that Sam no longer truly believed he'd done the right thing by marrying a woman he couldn't even pretend to love.

Charlie couldn't sleep.

She'd fallen asleep right after dinner, and now she was up, drifting about the house like a ghost at 4:30 A.M., trying to be quiet while Vince slept.

Of course, she could probably vacuum the bedroom rug and he wouldn't wake up. He *was* losing his hearing, despite his insistence that he wasn't. She was getting good and tired of repeating herself every time she spoke.

But whenever she brought up the idea of his getting fitted for hearing aids, Vince found some excuse to go out into the backyard — usually on the pretense of tending their garden.

Was it possible that he was in denial about growing old? She had to chuckle at that. His eightieth birthday was fast approaching. It was hard to pretend that you hadn't achieved elderly status when you hit the old eight-oh milestone, as she'd done three years ago.

Despite their advanced years, they were both in good health, and she thanked God each day for that. Their children and grandchildren were all healthy, too. Well, with the exception of Donny. And she'd long reconciled herself to the fact that he'd never be well.

God worked in mysterious ways, and for some reason He'd decided that Donny would be one of His special people.

Perhaps it was His way of reminding them that without sadness, joy wouldn't be quite as sweet.

Charlie had learned that lesson years ago. Firsthand.

She stopped her early morning waltz around this house — their "new" house — that she'd shared with her husband for the past twenty-five years, pausing by the picture of Vince in his Marine uniform. She picked it up from its place of honor on the fireplace mantel. It had been taken right after he'd signed up. The day after Pearl Harbor. The day after James had left this world.

Vince was grinning in the photograph, looking as if he were going to burst into merry laughter. He looked healthy and robust, with the very devil in his sparkling eyes.

It was true that the photo had been taken several years earlier, but it was a far cry from the intensely grim, hollow-cheeked young man who'd fainted at her feet in Senator Howard's office in January 1944.

As Charlotte had rushed to help him, Mrs. P. had started to phone for an ambulance. He'd revived almost right away, pushing himself up onto his hands and knees and insisting that he didn't need to go to the hospital.

It was then that Charlotte found out he didn't have a hotel room in the city. Apparently he'd been sleeping in churches. Lots of servicemen did, those days.

Those few men who didn't spend the night in Sally-the-upstairs-tenant's bed, that is.

And so Charlotte had done the only thing she could think of to do. She'd brought Private DaCosta home.

She and Edna Fletcher took turns sitting with him those first few nights. But the penicillin Dr. Barnes had prescribed won the battle with his infection, thank goodness, and it wasn't long before the young Marine was resting more comfortably.

By Monday, he was doing well enough that Charlotte felt able to return to work.

But for the first time in years, she actually put on her coat at 5:00. For the first time since the early days of her marriage, when James had been stationed here in Washington, she was not merely ready but eager to return home when the evening rolled around.

And it felt wrong. It felt as if she were being unfaithful. As she got off the bus and walked those last few blocks home, it felt like a terrible betrayal to James's memory.

By the time she went into the apartment and hung up her coat, she was good and upset.

And Mother Fletcher was singing — *singing* — in the kitchen as she prepared dinner.

Charlotte didn't say a word as she went in to help.

"He's much better," Mother reported. "He actually ate quite a bit at breakfast and again at noontime. And he even asked me to help him shave just a short while ago." She winked at Charlotte. *Winked.* "It's a good sign when a young man cares enough about his looks to ask for a shave."

"Good," Charlotte said tightly. "Then it won't be long before he's well enough to leave."

"There's no need to rush him out of here," Mother said calmly as she stirred the chicken gravy.

"You like having him here," Charlotte realized.

"Yes." She wiped her hands on her apron. "I do. He's sweet, he's smart, and he plays gin rummy. I have to admit, it's nice to have a young man around again, to take care of."

"He's not your son." Charlotte was almost frantically upset. She never would have dreamed of speaking to her mother-in-law this way if she weren't. "It's foolish to pretend he is."

Mother Fletcher's voice was sharper, too. "My son is gone. What's foolish is pretending that anything you or I can do will change that bitter truth. We are here. James is gone. He'll be gone tomorrow, too — whether or not we continue to show common decent kindness to this young man."

Charlotte turned and walked out of the room. She was up the stairs and through the door before she realized that she couldn't take solace in her bedroom — the room she'd once shared with James an entire lifetime ago.

Vincent DaCosta was sitting up in the middle of her bed.

Wearing a pair of James's pajamas.

She stopped short.

He was holding a book, but he wasn't reading. He was looking at her, a silent apology in his eyes.

Of course, he'd heard every word she'd said to Mother Fletcher downstairs. The same way she heard everything that went on in Sally Slaggerty's apartment upstairs.

"How are you feeling, Private?" she asked, trying her best to be polite, while wanting nothing more than to run away from him as well — while hating herself for noticing how much better he looked with some color in his face, for noticing that he'd washed and combed his hair as well as shaved. For noticing how handsome he looked without that constant haze of pain in his dark eyes.

"Much better," he said. "Thank you. I'll leave first thing in the morning, if that's all right —"

She cut him off. "Has the doctor said you were strong enough to leave?"

"No, but I don't think —"

"When the doctor says so, then you can leave. *If* you have a place to stay. If not, you should plan on staying here. I apologize, Private, if I made you feel unwelcome."

He shook his head. "I don't —"

"My husband is dead." It was not the first time she'd said those words aloud, yet their finality struck her anew each time she uttered them.

"I know." Vince closed his book, set it down beside him on the bed. He looked up at her, and she saw from his eyes that he truly *did* know. He'd been wounded fighting this lousy war. He knew what dead really meant in a day and age where bombs could blow a man to pieces, where shrapnel could shred him so that he bled to death inside even while he kept on fighting. "I'm sorry. Mrs. Fletcher — your mother-in-law — told me he was lost at Pearl."

She didn't want his understanding. "That's a stupid way of saying it," she said sharply. "Lost. As if he were misplaced."

He didn't hide from her flare of temper. "I think the word *lost* really refers to the survivors," he said quietly. "The loss is theirs. Yours. Mine." He met her gaze steadily. "More than eighty percent of my platoon was lost at Tarawa, Mrs. Fletcher. I, for one, will never be the same for having lost them there."

She didn't want to like him. She didn't want him to be anything more than an injured, anonymous soldier she was helping to nurse back to health.

But Vince DaCosta had stopped being anonymous the first day she'd brought an extra sandwich for him to share for lunch. As they'd talked, he'd

153

told her that he'd grown up on Cape Cod. That his father was a lobsterman, that he'd been raised half in the water. The only thing he could do better than swim was sail a boat.

He'd never been to college, but he was the first of the DaCostas to get a high school diploma — no small feat for a working-class family.

He'd gotten the rest of his education the same way Abraham Lincoln had, he'd told her. By reading any- and everything he could get his hands on.

Including, apparently, *Little Women*, the book resting now beside him on her bed.

It was an odd choice for him to have made, considering that all of James's far more masculine books, Jack London's stories and the complete adventures of Sherlock Holmes among them, were still on her shelves.

But perhaps Vince knew that seeing him in James's pajamas was quite all she'd be able to bear.

"It's time to change your bandages." She knew he hated that. He would lay back in the bed with his arm up and over his eyes, as if that could make him disappear. Blushing furiously the entire time.

Changing his bandages certainly could have waited until after dinner, but Charlotte desperately wanted him to transform back into a patient. He was much too difficult to deal with as a man.

The steady look that he gave her told her he knew darn well what she was up to. Yet she could see kindness, not accusation, in his eyes.

"I'm feeling well enough to do it myself now," he told her.

She challenged him. "Isn't that what you thought

the last time — and you ended up getting an infection?"

"I thought I'd nearly healed," he said. "And I had. I just . . . You're right, I should've taken better care of myself. I promise I won't make the same mistake again."

"The last promise you made was that if we let you stay here rather than sending you to a hospital, you would allow us to change your bandages every day," Charlotte stubbornly pointed out.

"Mrs. Fletcher," he said, "I really am feeling much better. Everything seems to be working the way it's supposed to be working again. Everything." He looked at her squarely, but a faint blush darkened his cheeks.

Perfect. Now she was blushing, too. She was about to matter-of-fact her way through it, though, when Upstairs Sally came home. Loudly.

Her sitting room wasn't directly overhead, but her footsteps still managed to sound as if she were flamenco dancing on Charlotte's ceiling.

The radio went on. Benny Goodman was at a high enough volume almost to mask the sound of voices. Sally's high-pitched laughter. And a second voice. A low rumble of a voice.

Her heart sinking, Charlotte looked at her watch. It was 5:45 in the evening. And Sally had already brought her date home.

Rapid footsteps sounded overhead and the laughter got louder. They were in Sally's bedroom now, and from the sound of things, Sally was being chased over and around her bed.

There was a sudden giggling shriek as the bedsprings above gave a loud creak.

Whoever he was, he'd caught her.

At this point, there would usually be a few moments of silence, as Sally and her friend undressed. But whoever this "friend" was, he was in a hurry. Because it wasn't more than five seconds before the bed upstairs started creaking. Rhythmically.

Unmistakably.

And the laughter turned to moaning.

Poor Vincent was as embarrassed as she was. Maybe even more so. If that was possible.

Charlotte all but ran for the door. "I'll go see about dinner." But then she turned back. The polite thing to do in mixed company was simply to ignore the fact that her upstairs neighbor was fornicating loudly, but unlike her, Vince couldn't run from the racket. She simply couldn't leave him there without saying, "I'm so sorry about this."

He'd already picked up the book again, but now he closed it, one finger holding his place. "It's not your fault that the walls and floors are so thin. He's probably home on furlough."

"Her husband died in the war."

That made him pause for only a moment. Then, "I guess everyone has their own way of dealing with their grief," he said quietly.

"Well, she 'deals with her grief' endlessly," Charlotte told him. "Nightly. It gets tiresome after a while. Trust me. The night can be very long."

"I spent a night pinned down by the enemy," Vince said. "We dug ourselves into the sand, on the beach. Me and a guy who'd had his leg . . . who'd been badly wounded. I spent the night listening to him crying for his mother."

Charlotte couldn't speak, couldn't move.

"*That* was a long night," Vince told her as Upstairs Sally achieved fulfillment with a quavering scream.

"I'm sorry," she managed to whisper, then pushed herself out the door.

EIGHT

"Rumor has it that your little 'oh, it was nothing' knee injury was in fact a broken kneecap," Joan said as Mike Muldoon approached.

He was wearing his uniform again today. It couldn't have been more white than anyone else's, yet on him, it truly seemed to glow.

For a moment he looked as if he were about to turn around and walk back into the restaurant's parking lot, where he'd left his truck. But instead he smiled. It was definitely forced. "There're always lots of rumors circulating," he said. "You've got to take 'em all with a grain of salt."

"So you didn't break your kneecap in Afghanistan," she clarified.

"No comment."

She rolled her eyes. This again. "I'm not the press."

"And I'm not at liberty to talk about where I may or may not have been and what I may or may not have done there, particularly in terms of the A-word," he countered. "Joan, do we really have to fight again today? Because I was kind of looking forward to having an indigestion-free lunch."

Joan was nervous, and it was true, she tended to pick fights when she was nervous.

158

It was weird. She'd purposely given Muldoon the kid brother speech last night on the phone, and he'd seemed to accept it readily enough. Except now she was the one who needed convincing. Seeing him face-to-face again, in all his shiny, youthful Navy SEAL splendor was enough to make her forget her own name, let alone her resolve not to wake up in a few weeks' time with a raftload of regrets and a new skeleton for her closet. She had career aspirations — and hers was a world where skeletons didn't stay inside of closets for very long.

She cleared her throat. "The men in your team really love you. Am I allowed to say that?"

Muldoon shook his head. "Definitely not. They can admire and respect me, but love? The word's not in the working SEAL vocabulary. At least not in reference to teammates, thank you very much."

She laughed. He was smiling, too, and this time it was more genuine. "I really am sorry about yesterday," he added as he held open the door to the restaurant, "and I really do appreciate your willingness to have lunch with me."

"I thought I already forgave you last night," she said, taking off her sunglasses and letting her eyes adjust to the lack of blinding sunlight inside. "Although, if you're really that contrite, I'll let you make it up to me by telling me where most of Team Sixteen were this morning, all morning. Training, I'll bet. But what kind of training?"

"Joan, there are things I can't tell you, no matter how contrite I am. You know this. Don't pretend you don't. I cannot answer any questions that are about past, present, or future operations." She

159

opened her mouth, but he stopped her. "Yes, you can shout about your security clearance until you're blue in the face. You can even proposition me — promise me kinky sex till we both drop from exhaustion — but it won't do any good. You can *marry* me, for crying out loud, bear my children, and spend the next fifty years with me. But I still can't and won't answer questions about operations." He stepped up to the hostess. "Table for two. Near the windows, please."

The young woman flashed her dimples at Muldoon as she gave him a very deliberate once-over. It took her far less time to size up Joan. "One moment, Lieutenant." She vanished into the restaurant, and Muldoon turned back to Joan.

Avoid, avoid, avoid his kinky sex comment. She had to ignore it as completely as she ignored that dismissive look from that hostess bitch. Don't take that bait, Joan. Don't do it. He was testing her, but she was strong.

"Okay," she told him.

Her surrender completely caught him off guard. The expression on his face was comical. "Okay? Just like that, okay?"

"Are you really going to argue about my agreeing with you?" she said. "Aren't you the one who wanted an indigestion-free lunch?"

"Yes, but —"

"If I ask you a question that you can't or won't answer, you just say pass. Is that okay? It's easier than me trying to figure out what I can and can't ask. This way I'll just ask everything and you can be the censor."

He was looking at her as if he were wishing he

could climb into her head to find out what she was really up to.

"Lieutenant Muldoon. What a pleasure."

Joan turned to see sheer perfection holding out a manicured hand and smiling up at Mike Muldoon. Petite and blue-eyed with perfectly coiffed honey-blond hair and a figure reminiscent of Pamela Anderson's, perfection wore Armani today and carried a handbag that matched her high-heeled shoes.

On closer inspection, perfection was in her early to mid-forties, but since she could probably still cause a riot by wearing a bikini, that quite possibly made her even more perfect.

Muldoon shook the outstretched perfect hand, morphing neatly into his too-polite evil twin. "Mrs. Tucker. How are you, ma'am?"

Tucker, Tucker. Joan had heard that name before. And she couldn't deny she got a charge of sadistic delight in hearing perfection get blatantly ma'am-ed.

"Call me Laurel, please, and I'm wonderful. Larry's gone to D.C. for a few days — it's always a nice break to have him out of the house." Her voice was as perfect as the rest of her. Musical and sweetly sultry. Shades of Barbara Eden's Jeannie. *Thank you, Master.* "You remember my daughter, Lindsey."

Lurking behind perfection was a skinny, freckle-faced teenager with short brown curls and a bad habit of biting her fingernails.

Muldoon nodded at the girl. "Yes, I do."

Oh, poor little Lindsey. Joan couldn't imagine how hard it would be to go through life with perfection for a mother. Talk about difficult child-hoods. How could the entire world not compare them and find the daughter lacking? The whispers and stares must be excruciating.

And poor Lindsey was too young yet to know that the best men, the worthwhile men — the ones worth having and sometimes even keeping — didn't want anything to do with perfection.

Muldoon, who was doing his SEAL robot im-pression with real finesse, turned to Joan with his polite smile carefully in place. "This is Joan DaCosta. She's on staff at the White House and in town for a couple of weeks."

Joan felt the warmth of his hand at her waist and realized that he'd actually put his arm around her. As if they were there on a real date. As if lunch weren't the most nonromantic meal of the day.

Perfect Mrs. Tucker — whom Joan finally re-membered was married to the skeevy admiral with the thinning hair — had a dead-fish handshake. "Lovely to meet you, Joan. I'm Laurel."

"Nice meeting you both," she said. Lindsey didn't seem to want to shake her hand. The girl was fiercely occupied by a hangnail.

"Lieutenant, your table is ready." The hostess bitch was back, holding a pair of menus.

"Please excuse us," Muldoon said. "Mrs. Tucker. Lindsey."

He kept his hand on Joan's waist all the way to their table, only letting her go to hold out her chair for her.

She waited until he'd sat down and the hostess had handed them both menus. By that time, her imagination had gone into overdrive.

162

"Don't you dare," she said, leaning across the table so that she could speak in a low voice, "tell me that there's something going on between you and *Laurel*." She imitated the way the woman spoke.

He laughed, and just like that the robot SEAL was gone and Mike Muldoon was back. "Why not? She's pretty hot. Don't you think she's hot?"

"Oh, my God, Michael!" She put down her menu without giving it a glance. "Were you . . ."

She shut her mouth, able only to make questioning, disbelieving eyes at him, as a waiter brought them bread and filled their glasses with water. Finally he left, and she leaned closer to Muldoon again, lowering her voice even more. "Were you trying to make her jealous or something? Was that what that was? You know, the arm around me thing?"

"Jealous? Wow, no," he said, with a laugh. "I was just . . . I don't know. She freaks me out a little. She's always there when I turn around, like she's maybe looking for some play, or . . . I don't know, it's probably just my imagination, but I thought if *she* thought I was involved with someone . . ."

"Like *that* would stop her. I thought she was going to drool on your hand. I mean, hello, subtlety! News bulletin just in: Larry's gone to D.C. for a few days. Why don't you come up and see me sometime, sailor? Talk about blatant. And right in front of her daughter. Shit. Ain't no *maybe* here, babe. She wants your ass."

Muldoon smiled weakly. "Maybe you're right."

"*Maybe* again." She couldn't remember the last time she'd laughed so much. "Come *on*."

"I'm pretty sure she's just playing a game. You know, just flirting with me."

"Honey, she was looking at you as if you were dessert, and today was National Break-the-Diet Day."

He glanced across the room to where Laurel and Lindsey were being seated with a woman who looked as if her bathroom mirror was a time portal to 1983. Big hair. *Big* hair.

"I don't know," he said, shaking his head. "Her husband's a player. I think on some level it would really appeal to her, you know, to sleep with a SEAL to get back at him for all the times he's cheated. Particularly since he's not a fan of SpecWar, and in particular since he's not a fan of Team Sixteen. Some of the guys think I should play out the scenario, see what she'd actually do if I responded to one of her innuendoes, but I can't do that. I mean, what if she's serious? Then what do I do? She's married. And I don't mess around with women who are married. Even if they are hot."

That was what was holding him back? She was *married?* "But, ew, isn't she, like, too . . ." Joan couldn't think of the right word.

"Old?" he suggested.

"Yes," she said. "Yes! Old. She's old enough to be your mother."

"Actually, my mother had me pretty late in life. She just turned seventy, so —"

"I didn't mean literally, Einstein. I meant in theory. Laurel Tucker's got to be fifteen or twenty years older than you. That's creepy."

"Why?"

He was serious.

"Because it is," Joan told him.

"No, it's not. Susan Sarandon's almost thirty years older than me. She's been my fantasy date for years. Still is. She's in her fifties and I'd do her in a heartbeat. Whoa, that was pretty crude. Sorry."

"Crude, schmood. I'm thrilled to death to find out that beneath that glowing exterior, you're a real, normal, red-blooded human male."

"Yeah, I'm not sure about normal," Muldoon told her with a laugh.

"Susan Sarandon, huh? That's . . . very interesting."

"Put her in black leather, and I wouldn't even care if she had a significant other or not. All rules would go right out the window."

Mike Muldoon — the closest thing to an angel in all of SEAL Team Sixteen, hell, in probably all of the SEAL teams on both coasts of the U.S. — liked black leather when worn by mature celebrities. Oh, dear. Joan didn't know whether to laugh hysterically or run out of the restaurant. "Next you're going to tell me you're into domination."

She'd meant it as a joke, but he just smiled. "Yeah, well, put a whip in her hand and I'm not running away."

She couldn't manage to keep her mouth shut or even change the subject to something more safe, more staid. "Susan Sarandon's skinny, isn't she? I thought you didn't like skinny women."

"Actually she's extremely curvaceous. Go rent *Bull Durham*. I think she was a few years older than you when she made that movie. That was the one that made me completely fall in lust with her." He held out the basket of bread to her.

It was Italian with sesame seeds on the top. Joan took a piece, and he did then, too.

God, he was about as subtle as Laurel Tucker with this talk of older women. She helped herself to some butter and tried to pass it to Muldoon, but he shook his head. "No thanks."

Joan knew exactly what he was doing here and it was not going to work. Even if he was sincere, which he certainly seemed to be, the rest of the world didn't have his open-minded perspective.

So, okay. Maybe she should try her "bad idea for people who work together to date" speech, because apparently the "little brother/let's be best friends" approach wasn't working. Or maybe it *would* work, if she just kept reinforcing it, the way she'd planned.

She buttered her bread. "What do you think about Brooke Bryant? Hot or not so hot?"

He didn't hesitate. "Very hot. Another woman who's not too thin." Or too young. He didn't have to say it — she could read that loud and clear from the look in his eyes.

"Actually, she yo-yos," Joan told him, ignoring both his eyes and his unspoken message. "I know her pretty well."

He didn't pick up the conversational ball. He just sat there, watching her and eating his piece of Italian bread.

"Don't you want to know what she's really like?" she prompted.

"Oh," he said. "Sure. I'm sorry, I'm . . . What's she really like?"

"She's very sweet," Joan said. "A lot more like her father than the newspapers and TV news let

166

you think. She tends to run a little too emotional, but you can't really blame her considering the kind of stress she's under — that constant public scrutiny. It would drive me insane."

"Yeah," he said. "I bet. That must be really hard." He cleared his throat. "Look, Joan —"

She cut him off. "I have a favor to ask you. A big favor."

"I'm here to help you," he said. "If there's anything in my power that I can —"

"There is," she said. "I need to find Brooke an escort to that party Admiral Crowley is hosting over at the Del on Saturday."

It was obvious that was not the favor he had been hoping to hear her ask. He carefully wiped the crumbs from his fingers with his napkin, then put it back in his lap. "I could help you find someone to escort her, sure," he finally said.

Enough already. "I was thinking of you."

"Me." He took a sip of water. "Why me?"

"Because I know if you're with her, she won't get into any trouble. Because I trust you. Because."

He took his time in answering her. "I don't know," he said.

"What's not to know? It's not like I'm suggesting an arranged marriage. It's just a date."

"What about you?" he asked. "Who's going to be your date?"

She was prepared for that question. "I don't need one," she told him firmly. "I'm not the President's daughter. Besides, I'll be working. I'll be busy running around. Please say yes. This would be such a huge favor . . ."

She'd come up with this last night, and had been

particularly pleased with the way it would underline to Muldoon just how determined Joan was about keeping their relationship brotherly. Sisterly. Non-loverly. As in *please date my friend.*

And best of all, if Muldoon was Brooke's escort, there was no way Joan would be tempted to do something completely foolish, like dance with him at the party.

She suspected that dancing with him would be very dangerous. "Please?"

"All right," he said. "I mean, yeah, sure. Twist my arm. Brooke Bryant. Wow."

Victory. Joan opened her menu. "You — darling dearest — are my new hero."

"Great," he said. "I'm . . . glad I can help."

Haley had gone down for her nap early.

Mary Lou had had her out in the backyard all morning long, so as not to wake Sam while he slept. They'd stayed there right up until the time he left for work at about eleven — because he didn't bother to come say good morning or even tell them he was up.

He just came out right before leaving for the base, to say good-bye, to smother Haley's cheeks with kisses, to make her laugh and chortle and shriek as he swung her around and tickled her.

Try changing her diaper after she poops, Mary Lou wanted to say, but she held her tongue.

"Gotta run" was all he'd said to her as he dumped Haley back into her arms, as he headed for his truck, leaving before she could even ask him what he might want for dinner.

Haley didn't want him to go — Mr. Fun, pop-

168

ping in to make her giggle and laugh — and she started to cry.

They'd gone inside then, and had lunch early. And while Mary Lou was washing up, Haley had started nodding off, despite the fact that she had a teething biscuit on her tray.

And then it was noon, Haley was sleeping, and Mary Lou had taken the baby monitor and gone out to bring in Donny's mail. It sure beat sitting in that living room that she'd always dreamed about having, wondering why she wasn't all that much happier than she'd been back when she was eight or nine and living in some bug-infested shithole with her drunk of a mother.

Donny had mostly junk mail — catalogues and invitations to apply for credit cards — in his box.

Mary Lou stood on his front steps and rang his bell, moving back slightly so that he'd be able to see from his windows that she wasn't one of the invading alien horde.

The curtain moved and she made herself smile. "Hi, Donny. It's just me with the mail."

But the door didn't open.

Mary Lou rang the bell again. Twice this time. "Donny, open up! It's Mary Lou. I'm worried about you, hon. I have a little extra time today, if you need anything from the grocery store. Or the pharmacy." Like a refill on your prescription of antipsychotic drugs.

When he took his meds, Donny was . . . well, the truth was he was never *normal*. But at least he was a much more manageable form of crazy.

She suspected, however, that he'd stopped taking his medicine some time ago.

169

She hadn't realized that yesterday when she'd gone and yelled at him, calling him nasty names. Oh, man, she was a total asshole, taking her bad shit out on this poor tortured soul.

"Donny, please, I'm really sorry about yesterday. I didn't mean what I said. Can't you let me in so we can talk about it?"

Nothing. No movement. No faint sound of chanting, even.

He had probably retreated to his walk-in closet. He'd made it into a kind of a mock bomb shelter — a small windowless room right in the center of the house, where he kept canned goods, a sleeping bag, his favorite comic books, a flashlight, and about a five-year supply of size D batteries.

Oh, yeah, and his laptop. He ran a cable extension from his bedroom so he could get online. Probably to visit the crazy people's chat room.

Since his closet was otherwise occupied, he kept his clothes in anal-retentive stacks around his bedroom. He had about fifty different sweaters. Apparently, that was the recommended Christmas gift for crazy relatives.

"What do you think Donny wants for Christmas this year, dear?"

"Who knows what he wants? He's crazy. Get him a sweater. Even crazy people get cold."

Of course, if they took the time to visit him, they'd know to get him books. He loved reading about military history, in particular about Navy SEALs. That was probably why he'd let Mary Lou into his house that first time. Because she was married to a Navy SEAL. Mary Lou wasn't sure if it was truth or some kind of made-up fiction, but

Donny was convinced that someone in his family had once been a SEAL.

Donny also loved music. Oldies. Like the Beatles.

He was also a whiz when it came to playing the stock market. Mary Lou didn't understand any of that stuff, but crazy Donny sure as hell did. He'd told her once that he'd made a million dollars the week before, and she'd thought he was just being his crazy, old, deluded self. But then one day she'd opened his mail for him and caught a look at his account statement from the bank. He had more than a half million dollars just sitting around in his checking account.

She'd warned him to keep his bank records in a safe place. Don't leave them lying around for any aliens — or people like the cleaning ladies who came in once a month — to see.

Mary Lou wasn't sure what kind of gift to buy someone who played the stock market other than a hat that said "I am richer than God."

But as far as deeply personal gifts for Donny went, a roll of heavy-duty aluminum foil would have been far more appreciated than any dumb sweater. Especially since, despite all of his clothes, Donny had two favorite shirts and two favorite pairs of pants. He wore each outfit every other day, day after day after relentless day.

Once a week, his grandparents would come to visit, and his grandmother would somehow manage to get him into something different — which lasted until about three minutes after they pulled out of the driveway.

Both she and Donny's grandfather were about a million years old. Mary Lou worried about what would become of Donny after they were gone.

She rapped on his door again. "Donny! Please open the door. It's me, Mary Lou. I just want to make sure you're okay."

Silence.

When he was like this, ringing the bell repeatedly would only make it worse.

"Dammit," she said, and turned around — to find Ihbraham Rahman, the yard guy, standing three feet away from her, at the bottom of the steps. She juggled Donny's mail with the baby monitor and dropped most of the mail. "Oh! You scared me to death!"

"I'm sorry." He helped her pick up the envelopes and catalogues. "I was working at the Bentons', and heard you over here and . . ."

Mary Lou could see his truck parked in front of the yellow house three houses down from the Robinsons'. So that was their name. Benton. She'd never met them face-to-face.

There were a lot of people in this neighborhood that she'd never met.

"Is everything all right with your friend?" he asked as he handed her back the mail. There was genuine concern in his eyes.

"I don't think so," she told him. "He won't answer his door. He's kind of crazy —" She lowered her voice and barely even breathed the word, just in case Donny was listening. "— even when things are going well, so . . ."

"Are you sure he's home?" Ihbraham asked, turning to look at the house. He was tall. Not as tall as Sam, but still, she had to tip her head back just to talk to him.

"Yes," Mary Lou said. "Considering that he never leaves. Ever. Besides, I saw him peeking out at me."

"Is there no one you can call?" He dressed kind of the way Jesus might dress if He were alive today. Loose pants made out of some kind of lightweight, flowing material, with a comfortably worn-out T-shirt. And of course those leather sandals.

"Well, he's got grandparents who don't live too far away. I suppose I could try to find their number. I'm not exactly sure of their last name, though."

"You could call the police," he suggested.

Mary Lou laughed. "Yeah, I don't think so. The last thing I want to do is get Donny locked up. He's not hurting anyone, here."

"Except maybe himself," Ihbraham pointed out.

Mary Lou sat down, right there on Donny's front steps. "Who gets to decide that? You know — whether or not he might be hurting himself . . . ? Because he might see it differently from the police or the doctors in the funny farm or even me and you. He's got food and water in there — enough so that he doesn't have to come out for years if he doesn't want to. Who are we to say that he doesn't have the right to spend the rest of his life in there with the shades pulled down if that's really what he wants?"

"May I?" Ihbraham asked, as if she owned the step.

"You don't have to ask just to sit down. It's a free country."

He sat. "Free more for some than others. I've learned never to assume."

Mary Lou looked at him, at his so very foreign-looking face. Dark skin. Thick dark slashes of eyebrows. Dark beard. Full lips that were nearly always smiling.

And those eyes, so warmly, richly brown and filled to overflowing with concern and kindness and a calm acceptance and wisdom.

When most people looked at him, unless they looked closely, they wouldn't see his eyes or his smile. And if those people were anything like her, they'd cross to the other side of the street when they saw him coming. They'd assume, from the color of his skin and from the way he looked, that he was dangerous.

She remembered all those nervous phone calls she'd made to her sister when he'd first started caring for the Robinsons' yard, and she was ashamed.

"I'm sorry," she told him, although she was certain it didn't make up for all the shit he'd no doubt been through since 9/11.

"It's okay," he said. "I have T-shirts that I sometimes wear when I go out. They say 'I am an American, too.' It's helped a little."

"Life really sucks," Mary Lou said.

"No," he said. He shook his head. "No. It *can* be hard sometimes, though."

And then they sat there for a moment in silence.

"I could really use a drink," she admitted.

"I know," Ihbraham told her quietly.

And she knew that that was true. He *did* know.

"Bottom line," Muldoon said as he watched Joan across the restaurant table. "We feel that it's

174

just not safe for the President to come here right now. At least not the way you want him to come here — with a demonstration that's open to the public. Crowd control will be impossible."

She tapped her fingers on her coffee cup. "So you're telling me Commander Paoletti would rather Team Sixteen not receive this citation from the President?"

"Yeah," he said. "If the choices are to do it at this dog and pony show here on the base or not at all, the CO would choose not at all because he values the President's — and the public's — safety over his own career. We'd be more than happy to go to Washington, though. I haven't cleared this with the commander, but I'm willing to bet he'd be okay with us giving some kind of a demonstration right there at the White House. On the President's — and most important the Secret Service's — own turf."

Joan looked out the restaurant window at the sparkling bay and the glistening skyline of San Diego. As much as Muldoon preferred the vastness of the open ocean, this was a pretty nice view. She gazed at it for quite some time, while he watched her.

They'd shared a dessert, two forks but only one plate, as if they were lovers. Or best friends. She'd made it clear both last night and today that they weren't going to be anything more than friends.

She'd begged him to go on a date with Brooke Bryant, which was freaking weird. Not just the concept of escorting Brooke to this party at the Del, but the idea that Joan had had to beg him to do it.

What was wrong with him, that he didn't jump at the chance?

Well, it was one thing to fantasize about someone like Brooke when she was three thousand miles away from him. It was another thing to walk into a party with her on his arm.

Especially when he wanted to walk in with someone else entirely on his arm.

Joan was supposed to have realized by now that she wasn't too old for him. She was, after all, much younger than Brooke Bryant.

But no. It was obvious that the problem wasn't that she was too old for him. It was that she thought he was too young for her.

So he was going to escort Brooke to some pain in the butt party where he'd have to wear his dress whites and keep up polite conversation and small talk all night long.

Which was something that he hated doing and completely sucked at.

God help him.

He'd lost the age battle to Joan right at the start of their lunch. And here he was — judging from the expression on her face — about to lose another.

He had to give her credit — she'd actually paid attention and heard him out. She'd listened carefully to what he'd had to say about the risks of going forward with the President's visit to Coronado.

"Well, I'll certainly bring your concerns to the President's attention," she finally said as she turned back from the view. "But I'm pretty sure I already know what his response is going to be. 'If I

176

can't feel safe within the gates of a military base on U.S. soil, where *can* I feel safe?' "

"It's not the base that's the problem," Muldoon told her. "It's opening up the demonstration to the public. There are known terrorist cells in —"

"San Diego," she finished for him. "Yes, and in every other major city in the United States, as well. But it's time to start campaigning for reelection, and I know for a fact that Bryant isn't going to sit in the basement of the White House, quaking with fear."

"He's the President," Muldoon countered. "He owes it to this country to stay safe."

"Actually, his policy has been 'Don't let the terrorists win,' " Joan shot back at him. " 'Go on about your daily lives. Be vigilant and alert, but fly, go on vacation, go to concerts and football games. Live on the ninety-eighth floor. Don't live in fear.' "

Muldoon nodded. "There's an FBI counter-terrorist team in town because there's some kind of threat to the area's commercial airports."

"Well, that's good news," Joan said, "seeing as there are no commercial airports on the base."

"Commander Paoletti hasn't put it into these words exactly, but I know he's had a bad feeling about this visit from the moment news came down from Admiral Crowley."

"That'll go over well. 'We need to cancel your visit to Coronado, Mr. President, because Commander Paoletti has a bad feeling about it.' " Joan laughed.

Muldoon didn't. "This is a man whose hunches you should trust," he told her. "Talk to your bosses."

"I will, but don't expect too much." She leaned slightly across the table, and for one brief moment, he thought she was going to take his hand. No such luck. Jeez, he really liked her. Every minute he was with her, he liked her even more. This was so totally not fair.

And meanwhile, on the other side of the room was Mrs. Tucker, whom Joan seemed to think was ready to blatantly proposition him if she had half a chance. Oh, boy, wasn't *that* perfect?

"My turn for serious conversation," Joan said. "I still want —"

"To see Team Sixteen in action, training." This time it was his turn to finish her sentence. "I know. So, okay."

"Okay? Just like that? Okay?" She was purposely echoing the words he'd used earlier and, he realized, quite possibly trying to imitate him with that wide-eyed look.

"Very funny. I've set up a simulated training exercise this afternoon. It's a beautiful day for a boat ride, so at 1600 hours I've got a bunch of volunteers — including Jenk, who publicly proclaimed his total devotion to you at a recent team briefing —"

"Jenk?" she said, laughter in her eyes. "Cherub-faced with freckles? Why is it that I seem to attract the children?"

Mark Jenkins was actually a little bit older than Muldoon — a fact he chose not to point out. "Cosmo volunteered, too."

"Old break-your-neck-without-a-sound Cosmo, huh? That's . . . lovely."

"He's a good man."

"I'll have to take your word for it. He's not exactly a glowing conversationalist."

"If you're done insulting my friend —"

"I wasn't being insulting," she told him. "Just observing. He also has very nice sunglasses. But that's all I know about him."

Muldoon had to laugh. "If you're done with your observation of Cosmo —"

"I'm done with everything I can say aloud without being accused of being harassing and sexist." She smiled at him, and he lost his train of thought.

What was she telling him? That she found Cosmo attractive? *Cosmo?*

He pulled himself back to the point. "Look, at 1600 hours, there're about seven guys willing to put in some additional time to demonstrate some helocasting and recovery techniques. Just for you. Is that okay?"

"Is that supposed to make me feel guilty?" she countered.

"No. Just maybe a little appreciative."

"I am. But I still think I'll keep my distance from Cosmo, thanks. What's helocasting?"

"It's an insertion technique," he told her. She wanted to keep her *distance* from Cosmo. He gave up trying to figure her out. "Helocasting is just a fancy name for jumping out of a helicopter and into the water. Of course, there are wrong ways and right ways of doing it. Hopefully this afternoon we'll demonstrate only the right ways. And we'll also show you a recovery technique — basically hooking the men in the water with a big rubber loop and yanking them up and into an inflatable boat. It's a tried-and-true method for getting guys out of the water, developed during the Second World War."

"Demonstrate," Joan said. "That means I watch, right? No one's pushing me out of any helicopters? I stay out of the water?"

"Lose the heels," Muldoon recommended, "and your chances of staying out of the water will greatly increase." He smiled at her. "But just in case, I'll make sure you have a life jacket on before we leave shore."

Joan looked at him. "Michael."

"Just in case," he said, and flagged down the waiter to get the bill.

"What are you doing here?" Donny pulled his laptop back as he scooted into the farthest possible corner, away from Vince.

"People worry about you when you don't answer the door. That's what I'm doing here." It smelled like a gym locker in there, but Vince shut the closet door behind him, hoping that would calm down his grandson. Way too much whites of his eyes were showing.

He sat down on the floor of the closet — which Don had completely covered, walls and ceiling, with aluminum foil. "Your friend — that gal with the southern accent — gave us a call."

"Did you lock the door behind you when you came in?"

"You know I did," Vince said. His grandson was wearing his favorite hat today. With that, the closet dwelling, and the rocking back and forth, Vince was pretty sure it was safe to assume that he'd been off his medication for at least a few weeks now. "You know, Don, you need a few pillows in here. Once you pass seventy, you start to bruise your own ass just by sitting on the floor without a cushion."

The rocking got more pronounced. "Don't let Gramma open any windows."

"No, son, she's not even here. She had a ladies' auxiliary meeting." Vince had gotten the call from that southern girl — Mary Lou — on his cell phone after he'd dropped Charlie at the church. "I can't stay long. I just wanted to stop in and make sure you're all right."

"I'm all right."

Yeah, if all right meant wearing an aluminum foil hat and living in a closet, Donny was stellar.

"Last time we were here, you told me you were taking your pills," Vince told his grandson as mildly as he possibly could. "Now, you know I've never judged you, Donny. I've never blamed you and I've never told you how to live your life. I've never done anything but be here in case you need me. So why would you want to tell me something that's not true?"

Tears welled in Don's eyes. "I can't let them know," he whispered. "Shh. Shhh. They got to my pills and switched them with their pills. But I found out and . . . Don't think it, don't think it or they'll find out. Don't think it . . ."

Beneath his aluminum-covered hat, Donny was starting to lose his hair. He was approaching forty, a beefy bear of a man, with about thirty extra pounds sitting around his waist.

Vince could remember him at five. At ten. A shy

kid with wide, worried brown eyes who only laughed if you really worked to entertain him. At fourteen, his focus in life was getting A's in school. He stayed in his room and studied as if he were chained to his desk, and everyone told Tony and Sheryl how lucky they were to have such a good son. By sixteen, though, they all knew something was very wrong with Don. By seventeen, he'd stopped leaving the house.

Medication worked well enough at first for him to be able to attend college. But instead of getting better, getting strong, he crumpled under the intense stresses of college. He got worse. And he went back home to live.

Which marked the official beginning of the end of Tony and Sheryl's already rocky marriage. Vince's youngest son and his wife had been struggling to stay together for years, and having to deal with a seriously mentally ill child broke the so-called camel's back.

Sheryl had moved with Donny here to California. Bought this little house, and then proceeded to die of cancer, breaking everyone's heart. Especially Tony's.

Charlie and Vince had wanted Donny to move in with them after the funeral, but Donny refused. And then surprised the hell out of them all by revealing that he'd been investing in the stock market via the Internet for years. He had enough money — a small fortune — saved to support himself in this little house for the rest of his life.

"Don't think it," Donny was still repeating.

A change of subject was in order. "Joanie — your sister — is in town."

The rocking stopped, and just for a moment, Don sat up a little taller. "Yeah, she E-mailed to tell me she was coming out to San Diego for a few weeks."

It was the brief glimpses of normal beneath the aluminum-covered hat that were sometimes the hardest to bear.

"She works for the president," Don continued. "She said the Secret Service makes sure that the aliens can't get to anyone in the White House. I need to ask her how they do that."

Of course, normal never stayed around for longer than a glimpse.

Vince glanced at his watch. He was going to have to scoot soon in order to get back to the church to pick up Charlie on time. "Joanie told me they all take this special pill that keeps them safe." He was glad Charlie wasn't here, because it drove her crazy when he played to Donny's illness. "How about I call her and ask her to bring you some?"

Donny started rocking again. It was pretty close to a nod yes.

"She'll come tomorrow morning," he told his grandson. "And if she's busy, I'll go to her and pick up the pills and bring 'em over myself. How's that?"

More rocking.

"Good." Vince creaked his way to his feet.

Donny didn't like being touched, so he gave the kid a mock salute. "I'll see you tomorrow, kiddo."

"You said Joanie would come."

"All right, then. Joan'll see you tomorrow."

Vince let himself out of Donny's house, locking the door behind him. He had his cell phone out and open before he got into the car, calling back Donny's doctor to give him the thumbs-up for that new prescription.

Joanie, he knew from experience, would be a little harder to reach.

NINE

Joan DaCosta was all right.

Sam had always thought that Muldoon's taste in women leaned slightly toward grim, whip-cracking Nazi types, but Joan spent most of her time out on the boat laughing. She wasn't afraid to let the salt spray whip through her hair, tying it back only to keep it out of her mouth. In fact, once or twice he'd caught her lifting her face to the wind, to get a good, solid noseful of ocean air.

She wasn't pretty, not by a long stretch. Her cheeks were too round, her mouth too wide, her chin too pointy. And her nose — he didn't know what the deal was with her nose. It looked like maybe it came from someone else's face entirely.

Yet, somehow, when she smiled, she was beautiful. It was pretty freaking weird, but within two minutes of meeting her, Sam knew exactly why Muldoon was dogging her.

Not that Muldoon was capable of getting into any woman's face far enough to call it dogging. He was more like casting wistful glances in her direction and kind of pathetically hoping she would notice him.

The good news was that she *did* notice. She played it really cool, laughing and joking and teasing everyone, but her female radar was up and working. And part of her was monitoring Mike Muldoon at all times.

She thanked them all after they pulled back into the dock, after the demonstration was over, calling each of the men by name and shaking his hand.

"Thanks for taking the time to do this, Lieutenant Starrett," she said as she shook his. "I think I've probably made you late for dinner."

Any reason not to go home was a good enough reason to stick around.

"No sweat," he told her. Just as he'd expected, she had a nice, solid grip. "Dinner's not that big a deal at my house."

Mary Lou usually ate early, with Haley. She saved a plate for him and heated it in the microwave when he got home. And then she sat there and watched him eat. It was weird eating with an audience like that. Every time he tried to make conversation, he was reminded of just how incompatible they were, which depressed the hell out of him. So he always just sat and ate as fast as he could.

He'd taken to arriving home minutes before she had to leave for her nightly AA meeting. That way she'd leave, and he'd heat the plate himself.

Of course, then he'd eat standing up, chasing Haley around the house. He hated the playpen that Mary Lou had bought and put front and center in the living room. Sometimes, if Haley was particularly energetic, he'd put her in there, but climb in, too, and just sit cross-legged while he ate his dinner, careful to keep his plate out of range of his daughter's grasping little fingers.

186

After dinner, he'd heat a bottle of milk in the microwave, then sit with Haley on the couch and watch hockey or baseball until she fell asleep, a warm little lump of life on his chest.

Lately, his timing had been off, and Mary Lou took Haley with her to her AA meetings. Which meant Sam got to come home to an empty, responsibility-free house. Which was what he missed, wasn't it?

"Regardless, I do appreciate your spending all this time with me," Joan told Sam now with a smile.

The sun was setting and it was about as romantic as it could get there by the water. Muldoon was hovering nearby, ready to walk her back to the parking lot.

"What time's that phone call you're expecting?" Sam heard him ask her.

"Ten o'clock eastern time, which is . . . help me out here. All of my already pitiful math skills completely vanished at the shock of watching you guys get lassoed out of the water at top speed by a guy with a rubber noose. I still can't believe necks don't get snapped when you do that."

"That's generally why we need to get an arm up in there, too," Muldoon told her.

"You can't be like normal people and stop the boat so the guys in the water can climb on? I mean, sure, it's not as flashy, but . . ."

"Stopping the boat can be a major liability."

"Why?" Joan asked as Sam gathered up the last of his gear.

"There're a lot of reasons, the biggest being that stopping can be bad for everyone's health if the enemy's shooting at you."

"Aha!" she said. "Civilian versus military reasoning. I wasn't thinking about any enemy or any shooting, because in my world, I get up and go to work, and occasionally I'll stop at a store on my way home, and there's never anyone shooting at me. But that's what you do when you go to work, right? Get shot at."

"Actually most of the time we don't get shot at, because the enemy never knows we're there," Muldoon said. "We usually sneak in and sneak back out. What you saw today was an extraction technique that pulls us out of an area quickly. Once the enemy does know we're there, we tend to use speed instead of stealth. I think I mentioned earlier that this technique was first used during World War Two."

No, no, no, boy wonder. Save the lecture for the classroom. Ask her about herself. Confess a secret. Make this sunset conversation count.

But Muldoon was an idiot. "See, Navy frogmen would swim all the way to the shore of an enemy-held island to find out what kind of underwater barricades had been constructed," he continued. "They'd do readings on tides and coral reefs and all that other stuff that really matters when you're about to attempt a full-scale invasion, right? The frogmen would check everything out, then swim way back out to a point where they'd be picked up. The idea was to get them out of the water without the boat being hit by enemy shells, and without the enemy catching on that there were swimmers out there being picked up."

"Gee, and I thought it was just something you did to show off."

Muldoon laughed. "No. Well, today it was."

She laughed, too. "It worked. I was impressed."

"There's probably not enough time to get dinner before you have to take that phone call, huh?" Sam heard Muldoon say.

Sam rolled his eyes. Amazing ineptitude. Way to give her an excuse not to share a meal with you, Mike, you flipping genius.

"Actually, I'm still reeling from lunch," she said. "I think I'm just going to get a salad from room service while I watch some CNN."

That sounds good. Mind if I join you? Come on, Mike. She obviously likes you, she's friendly . . . This was not that hard to do.

"The news is on all the time in my office," Joan continued as they started walking toward the parking lot. "I go into withdrawal when I'm away from D.C. because out in the real world, nobody's got the news on."

Sam didn't catch exactly what Muldoon said, but Joan answered by saying, "I'm having lunch with Commander Paoletti and his fiancée."

Obviously Muldoon, the fool, had given up on seeing her again that evening and had moved on to tomorrow.

"She's not in town for that long, blockhead," Sam muttered. "So make your move before it's too late."

"And you would be talking to . . . your invisible friend?"

"Shit!" Sam turned to see WildCard standing behind him. "Where the hell did you come from?"

"I am like the wind," the Card intoned. "I move silently across both land and sea."

189

"Fuck the wind. You up for getting a beer, Chief?" Sam asked.

"Since Savannah's in New York, yes, sir, I am." WildCard fell into step with him. "So. You've started talking to yourself, I see, Captain Queeg."

"I was talking to Muldoon. I wasn't talking to myself." Although Sam knew that if he could go back in time just a few years, he'd hunt himself down and start talking to himself in earnest. And he wouldn't stop until he was convinced that his younger, dumbass self wouldn't make the same stupid mistakes all over again.

Christ, speaking of mistakes, what the hell was he going to do about Mary Lou?

Sam finally called at 8:30.

Mary Lou waited for two rings before picking up the phone. It was an old habit from when she was a teenager, an attempt to come across as if she wasn't desperate, as if she wasn't eagerly waiting by the phone. Which she always had been. Which she still was even now — a pathetic thought since she was married. "Hello?"

There was a pause, then Sam's voice. "I thought I'd get the answering machine. I didn't expect you to be . . . Didn't you have a meeting tonight? It's me," he added, as if anyone else might ever call her.

"No, I, um, I didn't go tonight." Mary Lou looked over at the dinner table. She'd gotten out a linen tablecloth — a wedding gift from Sam's sister Elaine, who lived near Boston — and even put out a candle. The steak she'd finally decided on cooking for this "special" dinner was still marinating in Italian salad dressing — a trick Janine

190

had taught her back before she hooked up with Clyde-the-vegetarian and moved to Florida. Lord, she missed her sister.

"Is everything all right?"

"Yeah," she said. Haley was watching her, sitting in her swing, chewing on her plastic keys, so she forced herself to smile. "Are you still at the base?"

Another pause, apparently while he decided whether or not to tell her the truth. "No, I'm, uh, over at the Ladybug with Ken."

He'd gone for truth — at least partial truth. The big question was, who else was at the bar with him?

"We were helping Muldoon wrangle this public relations person from the White House," he told her, "and the maneuvers went kind of late. I figured you'd be at your meeting, and, you know, Savannah's out of town so . . ."

She *hadn't* known that Savannah, Chief Karmody's wife, was out of town. The only time the other SEALs' wives called her was if there was some kind of disaster. Like when that helicopter had gone down in Pakistan. Mary Lou had been glued to CNN, desperate for any news at all as to who might've been on board. Meg Nilsson had finally called to say she'd just heard from her husband that Team Sixteen wasn't even in Pakistan at the time of the crash.

That time, it was someone else's husband who had died.

"I just wanted to let you know where I was, and that I grabbed some dinner with Ken, so don't worry about me," Sam continued. "And don't wait up, okay?"

"Okay," Mary Lou managed to say. Her husband was spending the evening at the Ladybug Lounge — the meat market, low-rent, pick-up joint of a bar where she'd first met him. She could tell from the broadening of his Texas drawl that he'd already had a beer or two.

Oh, Lord, what she wouldn't do for a beer . . .

"Sam," she said, "I was thinking. You said you had relatives in Sarasota, you know, where Janine lives now, with Clyde?"

"Yeah," he said. "I have a bunch of cousins there."

"I thought maybe we could take a vacation. Go east and visit them all. Janine and your cousins, too."

Sam was silent.

"You still there?" she asked.

"Yeah," he said. "I just, uh . . . I don't think that's a very good idea. I don't think you would, um, like my cousins very much. But if you want to go see Janine, then definitely you should go."

Yeah, he'd like that, wouldn't he? To have Mary Lou and Haley go to the East Coast for a while while Alyssa Locke was in town. "I don't know," she said.

"Think about it," Sam told her. "I'll see you later." He cut the connection.

He would come home late, smelling like those really strong mints that came in a little tin box — as if they could somehow mask the scent of beer on his breath. As if that would somehow fool her into thinking that he hadn't spent the evening in a place where she couldn't so much as set a foot inside the door without risking her sobriety.

Don't wait up.

That was easier said than done, when she knew that even if she went to bed, she wouldn't fall asleep. No, she'd lie there, even after Sam came home and fell instantly and annoyingly unconscious, wondering who he'd danced with and who he'd wished he'd shared a bed with tonight.

As if *that* was such a mystery.

Mary Lou hung up the phone and plucked Haley from the seat of her swing. Her car keys were on the counter, and she grabbed them and was halfway out the door before she made herself stop.

What was she doing? Was she really going to drive over to the Ladybug Lounge to see . . . what? If Alyssa Locke was there, too? How would she know? The Bug didn't have windows. And she sure as hell didn't know what kind of car Alyssa was driving.

So what good would it do? It would probably only make her feel worse. Hearing the distant music and laughter. Watching people pull into the parking lot, ready to go inside and have a good ol' time, drinking themselves into oblivion.

She held Haley close, breathing in her sweet baby scent.

If she called ahead, she could probably arrange to drop Haley off at the sitter's for a few hours. As long as Mrs. U. was home, she wouldn't mind earning a few extra bucks.

And then Mary Lou could go over to the Ladybug, park her car, and go inside.

It was a bad idea.

No, it was a *terrible* idea.

She set Haley down in the playpen in the living

room, amid a pile of toys and stuffed animals, went to the phone, and dialed Rene's number.

Answering machine. Shit.

Mary Lou was doing what she was supposed to do — calling her AA sponsor in an attempt to keep herself from doing something really stupid. She was doing everything right, so why, why, *why* did this have to be so hard?

She called Janine and the line was busy. She dialed again. What, didn't vegetarians believe in call waiting? Shit.

She called Donny, but he was still in siege mode and not answering his phone. His grandfather had called her earlier to report that he'd stopped in to see Don, who was apparently disoriented from not taking his meds, but safe.

Mary Lou took a deep breath and called her mother — she was that desperate to talk to someone, anyone — and got another machine. Of course, it was much later out on the East Coast. In fact, it was getting pretty close to last call. Even if her mother *had* been home, she probably would've been too drunk to make much sense.

Mary Lou dug through her kitchen junk drawer, searching for her AA blue book — the schedule of all the regular meetings in town. Maybe there was something that started late somewhere in San Diego. Maybe . . .

A business card poked out from between a half-eaten box of Good & Plenty and the city's recycling schedule, and she pulled it free.

Ihbraham Rahman.

He'd been extremely nice to her over the past few days.

But why? What exactly did he want from her?

He wanted to fuck her. That was the obvious answer. Why else were men kind to women?

Except she hadn't even once seen that familiar, male, appraising, sexual edge in his eyes when he looked at her.

And why not? What was so wrong with her? Aside from the twenty extra pounds . . . Although, didn't foreign men like women with meat on their bones?

Not that it really mattered to her. Because unlike her husband who was obviously ruled by his dick rather than a sense of what was right or wrong, *she'd* never hook up with someone who wasn't white.

She still was in shock over the fact that Sam had actually considered marrying Alyssa Locke. Mary Lou had called him on it once, and she'd seen from his eyes that he honestly didn't see what was so wrong with that — a white man married to a black woman.

No, Sam couldn't see past the sex.

And aside from that, everything would be hard. Everything. All of their choices, all of their decisions. Where they lived, who they chose as their friends, where they went to church.

People would stare. Wherever they went, whatever they did, they'd stand out as different.

And their children . . .

It was hard enough being a kid in this shitty world and trying to fit in, without being forced to deal with two completely different heritages.

How would Sam, with his Texas white-boy upbringing, be able to relate to a black son and all the issues he would have to face as a young black man growing up in America, land of the free white male?

No, sir. Thank you very much. Jesus himself could come down from heaven, and Mary Lou wouldn't have to think twice about marrying him if he didn't have the same color skin that she had.

Life was hard enough without asking for trouble.

She dialed Ihbraham's number.

From where she stood, she could clearly see Haley happily chewing on Eeyore's ear.

"Hello?"

Oh, Lord. He was actually there. Unless he had a roommate . . . She cleared her throat. "May I speak to Ihbraham Rahman, please?"

"This is he. Who is calling, please?"

He sounded so different on the phone. So distant and formal. "Uh, this is Mary Lou Starrett. From next door to the Robinsons . . . ?"

"Ah," he said. "Of course."

Of course? What did *that* mean? That he'd expected her to call him? That she'd seemed so terribly desperate that her calling him was a given?

But then he asked, "Are you all right, Mary Lou?"

"Yeah," she said. "I just . . ." She closed her eyes. "Actually, no. No, I'm not all right. I'm terrible, actually."

"Are you sober?" he asked.

"Yes."

"That's good," he said. "I'm so glad you called before you did something that could not be undone. You're a very strong woman. Very strong."

It was entirely possible that by calling him she *had* done something that couldn't be undone. His musical accent wound itself around her, soothing her in a way that was dangerous.

"I'm not going to sleep with you," Mary Lou blurted. "I just want to say that up front."

There was the briefest of pauses. "Okay," he said. "It's good to make such things clear, I think. Although I wish to assure you I gave you my card only with hope of providing support to your sobriety. My intentions were not salacious."

Well, *there* was a word she'd never heard used in conversation. In a book, sure, but . . .

She didn't know what she felt more strongly — relief or disappointment at his lack of salacitude, or whatever the hell the word would become if it were a noun. Lord, she was fucked up. She absolutely would never in a million years become involved with this man, yet a solid part of her was actually upset that his intentions *weren't* freaking salacious.

What the hell did that say about *her?*

"Talk to me," Ihbraham said in his gentle voice. "Tell me why, no matter how terrible you feel, you aren't going to have a drink right now. Not for forever. Just for right now. Tomorrow's not to worry about. Tomorrow you'll handle when it comes, okay? But tell me why you're not going to drink tonight."

Mary Lou sat down in the doorway between the kitchen and the living room. The only reason she wasn't down at the Ladybug right now was deep in conversation with her Pooh Bear.

"You really want to hear this?" she asked Ihbraham.

"Yes," he said. "I do. I absolutely do."

Funny, he said it with so much conviction, she could almost believe him.

As Charlie headed upstairs, thunder rolled in the distance.

Vince had turned on CNN to get the latest on the war but she never watched past the headlines. All she needed to know was that the terrorists hadn't killed anyone else today.

As far as the details of the conflict went, well, back in the 1940s, she'd had enough details of war to last her a lifetime.

People died in war. That was the most important detail, and one that the news seemed to gloss over today. War wasn't this clean, tidy affair that CNN was seemingly reporting. It was filled with death and destruction. It was bombs falling and shards of metal screaming through the air and smoke and blood and fear and grown men screaming with pain.

It was waking up in the middle of the night to the sound of a Marine who was barely old enough to go into a nightclub shouting about getting to cover. It was about finding him panicked and completely disoriented underneath the bed.

All because they were having a thunderstorm in a city thousands of miles from the front lines.

Charlie now turned around and went back down the stairs. The book she was reading was out on the kitchen table, and she picked it up as she went past. Thunder rolled again, louder this time as she went into the den.

Vince looked up and saw her there. He knew

why she'd come back downstairs and his smile was still a little embarrassed. After all these years. "I'm okay," he said.

"I know." Charlie sat down next to him on the couch and squeezed his knee. He took her hand in his and, bringing it up to his lips, he kissed her as he watched the sports news.

He *was* okay.

She was the one who would remember forever that on July 17, 1964, Vince had finally been able to sit through a thunderstorm without getting tense. Sure, he'd always tried to hide it, and he did a good job, too. But for all those years after the war, he'd never been able to fool her.

And forget about the storms that crashed overhead in the middle of the night. For years, Vince had woken up disoriented and confused. She'd gotten into the habit of turning on the light at the first little rumble of distant thunder.

Sixty years later, and he still woke up and stayed up until the storm was through.

She gently disengaged her fingers from his and reached over and turned on the lamp that sat on the end table. It made the room just a little bit brighter. "Mind if read?"

" 'Course not."

Sixty years.

Charlie settled on the couch so that her shoulder touched Vince's as she opened her book and pretended to focus on the story.

Nearly sixty years of holding on to him, of holding his hand, without making it obvious that that was what she was doing.

Charlie prayed every day that the fighting in this

new war didn't escalate, that sixty years from today wouldn't find countless old women still worried about all those formerly young men who had served this country at such a personal cost. Of course, nowadays the young women were going, too. Who would hold *their* hands sixty years from now?

What a price to pay for freedom. All those years of life, irrevocably shaped by the sights and sounds of war.

And although the years flew by, some memories simply never faded.

That was as true for her as it was for Vince.

Charlie remembered that first time as if it were yesterday.

She'd sat up in the dark of the tiny extra bedroom in the house she shared with Edna Fletcher, awakened from a restless sleep by the sound of shouting.

"Not here! Not here! God damn it, go back! Go — For the love of God, don't you understand? You won't clear the goddamn reef!"

It was Vince.

Lightning flickered behind the curtains and thunder crashed again, deafeningly loud. The hot spell they'd been having for the past few days had brought them an electrical storm, despite the fact that it was only January.

"Noooooooooooo!" Vince shouted so loud and so long, Charlotte was out of the bed and down the hall almost before she knew it, running for his room. "They're drowning! Don't you see?"

She grabbed the light switch and cranked, but the power had gone out.

"Vince?" Lightning illuminated the empty bed. She tried to look around the room, but the flash faded too quickly. "Vince, where are you?"

Thunder cracked again, shaking the house.

"Get down! Dear God, keep your head down! They're throwing everything at us that they can!"

Charlotte crouched next to the bed and peered into the darkness underneath. Lightning flared and there was Vince, his eyes wild in his gaunt face, his dark hair a mess.

He grabbed her, and she shrieked as he pulled her onto the floor and yanked her underneath the bed with him. As the thunder roared, he rolled on top of her.

As thin as he'd seemed as she'd cared for him this past week, he was bigger than she was. In fact, from this perspective, he didn't feel frail at all. On the contrary, he was quite solid and heavy. And unquestionably male.

"Stop," she said, even though part of her had been starving for years for this very type of physical intimacy, for a body to cling to, to hold close, for someone else's strong arm tightly wrapped around her. "Get off me!"

But he didn't move. He tucked his head down close to hers. "Stay down!"

He was covering her from an imaginary barrage of shells, she realized. He was trying to protect her. This wasn't even remotely about sex.

"Vincent, it's just a thunderstorm." His ear was right by her mouth so she spoke as quietly and calmly as she possibly could, considering that her heart was racing.

She'd jumped from bed so quickly, she'd neglected to put on her robe. And she was lying there now, on the floor beneath him, in only her thin flannel nightie, which had ridden way up as he'd pulled her under the bed. She could feel his bare legs, warm against hers.

"Jesus God, Ray, keep your fucking head down!" His voice broke. His language should have shocked her, but it wasn't half as shocking as the raw pain and horror in his voice. "Oh, God, why didn't you keep your head down? Medic! I need a medic! Where the fuck is the medic?"

Charlotte did the only thing she could do. She put her arms around him and held him as tightly as he was holding her.

"Vince," she said. "Vincent. Listen to me. It's Charlotte Fletcher. Not Ray, *Charlotte*. We're safe. We're in Washington, and this is just a thunderstorm."

"Charlotte?" Edna called.

"Under the bed, Mother," Charlotte called. "Get candles! Bring as many candles up as you possibly can! Please hurry!"

"Where's Ray?" Vince asked. He was breathing hard, as if he'd run for miles. Or as if he were trying desperately not to cry.

"I don't know," she told him. "But I do know he's not here. Not now. You're here, Vince, and I'm here, and Mother Fletcher just went downstairs to fetch some light. You're in our house in Washington, D.C., and we're all safe. No one's shooting at us."

Light came into the room. Charlotte couldn't see the door from her vantage point under the bed, but she suspected Edna had simply grabbed the candlesticks from the dining room sideboard and set them here on the oak dresser.

"I'll get more," Edna said.

The light was faint and it flickered, but it cut through the darkness.

"Open your eyes," Charlotte commanded Vince.

He did, but she still wasn't sure if he could really see her yet. Lightning flashed again, but it was less jarring with the candles already lighting the walls.

Still, he tensed and ducked his head, pulling her closer to him, too, when the thunder came. It was less earthshaking this time — the storm was starting to move off, thank God.

"It's thunder," she said again, her face pressed against his neck. He was hot and he smelled like her soap. "Just thunder."

The sound of Mother Fletcher's footsteps hurrying up the stairs heralded the arrival of more candles, more light.

"Put at least one on the floor, please," Charlotte called. And then, alleluia, there was more light.

"Oh, dear," Edna said. Charlotte caught a glimpse of her mother-in-law's pale face as she peered under the bed.

"He thinks the thunder is shelling. He thinks we're under attack," she explained, her own face heating at the idea of what this must look like from Edna's perspective.

"How can I help?" Edna asked. She actually lay down on her stomach, on the chilly floor, in order to get closer, bless her.

"I don't know," Charlotte admitted. "I was hoping the light would help."

Edna pushed the candle even closer. "Young man, look at me. Look and see where you are," she ordered in that no-nonsense voice that had surely kept James hopping when he was a child.

It may have been Edna's stentorian tones, or the light from the candle burning right beside them, but this time when Vince lifted his head, Charlotte knew he was on his way back.

As Edna reassured him that the war hadn't yet come to 84 Chestnut Street in Washington, D.C., he looked at Edna, looked at the candle, looked at the bed frame above them. And then he looked at Charlotte.

She saw the exact moment he realized exactly where he was and that she was lying beneath him. The parade of emotions that crossed his so-expressive face would have been funny if she hadn't felt like crying in sheer relief.

Shock, horror, disbelief, embarrassment. Desire. She saw clearly from his eyes that she now wasn't the only one who was intensely aware of the way their bare legs were intertwined.

"Please tell me I didn't hurt you," he whispered as he quickly pushed himself off of her.

"You were trying to save me," she reassured him. Funny, but she didn't seem able to do more than whisper, either. She cleared her throat. "My dignity is slightly bruised, but that's the extent of any damage. However, I suspect we've irrevocably crossed over to that place where it's not just acceptable but rather necessary now to address each other by our given names."

He laughed at that, as she'd hoped he would. But then his face crumpled, just like that of the little boy who lived in the house next door, and he started to cry.

He tried to pull farther away, but this time she was the one who reached for him and wouldn't let him go.

There was nothing to say, nothing to do but hold him and cry, too. From all that he'd said tonight, she could begin to imagine the nightmare he — and thousands of other American boys — had lived through. And perhaps worst of all, she could begin to imagine what it had been like at Pearl Harbor when the Japanese had attacked. When James had died.

They both cried until they were exhausted, until Vince fell asleep. And then Charlotte cried some more.

And when she next looked up, light was coming in through the windows. She'd fallen asleep right there, in Vince's arms, on the floor beneath the very bed she'd once shared with James.

Edna was long gone, and the candles had all burned out.

Vince was sleeping, and she gently pulled free from his embrace and crawled out from under the bed.

By all rights she should have felt terrible, staying up so late, crying as hard as she had, and then sleeping on the hardwood floor. Every muscle in her body should have ached. Every bone should have felt bruised. Her head should have pounded.

But as she slipped out of the room to get ready to go to work, she couldn't remember the last time she'd had a better sleep.

Muldoon had had the evening from hell.

Mrs. Tucker had followed him into the grocery store.

It was like something out of a bad movie, and he'd had to dash down the dog food aisle to escape out the loading dock.

On his way home, desperate for a beer, he'd stopped into the Ladybug Lounge and come across a sailor going head to head with some bikers in the parking lot.

It took a full hour to get that straightened out.

He drove the kid back to the base, and then somehow found himself outside of the Hotel del Coronado, where Joan was staying.

He still wanted that beer, but more than a beer, he wanted to talk to Joan. Who wasn't answering her cell phone.

Muldoon used his own phone to call the hotel's main number as he walked toward the lobby. Thunder had been rumbling for the past hour or so and a sharp crack made the skies open. He ran, but it was hopeless. By the time he reached the hotel, he was soaked.

The front desk patched him through to her room, but she wasn't there. After four rings her voice mail picked up.

He didn't leave a message because he wasn't sure what to say. *Hi, I'm really not stalking you. Really. It's just that I can't seem to spend more than a couple of hours without desperately wanting to see you again.*

That would go over well.

There was a hotel directory in the lobby, and he

stopped and dripped for a moment in front of it, attempting to get his bearings. There were several different bars in the Del. The Palm Court had piano music, but the Babcock and Story bar had jazz guitar.

Joan was definitely the guitar type. He headed for the B&S.

Come on, Joan. Be there.

He stopped just inside the bar in part to let his eyes adjust to the dim lighting, in part in an effort to dry off a bit more, but mostly because he had absolutely no clue what he was going to say if he did find her there.

How about, *You aren't going to believe everything that's happened since I walked you back to your car this evening.*

Of course, that didn't explain what he was doing here at the Del.

I called your room, but you weren't there, and since I was driving past, I figured I might as well go out into the pouring rain to see if I could find you, because I have had one unbelievably freaky evening and all I want to do is look into your eyes and tell you about it and laugh. And then I want you to invite me back to your room so we can spend about seven hours straight having incredible, screaming monkey sex.

That last part might not go over so well, despite the fact that he now realized he'd gotten out of his truck not entirely in search of a beer.

No, a beer would certainly be nice, but it would be completely unnecessary if Joan were to appear before him and hold out her hand to lead him up to her hotel room.

And then, as if on cue, there she was.

He'd been squinting through the darkness at all the little tables that dotted the room, but she was sitting right there at the bar, sipping some kind of frozen drink from a straw.

And laughing into some other man's eyes.

Muldoon used the mirror behind the bar to get a better look at the man's face. He wasn't anyone he knew. In fact, the guy was wearing a business suit. He was in his fifties and was overweight and bald, but whatever he was telling Joan had her complete attention.

As he watched, something the bald guy said made Joan crack up. The man laughed along with her, and the sound of their two voices floating over the jazz guitar was enough to make Muldoon crazy.

Who was this guy? Was he someone she knew? Or was he someone who was just trying to pick her up in this hotel bar?

Or maybe she was the one who'd hit on him. Maybe she liked fifty-year-old bald guys. Maybe if Muldoon were a fifty-year-old bald guy, she'd be getting it on with him right this very moment.

If he were Sam, he'd push his wet hair back from his face and go and sit down on Joan's other side, order himself that beer he wanted. Introduce himself to Baldy.

But chances were that Sam hadn't had Muldoon's string of bad luck tonight.

Feeling decidedly pathetic, he cut his losses for the day and went back out into the rain, heading for home.

"I was just about to turn ten that summer," Mary Lou told Ihbraham, the telephone tucked under her chin as she sat on the floor in the archway between the kitchen and the living room and fed Haley.

Who'd finally fallen asleep, right at Mary Lou's breast.

"Janine was thirteen," she said quietly, looking down into her daughter's perfect face. "We were living in New Orleans, and my mother was working as a cocktail waitress. She was actually showing up for work for a change — she was working the late shift, which was just her speed. Have you ever been to New Orleans?"

"No," Ihbraham said. "I haven't."

"It's a crazy city. The bars stay open late, late, late — it doesn't matter if it's a Monday or a Friday. Every night is party night.

"We were living in an apartment that was really nice — it was a palace compared to some of the dumps we'd lived in. And it was huge — Janine and I each had our own bedroom. The only catch was that it belonged to this guy Lyle that my mother had met at the bar, and we had to be real quiet, tiptoeing around the house. He was kind of fat and smarmy, but he worked in an office and actually wore a suit and got a paycheck every week. Which he used to buy us things. Toys and pretty clothes. Books.

"Things were good. It was the first time I could remember that we didn't use food stamps. Maybe it was the only time . . .

"But Janine started acting weird. Like if I came up behind her and she didn't hear me coming, she would really jump. And she cried a lot — I didn't know what was wrong with her. Why was she crying when we had our new Fat Daddy buying us all those things?"

On the other end of the phone, Ihbraham sighed, and Mary Lou knew he'd guessed where this story was going.

"I remember being terrified that Mama would get tired of Lyle and we'd have to hit the road again. I told Janine that if she did, I was going to beg Lyle to let me stay here. I could keep his kitchen clean and do his laundry. And she got real angry at me. I didn't understand why, and she finally told me that if I really wanted to stay here, I'd have to suck on my Fat Daddy's thing, because that's what she had to do, every night after Mama went to work. That was the real reason he let us live here.

"I was shocked," Mary Lou told him. "I mean, I grew up knowing all there was to know about sex. Mama got drunk and brought men home and wasn't very good at remembering to close the bedroom door. And sometimes there wasn't even a separate bedroom."

She looked down at Haley, who was sleeping on her lap. How could her mother have done that? How could her mother not have loved her and Janine as fiercely as she loved this little girl? But Mary Lou knew that it wasn't that her mother had loved her any less. But rather that she'd loved alcohol more.

"I knew what Janine was saying was something that some men liked. And I also knew that some men liked little girls — enough of my mother's parade of boyfriends had waggled their things at us, starting back when we were real small. But once they did, and once we told Mama, she kicked them out on their butts faster than you could blink.

"And I have to confess, there was a time or two when Janine and I told stories that weren't true — like, Mama, he touched my booby! — just to get rid of a boyfriend that we didn't want hanging around.

"Well, when Janine told me this about Lyle, I went running to Mama. And I told her what Janine had told me, only Janine, she denied it. Flat out. She said I was making things up, that I was mad because Lyle bought Janine a new sweater and he didn't get one for me. And Mama believed her. I got sent to bed without supper for telling stories.

"Janine kept telling me, too, that she'd made it all up, but I knew she hadn't. I knew. So I pretended to go to bed early, and I hid in her closet. And sure enough, after Mama left for work, Lyle came into Janine's room. And sure enough . . ."

That image of Janine and Lyle was still crystal clear in her head, even after all these years. And it still made her sick. It still made her want to cry.

"What did you do?" Ihbraham asked gently. "Poor little one, only ten — what could you do? You had already told your mother. Who else was there to tell?"

"Well, hell, I told her again," Mary Lou said. "I went screaming out of that closet. Scared the shit out of Lyle — too bad I didn't give him a heart attack — and ran all the way to the Shamrock Café, where Mama worked. I told her what I'd seen.

"Only Lyle had called ahead with some story about a big fight I was having with Janine. Mama marched me back home and locked me in my

211

room. I was scared to death — I didn't want her leaving me there with him — but Janine just wouldn't tell the truth. I remember I was crying and saying, 'Tell her! Tell her!' She told me later that she was tired of always moving, and she figured this wasn't so bad — she could live with this."

Ihbraham sighed again.

"So there I was, locked in my room," Mary Lou continued. "I locked the door from my side, too, and I even pushed my dresser in front of it like I'd seen people do in the movies. And sure enough, Lyle came rattling my doorknob, talking about punishment, about how I was going to have to pay, about how he could do whatever he damn pleased and no one — no one — would ever believe me. He told me what he was going to do to me when he got that door unlocked, about what he was going to do to me every night from that night on." She paused. "I won't repeat it here, but I remember it. Every god-awful word."

"I'm so sorry," Ihbraham said.

"I would kill a man who said those things to Haley," Mary Lou told him.

"I know," he said. "And I would help."

"He tried to get into my room, but Janine hit him," she told him. "Over the head. With the biggest, heaviest cooking pot she could find. In the movies that usually knocks a person out. But all it did was piss Lyle off. I could hear him beating the crap out of her on the other side of that door. He beat her, and he raped her, and I was sure he was going to kill her. So I did the only thing I could do. I went out the window, and I jumped off the roof. I broke my wrist in the fall — Lord Jesus, did that

212

hurt — but I ran for Mama anyway, screaming bloody murder.

"Well, I guess third time's a charm, because this time she did believe me. And she grabbed this man who was the bouncer at the bar, and we all ran home. And one look at Janine . . . Well, there was no denying what had happened.

"And that was that," she said. "The end of our childhood. We moved out, of course. Moved back to Alabama. My mother pretty much quit on us after that — her drinking got crazy out of control. I think the guilt really ate her up inside. I did all the cooking and cleaning, because Janine had a whole lot of healing to do — she's still struggling, even now."

They were both silent for a moment.

"I would have killed him," Mary Lou said again. "A man who hurt my baby? He would not have seen another sunrise."

She watched Haley's eyes move slightly beneath her closed lids as she dreamed, a smile on her perfect little face.

"I would have killed him," Mary Lou said. "But my mother — all she did was try to drink her own self to death. I will not be like her. I *will* not."

At least not tonight.

TEN

Joan was waiting out in front of the hotel when Mike Muldoon pulled up in his truck.

"That was fast," she said as she climbed in.

"I don't live too far from here."

His hair was still wet from his shower and his cheeks were freshly shaved, making him look even younger than usual. He'd worn his uniform, as she'd asked, and he looked sharp and wrinkle-proof and completely awake despite the ungodly hour.

The cab of his truck smelled like freshly roasted coffee. There were two Starbucks cups in the holder that pulled out from the dash. "Oh, my God," she said. "Please say that one of those is for me."

He smiled. "One of those is for you."

"Have I told you yet this morning how much I love you?" she said as she fastened her seat belt and reached for the nearest cup.

"There's cream and sugar and a couple of scones in the bag."

Joan laughed. "Scones?"

"You seem the scone type." It was early enough that the streets were empty of traffic, and he did a smooth U-turn right there, heading back toward the causeway.

214

"The *scone* type?" The coffee was heated to near nuclear temperatures and burned all the way down. It was lovely.

"You know. A caffeine addict who can't drive past a Starbucks without stopping," he said. "You go in there often enough, sooner or later you're bound to buy a biscotti or a scone. I figured scone."

"We can't see each other anymore," Joan told him, taking another long sip. "The mystery has completely gone out of our relationship."

He had a really lovely laugh. And the way his eyes crinkled at the corners was lovely, too. And his teeth. Definitely straight and white and very lovely. In fact, the sunlight was sparkling in a lovely way off the gleaming and equally lovely hood of his truck. This entire morning had a lovely rating of about five million.

Except, of course, for the fact that she'd woken up at 4:30 A.M. because it was really 7:30 back in the real world. Which was decadently late for her.

She couldn't go back to sleep — not after last night's phone call from Gramps telling her that her brother Donny was wearing his foil-covered hat again.

As long as she was awake, she might as well get this visit over with.

"So where to?" Mike Muldoon drove like a young man. Like he loved driving his truck as only a still-young man could, carelessly caressing the wheel and the stick shift with his big, graceful hands, elbow resting on the open window. It was very different from the desperate way some men loved their sports cars when they hit middle age.

215

"I'm not sure how to get there from here," she admitted. "I have the address, but —"

"There's a city map in the pocket on your door," Mike told her, slowing down. "What's the street?"

"Westway Drive." There were a lot of maps in that pocket, including what looked like a detailed terrain map of Afghanistan. "This would probably be easier if I put down the coffee, huh?"

But he'd already sped up again. "Don't bother. I know where Westway is. Lieutenant Starrett lives over on Westway."

"Starrett . . . Mr. Texas, right?"

"Right." He shot her a look. "So what's my nickname today?"

Uh-oh. Joan played it dumb. "Your what?"

"Starrett's Mr. Texas. What are you calling me? Am I still Junior?"

At this moment, she thought of him as the apple in the Garden of Eden, perfect and shiny and treacherously tempting. But no way in hell would she ever tell *him* that.

"No more Junior," she said. "I think of you as 'Mike the adorable SEAL who brings me coffee even when I so rudely wake him up at four forty-five A.M. on a morning when he doesn't have to get up until eight.' "

He nodded. "It takes a little bit longer to say than Junior, but I definitely like it better." He glanced at her again. "Adorable, huh?" He cleared his throat. "You think?"

He was driving, so he couldn't hold her gaze. Still, Joan was grateful for the opportunity provided by the bag of scones. She dug into it. "You know damn well that you're adorable in every pos-

216

sible way, little brother. You want one of these?"

"Yeah." She put one into his outstretched hand and their fingers touched. "Thanks," he said. "Sis. Actually, when I think of myself, I think *math geek*. Not so much *adorable*."

Joan had to laugh at that. "No, no, no," she said. "Math geeks don't become Navy SEALs. They become accountants."

"I hate to break it to you, Joan, but when I was a kid, not only was I a math geek, but I was an overweight math geek."

"Really?" Now, wasn't that interesting? It certainly explained Muldoon's lack of strutting and posturing. Other good-looking men often came into a room and struck a pose. They had warped expectations based on years of being treated as special because of their glorious looks.

Not so Muldoon. He seemed completely surprised and taken aback by the attention he received. And his shy, gee-whiz thing wasn't part of an act. It was the real deal.

"I think you were probably just in your larval stage," she told him. "Fledgling," she corrected herself. "Fledgling is a much nicer word."

"Larval is more visually appropriate."

"Then larval it is. But from the looks of things, the metamorphosis was successful, my dear. The math geek is now most definitely an adorable Navy SEAL."

"The math geek is actually still a math geek who happens to excel at survival skills and military strategies and PT." He'd finished his scone and now held out his hand. "I think there're napkins in the bag," he said. "One of the problems of wearing

217

white pants — it's all over the instant you forget and wipe your hands on your legs. After a tragic pizza incident, I started carrying a spare pair here in my truck. Sometimes I think I should carry two."

Joan found a napkin and handed it to him.

"This is all way above and beyond the call of duty, you know," she said. "I purposely called your cell phone this morning instead of your home phone because I thought it would be off and I'd be able to leave voice mail. You really didn't have to volunteer to come out here with me."

"I know." He was signaling for a left turn, his eyes on the road. "I wanted to."

"You wanted to come on an emergency red-alert visit to my crazy-as-a-fruitcake older brother at the crack of dawn? Yeah, that's what I would do with my free time. Sleep is overrated, anyway."

"This isn't the crack of dawn," he told her as he took the turn. "This is halfway through the morning for me. Besides, I went to bed early last night."

"Still . . ."

"I'm happy to help," he said very firmly in what she was rapidly learning to recognize as his officer's voice — no room for argument.

"Well, thank you, just the same," she said. God, she had to tell him about Donny, so he'd know what to expect. But where to start? With the aluminum-foil-covered hat or the alien-repelling oils that her brother sprayed on his windowsills?

But before she could begin, he glanced at her. "Do you . . ." He cleared his throat. "Do you know, uh, many people in San Diego?"

His question was posed ultra casually, the way

218

people asked extremely important questions when they didn't want anyone to know how important the question was to them. Except, of course, they overcompensated in the casual department, and everyone knew anyway.

"Just my grandparents and my brother," she reported.

He nodded, but she could tell from looking that it was not the answer he'd wanted.

"So. Um." Here came another oh-so-casual question. Joan couldn't wait to hear it. "What did you do last night?" he asked.

What the . . . ? Why on earth did he want to know that? Joan watched him as she answered. "Not much. I took that phone call — which was a total waste of time — watched a little CNN . . . I got to bed pretty early, too." Again, this was not the information he was hoping for. She could see that in his eyes. "Why?" she asked. She didn't believe in casual questions. She always preferred those that were point-blank.

He glanced at her again. "I was just . . . you know . . . making sure you were comfortable — that you have everything you need."

She snorted. "Please. Don't insult my intelligence. Clearly there's something you want to know. Why don't you just spit it out instead of gingerly fishing for information? Which, by the way, you suck at doing. Your version of gingerly is the equivalent of fishing by throwing a grenade into a pond."

He laughed. "Well, jeez. Let me know what you really think, Joan. Don't hold back."

"That's right," she said. "*Don't* hold back.

That's what I'm trying to say to you. What are you trying to find out, Michael?"

"I don't know." He shook his head in disgust. At her or at himself? Maybe at both of them.

"Just ask," she urged him. "We're friends, right? You can ask me anything. Well, almost anything."

"I called, and you weren't in your room," he admitted. "It's not that big a deal. I was just . . . I had a really bizarre evening. Mrs. Tucker followed me into the grocery store —"

"She *did?*" Joan turned to sit sideways in her seat. "Oh, my God, you have to tell me *everything!*"

"I snuck out the delivery door —"

"You didn't!" This was just too good.

"After that, I stopped at the Bug for a beer and found this sailor, this kid, completely skunked and trying to pick a fight with a retired Ranger and his two very large friends in the parking lot. The Ranger had been in 'Nam — he could've eaten this kid for breakfast. What number Westway?"

"Four twelve," she told him. "What did you do?"

He pulled up in front of a little white house. Her mother's house. Donny's now. Joan didn't give it more than a quick glance. But even that was enough to make the beautiful morning significantly less terrific.

"After negotiating a peaceful solution to World War Three, I tried calling you. You weren't there, so I went home." He turned off the truck.

"You should have left a message, or called on my cell," Joan told him. "Although apparently there was some kind of satellite malfunction last night, so you might not have been able to get through.

But I was out of my room for twenty minutes, I swear. I went to get a soda from the vending machine, and halfway there figured what the hell, I could use something with a little more teeth. So I went down to the hotel bar and met some corporate someone from Des Moines who was all lit up because his daughter just had his first grandchild, like an hour earlier. He was so cute. But I only talked to him for fifteen minutes, tops. I must have just missed your call, poor baby."

He smiled. "It would've been nice to have a shoulder to cry on. But I survived."

"Tell me about *Laurel*. What did she say? I *knew* she was after your ass."

Muldoon laughed. "She didn't say anything. I saw her and ran. It was very undignified. Maybe I was imagining the whole thing, but I kind of freaked, since I'd seen her just a few minutes earlier, behind me at the gas station."

"She's stalking you!"

"I doubt it. And if she was, I think she might've gotten the hint when I ran away." He grinned. "Screaming in terror."

"Well, hey," Joan said. "Good morning to you. Your visit to the twilight zone isn't over yet. As if yesterday evening wasn't crazy enough, you're about to enter a world where hostile aliens from outer space lurk in every shadow, and apparently wearing aluminum foil on your head keeps those aliens from being able to read your mind. Don't move too fast or make any loud noises when we get inside, all right? And don't be shocked by anything I say. My goal is to get my brother back on his meds, and sometimes it helps if I play along. He'll

221

probably say some crazy things, and it's not important to convince him that he's wrong. It's not important to be right. I have to repeat that to myself over and over whenever I see him, because — believe it or not — I have this tendency to always want to be right."

Muldoon smiled at that. "I'm ready," he said. "Don't worry about me. I've gone into plenty of dark places, seen some pretty crazy things."

Joan nodded. "I guess it's just . . . hard when it's your own brother, you know?"

His smile faded. "Yeah," he said. "I can imagine. But I'll be right beside you."

He was actually serious when he said things like that. It made her want to cry. She gave him a bright smile and patted him on the knee. "Thanks, SuperSEAL. Let's get this over with."

Joan's brother Don was a pack rat.

His living room was stacked with books and magazines. Completely stacked in some places. As in from the hardwood floor right up to the stucco-patterned ceiling.

It was dark, too, despite the bright morning sunshine outside. All the shades were pulled down and the curtains were tightly closed.

After fetching an envelope of Don's medication that her grandfather had left for her in the mailbox, Joan had unlocked the door — a daunting task, since there were about a dozen different locks mounted there, and a half dozen different keys were needed to open them. After she unfastened the last of them, Muldoon stepped past her and went in first.

"Hey, Don, it's me. Joanie," she called out as she closed the door behind her.

The house was silent.

"Ah, this old house," Joan said, flipping her keys over and over, one finger stuck through the central ring. The keys jingled until they hit the palm of her hand with a smack. "My mother bought this house right after I left for college. My parents split up that same year, and Mom and Donny came out to San Diego because my grandparents lived nearby. Of course, they were my dad's parents — my mom's folks died before I was born — but my mom was closer to them than my dad seemed to be, and —" She went into the kitchen. *Jingle, smack.* "Donny, are you in here?"

Muldoon followed, but each time he got close enough to grab her keys, she moved out of reach.

"They moved in and fixed the place up. Well, she fixed the place up while Donny discovered Internet stock trading and made a fortune." *Jingle, smack.* She went down the hall and again he followed. "But then she got sick and went into the hospital . . . Well, I guess she was actually sick for quite a while. Stage four Hodgkin's disease doesn't just appear, like, whammo — one day you're fine, the next you got it. So I really should say that she *found out* how sick she was. This house was her last project — I guess that's why Don didn't want to sell the place and move in with my grandparents after she . . . Well. You know."

Jingle, smack. Jingle, smack.

She stopped outside a closed door. "I'm pretty sure he's in here. Sandbagged in, so to speak. Ready to repel an alien invasion. Donny DaCosta. In the closet. With his laptop and a funny foil-covered hat. Did you ever play Clue? Donny and I used to play Clue all the time when I was little." *Jingle* —

Muldoon caught the keys, then gently took the ring off her finger. He pocketed them, then laced his fingers with hers so that she was holding his hand instead.

"When did your mother die?" he asked.

"It was a long time ago," she said, looking down at their hands. "Twelve years. I was twenty." She looked up at him. "I'm okay, you know. At least, I should be. I paid enough for the therapy."

He smiled because she'd made a joke in an attempt to keep things light, and because she expected him to smile. "I think most people don't ever stop missing their mothers. It must be twice as hard for you to come here since this was her house."

She again tried to joke her way through it. "Yeah, well, what doesn't kill you makes you stronger, right?"

"Sometimes what doesn't kill you just plain sucks."

Joan laughed at that, but when she glanced up at him again, the look in her eyes took him by surprise. This was Joan without the crusty outer layer. A softer Joan. A vulnerable Joan. A Joan that completely took his breath away.

"I hate being here," she said softly. "Thanks for coming with me. Thanks for . . ." She squeezed his hand.

It was his big chance. Muldoon recognized it as a perfect opportunity to tell her he was smitten. To admit that he didn't think of her as any kind of a sister. Shoot, to grab her and kiss her.

But he was too busy standing there dumbstruck, like an idiot, gazing into her eyes.

She released his hand as she turned back to the door, squared her shoulders, and opened it. And the moment was gone. Joan the warrior was back, charging ahead.

"Donny, it's me."

The bedroom was dark, so she turned on the light. Stacks of clothes covered every surface, even half of the bed. Joan's brother had made his bedroom into the world's biggest walk-in closet.

"Who's there? Who's out there?" A gruff male voice came from the far corner of the room, from behind the closed closet door.

"It's Joan, you big dope. Open up."

With a hand on her arm Muldoon stopped her from going toward the door. When she'd first described her brother, he'd imagined a pencil-necked, bespectacled, timid sort of man. But that voice he'd just heard came out of an ogre. Sure, the ogre happened to live in a walk-in closet, but . . . "There's no chance your brother is armed, is there?"

"God, no," she said.

"Joanie?" her brother growled.

"Yep, Don. It's me."

Muldoon didn't let her go. "You're sure?"

"He's not dangerous," she told him. "Honest. I wouldn't have let you come here if I thought for one second that he was. The worst that's going to happen is you might get sprayed with Alien Be Gone, and I'll pay your dry cleaning bill and buy you dinner a few times next week, because God only knows what he actually puts in those spray bottles of his because it sure as hell smells like rabbit urine. That's one childhood odor I'll never forget." She turned to the door, raised her voice. "Can I come in?"

"Joanie, is that really you?"

"Yes, it is, and I'm coming in. Here I come. I'm turning the knob and — Whoa, baby, change your socks recently?" She turned and made a face at Muldoon that her brother couldn't see. "I brought my friend Mike to meet you, but he might want to wait outside, because, Jesus God, Donny, it stinks like feet in here."

"It doesn't bother me," Muldoon told her, following her into the closet. He'd smelled odors far worse than that of an unwashed man. "Hi, Don, I'm Mike."

"A Navy SEAL." Don DaCosta had Joan's brown eyes and a slightly similarly shaped face, but that's where the resemblance ended. He was a big man, as his voice had implied, with quite a bit of extra heft to him. It was hard to tell how tall he was, because he was sitting down. He was wearing what looked to be some kind of magician's or witch's cape with a silvery lining — something from a Halloween costume — as well as a fedora completely covered in shiny aluminum foil. He had about a week's worth of beard growing on his pasty face and wore olive drab pants and a T-shirt that he definitely hadn't changed in many, many days. He turned to look up at Joan in wonder, with eyes that were rimmed with red. "You brought a Navy SEAL for me, to guard me while I'm sleeping?"

"Oh, honey, I'm afraid neither of us can stay for very —"

Muldoon interrupted her with a touch, his fingers briefly pressing her arm. "When's the last time you slept?" he asked, lowering himself to the floor so that he was on Don's level.

Don rocked slightly. "Oh, no. If I sleep, they'll get in here."

Jeez, was it possible Joan's brother hadn't slept since the last time he changed his clothes? Muldoon knew that had to be the case. "You must be pretty tired, huh?"

"My grandfather was a Navy SEAL."

Joan looked pointedly at Muldoon, shaking her head no, then sat down next to her brother. "D'you see that program about Navy SEALs that was on the Discovery Channel last week, Don?"

"You think I'm making it up," he said, turning to look at her with exhausted eyes. "But I'm not."

"If Gramps were a SEAL, don't you think he might've mentioned it to me at *least* once?" she countered.

"He doesn't like to talk about it."

Joan opened her mouth as if she were about to argue, but then closed it, briefly closing her eyes for a moment, too. Muldoon knew exactly what she was thinking. It wasn't important to be right. When she opened her eyes, she leaned over and patted Muldoon's leg. "Well, you were right about Mike. He's a Navy SEAL, too."

"You know, you live right next door to one of my teammates," Muldoon told him.

"Really?" Joan said. "Who?"

"Sam Starrett."

"No kidding. *Right* next door?" Joan turned

227

back to Don. "That should make you feel pretty safe, huh?"

Don rocked. "They don't go into his house. They stay on his driveway or in his garage. I've seen them. They come over here, too, pretending to be the mailman. Or Mary Lou."

"Mary Lou?" she asked.

Muldoon answered. "Sam's wife."

"But I know better," Don continued. "They want my house, so they can watch him. But I won't let them in." He looked at his sister, alarm in his eyes. "Did you lock the door behind you?"

"Yes, I did," she said.

He rocked harder, starting to work himself into a lather. "Are you sure? You're absolutely sure?"

"How about if I go check?" Muldoon said.

Joan nodded at him as she reached for her brother's hand. "Donny, it's all right," he heard her say as he pushed himself to his feet and slipped out of the closet. "You're safe. I promise. Mike's here, right? He's not going to let anything bad happen. He promises me that all the time."

The house was eerily silent as he made his way back to the front door and threw the half dozen or so extra bolts that Joan hadn't bothered to lock after coming in.

A clock ticked in the living room from its place on an end table alongside a standing photograph of a young, dark-haired woman with a chubby-cheeked toddler laughing in her arms and a big-eyed, pinch-faced boy standing solemnly at her side.

The woman — Joan's mother, had to be — was kneeling beside the boy — Don. Her other arm

228

was around him, and her attention was focused on him, despite the much younger child on her hip.

Don DaCosta's mental illness had, no doubt, not been a whole lot of fun for anyone.

Muldoon went back down the hall, back into the bedroom. He knocked softly on the closet door.

Joan opened it and stepped outside, trouble in her eyes.

"Don's willing to take the medication — except for the fact that he's afraid it will make him fall asleep," she reported. "Apparently his experience with meds is that they usually make him drowsy."

"He looks like he's at the point now where just about any change in his state will put him to sleep," Muldoon told her. "He's probably starving and needs to go to the bathroom, too, but he's afraid if he's any less uncomfortable . . ." He could relate. He'd been in that place a time or two while on recon. "Look, is the grandfather he's talking about the one who lives nearby?"

"Has to be. We never knew my mom's parents," Joan told him. She sat down on the edge of Don's bed. "What are you thinking?"

"Call him," Muldoon told her. "See if he can get over here within the next few hours and plan to stay maybe even overnight. If he can do that, I can stay and, you know, stand guard so to speak until he gets here. That way Don can take the pill and get some sleep."

She was already shaking her head. "I can't ask you to do that."

"Yeah," Muldoon said. "I know. But you're not asking. Just call him, all right? And if he really wasn't a frogman — that's what the SEALs would

have been called back when he probably served —
tell him to keep it to himself. Between the two of
us, we can let your brother get a solid night's sleep,
which might help calm him down."

Joan took out her cell phone and dialed. "You
know," she said, "I'm beginning to understand exactly why all of the admirals' wives want to have
sex with you."

Hey, hold that thought, Muldoon was just about
to say, but she held up one finger, then spoke into
her phone.

"Yeah, Gramma, it's Joan. Sorry I'm calling so
early, but I'm over here with Donny, and . . . Yeah.
Yeah. I know. He's going to be okay, though. I
promise. Listen, is Gramps around?"

Vince didn't have time to do more than shake
the young man's hand before Joan hustled Lt.
Mike Muldoon back into his truck.

"He's got to be back on base in twenty minutes,"
she gave as the explanation, but he knew better.
Despite the "This is my friend" introduction,
Joanie liked this man, and thus couldn't deal with
the idea of introducing him to her extended family.

Yes, he knew the girl well. Took after her grandmother, God help them all — particularly Lieutenant Muldoon, poor guy.

Joan looked good. A lot more energized than he
would have thought considering she'd spent most
of the morning in Don's little airless hidey-hole.
She had a new hairdo that made her look really
pretty — and a lot like her mother.

"I'll call you soon," she promised, after giving
both him and Charlie a quick hug and kiss.

Charlie went inside to check on Don while Vince spent a few minutes inspecting the flowering shrubs he'd put in on the side of the house three months ago. This batch was going to survive. Of course, it would help if they'd get just a little more rain.

"Mr. DaCosta."

He turned to see a young woman stepping out of the kitchen door of the house next door. She was wearing some kind of restaurant uniform and carried a child — a little girl from the looks of the ribbons and curls — in her arms.

"I'm Mary Lou Starrett." She introduced herself in that same thick southern accent he'd noticed on the phone. He moved closer, because she was hard to understand. "I'm the one who called you. How's Donny?"

She was ridiculously young, hardly old enough to leave her own mother, let alone be one.

"Well, it's too soon to say that he's back on his medication, since he's only had one dose, but he has had that one. It's a start," he told her. "Thanks so much for looking out for him."

"It's no trouble," she told him. "He's a friend." Her cheeks dimpled as she smiled. "An unusual friend, but . . . he's a good guy. I feel badly for not calling you as soon as I noticed he was acting strangely — more strangely than usual, I should probably say."

"It shouldn't have to fall on you," Vince told her. "We call Don every day, but he only wants us to visit once a week. I'd suspected he'd gone off his meds, but I didn't try to push it because disrupting his schedule sometimes makes things worse. Sometimes he just goes into a decline and comes back out on his own. I guess we were just doing a lot of wishful thinking."

She opened the door of her car and put the baby into a car seat in the back, and he completely lost her reply.

"What's that?" he said.

She straightened up, smoothing down her shirt from where her daughter had grabbed hold of it. "I said, that's understandable. I have to get to work, but please don't hesitate to call me anytime — even for little things, like . . . what to get him for Christmas."

Vince had to smile at that. "Well, thanks, but that's an easy one. Stock in an aluminum foil company."

She laughed as she got into her car and said something that he didn't catch.

"What's that?" he asked, bending down to look into the passenger window.

"I said, it was nice meeting you. You have a nice day, now, Mr. DaCosta."

"You, too, dear," he said, stepping away from the car so she could back out of her driveway.

It was *nahce* meeting *yew*. Vince had to laugh. Of course. That was who this Mary Lou had reminded him of. Sally Slaggerty. Whatever little southern town Mary Lou had come from, he would bet big bucks that it wasn't too far from wherever Sally had been born more than eighty years ago.

Sally Slaggerty, who'd lived upstairs from Charlotte and Edna Fletcher, who'd entertained GIs and sailors in an intimate fashion on damn close to a nightly basis.

Vince grew to dislike poor Sally pretty quickly, because whenever she came home in the evening, gentleman du jour in tow, Charlotte would make a fast exit from his room.

But then there was that one time.

It was late — close to midnight — when ol' Sal got home. Vince had been lying there in the dark for about an hour, thinking about how Charlie had smiled as he'd made his first triumphant trip down the hall to the bathroom just a few hours earlier, when suddenly Sally's radio went on.

He'd learned a hell of a lot about sexual relations over the week or so he'd been there. He'd learned that some men did the deed as if they were running the twenty-yard dash and trying to break the world record for speed. Others — and they tended to be the repeat performers, invited back for two or three nights until they shipped out — kept the bed-springs squeaking and Sally moaning for close to an hour at a time.

An hour could be unbelievably long when there wasn't much else to do but listen — with the knowledge that Charlotte Fletcher was in the next room over, listening to the very same sounds.

Vince would lie there in that bed — her bed — and try not to remember that night that he'd found himself beneath the bed, with Charlie beneath him. He'd try not to remember the way she'd held him as he'd cried, or how sweet she'd smelled, or how soft her lips had felt as she'd kissed his forehead.

That night, Vince tried to focus on the fact that his trip to the bathroom had been a triumph. He was feeling much stronger. It wouldn't be long before he was up and out of bed for good. Which put him that much closer to the meeting Charlotte had set up for him with Senator Howard. It was still some time away, but he wanted to go in there looking strong and capable.

He'd barely recognized his reflection in the bathroom mirror, he was so pale and wan.

He tried to block the murmur of voices coming from Sally's room upstairs, but the crashing sound of breaking glass made him sit up in bed.

It was nothing entirely new. There'd be giddy laughter now . . . Except there wasn't. Just that murmur of voices. Sally's low and intense, her words indiscernible, the man's louder, suddenly clear.

"If you're not going to give it back, I'll leave when I'm goddamn ready to leave."

Another crash. And this time Sally cried out in pain or fear, it was hard to tell which.

Vince was up and out of the bed, standing on wobbly legs that hadn't made it farther than the bathroom and back in over a week.

Another crash and another. Jesus, this guy was beating her! Where the hell were his pants? "Charlotte!"

The light went on in the hallway, and Charlie pushed open his door, her mouth grim. "I'm calling the police." Wrapping her robe around her, she vanished toward the stairs.

Upstairs, it sounded as if Sally had locked herself in her bathroom. Her "friend" was now beating on the door instead of her, thank God, but Sally was sobbing, begging for some one, anyone, to help her.

To hell with his pants. To hell with the police, too — they weren't going to get here in time to help at all.

Vince took the stairs down to the front door faster than he should have and fell the last few steps. Charlie was beside him then, all soft flannel and sweet-smelling hair.

"Don't," she said. "Don't, Vince — I'll go!"

"Like hell you will!" He somehow pushed himself up and toward the door. "Call the police and stay here!"

The night air was cold and bracing. Sally's door was around the side of the house and up a rickety flight of outside stairs. It had a wooden railing on both sides, and he was able to pull himself up mostly using his arms, two steps at a time.

By the time he reached the top, Charlie was behind him again, pushing something into his hands.

A baseball bat.

James's, no doubt. Thank you, James, you old son of a bitch.

"Stay back," he told her again as he hobbled toward Sally's door.

But she didn't. She followed him.

The damned door was locked.

He could see through its window, through a gauzy curtain, into Sally's living room. It was a homey, tidy little room with a rocking chair knocked over from its place next to the radio, a braided rug, and a crocheted blanket thrown over the back of the sofa.

The man pounding on the bathroom door was a behemoth, but a behemoth with a swollen, bloody lip — good job, Sal!

"Go back downstairs," he said, trying one more time to convince Charlie. If he was going to have to fight with this giant, he wasn't going to be able to fight fair, and he didn't want her to watch.

She shook her head. "I'm not leaving you, Vincent."

It was a moment he would have liked to savor — with her genuine concern for him filling her eyes, her face scrubbed clean of all makeup, her usually tidy hair a golden cloud around her staunchly squared shoulders.

But damn, that bathroom door wasn't going to stand much more abuse.

Sally screamed again and Vince didn't hesitate. He swung hard and put that bat right through the window. The crash of breaking glass resonated through the night, and somewhere in the neighborhood a dog started to bark. Across the street, a light went on. Good. The sooner the police got here, the better.

He reached through the broken window, unlocked the door, and went inside, trying his best to sidestep the broken glass, which was pretty much impossible.

"Don't come in," Vince warned Charlie, but of course, she ignored him again. Thankfully, she had slippers on as the glass crunched underfoot.

"Who the hell are you?"

No doubt about it, Vince had definitely caught the attention of Sally's friend. The man was wearing a disheveled but otherwise gleaming new Air Corps uniform with a first lieutenant bar on his shoulder. He was an officer but clearly no gentleman, and obviously far more than three sheets

236

to the wind. He wiped his bleeding lip with the back of one hand as he sized them up, his gaze lingering on Charlie's thin bathrobe.

Vince stepped in front of her, planting himself and praying that his knees wouldn't give way. Not now, please, Lord. Her fingers tightened on his arm and he knew that she'd just realized how big this guy was.

"I'm a Marine who fought hand-to-hand on Tarawa," Vince told him evenly, told Charlie, too. No doubt she'd forgotten exactly how he'd received those wounds that had kept him confined to her bed for so many days. "I suggest you leave, Lieutenant. I believe you've worn out your welcome here."

"Oh, you do, do you?"

"Sally, are you all right?" Charlie raised her voice to be heard through the bathroom door. But all they could hear was the sound of the woman sobbing.

"That fucking whore stole my wallet," the behemoth said as if, even if it were true, that gave him the right to beat her.

"Watch your mouth around the lady," Vince countered sharply.

"Yeah, if she's friends with Sally, that ain't no lady you're with tonight, pal. Make sure you bang her hard and get your money's worth. That's all I'm trying to do here. Get my money's worth."

Vince didn't raise his voice. "Listen carefully to me. You are not worthy of breathing the same air as either of these two women — both of whom have lost husbands in the war, and neither of whom have ever stolen anything in their lives — a fact I would swear to on my sainted mother's grave.

"So I'm going to start to count. And if you're not on your way out the door and down those stairs by the time I get to three, I'm going to kill you."

"Oh, yeah?" the man scoffed.

"Yeah," Vince said. "Look into my eyes. I *will* kill you. I'll probably even enjoy it. God knows I've killed far better men than you.

"One."

The behemoth stared from Vince's face to the bat and back.

"Two."

Whatever darkness he saw in Vince's eyes apparently worked. The man moved, fast, but it wasn't an attack. He headed for the door, skidding slightly on the broken glass, and slamming it closed behind him.

Charlotte rushed for the bathroom door. "Sally, he's gone. Open up!"

Vince sank down into one of Sally's kitchen chairs, exhausted and aware that even though he hadn't been forced to fight, he'd revealed far more of himself to Charlie than he'd ever intended.

He stared at his feet, cut from the glass and bleeding. Funny how it didn't really hurt.

"Vince bluffed him into leaving," Charlie told Sally through the door, but as she glanced back at him, he could tell from her eyes that she knew the truth. It had not been any kind of bluff at all.

He *would* have killed that man. Without blinking.

Mary Lou was on her way in to work, dropping off Haley at Mrs. U.'s, when she saw it.

She was getting the stroller out of the trunk of

238

her car because Mrs. U. and her four-year-old, Katie, wanted to take a walk with Haley down to the doughnut shop.

Of course, another doughnut was the last thing both Mrs. U. and Katie needed, but Mary Lou kept her opinion about that to herself. Particularly when, after setting up the stroller on the sidewalk, she went to close her trunk and saw it.

It was wrapped in some kind of fabric — oil-cloth, she thought it was called — and pushed way into the back, behind the jumper cables she always carried and had used on more than one occasion.

She reached in and pulled it toward her and un-wrapped it.

And found herself staring at a deadly looking au-tomatic weapon with a spare banana clip.

"Someone wants to give her mommy another kiss," Mrs. U. said from right behind her, and Mary Lou quickly wrapped the big gun back up, shoving it behind the cables and slamming the trunk closed.

God damn Sam! What was he thinking, leaving a gun like that lying around where anyone could take it? Her trunk didn't lock. Anyone could just open it up and help themselves.

Inwardly fuming, she forced a smile and gave Haley another hug and kiss good-bye.

She headed to work, remembering Ihbraham's words from last night, when they'd talked on the phone.

"If you don't tell him that you are unhappy," he'd said, as they talked about Sam, "then how will he ever know?"

She'd told him she'd been working overtime the

239

past few months to be compliant and agreeable. She was trying hard not to stir things up, for fear of driving Sam away.

"But is this thing you fear," Ihbraham had asked, "this being alone again, is it really so much worse than the being alone that you already have?"

She'd thought about little else all night — especially when Sam finally did come home. He climbed into bed beside her and fell immediately asleep. And Mary Lou lay there, still as completely alone as she'd been ten minutes earlier.

This gun in the trunk had to be mentioned. There was no doubt about that.

The guard at the gate of the base waved her in. And Mary Lou parked in her usual spot alongside the Dumpster.

She marched into the McDonald's, tired as hell of being alone.

ELEVEN

Joan was slipping into a clean blouse when there was a knock on her hotel room door. She peered through the peephole and saw Muldoon standing in the hall.

"What are you doing back so early?" She left the door open so that he could come in as she buttoned the last of her buttons, heading for the car keys that she'd put on top of the TV cabinet.

They'd stayed so long at Donny's, Muldoon had gotten to the base a mere four minutes before an important meeting started — a meeting that he couldn't tell her anything about. Instead of taking the time to drop her here, they'd gone straight to the base and she'd dropped him instead. He'd insisted that she take his truck and drive herself to the hotel.

"May I come in for a minute?" he asked now, still planted securely out in the corridor.

"Of course," she said, tucking her blouse into her pants and grabbing the keys. "But I'm a little crunched for time right now, so I can really only spare a minute." She tossed him the keys to his truck as she swept into the bathroom and raised her voice so he could still hear her. "I'm meeting Commander Paoletti and his fiancée for lunch, and I seem to have misplaced my fairy godmother, so I'm going to have to rely on makeup and this curling iron — ouch! — to transform myself into something presentable."

Said curling iron was hot enough to require sticking her finger under cold running water after touching it — dumb move.

Joan leaned in toward the mirror for a closer look at the dark circles beneath her eyes. "God, I hate jet lag. I need some of that special makeup — you know, the kind that you buy after you get into a car accident and meet your airbag face-to-face . . . ?" What she really needed was a longer nap. She shut off the water and dried her hands.

"Actually," Muldoon called back to her, shutting the door behind him with a click, "you can relax, because your lunch date is about to be postponed."

The phone rang. There was an extension right there in the bathroom, but Joan stuck her head out the door to look at Muldoon. What, was he psychic or something?

He was standing politely by the door, but was looking around her room, at her laptop set up on the desk surrounded by an embarrassing number of empty coffee cups, at the silk dress on a hanger that she'd decided not to wear to this lunch because it was a little too youthful and flirty, at the still-unmade bed that she'd crawled back into for an hour after spending that exhausting morning with her crazy brother.

And with Muldoon. She'd spent the entire morning with Muldoon, too. It was entirely possible that the most exhausting part of the morning

242

had come after he'd stripped down to his T-shirt and muscled Donny into the shower, then into his pajamas and, once clean, into his sleeping bag on the closet floor.

Because then there they were. Standing guard against the hordes of roving aliens while Donny slept the sleep of the dead.

Alone in her mother's house, in her tomblike living room, where that stupid clock — the loudest clock in the entire damn world — ticked.

Joan had always hated that clock.

They'd sat there, surrounded by that infernal ticking, and Joan had babbled on and on about God knows what, talking about anything and everything to avoid discussing the subjects that really mattered. Like how completely freaked she got whenever she came into this house that she had no choice but to come to at least once a year because Donny never left. How awful it had been growing up under the shadow of Donny's illness. How badly she wanted Muldoon to tear her clothes off in a fit of passion that was violent enough to knock over that stupid clock, or at least noisy enough to drown out the ticking for a little while.

He now met her eyes as if he could read her mind, and she retreated back into the bathroom and picked up the ringing phone. "DaCosta."

"Hey, Joan, it's Tom Paoletti. I'm glad I caught you."

"No lunch today, huh?"

"Yeah, sorry about that. We'll have to reschedule. My timetable for a certain . . . project has just shifted, and . . ."

Joan shut off her curling iron. "It's not a problem, Commander."

"Good. I've made arrangements for you to have access to the base while we're gone through Lieutenant Steve McKinney, from the public affairs office."

"Gone?" she repeated. We, he'd said. She stretched the headset cord so that she could again lean out of the bathroom and look at Muldoon. "Are you going somewhere?" she asked.

Muldoon nodded while Tom answered. "Training op. We'll be off base for about forty-eight hours — we'll be back before you know it. Steve's a nice guy. He'll be able to answer any questions and even help you set up some of those photo ops you're looking for."

"Steve McKinney." Joan went back into the bathroom and wrote the name on a piece of toilet paper with eyeliner, digesting what Tom had just told her. Muldoon was going to be gone for forty-eight hours. And when he came back, Brooke would be in town.

Shit.

"I also wanted to leave you Kelly — my fiancée's — cell number," Tom told her. "She didn't want to call and bother you, but she asked me to let you know that she's having an impromptu dinner — really casual — at our place tonight. It's something some of the wives and girlfriends like to do when we go wheels up like this. She told me to tell you that you're welcome to join them — you know, get a glimpse of that aspect of military life, if you want."

"That's . . . very nice," Joan told him as she wrote

down the number he rattled off. It was more than nice, it was brilliant. She could picture Brooke surrounded by a group of wholesome-looking young women, bonding over coffee. Myra was going to love that. "I'll definitely give her a call."

"Great. Again, I'm sorry about lunch."

"You're forgiven."

His laughter was a warm rumble in her ear. "I'm glad. Look, Joan, as long as I have you on the phone . . . I know Lieutenant Muldoon spoke to you about this, and I understand you don't have the authority to make these kinds of decisions, but I really think this is the wrong time for President Bryant to come out here to the base. I mean, a low-profile tour would be one thing, but for the kind of dog and pony show that the White House is looking to put together . . . ?"

"I'll do my best to see that your reservations are brought to the attention of as many decision makers as possible, Commander," she told him. "At least then you'll be on record. And if something does go wrong —"

"I can say I told you so?" he interrupted. "That's not what I'm looking for. That's not good enough."

"I'm sorry, sir," she said. "But I just don't have the kind of influence to help you out."

"Do the best you can," he told her. "And if you see Muldoon, tell him to get his butt back to the base, ASAP."

"Good luck — wherever you're going," Joan said.

"Thanks. Catch you later."

Joan hung up the phone and went out of the bathroom.

Muldoon was still standing by the door.

"Is this really just a training op?" she asked him.

He looked her in the eye. "Yes, it is."

"Which is what you would tell me even if it wasn't, right?"

Muldoon nodded. "Yeah. But this one really is training."

"Which is also what you'd say," she pointed out.

"Yeah."

"Where are you —"

"I can't tell you. You know that."

"Yes," she said. "Of course. I'm sorry. I'm just . . ."

He was looking at her a little too intently, so she forced a smile despite her sudden realization that any given moment this man — and Cosmo and Gillman and Jenk and Sam Starrett and all of the other fabulous, wonderful men of Team Sixteen that she'd met over the past few days — might be thrust into any one of the numerous hot spots around the world where the U.S.'s Special Operations forces were going head-to-head with terrorists.

Forty-eight hours from any given moment, Joan could well be attending Mike Muldoon's funeral. She suddenly wanted to sit down, but she forced herself to stay standing, to keep smiling at him.

"You have my cell phone number, right?" he asked. "In case you need me? I mean, I'm sure Steve McKinney will be able to handle any problems, but . . ."

"I'll be fine," Joan told him. "Just . . . be careful, okay?"

He took a step toward her, and she turned away,

suddenly afraid of what he had seen in her eyes.

God, what *had* he seen in her eyes?

Lust? Probably, God help her. He certainly was attractive, with his quiet, clean strength and the intelligence that lurked in those pretty blue eyes.

Longing? For sure — and that was even worse than lust. She could feel it still, bubbling within her, a rolling boil of feelings and emotions she was afraid to examine too closely for fear of what she might find.

It gave her a sense of immediacy, a sharp awareness that tomorrow was not always guaranteed.

It made her want to throw herself into Muldoon's arms and cling to him and beg him to come back in one piece.

It made her want him.

Yeah, right. Like she hadn't wanted this guy — Lieutenant Young and Perfect — before this. Nice try at fooling yourself, Joan. Still, here it was. Up at the surface. Impossible to ignore. Everything she'd spent the past few days running from.

This — what she was feeling right now — was why all those women married men they'd known for only a few days during World War Two.

Of course, this man wasn't exactly asking her to marry him, now, was he?

Joan briefly closed her eyes and lived their entire potential love affair in the space of three heart-beats. She could — right now — turn back to him and meet his eyes and let him see what she was thinking, what she was feeling — all of her concern and lust and longing and fear that this might be the last time she saw him alive. She didn't doubt at all that within ten seconds she would be in his arms, kissing him.

And oh, God, just thinking about kissing him, about losing herself in him, his mouth on hers, his tongue, his . . . It almost made her turn around, but in her mind that kiss became lovemaking and that lovemaking became an ill-thought-out, awkward, ill-timed, mismatched relationship based on physical attraction and temporary insanity, with all of its missed expectations and pressures and failures and bitter disappointments.

Joan stood there with her back to Mike Muldoon and knew if she turned to face him that their friendship would turn from a thing of joy and laughter to a hardened, blackened little lump of resentment and pain. Sure, it would take slightly longer than three heartbeats to do so, but it would happen just the same.

She liked this guy.

That wasn't the big news flash here. The news flash had to do with just how *much* she liked this guy.

Enough so that her feelings for him trumped all of the confused emotions that came with that lust and longing. She had to smile at the irony of that. The truth was that she liked Muldoon way too much to sleep with him. If she didn't like him so damn much, she'd *do him*, as he'd so eloquently put it yesterday at lunch. What would he say if she told him that?

But instead of revealing intimate secrets that were best kept to herself, Joan opened her eyes and found herself gazing at her laptop.

"Will you be back in time for the admiral's

party?" she asked, able to turn and face him now that her anxiety could be blamed on a far more reasonable fear — that Brooke Bryant would be without an escort for a very important social event.

It was actually laughable how little she cared about that right now, but he didn't know that.

"It'll be tight, but yeah. I'll make it," Muldoon told her. Now if she could only make him stop looking at her like that — as if he wanted to throw her down on her bed and . . .

"Good, because I emailed Brooke and, you know, told her all about you. She's really looking forward to meeting you. Very enthusiastic." Joan didn't bat an eye as she spun Brooke's emailed response of "Whatever" into something that sounded more enticing. "I told her to bring her whip. She emailed back and asked which one."

Surprise took over everything else that was written on his too-expressive face. But then he laughed. "Very funny, Joan."

She forced herself not to smile. "Hey, I'm serious."

"Right."

"I am."

"Okay, fine," Muldoon pretended to surrender but then counterattacked. "Give me her email address so I can write to her myself. I want to help her pick one out from her vast S and M collection."

Joan was so busted, and they both knew it. But she refused to quit the game, giving him a holier-than-thou look instead. "I'm afraid I can't give out Brooke Bryant's email address to just anyone."

"Give me yours, then," he countered. "I'll email you and you can forward it to Brooke. If she wants to write back to me, then she can. If not . . ." He shrugged.

"You'll have access to email where you're going?" She fished through her handbag, searching for one of her business cards.

"Yeah," he told her. "At least part of the time."

She handed him her card with her email address on it. "It *is* just training you'll be doing, isn't it?" She tried to see inside of his head.

Muldoon just smiled as he glanced at her card, then tucked it into his pocket. "I'll call you later to make sure Steve's getting it done for you." He opened the door to let himself out, then turned back to add, "I'm still your official liaison. You have any trouble, call me, Joan. I'll get back to you as soon as I can."

"Be careful," she said again.

"Being careful isn't quite part of the job description, but we work hard to make sure all the men in the team are as safe as possible."

"Good," Joan said. "That's good. That's . . . good to hear."

He stood there, then, just looking at her, halfway out the door.

"Thanks again for this morning," she told him. It wasn't too late to rush toward him and kiss him.

Muldoon nodded, lingering just a moment longer as if he knew she was weakening in her resolve.

But she wasn't. She was strong. She gazed back at him and let herself like him. A lot. Too much to move and blow it.

A year from now she still wanted him to be her friend and not a former lover that she was too embarrassed to call and talk to.

"I'll see you on Saturday," he finally said, and shut the door behind him.

Mary Lou was waiting for him, right there in the corridor of the Team Sixteen building.

Jesus, Sam couldn't believe it. She was right outside of Lieutenant Jacquette's office.

Several weeks ago, the XO had spoken to Sam about Mary Lou's relentless on-base visits. "Tell your wife that the proper time for her to talk to you is when you're home. Tell her that other officers — higher ranking officers on base — are starting to comment on the fact that she's always here, checking up on you, distracting you and everyone else, making it impossible for you to do your job. Tell her how bad it makes you look when she comes here like that."

Sam had told her. But here she was. Back again. God damn it. And Jazz Jacquette was walking down the hall. He gave Sam a long, pointed look before going into his office.

"You're not supposed to be here." Sam was all but drowning in frustration. "I thought we got this settled weeks ago, Mary Lou. What do I have to do to get through to you?"

"I got your message. About you going out of town? But I needed to talk to you before you left." She must've just gotten off from work. She was still wearing her uniform and her hair was limp around a face slightly greasy from hours at the french fry machine. Her makeup had long since worn off from the heat and she looked even younger than twenty-two years old.

As if twenty-two wasn't ridiculously young enough.

Sam felt a twinge of guilt. This was his fault. He'd known she was young that first night he picked her up at the Ladybug Lounge. Young, with a lousy education, and a lousier childhood.

She'd never told him about it specifically, but he'd gathered early on that she and her mother had had some kind of falling out quite a few years ago. There had been some kind of betrayal — exactly what, he wasn't sure. The time he'd brought it up, shortly after their wedding, she'd changed the subject and started talking about the curtains she was planning to hang in the kitchen.

Curtains. Jesus.

He couldn't count how many times he'd tried to talk to her about real things, serious things that mattered to him, but she quickly brought the conversation back to such important topics of discussion as when was it time to cut the baby's toenails or the difference between using green or yellow split peas in pea soup.

Of course, it wasn't her scintillating conversation that had drawn him to her in the first place. It was the way she'd looked out on that dance floor in those cutoff jeans and an overburdened tank top.

She was the anti-Alyssa, telling him in her southern sugar pie voice how she was a regular winner in all of the local wet T-shirt contests as if that were something to be proud of, and, yes, he'd pursued her precisely because of that.

Although Mary Lou had been as eager to take

him home that night as he'd been to go there. That part wasn't his fault. It was the other nights, after he'd realized that she'd cast him in the role of Prince Charming, after he knew she didn't see their casual sex as either casual or mere sex, that he was to blame.

To give himself a little credit, he'd ended their affair when he realized she was actually hoping he'd marry her. He wasn't a total shit. Just a partial shit, with a run of some very bad luck.

A partial shit who'd found out the hard way that getting fucked turned into a negative, soul-sucking experience if there wasn't love or at least genuine caring involved. A loser who had learned that hero worship wasn't love. That it wasn't even close.

There was an op last year in Afghanistan that went really wrong. Sam had led a squad — Muldoon, Gillman, Izzy, Jenk, and Cosmo — that got hit by an al-Qaeda ambush. The ambushers were amateurs and didn't wait until the SEALs were close enough to wreak real havoc. Cosmo took a hit, but the bullet was spent and didn't do much damage.

When the SEALs returned fire, the tangos turned tail and ran, but Sam gave the order to engage the enemy — to go after them and either bring them in for questioning or eliminate them.

The terrorists didn't go for plan A, opting instead to fight to the death.

Which the SEALs did, quickly and efficiently, only to find that two of their ten attackers couldn't have been more than eight years old. As for the others, the oldest was maybe eighteen.

Amateurs, indeed. They were children. And now they were dead children.

The CO had made them all go in for a couple of extra sessions with the shrink after that one.

It had been Mike Muldoon's personal nightmare — engaging the children who fought as terrorists, and God knows there were a lot of them in al-Qaeda, may their parents burn in hell — and Sam spent hours with the younger man, just letting him talk it out, just listening.

But eventually Sam had gone home to a hot dinner that Mary Lou cooked for him.

He couldn't choke it down. He'd needed to talk about it, too.

And there was Mary Lou. His wife. Sitting across the kitchen table.

He'd reached for her hand.

"Who would teach their children to hate and to kill like that?" he'd asked after haltingly telling her as much as he was allowed to about the op, about how sick he'd felt looking into the faces of those dead little boys.

And Mary Lou had started to cry.

Her tears, however, were not in sympathy. No, in fact, she was upset with him, and she pulled her hand away. This was in the days when they still fought regularly. It was before she started trying to please him at all costs.

"Don't talk like that," she'd told him. "You're a SEAL. You shouldn't be talking like that, like they didn't deserve what they got. I'm the one who suffered. I was scared — terrified — when that helicopter went down in Pakistan. I'm the one who sat in front of the TV for eighteen hours, waiting for a

254

scrap of news that would tell me if I was going to have to raise our baby girl without a daddy. You wanted to go there. You wanted to fight. I hear you say that all the time. You want to feel bad for someone? Feel bad for Haley, who spent the past four weeks without her father!"

Needless to say, their conversation hadn't gone any further.

That was the day he had understood that she didn't love him any more than he loved her. She loved the *idea* of him, sure. She maybe even loved the image she'd built of him in her head — some superman who never doubted himself, never faltered, and never failed.

But that sure as shit wasn't him.

Truth was, Mary Lou didn't give a damn about him. She had no real desire to get to know him — especially if the real him deviated from the picture-perfect super-him she held in her head.

From that day on, Sam had given up trying to make his marriage work. He stopped attempting to be interested in the differences between green and yellow split peas or how many pies to bake for the church bazaar, and started merely to endure.

"Come on, I'll walk you back to your car," he told Mary Lou now, aware that Jazz's door was wide open.

"I wouldn't've come here if it wasn't important," she told him as they headed for the stairs. "I've been trying to be patient about a lot of things, Sam, but this is something I cannot abide."

Sam fought to suppress a surge of frustration and anger. Getting angry at Mary Lou only made things worse. She'd start to cry and it would be twenty minutes instead of five before he was back upstairs. "This is about Alyssa, right? Well, stop right there, because she doesn't have anything to do with the reason we're going wheels up —"

"No," she said. "It's not —"

He plowed right over her as he held open the door that led outside to the parking lot. "The FBI isn't part of this operation, so you can sleep a little easier — never mind the fact that I've told you, I've given you my fucking *word,* at least two million times that I haven't so much as touched her since we were married. So just go home, Mary Lou. Go the hell home and get over it."

Her cheeks flushed. "This isn't about her. I'm not going to fight with you about her anymore. I'm not."

"Then what *did* you come here to fight with me about?" Sam spotted her car over by Muldoon's truck near the building's entrance.

"I didn't come here to fight with you at all. I came to tell you that the lock on my trunk is broken. Anyone can get in there any time they want."

Sam clenched his teeth against a stream of foul language. He was going to have to endure one of Lieutenant Jacquette's lectures because the fucking lock on the fucking trunk of her fucking car was fucking broken. A lock that had been broken long before Mary Lou's sister Janine had given her the car.

The muscle in his jaw was surely jumping, but Mary Lou didn't appear to notice. She was busy opening her trunk.

"I came here to tell you that I don't want you

leaving things in my car," Mary Lou told him, chin held high for a change. As much as she was pissing him off right now, it was refreshing to see her show some backbone after spending the past few months with the Stepford Wife clone. "And especially not *this*." She gestured to the trunk behind her.

Sam knew he was supposed to look inside, so he did. "I thought you *wanted* jumper cables in there, in case you needed them again."

"Look beneath them," she ordered tightly.

Sam looked. He even picked up the cables and shook them. "Trunk's empty, hon," he told her.

"What?" She turned with a gasp, and then started searching the wheel well. "No, it was just here . . ."

"I don't know what you thought you saw in here," Sam told her as she even looked beneath the spare, letting it fall back into place because — surprise, surprise — nothing whatsoever of his was in there. "But if I'm going to have any hope at all of getting promoted, from now on in you're going to have to wait to have your hallucinations *after* I come home at night."

And *that* was cruel.

Mary Lou's eyes filled with tears, but her chin stayed high as she dug through her purse for her keys. Without another word to Sam, she took the jumper cables from him, tossed them back in, and slammed the trunk closed, leaning on it to make it latch. She marched around and climbed into the car, slamming that door behind her, too, and starting her piece-of-shit-on-wheels with a roar.

Ah, fuck.

Sam knocked on the window, and she rolled it down a meager half inch so she could hear him.

"Look, why don't you take my truck home." He held out his keys. "I know a guy — Al Speroni, remember him? He owns that body shop next to the video store. I'll give him a call, ask him to come pick up your car and either fix the lock or replace the entire trunk lid — he owes me a big enough favor. You can drive my truck until I get home. How's that sound?"

Apparently it sounded good enough to Mary Lou, who turned off her car and rolled the window down a little farther so that she could take his keys.

"Leave your keys under the mat," he told her. "Just the car key, not the house key, okay?"

She nodded.

"I've got to run," he said. "Give Haley a kiss for me."

She turned to look up at him. "I wasn't hallucinating, Sam."

He was already backing away. No way was he going to talk about this anymore right now. He was already screwed as it was. "I have to go. You take care, all right? One day at a time. I'll see you in a few days."

Sam ran for the building, free for the next forty-eight hours.

The feeling was a good one, despite the reaming he'd yet to receive from Lieutenant Jacquette.

Jesus, maybe he should put in for a transfer to another team — something that would put him in some hot spot on the other side of the world, where Mary Lou couldn't come with him.

Shit, she'd probably be happier with that arrangement, too. She'd get her superhero without having to clean up his all-too-human mess day after day.

He'd miss Haley, though. And the guys in Team Sixteen.

And Alyssa Locke, a little voice — persistent fucker — inside of him chimed in.

He was as pathetic as Mary Lou — still in love with his fantasy of Alyssa, despite finding out that she was someone else entirely.

Sam went inside and took the stairs two at a time, and went directly to Lieutenant Jacquette's office, knocking on the open door. "Sir. Got a sec?"

Jazz Jacquette looked up from his desk. His default grim expression got even darker when he saw that it was Sam.

"Sir, she doesn't get how the military operates," Sam told him. "I assure you that I've tried and tried to explain that —"

"I'm sure you have." The XO sat back in his chair, shaking his head slightly as he looked up at Sam. "It's a shame she won't listen, because it is hurting you, Lieutenant."

Sam nodded. "I know that, sir. I'm thinking about asking for a transfer. I think it might be a good idea if I went overseas."

The expression in Jacquette's eyes was impossible to read. "That would be a serious loss to this team."

"Thank you, sir, but I don't know what else to do."

"I've heard the rumors, but . . ." Jazz cleared his throat. "You married her because she was pregnant, is that correct?"

Sam laughed, but there was no humor in it. "Gee, I thought that went from rumor to verified fact a *long* time ago. Yes, sir, it is correct."

Jazz nodded solemnly. "Sam, I'm speaking to you not as your XO right now, but as your friend. You married the girl because she was pregnant, but she's not pregnant now, is she?"

Sam understood the implication. As unsavory as it was, the possibility of divorce had popped into his thoughts way more than a time or two. But, "Am I supposed to just ignore Haley? She exists. I'm her father. If I divorce Mary Lou, I'll be divorcing her, too. There're no two ways around it."

Jazz bounced the eraser end of a pencil on the file on his desk. "You know, from the way I hear it, you already are pretty much ignoring Haley. Of course, that could just be a rumor, too."

Sam clenched his teeth over a completely inappropriate reply to an executive officer.

Another deep sigh from Jazz. "Sam, these past six months now, your head has been somewhere else. I don't know where you've gone or, really, what's going on with you, but I do know this. I don't want you transferring out of this team. I want you back. I want my best officer back to giving a hundred and ten percent, not this half-assed fifty or sixty that you've been delivering lately."

His best officer. Holy fuck. Lieutenant Jacquette didn't use words like *best*. Ever. Sam didn't know whether to shit or go blind. So he just stood there.

"Tell her to stay away, Lieutenant," Jacquette said. "Next time I see your wife in this building, I will call the shore patrol and they will physically remove her *and* charge her with trespassing. You

260

might want to warn her about that, because it will *not* be fun for her."

Jesus. "I'll tell her that, sir."

"Good." Jazz was already once more buried in his files. "By the way, if you tell anyone that I called you my best officer, I will deny it completely."

Sam had to smile. "If I told anyone, sir, trust me, they wouldn't believe me."

"Depends on whether or not they knew you, Lieutenant," Jazz said. "If they've served with you, they'd believe it." He looked up. "Don't you have things to do?"

"Yeah," Sam said. "I'm just temporarily over-come by a case of the warm fuzzies. I thought I'd bask in the warmth of your love a little bit longer, sir."

Jazz didn't smile. In fact, his legendary glare was pretty damn daunting. "Let me put it into language that I know you can understand. Get the fuck out of here, Starrett."

"Aye, aye, sir." Sam got. But as he walked away, he could have sworn he heard Jazz Jacquette laugh.

TWELVE

Charlie sat in the lounge chair on Donny's screened-in porch.

She and Vince had bought this furniture for their grandson several years back, and at the time, she'd protested. When would he ever use it? The porch was off-limits to him because, although there was a ceiling and roof overhead, apparently aliens were capable of squeezing their way through the tiny holes in the screens.

But Vince had just smiled the same way he'd always just smiled all those decades they'd been married. "The chairs are for us, Charles," he'd said.

And, indeed, she'd spent quite a bit of time sitting out here since then.

Inside the house, Donny was still sleeping, and Vince was still standing guard, as he'd promised.

Of course, aliens could attack and Vince would never hear them coming. Unless they brought a marching band with a big bass drum with their assault team.

She should talk. Her own ears weren't what they used to be, either.

Sixty years ago, she could hear every word spoken — no, whispered — from well down the hall.

"I, well, I just wanted to come over here to thank you

*for what you did last night — you know, coming to my
rescue like that.”*

Charlotte had been lying down in that spare
bedroom, in that apartment she'd once shared
with James, exhausted from the explosive events of
the night before, when the sound of quiet voices
awakened her.

It was no wonder she was so tired — she'd sat
with Sally until the police arrived, and then she'd
brought Vince back to bed and cleaned and ban-
daged his feet, cut from the window glass he'd
shattered to get inside Sally's apartment.

Then, before she went back to her own bed,
she'd insisted he show her his wounds. She wanted
to see with her own eyes that his trips up and down
the stairs hadn't torn out his stitches.

It had taken her bursting into tears to get him to
comply — an outburst that had been as completely
unexpected to her as it was to him. She was not
prone to such emotional demonstrations. In fact,
she hadn't even cried — not noisily like this —
when that telegram about James arrived.

Idiotically, she cried again from relief when she
saw that Vince had, indeed, not injured himself
any further.

He'd reached for her then. Somehow he knew to
say nothing, just to hold her and stroke her hair.

And when she was done crying, Charlotte lay
there, on her bed, wrapped in the arms of a man
that James wouldn't've given a second glance. An
enlisted Marine, without a college education. A
lobsterman from Cape Cod, with the kind of name
— DaCosta — that wouldn't go far in the political
arena to which James had always aspired.

263

Charlotte lay for hours in Vince's arms, staring out the window at the night, listening to him breathe.

Exhausted himself, he'd finally fallen asleep, and when he did, he pulled her closer to him. As much of a gentleman as he was in the daytime, in sleep his body betrayed him, reacting unmistakably to her nearness.

Dear Lord Almighty, give her strength. It was all she could do to keep herself from reaching for him, the way she'd reached for James when she'd awakened in the night to find him wanting her.

Although maybe she should just fall asleep, too, and let their two desperate bodies do their will, because, oh, James, forgive her, she wanted to lie with this man. If she hadn't before tonight, well, seeing him charge up those stairs to come to Sally's aid with such little regard for his own health and safety had clinched it.

Hearing Vince's words of warning, his quiet, almost matter-of-fact threat that revealed that the worst of his wounds from Tarawa were not wounds to the flesh but rather wounds to the soul, cemented her longing.

She wanted to share the same sweet intimacies with him that she'd shared with her husband. She wanted the laughter that came with it, and the hope and promise and the joy of giving and taking. The connection of hearts, the touching of souls.

She wanted something she couldn't have, because how, how, *how* could she ever laugh like that again while knowing that James was lying cold in his grave a half a world away?

Charlotte started to cry, deep welling sobs of a grief that she'd held in for much too long, and Vince woke up, holding her even closer, trying to comfort her. "I'm sorry," he whispered. "Charlie, I'm so sorry."

"Help me," she sobbed. "Please . . ."

"I will," he said. "I want to. Just . . . tell me how. Tell me what to do. What can I get you? How can I help?"

But there was nothing he could do. Nothing anyone could do. "I don't want to live without him," she wept. "I'm so tired of living without him."

"Oh, Charlotte, don't say that." He tried to hold her more tightly, but she suddenly couldn't stand to feel his arms around her and she struggled to get away from him, pulling so hard that she tumbled off the bed and onto the floor. She hit with a jarring thud, but it didn't matter. Nothing mattered anymore.

"Charlotte." Vince followed her to the floor, but she swatted at his hands.

"Don't touch me! Just go away!"

He went, but the light went on in the hall, and he came back a few moments later with Edna Fletcher.

"Oh, dear. I knew sooner or later it would all have to come out. She was so stoic when we got the news." Her mother-in-law's hands were warm against her back. "Just cry, sweetie, just go ahead and cry," she crooned. "That's a good girl."

Somehow, sometime last night, Charlotte had made it back into the narrow little bed in the spare room. She woke up in the morning feeling horribly hungover from her tears, but she forced herself to dress and go in to work. Her job for the senator was an important one.

But by lunchtime it was clear that she was doing no one any good, so she returned home, crawled into her bed, and slept deeply and dreamlessly.

Until a voice woke her. A female voice. Sally's, from upstairs.

"I also wanted to let you know that Morton's wallet was found," she was telling Vince. She was here with him. In his bedroom. *Charlotte's* bedroom. "That was his name. Lt. Morton Peterson from St. Louis, Missouri. The police called to tell me they found it outside of the Golden Goose bar. That's where we met — he must've dropped it before we left. You can call the police, if you want, to verify that I didn't —"

"I know you didn't steal anything," Vince interrupted. He sounded both so matter-of-fact and so quietly certain. Charlotte could picture his gentle, reassuring smile. "I don't need to call anyone."

"Well," Sally said. She cleared her throat. "That's . . . refreshing."

"You need to be more careful in choosing the company you keep," he said, again without a trace of judgment or disapproval in his voice, as if he harbored not even one negative thought about the woman. How did he do that?

Last night, even as Charlotte was helping Sally put ice on a very painful-looking and swollen eye, she had found herself thinking, You reap what you sow.

"I . . . I know," Sally said now. "I will. I just . . ." She laughed. Or maybe she was starting to cry.

Charlotte couldn't quite tell. "And so I tell myself the very same thing every day. But then I get out of work, and the evening stretches out ahead of me, like the entire rest of my pathetic, lonely, miserable life and . . ." She was definitely crying now. "I can't help it."

"Hey," Vince said. "Shhh. It's okay."

He was comforting Sally, no doubt holding her the way he'd held Charlotte just last night.

"I'm sorry," she said. Apparently it was the refrain of war widows all across the country.

"It's all right," Vince said. He should go into business, charge a fee for the comfort of his arms. "Where'd he die?" he asked her gently. "Your husband."

"He was in the Merchant Marine," Sally told him between snuffles. "His ship went down in the Atlantic, torpedoed by a U-boat." She made a sound that might've passed for laughter if Charlotte didn't know just what she was feeling. "No one ever asks about him, you know. Sometimes it feels like I imagined him. Like he was never really real."

"What was his name?" Vince asked.

"Frankie," she told him. "Not Frank, Frankie — isn't that a hoot? He had all these tattoos — such a big, burly man — and he insisted on being called Frankie because that's what his mother called him right up to the day she died. Oh, he loved his mother, my Frankie did."

"I'd bet a year's pay that he really loved you, too," Vince said.

She laughed. This time it was definitely a laugh. "Sugar darling, you'd win that bet. He was the sweetest man." She was silent for a moment. "An

267

awful lot like you, you know — although you are a young one, aren't you?"

"No one's young anymore," Vince said quietly.

"It's a crying shame. The only boys who stay young are the ones who come home in a box. And they never grow another day older, do they?" She was silent for a moment, then she laughed. It was forced, ringing with the same kind of false merriment Charlotte recognized from all those nights she'd entertained upstairs. "Well, *there's* a reason, if I ever heard one, to live for today. What do you think about that, sugar darling?"

Vince laughed, too. It wasn't forced, but it was definitely odd. Embarrassed, maybe. "Well, I —"

There was silence then. But not quite total silence.

Charlotte sat up in her bed. Was he . . . ? Were they . . . ? Dear God, was she going to have to sit here and listen to Sally and *Vince . . . ?*

But then Vince spoke. "Wait," he said breathlessly. "Whoa. *Whoa.* Hold on."

"Shhh," Sally said. "Just relax, hon. I'll make you feel good."

He laughed again. "You know, actually, I'm feeling just fine already today as it is, so —"

"Yeah, I can see how fine you're feeling, big boy. How long's it been since you . . . ?"

Vince laughed again, even more uncomfortably this time. "Look, Sally, I appreciate the thought, I really do, but —"

"Oh, my goodness gracious," she said. "You've never . . . ." Her laughter was incredulous now. "You haven't, have you?"

"Well, no, not exactly, but that doesn't mean —"

"Hush up, sugar, and let me thank you properly for what you did last night. It's about goddamn time *some*one taught you a thing or two."

After all those nights of intimate noises coming through the thin ceiling and walls, someone — namely Sally — already had taught him quite a bit.

Charlotte sat there, more upset than she had the right to be, telling herself that this wasn't jealousy she was feeling. She was upset merely because Vince had never been with a woman. He'd faced the horrors of war without having known how beautiful love could be.

And that wasn't fair. Nothing about this world, this war, was fair.

"Wait," he said now. "Stop. I'm serious, Sally. *Stop.*"

"What are you so worried about?" she said. "You told me there's no one else home right now, that the old lady and the frigid nun are both off at work."

Nun? Sally thought of her as *the frigid nun?*

"Who's going to care if we make a little noise?" Sally persisted. "Who's even going to know?"

"I will," Vince said quietly. "I'll know — and I care. And you'll know. And you care, too. I know you do, as much as you pretend otherwise. And just so you know, Charlotte's not a *frigid nun.*"

"Ahh," Sally said, drawing the word out. "I see. Charlotte, huh? She lets you call her by her first name? How daring of her."

"That's not funny," Vince said.

"Yes, it is." There was a pause. Charlotte could picture her gathering up her jacket and purse.

"Well, I'll just let myself out. No point in staying where I'm not wanted."

It was a good idea, one of which Sister Charlotte definitely approved.

"Please don't be offended," Vince said. "It's not that I don't find you attractive. You're a very beautiful woman, a very generous woman — maybe a little too generous at times, but —"

"But you're saving yourself for Charlotte. Which is very sweet, but, honey pie, I feel obliged to tell you that last night — you know when she was sitting with me in the powder room? — I'm sorry, but she made it very clear to me that there was nothing — absolutely nothing — going on between you and her."

"Her husband's name was James," Vince said. "He died at Pearl. She loved him very much."

There was silence for a moment. Real silence, and Charlotte used it to try to make sense of the conversation she'd just heard. Vince didn't want to be number four hundred thousand and three in a steady stream of soldiers and sailors who appreciated Sally's charms because of . . . *Charlotte?*

Then Sally said, "You think if you wait around long enough, she'll get over him." She laughed, but this time it was flat, totally devoid of humor. "Well, guess what, sugar darling? She won't. And that's going to make you the oldest virgin in the Marine Corps, because she's not the type to mess around — not without getting married first. Those knees are glued together, and they won't pop open until she says *I do.* Which'll never happen, mark my word. You don't really think she'll marry you while in her heart she's still married to her James, do you?"

Vince was quiet. "I can hope, can't I?" he finally said.

"You can indeed," Sally agreed. "But, honey, if you change your mind before it's time for you to go back to the fighting and this time maybe get yourself killed, well, you know where to find me."

Charlotte heard the sound of Sally's heels as she clicked her way down the hall, down the stairs. The front door opened and closed; the screen door banged.

And then the house was silent. So silent she could hear the infernal ticking of that blasted clock of Edna's from down in the parlor.

From the other room, she heard Vince shifting in his bed. There was a thud, and Charlotte realized that he was coming down the hall, heading for the bathroom — and to get there he'd have to walk right past her open door.

She didn't have time to lie down and pretend to be asleep. She didn't have time to do anything but sit there like an idiot and stare back at him as he caught sight of her and froze.

"Oh, Christ," he said, his voice cracking slightly with mortification. "I didn't know you were home."

"I am," she said inanely.

He closed his eyes briefly, and when he opened them, he forced himself to look at her. "I suppose it's too much to hope that you didn't hear all of that . . . ?"

Charlotte shook her head, feeling her face heat with a blush. She couldn't hold his gaze.

"Yeah," Vince sighed, but then forced a smile. He was blushing, too. "I didn't think so."

271

She made herself look back at him. "I can't marry you, Vincent."

"I know," he said. "I do know that. I just . . . Well . . . A guy's allowed to dream, right? Excuse me," he added with a nod, and headed for the bathroom.

Mary Lou had been driving her husband's truck as she left the base, and, wary after she'd found his parcel in the trunk of her car that morning, Husaam Abdul-Fataah spent the afternoon ready to run.

But nothing happened.

He had people keeping their eye on both the Navy base and the San Diego FBI headquarters, and there was no indication whatsoever that they'd moved to a state of higher alert.

Mary Lou wasn't pulled in for questioning — always a good sign that the authorities hadn't been tipped off to anything unusual.

It was possible that she'd thought the weapon belonged to her husband. It was possible she hadn't mentioned it to anyone — or if she had, they hadn't listened.

He had a feeling Sam Starrett didn't spend much time listening to his wife.

As Husaam had followed her, she'd picked up her kid and gone directly home, bypassing her usual grocery store run. But that and the truck were the only signs that things weren't absolutely run-of-the-mill normal.

One of his pairs of eyes running free on the Navy base reported that the SEALs of Team Sixteen gathered in combat gear with their duffel bags packed. They boarded a transport plane, taking off for parts unknown.

Shortly after that two men arrived in a truck marked "Al's Body Shop," and one of them drove Mary Lou's rattletrap of a car out of the parking lot next to the Team Sixteen building.

He'd relaxed even more at that news.

Starrett was going to be out of town for a few days, so Mary Lou was using his truck while her car went in for repairs.

It was nothing to worry about.

In fact, aside from the obvious problems it caused, it was a good thing — Starrett being out of town like that. He'd use the opportunity to get closer to Mary Lou. It was laughably perfect.

At one point, he'd been tempted to stay away from her completely — especially after discovering the broken lock on the trunk of her car. It seemed a gift from heaven.

But he knew it wasn't. It was a fluke. And he'd gone ahead with his strategy to befriend the woman. Because, after all, it was Mary Lou who went into the base unquestioned several days a week. There was no guarantee she'd always be driving that same shitbox of a car.

And indeed, as he'd watched her driving her husband's truck, Husaam was very glad that he'd stuck to his first plan.

Now, later in the afternoon, after nap time was over, he watched as she loaded the kid back into the truck. He followed her into town, to the grocery store.

Unhampered by a small child, he made it inside before she did, grabbing one of the plastic baskets by the door and heading to the frozen-food section of the store. Nothing like a pathetic single man with microwave dinners in his future to evoke a little extra sympathy.

He grabbed four or five and was just about to round the corner — *Wow, what a coincidence, Mary Lou, running into you here!* — when he heard her say, "Hey, how're you doing?"

"Oh, hi, Mary Lou. I'm fine, thanks. Hi, Haley. Wow, she's gotten big."

It was Kelly Ashton, Tom Paoletti's not-quite-wife. A month or so back, when he'd thought she'd be his best candidate for this operation, he'd gotten to know her. And he still kept tabs on her.

He was going to have to get out of here. If he bumped into them now, while the two women were together, Kelly might think it odd that he was on such friendly terms with Mary Lou.

"She's just started walking," Mary Lou said. "Getting into everything, you know?"

"Oh, yeah," Kelly said. Even though she didn't have any children of her own, she was a pediatrician. "Time to childproof the house. Lock up that cabinet under the kitchen sink in particular."

"I already did," Mary Lou said.

"That's good. Well, it was nice seeing you." Kelly's words were a polite dismissal, and he knew he had to get out of there before they went in two separate directions.

But Mary Lou kept the conversation going. "I never know what to buy for food when Sam deploys," she said. "I never know when he's going to be back, so I don't want to buy my regular amount of food in case he's gone for a while. But if I buy only a little, that almost guarantees that he'll be back tomorrow."

He took a quick look around the corner to see where they were standing, to try to figure out which was his best way out of the store — front door or back. Both women had shopping carts. Haley was strapped into the seat of Mary Lou's. Kelly's was filled with food.

"I always just buy a little," Kelly admitted. "For exactly that reason. I'm sorry, I'm running a little late. I better get onto the checkout line. I hate to have to run, but —"

"Are you having a party?" Mary Lou asked. "Or do you just like chips and salsa a whole lot?"

"Oh," Kelly said. "No, not a party. Nothing official, that is. I'm just having a few friends over tonight to watch a video. It helps to do that when, you know, Tom's out of town."

"Oh," Mary Lou said. "Yeah. I know what you mean. It's kind of hard not knowing exactly where they are or what they're doing, or . . . what have you."

"Yeah," Kelly said. "It is."

Mary Lou's voice sounded a little tight. "Well. Have a nice time. Like you said, you're running late."

"You know, you could come, too," Kelly offered. "I mean, if you're free tonight. If you can find a sitter."

So much for tonight's plan — there was no way Mary Lou was going to turn *that* invitation down. So unless he could figure out some way to intercept her on her way home . . .

"Oh," Mary Lou said. "Wow. That's real sweet

of you. Thanks. Wow. I'm sure I can find a sitter. What time?"

"Five-thirty. I'm afraid it's on the early side," Kelly told her. "I have an early morning tomorrow."

It was pretty close to 4:30 right now.

"Five-thirty's great," Mary Lou said. "I'll see you then."

"Great," Kelly echoed. He'd spent enough time watching her to know that her enthusiasm was forced.

As she headed for the checkout, Mary Lou headed for produce, leaving him a clear exit route out the back.

It was time to regroup, rethink, recalculate.

In a way it was refreshing, because up to this point, Mary Lou and her humdrum life hadn't been very much of a challenge at all.

Joan answered her cell phone on the first ring. "DaCosta."

"Hey, Joan," Muldoon said, sitting down on the dusty ground because out here a step in the wrong direction could make the signal fade. "It's Mike Muldoon. How's it going?"

"Everything is incredibly groovy, Mike Muldoon," she answered. "I'm about five minutes from some kind of social thing at Commander Paoletti's house. Some kind of wives and girlfriends hanging out, drinking lots of wine, and watching Jane Austen movies while you brave gorilla he-men save the world thing. Personally, I think we'll be having more fun."

Muldoon laughed. "I'm not so sure about that.

We're using some pretty cool toys tonight and tomorrow. I can't tell you about it, but trust me. The fun factor is high out here."

"Said the man who's definition of fun has nothing to do with Colin Firth," she countered.

A wives and girlfriends gathering. Wasn't it interesting that she'd been invited to that? And wasn't it twice as interesting that she'd go?

"So you're going to this thing because . . . ?"

"I've accepted Jenk's marriage proposal."

"Ha-ha," he said. "Very funny." She was kidding, wasn't she?

"It's work, Mike," she told him. "I thought — if Kelly and the other women are okay with it — we might set up a similar get-together when Brooke comes to town. I know it's not on her planned schedule of events, but it would make for a great photo op."

"Except for the fact that there's not a man on this team who would want his wife or girlfriend's picture on the front page of a newspaper," he pointed out. "You know, for the same reasons they don't want 'em wearing Navy SEAL T-shirts or hats. There are enough people on this planet who would love nothing more than to retaliate by targeting the loved ones of the SpecWar team members who are making their lives so miserable right now. Let's not make it any easier for that scum to ID them, please."

"Oh, shit." He could hear Joan's good mood evaporate. "You're right, SuperSEAL. God, I never even thought of that."

"Sorry," he said.

"No," she said. "Don't you dare apologize. What

a mistake that would have been. I would have put those women in danger and had a team of pissed off Navy SEALs coming after me. I think you just saved my ass."

Now was when, according to words of wisdom he'd recently received from Sam Starrett, he should make some kind of comment broadcasting his interest. Like, *And a mighty fine ass it is, well worth saving.*

"What did you just call me?" he asked instead.

"Nothing," she said. "Probably Muldoon. Or Michael. Or Mike. Or —"

"SuperSEAL?"

"Oh, that."

"You've called me that before."

"Yeah. You have a . . . man of steel thing that you sometimes get going. It's . . . amusing."

That wasn't the word he'd hoped she'd use. "Gee, thanks. Nothing I love more than amusing you. Ma'am."

"Watch it, Baby Huey."

"Oh, my God. How did you . . . ?"

"People like me," Joan said, laughing. At him. "People talk to me. People tell me all their secrets."

"And all of everyone else's secrets, too, apparently." Muldoon amused her — wasn't *that* just great? Still, he had to laugh. His luck was just unendingly bad. "Who told you about Baby Huey? Because now I have to go and kill him."

"So it's true," she said. "That really was your nickname while you went through BUD/S?"

Yeah, and for a long time after. "No," he said now. "Absolutely not. It's a heinous lie."

She laughed again. God, he loved it when she laughed.

"Oh, I got your email," she told him. "And I forwarded your message on to Brooke."

Come on, brain, don't stall. This was one of the reasons he'd called. Stick to the plan — even if she did find him *amusing*. "Did you read it?"

"Yes, I did. You didn't really think I'd forward something to the President's daughter without checking, did you?"

"Was it okay?"

"It was —" She hesitated for just a fraction of a second. "— very friendly."

No kidding, it was friendly. Muldoon had labored hard, putting just the right amount of subtle sexual innuendo in the message to Brooke — because he knew Joan would read it.

Hello, Brooke. Mike Muldoon here. I'm a lieutenant, junior grade, in U.S. Navy SEAL Team Sixteen. I'm really looking forward to acting as your escort to the Admiral's party Saturday night. I hope you'll let me make your evening — and the rest of your time in Coronado — as pleasurable as possible. I stand ready to take you wherever you wish to go whenever you wish to go there.

Wink, wink. Nudge, nudge. Hubba hubba.

"Any response?" Muldoon asked.

"Yeah," Joan said. "I forwarded it to you. I don't know why she wrote back to me instead of just zapping it directly to your email address. But she did. So I forwarded it."

"What'd she say?"

"What am I, your secretary? Go read your email, my brother from another mother."

"Aw, come on. I don't have time to sign online right now. Did she really write back, or did she send a form letter? 'Thank you so much for emailing the daughter of the United States' President . . .' "

"It was . . . Well, it wasn't a form letter."

"So what'd she say?" he asked again.

"What do you think she said? 'Dear Mike, I've seen your picture and I can't wait to jump your bones . . .'?"

Muldoon knew Joan said it just to be funny, just to tease. She had no idea how close it cut to a truth that made him uncomfortable in a decidedly perverse way. Perverse because although he hated it, he continued to use his looks to his advantage.

He'd have used them with Joan by now if he could have.

"*Talk* to her when you talk to her," Sam Starrett had said to him just a few hours ago on the transport plane — Muldoon's own Texas-style, six-foot-three-inch, shaggy-haired, stubble-chinned Dear Abby.

"You know, I can't remember the last time I was with a woman who wanted to sleep with me because of me," he told Joan now. "You know, not because of what I look like, but because of who I am. Frankly, I'm tired of it." As soon as the words were out of his mouth he regretted saying them. Way to sound pathetic and stupid. "I'm sorry. Look, I need to go."

"Whoa," Joan said. "Whoa, whoa, whoa there, my friend. You can't just say something insightful and extremely mature — and personal, might I add? — and then run away."

"It didn't sound mature to me — it sounded pretty stupid and whiny. Like, you know, poor me. I can't walk into a bar without a dozen women wanting to get naked with me. Life sure is rough." He rolled his eyes in disgust at himself.

She laughed. Apparently he was continuing to amuse her. "Yeah, well, I can imagine that would get old after a while. Maybe. But the truth is, Michael, that lots of people are easily attracted to superficial things. A pretty face, a nice body, money, a position of power. You know, I've been romanced by men who just want a connection to the White House. You learn to be careful. You learn to identify the insincere pieces of shit from the real deal. And real people *are* out there."

"Yeah," he said. "I know. I just haven't found that many of them." And none of them — like her — was even remotely interested in him. That *was* a pathetic thing to say. Fortunately he shut his mouth before it came out.

"Keep looking," she told him. "They're out there."

"Yeah," he said. "I guess." He didn't want to keep looking. He liked what he'd already found. "Look, I really do have to go now. Are you sure you won't tell me, just real quick, what Brooke said in her email?"

"She asked you a bunch of questions. What's your favorite movie, what's your favorite color? That sort of thing. Jeez, I don't know exactly. With Brooke you never know what she's going to say just to shake you up a little. Like, what's your favorite sexual position?"

"*Star Wars*, red, and on my back."

"O-kay," Joan said. "Well now. Thanks so much for information I didn't need to receive."

"Hey, you asked."

"No, *I* didn't ask. *She* asked. And she didn't even ask. I was just speculating what she *might* have asked. God."

"Feel free to pass the information along," he said.

"Oh, ew," she said. "She's too old for you. Don't gross me out, Muldoon. Besides, didn't you just get done telling me how tired you were of superficial sex?"

"Yeah," he said. "But when the choice is between superficial sex or no sex, well . . . I *am* a guy."

"One whose maturity points have all just been erased," she informed him. "Okay, I'm here. At Tom and Kelly's. I've got to go drink wine. Thanks so much for checking in, Lieutenant Icky."

"Hey," he said, suddenly afraid he'd gone too far, despite Sam's advice. What did Sam Starrett know, anyway? "I didn't mean to offend you."

Joan definitely had the greatest laugh. "What, by telling me *Star Wars* is your favorite movie? That *is* kind of offensive, Mikey. Everyone knows that *The Empire Strikes Back* was the best."

Muldoon laughed, too, relieved. "Tell everyone we're here, we're safe, and we'll be back in plenty of time for the admiral's party on Saturday night. I'll check in with you again tomorrow."

"May the force be with you, SuperSEAL," she said, and cut their connection.

THIRTEEN

Charlie was quiet in the car on the ride home from Don's.

The kid had woken up a little after 5:30, and he'd actually ventured out into the kitchen to get something to eat. It was then, while he ate the dinner Charlie had prepared, that he asked them to go home.

Charlie had looked over at Vince, a question in her eyes. Would he be okay on his own? Was it possible the medication had begun to work that quickly?

Vince had nodded yes. Actually, the doctor had prescribed a powerful, temporary antipsychotic in addition to the kid's usual meds. The new drug had a calming effect, the doc had said. It would ease Donny's anxieties, so much so that they'd see an almost immediate result.

The proof was right here, in his emergence from the closet.

Of course, now Don was in the process of getting worked up over the fact that his grandparents were there outside of their regularly scheduled weekly visit. So maybe it would be best if they did leave.

The kid preferred to be alone. He liked his regular routine — which involved a lot of time spent by himself, on the Internet.

Vince suspected that his grandson was a regular surfer at certain webcam sites and other cyber locations. And it wasn't necessarily the real-time world of naked cavorting women that kept Donny glued to his computer screen. It could just as well be video of a newborn giraffe from the San Diego zoo or a D&D gaming room that had caught his obsessive-compulsive attention.

After making it clear to Don that they'd be back in the morning to make sure he took his medication, Vince and Charlie hit the road.

"I understand why Tony doesn't come to visit very often," Charlie said now. She sighed. "And I thank God every day that Don doesn't want us to visit more than once a week." She looked at Vince. "Am I a bad person for thinking that?"

Vince smiled at his wife. "No, you are absolutely not."

"Hmmm," she said, clearly not agreeing with him.

"Maybe you shouldn't go back tomorrow," he said. "I know how much it gets to you. And then, you know, that upsets Donny. It kind of feeds on itself. You're upset, so he gets upset, which makes you even more upset, which et cetera, et cetera. It's the same thing with Tony when he comes. Hey, Don told me just today that Tony's been emailing him lately."

One of Tony's biggest difficulties had been accepting that he and Don were never going to have a traditional father-son relationship. He'd dropped completely out of Donny's life for a while.

Vince had been glad to hear that Tony was making an effort at having some kind of relationship with his son, and that he was astute enough to attempt to fit it into a format, like email, that Donny could handle without a lot of additional stress.

Although it was entirely possible that this contact from his father had been the straw that broke the camel's back — or the straw that made the camel flip out and stop taking his meds, as it were.

"And you were going to tell me this about Tony . . . when?"

Oh, danger, danger, Will Robinson! Sweet Charlotte was looking for a down and dirty fight.

"Right after we got into the car," he answered. "Which is right now. Which is when I just told you. It's good to hear, isn't it? Although, to be honest, Donny didn't seem particularly excited. Could be the meds. He was moving pretty slow. Remind me to ask him about it again in a coupla weeks, when he's up to speed."

"He's never up to speed," Charlotte said darkly.

"Up to *his* speed," Vince corrected himself.

"How do you do it?" she asked him. "How do you just sit there and accept him exactly as he is, without ever letting it get to you? You don't get angry, you don't get upset — you know, I can count the number of times you've lost your temper on my fingers. Nearly sixty years and . . . It's really starting to piss me off, Vincent."

He laughed at those words coming out of this woman's extremely proper mouth. Unfortunately, she hadn't said it to be funny.

"And you know what else? I'm getting good and

tired of shouting all the time," she informed him tightly. "We have plenty of money. Will you just go and buy some hearing aids, for goodness sake?"

This wasn't about his hearing or alleged lack thereof. It was about Donny. It was about how hard it was for Charlotte to acknowledge the fact that their grandson was never going to have the kind of life they'd always dreamed he'd have, back when he was a wide-eyed, sweet-faced ten-year-old. He was never going to have a family. He would most likely never find the kind of love and companionship they themselves had shared for all these years.

It was a difficult thing to come to peace with and accept.

"I think Donny's okay, Charles," he told her now. "I think he's okay with his life. He *likes* being alone. And the Internet allows him to be social on certain levels — levels he can deal with, with limits he can handle. When he's taking his meds and his biggest anxieties are under control . . . he's okay. I would even dare to suggest that he's happy."

She was silent for the rest of the ride home. But when he pulled the car into their driveway, she asked, "You really think he'd be better off if I didn't go tomorrow?"

"I wouldn't say better off," Vince told her as they climbed out of the car. "He loves you and he knows you love him. But I do think it might help keep him calmed down right now, while he's still unstable."

Charlie nodded. "I'll go, but I'll stay in the car."

Her reason for going along tomorrow might've been so that she wouldn't feel completely helpless and unnecessary when it came to assisting Donny. She'd be there in case Vince turned out to be wrong, and Don *did* need her.

But he would bet big dollars that her real reason for wanting to go was so that he wouldn't have to drive over there alone.

Vince unlocked the kitchen door, holding it open for her. "Okay," he said easily. "That sounds like a good plan."

"I'm going up to take a bath," she informed him as she headed for the stairs.

"Charlotte." He stopped her. "You *have* seen me angry more than ten times."

She thought about it. "No, I don't believe I have."

"When Upstairs Sally brought home that guy who lost his wallet . . . ?"

"That was the first time," she said. "But even then I think you were more upset than angry. But all right. It counts."

"How about when Tony was fifteen and he came home completely drunk and threw up on the brand-new living room rug . . . ?"

"Oh, yes. Two. And three — when Lexie was in that car accident, and that nurse wouldn't let you into the emergency room," Charlotte said. "That was very impressive."

"When Wendy lit the back deck on fire."

"That's definitely four." She couldn't keep from smiling. "Although I think even though you yelled, you were secretly impressed she'd managed such an accomplishment."

Vince grinned. "How *did* she do that without lighter fluid?"

"You also got good and mad at the high school when the band director was laid off," Charlotte said. "That's five."

"I was angry when you wouldn't marry me," he told her.

"No, you weren't. You were hurt."

"I was angry, too," he told her. "I just didn't broadcast that fact."

"Well, that doesn't count, because you didn't come across as angry."

"Well, I was."

"Well, you should have shouted, then," she countered. "Even if I let it count, that's only six times."

"There were definitely others."

She gave him her *Oh, yeah?* look. "Name 'em."

"Well . . ."

"Hah. You can't."

"Sure I can." He was angry a lot during the war. Surely he'd lost his temper more than once during those first few weeks he'd met Charlotte, when he was staying in her home. "I know — I was angry that day you came home and told me that Senator Howard was going to Hawaii, and that you'd been told to clear his calendar."

Charlie and the other secretaries had been ordered to contact everyone who had an appointment with the senator and reschedule. After waiting all that time, he was going to be shut out.

"No," she said now. "You weren't. You got a little grim, but . . ." She shook her head.

"If I remember correctly, there was an awful lot of yelling going on that day."

"That was me," Charlotte told him. "I was the

one doing the yelling. I was the one who was furious. Remember?"

He did.

"You want to do *what?*" He could still see her, standing in the bedroom that she'd so graciously given up for him, absolutely livid.

"Only six times," Charlie said now, continuing on up the stairs. "That's once a decade, Vince. Good thing I'm not prone to delusions or I'd think you might be one of those alien life-forms Donny sees all over the place."

Vince laughed and let her win. Surely he'd lost his temper more than that, but if she chose not to remember those times, well, that was just as good for him.

He went back into the kitchen and got a beer from the refrigerator door. Truth was, he'd had very little to get angry about these past sixty years. Truth was, he'd used up all of his anger during the war. It was hard to get too mad about a child's mischief after having lived through the three solid days of hell that was Tarawa, and all the other killing he'd seen.

Charlotte didn't think he'd been angry that day she'd come home from work to tell him that his appointment with Senator Howard — the one that he'd waited weeks for as he convalesced — was not going to happen.

And yeah, maybe she was right. He hadn't been angry. *Angry* wasn't a big enough word for what he'd felt. *Anguished* was perhaps more appropriate.

"We've been told to reschedule, starting in March," she told him, and he'd wanted to cry.

"I don't have till March," he told her tightly. "I'm

289

due back in California a week from tomorrow."

"What?" She sat down heavily in the chair by the door. "I had no idea you had to go back this soon."

"All I want is a few minutes of his time," Vince said. "Is that really too much to ask?"

He was going to have to start writing letters. He should have started weeks ago. But the truth was, he couldn't write to save his life. Who would take his misspelled letters seriously?

"You're barely recovered," she said. "You need more time."

"Charlotte, if I sent a letter to the senator, would he read it?"

She blinked at him. "He might not find the time to read it himself, but someone on staff certainly would. Depending how important it was, it might eventually make its way to his desk, so yes. It's possible." She leaned forward. "Vincent, don't they understand you've been sick? What good will it do to send you back to the fighting too soon?"

"It's not too soon," he told her. He was getting stronger every day. "In fact, if I don't get out of here, your cooking is going to make me too fat to fit into my uniform."

She didn't laugh at his pitiful attempt at a joke. She was just sitting there, looking at him as if he were a stranger — someone she'd never met. He wasn't quite sure if that was good or bad.

"Will you help me?" he asked her. "I need to write a letter that's so good the senator will read it before he leaves."

She was silent.

"Will you help me write it?"

Charlotte finally shook her head. "Vince, he's leaving the day after tomorrow."

"Okay, so it's got to be a really good letter."

"How can I help you when you won't even tell me why it's so important that you talk to him?" she asked.

Yeah, that was the part that wasn't going to be easy. He was going to have to tell her about Tarawa.

But not all of it. There was no way he would put the terrible details of that battle into a letter that Charlie might see.

"Mistakes were made at Tarawa," he told her, choosing his words carefully. "Big mistakes. I'm guessing there were lots of holes in the information given to the officers who planned the invasion. It was . . . well, it was a slaughter, Charles. You know that. But the newspapers wrote about it as a battle that needed to be fought. A necessary victory that had a terrible price. But I honestly think that price could have been a whole lot lower. I think that flat-out slaughter could have been prevented."

He had her full attention now. "How?"

"By filling in those holes," he told her. "By providing information about that beach, about the tides, about the underwater fortifications, including that goddamn coral reef — excuse me — that did more damage than any mines the Japs planted." He could see from her face that she didn't understand. "Charles, our Higgins boats were filled with Marines heading for that beach — but their hulls didn't clear the reef. They got caught up. Most of 'em got stuck there. Talk about sitting targets for the Japanese artillery. Whole platoons of Marines had to wade in, through waist- or even chest-deep water, more than five hundred yards to shore. We had no cover. We had no prayer. You could almost hear the Japs laughing as they mowed us down."

Charlotte's face was pale, and he realized he'd probably told her too much.

"There are dozens of islands in the Pacific that the Marines are going to take back from the Japanese, one bloody battle at a time. But we can't go in like that again. We need to get our men all the way to the beach. If there's a coral reef like Tarawa's out there on that next island, we need to rig it with explosives and blow a hole into it before the landing craft are on top of it.

"So, see, I've been thinking. I'm a strong swimmer. And I'm sure there are other men who grew up near the water. Ten or twelve of us could swim to shore and get a firsthand look at both the beach and the fortifications. We could carry explosives — I know there are some that work underwater. We could rig any obstacles that we find and blow 'em sky high. We could use snorkles so the Japs wouldn't even see us out there."

Charlotte's mouth was hanging open. "But if they did . . . ?"

He met her eyes. "Chances are, with a dozen small targets, at least one of us would make it back to the fleet with the information we gathered."

She stared at him, incredulous, slowly rising to her feet. "You're serious, aren't you? You want to write this letter to Senator Howard to involve him in setting up some kind of swimming Marine *death* team. Dear God, Vince!"

"No," he said. "Charlotte. Death team? That's not what I have in mind."

"It sounds to me like you're *out* of your mind! Swimming to shore? How could you swim all that way with a gun?"

It was a good question. One he'd thought long and hard about. "We wouldn't carry guns. It wouldn't be worth the drag or the weight, especially if we're carrying explosives. See, I'm talking about trying to make it to shore without the enemy seeing us, about swimming quite a distance and —"

She laughed, but it wasn't because she thought any of this was even remotely funny. In fact, she was furious. "You are . . . you're completely insane!"

"No, I'm —"

"Yes! You want to swim with a handful of other men to a Japanese-held island without a single gun. What do you think they're going to do when they see you, Vince? Wave to you? Offer you some sake?"

"Well, that's just it. They won't see us. We'll go in at dusk, swim back at night."

"Oh!" She was shouting now. "Now you're swimming across the ocean at *night!* Do you know how big the ocean is? Do you know how hard it is to swim at night? And it's not like the boat that's waiting for you will have running lights! You know, there are much easier ways of killing yourself. I'm sure you can find one that doesn't involve wasting the senator's — or my — time!"

"I'm not trying to kill myself. I'm looking to save lives."

"By sacrificing your own!"

"You see this?" He pushed himself off the bed and grabbed his uniform out of the closet. "Look at this. It looks like a uniform, but it's so much more. Every single man who gets dressed in one of these — Army, Navy, you name it — every man, both officer and enlisted, knows that. It's all about sacrifice. Those Marines who died at Tarawa weren't running away from the Japanese! They were running *toward* them. Do you think we didn't know we were already dead when those boats got caught on that reef? But we were wearing the uniforms of the United States Marines, and we did what we had to do for our country. Most of us died, but some of us made it through. And those of us who made it through, well, we didn't let the others die in vain. Yes, it's a sacrifice, Charles. I don't want to die — *no one wants to die* — but I will goddamn do what I have to do to keep my country safe."

There were tears brimming in her eyes and, as he watched, they spilled over and ran down her cheeks.

"I don't want you to go back," she whispered. "I don't want you to die, somewhere, all alone, so far from home. I dream of James almost every night. He's alone and dying and calling out for me. It haunts me, Vince. I couldn't bear it if you haunted me, too."

He couldn't look at her. He had to turn away, to put his uniform back in the closet, or else he'd do something stupid, like reach for her. But she didn't want him to reach for her. She wasn't going to let herself love him.

He didn't blame her.

294

"Well, I don't want to go back, either," he told her quietly. "But I have to."

"Maybe you don't," she said.

"Yes," he said. "I do. Will you help me write that letter, Charles?" He finally turned to look at her. "Please?"

"No," she said, and walked out of the room, shutting the door quietly behind her.

Mary Lou's heart sank as Kelly held open the door for her with a smile and a glass of beer in her hand. "Come on in." She turned toward the kitchen. "Hey, everyone, Mary Lou is here."

The friendly smile sure was nice, but oh, Lord, she hadn't even considered the fact that there'd be alcohol at this thing.

Mary Lou clung to her handbag as she followed Kelly into a brightly lit kitchen that opened into a living area on one side and a dining area on the other. Surprisingly, it wasn't all that much bigger than her own house.

The windows were bigger, though.

Sliding glass doors in both rooms opened onto a deck and framed a view of a neatly kept backyard filled with flower gardens and surrounded on all sides by other neatly kept backyards.

"Hey, Mary Lou," Lt. John Nilsson's wife, Meg, greeted her with a wave of a corn chip from her perch at the counter that separated the kitchen from the dining area. Her baby girl, Robin, was just a few months older than Haley, yet somehow Meg had managed to slim right down to her pre-pregnancy weight without any trouble at all.

Despite her apparent diet of corn chips and beer.

God, Mary Lou hated her. She gave Meg a big smile. "Hey, Meg. How's Robin and Amy?" Meg was also more than ten years older than Mary Lou, with a twelve-year-old daughter from her failed first marriage.

"Let's just say that it's three years, ten months, and fourteen days until Ames learns to drive, and between now and then I'll clock three hundred thousand miles," Meg said. "Sailing lessons, dance, theater classes, soccer . . ." She laughed. "I'm not working at all right now, and to be honest, I love every minute of it."

She exchanged some kind of pointed look with Kelly — obviously there was an unspoken understanding between the two women. Mary Lou felt a yawning, empty hole in her chest.

Why couldn't Meg be her best friend? What was so great about Kelly Ashton, who wasn't even married to Commander Paoletti?

Somewhere outside, a lawn mower started with a roar.

"Everyone, this is Mary Lou," Kelly announced, crossing to the sliders and pushing them closed against the noise.

There were five women in the kitchen and the only one Mary Lou knew besides Meg was Teri Wolchonok, beauty to the beast who was the SEAL team's heart-stoppingly scary Senior Chief Stan Wolchonok. Delicately pretty Teri actually flew helicopters — helos, as the SEALs called them — for the Coast Guard.

"You know Meg and Teri," Kelly said to Mary Lou. She gestured to a slender young woman who looked an awful lot like Gwyneth Paltrow, only with darker hair. "This is Christy, who's dating Mark Jenkins, and Shonda —"

"Who used to date — past tense, honey — Chief Wayne 'the Duke' Jefferson. 'The Duke.' Can you believe that?" Shonda was a very dark-skinned African-American woman with short-cropped hair that she'd dyed blond, and a wide smile that lit her from within. "What kind of grown man walks around calling himself 'the Duke'? I gave him up last year for Lent and decided to make it permanent. I come to these 'Wheels Up, Whoops, I'm Sleeping Alone Again Tonight' parties to remind myself that my decision to ditch the man was a smart one."

"Instead you sleep alone every night," teased a woman — a girl, really — who was still dressed in a waitress uniform. She held out her hand to Mary Lou. "I'm Ellen."

"What do you know from sleeping alone?" Shonda countered. "Ellen's spending time with Jay Lopez — and everyone and their baby sister knows our little Lopez has taken a vow of celibacy." She turned to Christy. "Or was that Jenk?"

"No, it definitely wasn't Mark." Christy laughed as if that were a very funny joke.

"Well, it sure as hell wasn't 'the Duke,' " Shonda said. "And check out that look on Joan's face. She's thinking '*What* are these lunatics talking about?' "

"Joan DaCosta's visiting from Washington," Kelly told Mary Lou. "She works at the White House."

"So ix-nay on the President Bryant okes-jay," Shonda said.

"Who's celibate?" Joan asked. "I definitely

missed something here. Slow it down a little. Have mercy on me and explain some of these inside jokes."

Joan DaCosta — thank the Lord — had an even bigger butt than Mary Lou. She really hated being the fattest woman in the room.

She moved over to the windows as the women continued their banter, feeling decidedly like an outsider. Even Joan, a visitor from the East Coast, was more comfortable here than she was.

"Jay Lopez is celibate, and Christy had breast implants," Kelly was explaining.

"Yeah, right," Christy said with a snort. "I went to the plastic surgeon and said, 'Gee, Doctor, I long to be a whopping 32B. Can you help me out?'"

The room erupted in laughter.

"Mike Muldoon is gay," Kelly continued, "and Cosmo Richter . . . Say it with me, now!"

"Was recruited to join the SEALs from his cell in the lifers wing of a federal penitentiary." Nearly all of the women finished in unison before dissolving into more laughter.

"Well, I kind of believe the one about Cosmo," Joan said. Despite her big butt, she was really very pretty when she laughed.

Outside the sliding door, in the next yard over, a man was cutting the grass. Was that . . . ? Could it be . . . Ihbraham? Mary Lou tried to look closer just as he disappeared behind some shrubbery, and knocked her head — pretty hard — against the glass. Which, of course, Kelly and Meg both noticed. They pretended not to, but Mary Lou knew they saw.

God, she was an idiot. Way to fit in. She moved away from the slider, rubbing her head when no one was looking.

"You wouldn't believe the rumors out there," Teri was saying to Joan. "Stan and I have a hot tub in our backyard, where apparently we have orgies every weekend."

"But you never invite me," the other women all said in unison.

More laughter. Mary Lou forced a smile.

There were four different bottles of wine out on the kitchen counter, along with glasses.

"Help yourself, Mary Lou," Christy said to her with a smile. "It's a self-serve party. You want it, you get it yourself. Beer's in the fridge."

Kelly slapped her forehead. "Oh, shoot!"

"What?"

"Mary Lou, I'm pretty sure there's some soda in here." Kelly opened the refrigerator. "Tom actually likes to drink that high octane root beer, or . . ." She opened the freezer. "I could mix up a can of lemonade?"

Mary Lou moved into the kitchen area. "I'll just have water."

"We have cranberry juice . . . ?"

"That would be great," she said. She hated cranberry juice, but Kelly was determined to offer her *some*thing.

"I'm really sorry." Kelly poured the juice into one of the wineglasses.

"It's all right," Mary Lou said as she took the glass, even though the sight of those wine bottles on that counter were driving her crazy. God, she needed some air.

But Kelly closed the kitchen window as the sound of the lawn mower got louder. "Figures Ihbraham would show up today."

Mary Lou stopped looking at the bottles of wine. "Ihbraham Rahman?"

Kelly laughed in surprise. "Yeah. Do you know him?"

"He does yard work in our neighborhood. He's really good."

"And apparently quite reasonable. He's out here two or three times a week. Everyone's hiring him."

"I'm glad to hear he's doing so well," Mary Lou said. "He told me that his business is pretty new. He's been working hard to get clients."

Kelly laughed. "Yeah, he keeps telling me two months are free with a yearlong contract. But Tom's really into gardening. It's therapeutic, believe it or not. The flowers out there are his."

Mary Lou moved to the window to look out. "Wow." Their gardens were quite lovely. She never would have guessed in a million years that Commander Paoletti liked growing flowers.

"I've got a total brown thumb," Kelly said. "I told Ihbraham I'd definitely call him if Tom's ever out of town for any length of time."

With a smile, she led Mary Lou back toward the rest of the women. They were still talking about the rumors that were constantly being spread about the SEALs.

"What I want to know is, has anyone ever seen Mike Muldoon with a woman?" Ellen asked.

"I think he really is gay," Christy agreed.

"Why do you think that?" Joan asked. "I've

spent some time with him lately, and I don't get that impression at all."

Teri cleared her throat. "He's not gay. I went on a date with him once."

The entire group turned to look at her. They all started talking at once, but Shonda was the loudest. She whooped. "The quiet women always have the biggest secrets! When was this and why is the man still alive? I would have thought dear ol' Stanley would've killed him and scattered his various body parts clear across the state by now."

"Actually, Stan set us up," Teri said. "It was . . . a while ago. Back when he was a little confused about our relationship. Back when he thought it was just a friendship." She smiled. "Back before I convinced him he was wrong."

"So did you and Mike . . . you know?"

"No!" Teri said, laughing. "It was just a date. Nothing happened. We had dinner. We talked. Mostly about Stan."

"So didn't he, like, make a move on you?" Christy asked. "Like, hey, baby, you show me yours, I'll show you mine?"

"No, he didn't," Teri said. "He's pretty shy. He was very nice."

"So how does that prove anything?" Shonda asked. "He was very nice. Hmmmm. Nice. In fact, I think it proves that he *is* gay."

"No, it doesn't," Kelly said. "It proves that he's polite and respectful of women. Some men just need a little encouragement in the love department."

"I'd like to meet one of them for a change. The

men I know need encouragement only when it comes to picking up their laundry and putting the toilet seat back down," Shonda said, and everyone laughed.

"You're Sam Starrett's wife, right?" Joan asked Mary Lou. "I met him yesterday. He's . . . impressive. There's got to be a lot of rumors circulating about *him*, huh?"

The room fell instantly silent.

No one looked at Mary Lou. It was worse than if they'd all stared at her, because this way she knew they'd actually heard the rumors. And this way she knew they thought those rumors were true. She wanted to shrink down to about an inch tall and run underneath the sofa.

"There's always a lot of rumors about everyone associated with the teams," Kelly said brightly. "How about we decide what we want on our pizzas?"

Shonda and Christy started arguing about anchovies, and the moment passed.

"I said something really wrong, didn't I?" Joan asked Mary Lou in a low voice. "I'm sorry about that. I didn't mean to . . ."

"The rumor is that I purposely got myself pregnant so Sam would have to marry me," Mary Lou told her just as quietly.

Joan cringed. "Ouch. That sucks."

"Yeah," Mary Lou said. "Excuse me."

She went into the kitchen, where Kelly was making a list of the various pizza toppings over by those fucking too-tempting bottles of wine. "What do you like on your pizza?" she asked.

"I'm sorry." Mary Lou set her untouched glass

of juice down on the counter. "I really can't stay. I promised the sitter . . ."

That was a very transparent lie, and Kelly wasn't fooled. "I'm sorry, too," she said quietly. "I wasn't thinking. We just always have wine and beer and . . . Sam says you're really doing well. Eighteen months sober is really great. It's quite an accomplishment."

"Thanks." Of course it didn't really compare with Kelly's accomplishments — going through medical school and becoming a doctor. Sure, she sounded sincere instead of patronizing, but Mary Lou didn't trust her. She didn't trust any of them. And she wanted to get the hell out of there.

Now.

Before she burst into tears.

"You know, I can order bottles of soda with the pizzas," Kelly suggested. "We'll put the wine and beer away and —"

"Oh, no, I don't want you to do that. It's really not a problem for me," Mary Lou lied. "It's just . . . I'm on a diet and pizza isn't . . . besides, Haley was really cranky when I dropped her off at the sitter's and . . ."

Kelly was dubious. "Are you sure? We can —"

"Very. Thank you so much for inviting me."

"Well, it was nice seeing you."

Yeah, they were both lying their asses off now. Mary Lou could practically smell the other woman's relief that she was leaving. "I'll let myself out. Please tell everyone that I'm sorry I couldn't stay."

And with that she was out of there. She practi-

303

cally ran down the hall and pushed her way out the front door.

She ran down the driveway and stood there for a moment, stunned that her car wasn't there, until she remembered she was driving Sam's truck.

The relief that flooded her was too much, and she stood there, at the end of the driveway, taking big gulps of fresh air as she tried not to cry.

Lord, was it too much to ask to have a friend? The only person she could really call her friend was Janine, who had moved across the country to Florida, leaving Mary Lou here, all alone.

"Mary Lou?"

Ihbraham's truck was parked in front of the house next door. He had just finished loading his lawn mower into the back, and he came toward her now, both glad to see her and puzzled as to what she was doing there.

Ihbraham was her friend.

He actually liked her. He honestly cared about her.

The realization hit her and she burst into tears.

"Wow," he said. "Do I smell that bad?"

But there must have been something in her eyes or on her face that told him it was time to kick aside the boundaries that he'd set between them. He hesitated only slightly before he reached for her.

Mary Lou clung to him, her arms tight around his waist as she sobbed into his shirt.

"Oh, wow," he said again in his lilting accent. "What's going on? Are you okay?"

For someone who was so thin, he was solid. Beneath his flowing clothes, he was all lean muscle.

And he smelled so good. Like fresh-cut grass and some kind of exotic fragrance — sandalwood. Janine used to burn sandalwood incense back when she was into psychedelic drugs.

"I need to go to a meeting," Mary Lou said, her voice muffled.

"Ah," he said, his hands warm against her back, against her head as he gently stroked her hair as if she were a young child. "That's always a good idea. Shall I help you find one? I have a blue book in my truck."

Mary Lou lifted her head and looked up at him, wiping her nose on the back of her hand. "Will you go with me?"

This time he didn't hesitate at all. "Of course."

"I *hate* this fucking *shit.*"

Muldoon didn't have to turn around to know it was Sam Starrett who was standing behind him, stripping off his rebreather and other diving gear.

"You know what lives in caves?" Sam asked. "Bats — which are *the* fucking creepiest mammal on the face of the earth, except they don't live on the *face* of the earth, do they? They live *beneath* it."

Bats were actually kind of cool, considering they used sound waves to navigate as they moved through the air at high speeds. But Muldoon kept his thoughts to himself, seeing how Sam had come up against about a hundred of them flapping in his face just a few hours ago without flinching or making a single sound. He was allowed to rant about it now.

"And those white bugs," Sam continued. "And fish and lizards. White with no eyes. Jesus." He laughed. "Listen to me complain. Like I wouldn't give damn near anything to be able to stay here and just keep training like this for the next, oh, five, ten years. Or better yet, go directly from here to Afghanistan to kick ass. Yeah, give me angry terrorists. Just please don't make me go home."

He'd sat down to strip his wet suit from his legs, and now he just sat on the ground, rubbing his forehead as if he had a massive headache.

"Anything I can do?" Muldoon asked.

Sam laughed, a burst of disgusted air. "Yeah, I wish. Make my life go away, will you?" He stopped himself, running one hand down his face. "Shit — sorry, Mike."

"Are you sure there's not —"

"Yeah, I'm sure." Sam cut him off. "I'm the one got myself into this mess, I'm gonna have to get myself out. It's just . . . it's not going to be fun."

Muldoon nodded. "I'm here if you want to talk."

"Right," Sam said, hauling himself up off the ground. "Talking will really help."

"Hey, you were the one who told me to talk to Joan," Muldoon pointed out.

"Yeah, how's *that* going?"

"Not so good," he admitted.

"What a fucking surprise." Sam gathered up his gear, and with a nod, he vanished into the night.

FOURTEEN

"Got a minute?"

"Heck, Mike, I've got a full hour," Joan said into her cell phone, reaching for the remote control and muting CNN. "And the only reason I can't talk longer is because I'm meeting my grandparents for lunch."

"That's great," he said. "I'm glad you found the time to do that."

She kept her eye on the headlines that ran constantly beneath the news. "Yeah, I'm smack in the middle of what we in this business call 'the lull before the storm.' Just try talking to me tomorrow, bub. In fact, let me apologize now for the fact that I'm going to be able to give you only twelve and a half seconds when you return from wherever it is that you are right now — that unnamed, secret place where you and your brothers in arms are doing unnamed, secret things that will help you be better prepared to fight terrorists."

Muldoon laughed. Even over the less-than-perfect cell phone speaker his laughter sounded too rich and warm. He sounded close, too — as if he were curled up inside of her ear.

"What's up, my brother from another mother?" she asked.

"I'm really just checking in," he told her. "I've got a little time to kill, too. I guess I just wanted to make sure that Steve was still getting the job done for you."

"He is," Joan said. "He's been very nice. Not as nice as you, but . . ." CNN cut to commercials and she was able to drag her eyes away from the screen. "Speaking of nice, do you know there's a rumor going around that you're gay?"

Muldoon choked. *"What?"*

Boy, he actually sounded surprised. She was sure he'd just laugh, sure he'd be aware of the rumors. "Oops. Never mind."

"Hold on," he said in his commanding officer's voice. "Wait. You can't drop a comment like that and then go *never mind*. Where did you hear that?"

"Is it true?" she asked.

He laughed in disgust. "What do you think?"

"I think if it's not true, why do you care where I heard it?" she countered.

"I'd kind of like to know who's spreading rumors about me."

"What are you going to do, go beat 'em up?" she asked. "Or — I know — hah! Go have heterosexual sex in front of them?" She laughed.

"Yeah, right," he said. "You are so not funny this time."

"Oh, but I am. I crack-a myself-a up," she admitted. "I was just picturing . . ." She laughed harder.

"What?"

"I was just picturing . . ." She couldn't stop laughing.

"What?"

"We were looking for a really flashy way to kick off the President's appearance next week, thinking about some kind of SEAL demonstration, and John Grotto, he's a major player in the White House communications office, he kept saying, 'We want to do something unusual. Something that's never been done before.' Quick, let me send an email to John suggesting . . . Wow, it puts a new spin on the idea of a demonstration, doesn't it?"

He laughed, and she could almost see him roll his eyes. "I'm so very glad I amuse you."

"Don't take it personally. It's really just . . . Sex is really very funny, don't you think?"

"*Funny* isn't the word that comes to *my* mind —"

"No," Joan said, trying her best not to start laughing again. "I know. You're right. When it's just two people and there's passion and maybe even real, honest love and the room is dimly lit — very dimly lit — then it can be pretty serious. But *public* sex? No, thank you. No way. It's just not . . . I mean, have you ever watched a porno flick?"

"Um . . ."

"Of course you have. Everyone's seen at least one and probably only one because, let's face it, you watch one and you never want to have sex again, let alone ever watch another porno movie. It's not sexy at all. It's hideous. At best, it's funny — *laughably* funny. There's lots of odd positions with strangely placed and therefore freakish-looking naked body parts. And there's grunting and all kinds of strange and very unsexy noises and . . . Have you ever watched yourself have sex?"

"Uh . . ."

"Well, no. Bad example," Joan said. "Because look at you. You probably don't have a bad side. You probably look terrific from all angles. But I had a very intense relationship in college with a guy who liked mirrors and I swear to God, I had to keep my eyes closed or I wouldn't be able to stop laughing. I was like, *'God!* What the *hell* is *that?'* "

Muldoon was laughing. "I think laughter is an important part of sex."

"Laughter, yes," she said. "But mirrors, cameras, or twenty thousand people watching from the bleachers — no, thank you. Kind of ruins the moment for me."

"Ruins the moment," he repeated. "I think most women have very definite ideas about what sex should or should not be. I mean, without a preconceived notion of exactly what the moment should be, it can't be *ruined,* right?"

"I can't decide whether to flambé you for being sexist or admit that you're on to something there, considering that most men are idiots and will do it anywhere, anytime, and with anyone."

"Nah, that's not true," Muldoon countered. "At least not the anyone part."

"Yeah, some guys draw the line at elderly women. But everyone else in a skirt is fair game." The running headlines were back on CNN, but they were all repeats.

"You know that's not true."

"Oh, excuse me," Joan said. "For some men, *married* women are on the untouchable list, too."

"Ms. Funny strikes again," he said. "Maybe you're right. Maybe men err on the side of being open to far more possibilities, but women . . . It's been my experience that most women have their fantasies practically scripted. This has got to happen, and then this, and then that, and the list goes on and on and on. As a guy, you need to play the game — and God help you if you accidentally throw in a little unwanted improv. But after a while, you learn your cues. It gets so you know exactly what they want to hear and when they want to hear it."

"If I'm Ms. Funny, you're Mr. Jaded."

"Maybe." He paused. "So tell me this — what is Brooke Bryant going to want to hear?"

Joan stopped watching the headlines. "Are you serious?"

There was another pause and then he said, "Yeah."

"You honestly want to start something . . . like that . . . with Brooke?"

"I like her," Muldoon said. "She writes a mean email. She comes across as smart and funny and, well, you know. Hot."

Oh, shit. Joan sat up. "Hot," she repeated. "You think that she's *hot* from the way she writes *email?*"

"Yeah," he said. "Yeah, you know, I do."

Joan closed her eyes. She wrote that email. All of it. All seven of them.

In the past twenty-four hours, she and Muldoon had exchanged seven different emails. God. What had she been thinking?

She'd forwarded Mike's first email to Brooke, who'd sent a reply directly to Joan.

What are you doing, sending this to me? Brooke wrote. She sounded brittle. Extremely stressed. *Who is this guy? I don't have time for this right now.*

Handle this, Joan, please. Write something back to him and say it's from me. In fact, send it from my official White House screen name. You know my password. I never have time to check that address anyway. Just deal with him!

"Look," Muldoon said. "She wrote me some really great email, and I really like her, and, well, I don't want to blow it."

"Wow. Well, okay." God, was she really jealous? She was. Which was stupid, since this was what she wanted, wasn't it?

"So how do I do it? How do I make sure she'll agree to see me again? I mean, I'm pretty sure that she thinks of me as being too young or —"

"Well, you *are*," Joan interrupted. "She's forty; you're twelve!"

"Twenty-five."

"I know," she said. "I was just being —"

"Narrow-minded," he said.

That stopped her cold. "You think I'm —"

"Yes," he said. "I do."

"She's old enough to be your —"

"Lover," he said. "We've exchanged lots of great email in a very short amount of time, Joan. I'm pretty sure she likes me, too. You know, she's really a great writer and a great person and . . . I need you to help me here."

Joan stood up and walked across the room to the window, with its view of the Pacific Ocean. He thought she was a great writer. "How?"

"I'm not sure," he said. "See, I've never done this before. I've never, you know . . ."

"No," she said. "I don't know. Spit it out, Muldoon."

"The number of times I've asked a woman out are in the single digits," he said. "I just . . . I've never had to, you know . . ."

"No," Joan said again, more irate than she had the right to be. "I *don't* know. For God's sake —"

"Women come to me," Muldoon told her. "If I want to be with a woman, I go someplace where women hang out — a bar, a party, an aerobics class, the grocery store produce section . . ."

"Oh, my God," she said. "You're really not kidding, are you?"

"No," he said. "Women approach me. All the time. I basically just say yes or no. I mean, obviously it's not as blatant as that. There's a whole game to it — or maybe dance would be a better way to describe it — but . . ."

"Well." Joan leaned her forehead against the coolness of the glass. This was crazy. What was she supposed to say to him to help him snare Brooke Bryant? "It sounds like you've had a lot of experience from the pursuer's perspective. What makes *you* say yes?"

He was silent.

"Other than the size of her breasts?" she added tartly.

"I don't know," he said. "I guess I say yes when she looks me in the eye and doesn't pretend it's going to be anything more than what it's actually going to be."

"So make sure you look Brooke in the eye," Joan said. God, she couldn't believe she was doing this. "You know, Mike, she's got a lot of issues, a lot of luggage. I'm not sure you really understand —"

"I look her in the eye and say . . . what?" he asked.

"God, I don't know. 'Wanna do me, baby?' "

"Hey, I'm being serious here. Help me out," he said. "Tell me — I don't know — is there some kind of line or approach that gets you every time? Something you can't turn down?"

"Honesty," she told him. "Kind of the same as you, you know? With the not-pretending thing. No lines. No bull. I like men who can hold my gaze and tell me that they like me — and mean it. Kissing works, too," she admitted.

"Kissing."

"Yeah, I'm not talking 'let me see how far down your throat I can stick my tongue.' I'm talking artful kisses. Persuasive, persistent kisses. Sweet kisses. There's a message being sent there — a very subtle message that says, 'This is not just about me getting off. This is about *your* pleasure, too. And see how good I am at that?' "

"Hmmm," he said. "Yeah, that's . . . good to know."

"It's a positive message to send to a woman. Of course, you could be less subtle and throw yourself on your knees before her, proclaim her your goddess, and beg to be her personal slave. That one gets me every single time."

He laughed.

"Michael, it's entirely possible Brooke was just messing around with that email. I've heard some stuff recently — rumors — that make me think she might be involved with someone right now."

"Yeah," he said. "And we all know how true most rumors turn out to be. Hey, whoops, I've gotta go. Thanks for talking, Joan."

"Mike," Joan said, knowing that she had to tell him the truth about who wrote all that email, but he was already gone.

"I'm so sorry I'm late." With Haley tightly secured on one hip, Mary Lou pulled a stray strand of hair out of her mouth and back from her face as she tried her best to smile.

Bob Schwegel, Insurance Sales, held his own against the embellishments several days of imagination had added to her memory of the man.

His blond hair gleamed in the sunshine, his chin was smoothly shaved, and his shirt was crisply white — obviously freshly laundered beneath his well-tailored business suit.

Mercy! Not only did he hold his own, he knocked that memory clear out of the park because he smelled so damn good.

"No problem. I always have plenty of files to read. Besides, you're doing me the favor, right?"

Mary Lou wondered if the makeup she'd bothered to put on this morning had already run down her face from the marathon she'd just raced — thanks to Haley's waiting to poop until they were out the door and halfway in the car seat and already five minutes late.

He smiled, his perfect teeth gleamingly white against his perfect tan. "You ladies look particularly lovely today."

He was still slinging the BS with an elephant-sized shovel, same as he had when they'd met at the library. Haley was mottled from crying, her eyes red and her entire face runny, and Mary Lou . . . Well, God only knew what she looked like now.

"Hi, Haley," he said directly to the baby. "How are you today? A little grouchy, huh, kid?"

He saw that Mary Lou was juggling her car keys and her purse, and he reached over and plucked Haley from her arms, snot and all.

"Don't let her get your —"

"I've got it." And he did. He was actually carrying a handkerchief in his pocket and he whipped it out and expertly wiped Haley's face and nose.

Mary Lou put away her keys and pulled the straps of her purse up onto her shoulder. "I didn't think men knew how to do that," she said, as she reached for Haley, who was starting to come out of the shock of being held by a strange man and beginning to look as if more tears were imminent.

"Back to your mommy," Bob said, smiling at Mary Lou and slipping the handkerchief into his jacket pocket.

"Thank you," she said.

"My pleasure." His eyes actually twinkled as he gazed down at her.

After picking up Haley from Mrs. Ustenski's, Mary Lou had come home from the AA meeting last night to find a message from Bob on the answering machine.

"Mrs. Starrett, this is Bob Schwegel from Medway Insurance," he'd said. "We met at the library a few days ago. I helped you carry your books out to your car? Forgive me for calling you like this, but I think I might've left my book with yours."

He'd left his number.

Mary Lou wrote it down and was about to erase the message on the machine because what would Sam think? But on second thought, she left it there. Let him think whatever he wanted to think. Of course, that was assuming he ever thought of her at all.

She'd called Bob back this morning to tell him that his book wasn't in her pile. In fact, she'd already returned most of those books to the library.

He'd asked her, please, if she didn't mind too much, to check in her car. Maybe it had slid underneath the seat. Unfortunately, it was a forty-five-dollar book . . .

But Mary Lou couldn't check. Her car was in the body shop.

That was when they'd made plans to meet here.

Mary Lou led the way into the cluttered shop office, where a biker type looked up from a stack of grease-smudged papers.

"Hi," Mary Lou said. "My husband brought my car in for a repair to the trunk, but I need to see if I maybe left something in it . . ."

"Starrett, right?" the biker said, glancing from Mary Lou to Haley to Bob and back. "That's done. We replaced the entire trunk lid." He rolled in his office chair to a rack on the back wall and plucked a set of keys from among dozens hanging there, then rolled back. "Our key machine's down, so there's only one key to the trunk. You might want to get that copied." He handed the ring to Mary Lou. "It's in the back lot. Row D."

"But . . . my husband's away. I have no way of getting the car home right now," she told the man.

"Sure you do," Bob said. "You drive the truck home, I'll follow, and then I'll drive you back here for your car."

"I can't ask you to do that," Mary Lou said, letting Haley hold the keys but keeping her from chewing on them.

"You can leave it here for as long as you like," biker man said.

"Thank you," she told him as she followed Bob out of the office.

"Say hi to Sam for me," the biker added. "Tell him I said we're even."

"I will," she said.

"I really don't mind helping you out," Bob told her as they headed past rows B and C.

She shifted Haley to her other hip. "I hate to break it to you, Mr. Schwegel, but my husband's a Navy SEAL. Believe me, we've got our insurance needs handled."

Bob laughed. "You think this is about me selling you insurance?"

"Isn't it?"

"No. It's just me doing you a favor after you did a favor for me. Very innocent. Just two people being friendly. No ulterior motives. And the name's Bob."

And there was her car. "Oh, drat!" With a new maroon truck lid that was a dark contrast to the light blue body. There was no doubt about it any longer. She drove a white-trash-mobile. She wanted to cry.

"Hey, it just needs a paint job," Bob said, touching her lightly on the arm. "It'll look great — you can have the whole thing done in maroon. It'll be almost like having a new car."

"Yeah, sure," she said unenthusiastically. The paint job would never happen. She'd make some calls, get some estimates, and be stunned at how expensive it would be. Sam would tell her to go ahead and spend the money, but she'd be unable to. She'd spent too many years with her mother and then Janine, counting nickels and dimes, to be able to spend any money at all on something that foolish.

It ran, didn't it? It got her and Haley where they had to go. That's what really mattered.

Still, the crappy way it looked depressed the hell out of her.

Mary Lou unlocked the passenger's-side door and stepped back to let Bob look for his book.

With a triumphant "Aha!" he pulled it out from underneath the seat. "Thank you," he said, "so much."

"You're welcome," she said, trying out the key on the trunk. It popped open.

He took the keys from her. "Here's what we'll do. You take the truck, I'll drive this car home, then you can drive me back here to get my car. That way you don't have to move the car seat out of the truck. Smart, right?"

"Oh," she said. "I'm sure you don't have time to —"

"My next appointment's not until two-thirty," he said. "Not only do I have time to help you get your car home, but I have time to stop for lunch, too, preferably with a little company for a change." He opened the driver's-side door and slid in behind the wheel. "I'm not going to take no for an answer to either suggestion."

Bob started her car with a roar and, bemused, Mary Lou started backing away.

He made an impatient face at her through the

windshield, motioning her to move faster with his hand, and laughing, she turned.

She could feel him watching her as she walked to Sam's truck, and when she glanced back at him, she caught a definite glint of admiration in his eyes.

Sam probably wouldn't like the idea of her having lunch with a relative stranger. He was always full of warnings — don't do this, don't do that.

But right about now, with a handsome man checking her out for the first time in a long time, Mary Lou didn't give a good goddamn.

"I've always loved your house," Joan said as she helped clear the table after lunch.

Charlotte looked up at her granddaughter, who laughed and held up a hand.

"I know," Joan said. "You don't need to say anything. I remember the hissy fit I threw when you moved here, too. What was I? Eight years old?"

"Seven," Charlie told her as she put the leftover chicken salad into a bowl. "And it wasn't a hissy fit. It was more of a tragic pout. Deep sighs and big, sad eyes. Very melodramatic. It was all Gramps could do to keep from laughing whenever you came over."

Joan remembered which drawer held the lids and fished out the right one. "He finally yelled at me. That was a little scary. Gramps mad. I almost fainted."

"He wasn't really mad." Charlie took the lid from her and sealed the bowl, popping it into the refrigerator.

"Yeah, I know," Joan said. "He was just ready for

me to snap out of it. Your old house was great, though."

"It wouldn't have been after they widened the street."

"I know. I drove past it last time I was in town. The traffic's terrible over there. Really noisy. And the entire front yard is gone."

"I do miss that pantry," Charlie admitted.

"And the dumbwaiter, and the front and back staircases," Joan said, remembering. "It was a great house for hide-and-seek, but that's not what made it magical. You and Gramps did that. And when you moved, the magic came with you."

Charlie hugged her. "What a lovely thing to say."

"It's true. I couldn't see it back when I was seven, but I finally caught on."

"There are some truths we're just not ready for," Charlie agreed. The coffeemaker was finally done dripping, and she poured them both a cup. "Are you still drinking this black?"

"Depends on how many calories I had for lunch," Joan admitted. "And today I had way too many, so yes."

"You don't need to diet. I think you look wonderful," Charlie told her, leading the way out onto the porch.

"Thanks, Gramma, but —"

"Tell me about this Lieutenant Muldoon."

Joan laughed and rolled her eyes. "Still trying to get me married, huh? I knew this was coming as soon as Gramps made himself scarce."

It was a habit Charlie and Vince had fallen into over the years, after Sheryl had died. Vince would disappear for a while so that Joan and Charlie would have a chance to talk privately. She didn't think for one moment that she could take the place of Joan's mother, but still, she hoped that being available to listen made things a little easier for her granddaughter.

These days it was tougher than ever to be a young woman.

"He's just a friend," Joan told her.

"Have you told him that? I may be old, but I still know smitten when I see it."

Joan shook her head as she smiled into her coffee. "Gramma, he's a twenty-five-year-old man. He wants to sleep with me. But he wants to sleep with me because he wants to sleep with everyone. That's what twenty-five-year-old men do."

"Yes, and I've heard that most young men have found that the quickest and easiest way into a woman's bed is to get up at the crack of dawn and spend five hours — or was it six? — at the home of her mentally ill brother. Oh, but wait. That's neither quick nor easy nor particularly fun — especially compared to picking up a woman in a bar."

"Gramma —"

"Some men aren't jerks, Joanie, even if they are only twenty-five years old. You know this man far better than I do, I'll grant you that, but if first impressions count for anything —"

"They don't. My first impression of him was —"

Charlie plowed right over her. "When he shook my hand, he looked me straight in the eye, and I thought, He's the one Joan's been waiting for. I know that sounds silly —"

"It does," Joan said. "He just has really pretty

eyes. Pretty everything. Maybe *you're* the one who's smitten."

"You whisked him out of there so quickly, I was sure you were intentionally hiding him from us. Even Gramps noticed."

Joan put down her coffee cup. "I was," she said. "I was trying to avoid this very conversation." She sighed. "Look, Mike is a really nice guy, all right? *Really* nice. Stupidly nice, in fact. I really like him. I do. But I can't think about him in terms of any kind of a real relationship."

"Why not?"

Joan rolled her eyes. "Do you have three hours? The list of reasons would take that long to work through."

"Abbreviate."

She sighed again.

"Come on. Humor your old gramma."

Joan laughed. "You're impossible."

"That's what Vince tells me. Tell."

Another big sigh, then, "First of all, he lives in California. The last time I checked, the federal government had no plans to move the nation's capital from Washington, D.C., to the West Coast. And if that's not enough, he's a Navy SEAL — who needs *that* aggravation? You should know what that's like more than most people. And, oh, didn't I mention that he's twenty-five years old? He's a baby. Even if I completely lost my mind and wanted to start a relationship with a man who lives three thousand miles away from me and risks his life regularly as part of his job, I can't get past the age difference. Everyone will look at us. Wherever we go. They'll wonder why he's with me."

Her cell phone rang before Charlie had a chance at rebuttal.

Which was probably for the best. There was no point arguing over a truth that Joan wasn't ready to hear.

What Charlie did say when Joan closed her cell phone was, "Gramps is quite a few years younger than me. Did you know that?"

Joan shook her head. "Three years isn't —"

"Seven isn't either."

She just laughed as she gathered up her handbag. "I have to get back. Apparently there's some kind of problem with Brooke — what a surprise. I'm needed back at the hotel. I swear, I'm really starting to dislike that woman, even though she is my President's offspring. Don't get up." She gave Charlie a kiss. "Tell Gramps I'm sorry I had to miss our card game. After this thing with Brooke is over, probably by next Thursday, I'll be around more often." She snapped her fingers. "Oh, I meant to ask you. Dick Evans told me you were invited to next year's anniversary ceremony at Pearl Harbor, that they'd asked you to speak on behalf of the families of the men who were lost."

"I'm not sure yet if we're going," Charlie said. "That's more than a year from now."

"A free trip to Hawaii?" Joan laughed. "I think you're going."

"We'll see." She hadn't even mentioned it yet to Vince. She didn't know how he'd react. Of course, he'd never say a word in complaint, but she'd suspected he'd been bothered by that interview she did last week for the History Channel. He was still pretty subdued, still oddly quiet at times, and it had been days.

And she wasn't quite sure how to broach the subject. *Are you still jealous of my dead first husband?* It was so absurd, it seemed impossible, after nearly sixty years of a good marriage. And yet . . .

"Dick also asked me to ask you if you'd come to this thing in Coronado next week — the SEAL demonstration — as a guest of President Bryant's. Sit on the riser with the other VIPs . . . ?"

"She'd love to."

Charlie turned to see Vince standing in the open sliding door.

"The invitation is for you, too, Gramps," Joan said.

"Then *we'd* love to." Vince smiled at Charlie. "Even though we didn't vote for the guy. Just tell us where and when and we'll be there."

"You'll get an official invite, probably tomorrow, but Dick wanted to be able to give the news agencies something on the local angle. So don't be surprised if you get a call from the *San Diego Union-Tribune.*"

"Oh, goody," Vince said. "Reporters. Let's see what they get wrong this time."

"Easy there, you," Joan said, and gave him a kiss. "Reporters are our friends. I've got to run. Bye, Gramma."

And then she was gone.

Vince shook his head. "At least we got her to sit still for a few hours."

"She's not dating that Navy lieutenant," Charlie told him. "They're just friends."

Vince laughed at that — a sharp burst of merriment. "Yeah? The way *we* were just friends, I bet, huh? Did you see her looking at him?"

"Did you see him looking at her?"

"Yes, ma'am, I did," Vince said. "I give 'em till the end of the week, tops."

FIFTEEN

Commander Paoletti, Lieutenant Jacquette, and Senior Chief Wolchonok, the mighty trinity of SEAL Team Sixteen, were deep in discussion.

Or rather, Tom Paoletti — looking pretty grim considering that their exercises in the cave had gone as well as they possibly could have — was talking, and Jazz and the senior were nodding in solemn agreement.

As Sam watched, Paoletti turned and briefly made eye contact with Mark Jenkins, who immediately approached the three, clipboard in hand. Hah. So that's how Jenk did it. Sam had always thought the freckle-faced petty officer had some kind of Radar O'Reilly–type telepathic abilities, but apparently he just kept his eyes open and stayed alert, ready to leap into action.

Sam watched Jenk nod and take notes as both officers and the senior chief gave him instructions.

No doubt about it. There was going to be a detour. They weren't going straight back to the base. Which was fine with him. The later he got home tonight, the better.

"What's up?"

He turned to find both Muldoon and Cosmo beside him, also watching the team's senior officers.

"I don't know," Sam admitted.

But then here came Jenk, trotting briskly toward them.

"Target practice," he announced.

"Now?" Muldoon asked. "Here?"

"The CO wants us to do some shooting from on board the helos," Jenk answered on his way past. "So, yes, now, but not quite here. We're going home via Caliente."

Caliente was the team's nickname — courtesy of an incident involving the usually taciturn Jay Lopez, some extremely hot shell casings, and a lot of shouting — for the CO's favorite firing range out in the desert, north and west of San Diego.

"Thought Black Lagoon was covert," Cosmo commented, his eyes hidden behind his sunglasses.

"It is," Sam said. Sure, they'd practiced close quarters combat in the cave, but firing weapons on an operation like Black Lagoon was always considered a last resort. Where they were going — and their insertion point hadn't been revealed but Sam had a strong sense that it wasn't going to be in Afghanistan, so it really had to be hush-hush — no one was going to do any shooting from any of the extraction helos whatsoever.

Besides, the helos that carried the SEALs away from an op were always armed with shooters — and good ones — of their own.

Mike Muldoon had a funny look on his face.

Sam nudged him. "What?"

But Muldoon just shook his head. "Nothing."

"We're gonna insert via two helos at the dog and pony show for President Bryant," Cosmo reported. "Call came in this morning. Date's set in stone. They don't want the Leap Frogs, they want us. We'll be fast-roping in from two Seahawks."

Sam looked sharply at Muldoon. "Is that true?"

Muldoon nodded. "Yes, sir." He didn't look happy as he watched Paoletti, who was still deep in a very serious discussion with the senior chief.

"Fuck," Sam said under his breath. Was it possible that Tom Paoletti thought there was going to be serious trouble during the President's visit to Coronado?

If so, that was one fucking serious discussion Paoletti and his senior chief were having, indeed. A little piece of paper called the Constitution made it very clear that the U.S. military could not take up arms against the civilian population. Repelling a terrorist attack on U.S. soil would be the job of the FBI and the Secret Service.

Of course, if the FBI invited the SEALs to join in, that would be a different matter altogether.

Never one to take a sense of foreboding lightly, Commander Paoletti no doubt was making sure his team was going to be ready for anything.

Feeling positively light-headed, Joan dropped the morning edition of *USA Today* onto the table and speed-dialed first Myra's and then Dick's phone numbers.

Both of her immediate superiors' phones were busy, so she called Meredith, back in D.C.

Who was in her office and answering her phone, because although it was early here, it was, thank God, three hours later there.

"There's a picture," Joan said, "of two Navy

SEALs in combat. On the front page of *USA Today*. Have you seen it?"

"Hoo-yah," Meredith said. "Isn't that what SEALs say? Talk about a pair of hunks and a half. You know, if I weren't afraid of giving Mrs. Alison a heart attack, I'd scan it and make wallpaper for my —"

"No." Joan cut her off. "There is nothing even remotely worth joking about here. This is very serious, Mere. I need to know — ASAP — where the hell this picture came from and who the hell authorized its release to a freaking national newspaper!"

"Whoa," Meredith said. "Joan. Relax. This is *the* most positive story connected to Brooke Bryant that's ever been printed. *Ever.* Apparently she's dating a real hero. That's great stuff. Even though the picture's not ours, we've been getting high fives all around for a job well done."

"It's not a job well done," Joan told her. "It's a major pooch screwing! Muldoon is active duty special operations — counterterrorist! It's bad enough that his name was released to the press — I never authorized that! He was supposed to be 'an unnamed U.S. Navy lieutenant' in the press release — but to have his picture in the paper for everyone in al-Qaeda to see? Do we want someone to target this man? This is *bullshit!* It shouldn't have happened, and I can tell you right now, there's going to be one freaking bad spin on this story if this hero becomes a dead hero. Now, are you going to help me find out who released this photo so we can cut them off at the knees?"

Meredith had gotten real sober real fast. "I'll get right on it."

Joan hung up the phone, dialing Myra again as she unfolded the paper and flattened it out.

Busy. Still busy.

It was definitely Mike Muldoon in this photograph. He was lit as if by a nearby explosion. He was dressed in black, wearing something that had to be one of those combat vests he'd described to her during her tour of the base. One arm was wrapped around the neck of another man who was dressed just as he was — Joan wasn't sure, but she thought it might be the chief whose nickname was WildCard. The blurb beneath the photo didn't identify anyone but Muldoon, thank God for small favors.

As angry as she was at its existence, it was an incredible picture — a fabulous action shot.

Muldoon held a weapon in his other arm, and he was gesturing with it to someone outside of the picture's frame as the two men ran down a rocky trail.

It was the expression on his face that made the picture so powerful. His mouth was open, as if he were shouting orders, and his eyes held a fierce intensity. He was determination personified.

Boy, was it possible she'd never really gotten to know Mike Muldoon at all? Back when they were first introduced, she never would have believed the man in this photo and the handsome young officer with the polite smile and stiff stance were one and the same.

And that was what kept her from having a total coronary about this. The Muldoon in this picture looked pretty different from the Muldoon who walked around the Navy base, who gave tours and had lunch in town and kept his white uniform sparkling clean.

Someone looking for the man in the photo would be challenged to find him.

However, it would probably be wise for Muldoon to stay someplace besides his apartment for a while. Like until the entire al-Qaeda network was wiped out.

Oh, God, he was going to be *so* pissed.

Joan looked at the photo again. This was not a picture taken during a mere training exercise, that she knew for sure.

Her phone rang. It was Meredith, sounding out of breath.

"Photographer's name is Camile Lapin," she reported without taking the time for a greeting. "She's French; she's with an extreme right-wing weekly newsmagazine based out of Paris. Our sources verify that she *was* in Afghanistan several times over the past year. Let's see, name of her paper translates roughly to *The Truth,* yada, yada . . . Oh! She just did an interview with CNN in which she alleges that this picture was taken in Afghanistan late last year. She says Lieutenant Muldoon — he's the one with the —"

"I know quite well which one he is."

"Well, she says he was in charge of some kind of secret military operation helping destroy one of the major al-Qaeda hideouts in the eastern part of the country. She says he risked his life to save her from, quote, certain death, end quote, and that this picture was taken — and I'm sorry, but I find this really hard to believe, because if you look at that picture, those guys are really hauling ass — after the lieutenant broke his knee?"

"Kneecap," Joan corrected her. That was why Mike was leaning on WildCard. Holy God, he was running down the side of a mountain, in a full, major stride, with a freaking broken kneecap.

She sat down because her own knees suddenly couldn't hold her up.

"Does she have any other pictures?" Joan asked.

"She says no, that this was the only one that came out. Apparently it was a dark night, and it's not easy to get your camera shots lined up with the rockets' red glare and bombs bursting in air."

"Cut the jokes, Mere. This is still not funny," Joan warned her. "How did this happen? Wasn't her camera and film confiscated after she was brought to safety?"

"Yes. But this one roll . . ." Meredith paused delicately. "How do I put this? Or rather, how do I tell you where she alleges she put it?"

Oh, God. "*That's* going to be fun — explaining that to Muldoon. Do we know why she held the photo until now? I mean, what kept her from going public as soon as she returned to Paris?"

"She says *The Truth* ran the photo on their front page the day after she left Afghanistan. But both the photo and her story weren't picked up by the Associated Press. Probably because *The Truth* had recently been discovered printing a whole series of photos from 1991 taken during Operation Desert Storm, that the paper claimed were from the current conflict." Meredith laughed. "It's the classic Boy Who Cried Wolf syndrome. Serves 'em right.

333

Although the fact that the photo was first printed last year makes me think Lapin's telling the truth about it being the only one. If she had other pictures, they would have been plastered all over *The Truth,* too."

"Yeah," Joan said. "Okay."

"So what now?" Meredith asked.

Good question.

"We're going to have to get Muldoon a room at the hotel," Joan decided. "And Secret Service protection if he wants it."

"You really think he'll need his own room?" Meredith asked. "I mean, if he really is Brooke Bryant's newest hottie . . ."

"Get him a room," Joan repeated, and hung up.

She dug through her handbag for her bottle of pain reliever as she dialed Muldoon's cell phone number.

This was not going to be fun.

She held her breath, but he didn't pick up.

All that non-fun was going to have to wait. Muldoon's voice mail went on, brief and to the point. "Leave a message, I'll call you back."

"Mike, it's Joan." Good start, but there was no way she was going to be able to leave him a message about this total fiasco. "Call me as soon as you get this message, all right? It's very important that we talk."

She flipped her phone closed. And picked up the newspaper to look at that photo again.

He was going to be really angry about this. Who wouldn't be?

But a man who could run with a broken knee-cap . . . Now, *there* was someone who had access to all kinds of self-control and normally untapped resources. There was no way that a man like that would stay angry at her forever.

Was there?

"Whoa," Cosmo said.

There was more emotion packed into that one little word than Muldoon had ever heard the petty officer utter in all of the years they'd both been with Team Sixteen.

He turned to find Cosmo staring up at the TV that was tucked in the corner of the sandwich shop.

Instead of eating more MREs — meals, ready-to-eat — they were here, having a real lunch of real food because Commander Paoletti loved them. This sleepy little California town was accustomed to the SEALs fast-roping down from helos to grab some grub. Most of the SEALs were over at the Mexican restaurant across Main Street, but Muldoon — forever and always watching his weight — wanted a turkey on whole wheat.

Besides, he had plans for tonight that didn't include the aftereffects of eating beans for lunch.

"You're on the news, sir," Cosmo said. He smacked the counter with the palm of his hand. "Hey, Frank, give us some volume here!"

But Frank was in the back room. "Be out in a sec!"

Muldoon took a step toward the TV and then another. Jesus, was that really a picture of Wild-Card and . . . ? It was. It was him. A photograph of Muldoon in action, his arm looped around the chief's neck, right there on the cable news.

But then the video cut to a slender young woman with closely cropped bleached blond hair and heavy black eye makeup.

"Shit, it's Camile." Unwilling to wait a second longer, Cosmo dragged a table up to the TV, climbed up, and cranked the volume himself.

"Who's Camile?" Sam Starrett asked, leaning back against the counter.

But whatever Camile — who looked vaguely familiar — had to say was done.

". . . in Afghanistan" was all they heard in her heavily accented English.

"Camile is that French reporter, wanted to interview that scumbag Zeeshan when we were taking out that cave last year," Cosmo said, and everything fell into place.

Her hair had been black back then, but it was definitely her. "How the hell did she get that photo?" Muldoon asked Cosmo. "I thought she was searched."

"She was. Shit, sir, I searched her myself. Confiscated her camera and four rolls of film."

"You should have called for a cavity search," Sam said. Easy for him to say. He hadn't been there — hadn't met the woman.

"Guess so," Cosmo said grimly. The muscle jumped in his jaw as he took off his sunglasses and faced Muldoon. "I'm really sorry about this, sir."

"Who knew?" Muldoon said. "Don't sweat it, Cos. It's not so bad. It's been months since that picture was taken. It's not like the info that we were there on the ground during the air strikes hasn't already been leaked."

The news anchor, perky and bright-eyed, was talking about the important role of SEALs and other "special forces" in the war on terrorism, and getting just about all of it completely wrong. Which was probably just as well. The less secrets given away, the better.

But then the anchor said, "As the war continues and stories of heroism and courage are reported, more and more people are clamoring to find out more about the men who wear the uniforms.

"Apparently Brooke Bryant, the President's wild child, was among the curious. Sources at the White House say she's been corresponding through email with Navy SEAL lieutenant Michael Muldoon for quite some time."

What?

"Whoa," Cosmo said again. "Have you really?"

Even Sam was now standing up straight.

And the photo of Muldoon and WildCard was back on the TV screen.

"No," Muldoon said. *Sources* at the White House . . . He felt sick. "I mean, yes, but —"

"Shh!" Sam said sharply. "I want to hear this."

"Ms. Bryant arrives in San Diego this afternoon," the bubbly anchor said in a voice-over, "where she'll attend a black-tie banquet, escorted by Lieutenant Muldoon. Lieutenant Muldoon is the SEAL officer on the left in this now famous photo."

Someone — a *source* from the White House — gave CNN his name and released that photograph . . .

The anchor was all dimples. "A well-recognized

337

aide to the First Daughter was reportedly over-heard investigating the preparations needed for a full fanfare military wedding. Sources have neither confirmed nor denied any rumors of impending nuptials, but there definitely appears to be romance in the air today at the White House.

"Coming up, we'll take a look at the latest in the automotive industry's —"

Cosmo was back on the table, turning the volume down.

Sam looked at Muldoon. "What the fuck is that about?"

He shook his spinning head. "It was Joan," he said. "I emailed Brooke Bryant, yes, but . . . I'm supposed to take her to this thing tonight. But I'm just her escort — I've never even met the woman. So I emailed her, mostly to try to get a rise out of Joan, because I was sending it to Brooke through Joan's email address and I knew she'd read it . . . But it was Joan who wrote back. I'm sure of it. It was definitely Joan. I mean, she was trying not to sound like herself, and she was using Brooke's screen name, but . . . I know that it was Joan."

"Jesus Christ," Sam said, laughing in amazement. "You know, for a smart guy, you are dumb as a stone. Were you really trying to make Joan jealous?"

"No," Muldoon said. "Yes. God, I don't know." He didn't know anything anymore.

Sam laughed. "Well, shit, Muldoon, *that* worked really well. Congratulations on your impending engagement to the President's daughter."

"This isn't funny, sir," Muldoon said stiffly.

"Sorry." Sam stopped laughing. "You're right. It's not funny. It really sucks to be used, doesn't it?"

Muldoon nodded. "Yes, sir."

Joan had to be one of those White House sources mentioned on the news. She'd probably set him up for this, right from the start. He just couldn't believe she'd leak his name. And yet, there it had been. Lt. Michael Muldoon. All over the news. And his picture, too.

So much for thinking she was his friend. Or more . . .

"Well, screw her stupid party," Sam said. "Who needs that kind of hassle, right? When we get back to Coronado, what do you say we head over to the Ladybug and spend the night playing pool and doing shots? How about you, Cos? You in?"

"Absolutely, sir."

Muldoon shook his head. "I can't," he said. "Thanks, Sam, really, but I promised I'd be there, and I keep my promises." Unlike some people who worked in the White House and promised not to turn him into a news story. He looked from Sam to Cosmo and back. "But save me a seat at the bar. I'll definitely be there as soon as I possibly can."

Donny DaCosta actually answered his door when Mary Lou brought him his mail.

He was moving slowly and his eyes looked a little bit as if he'd just spent twelve straight hours on Bourbon Street in New Orleans — the result of his medication, no doubt — but the door opened and he even reached his hand out.

339

"Thanks," he said as he took the pile — now quite large — from her.

"I'm sorry if I hurt your feelings," she said, knowing it was too soon to ask if she could come in. "I didn't mean what I said, Don. I was just . . . wigging out."

He nodded, apparently extremely able to relate to the phenomenon. Or maybe he was nodding merely because it was the easiest and quickest way to get rid of her.

"Let me know if you need anything, hon," she said, as he closed the door.

Mary Lou heard him throw all the locks and bolts as she bent to pick up the baby monitor she'd set down on the steps in order to have both hands free to hand him his mail.

And so life in this neighborhood was returning to normal.

Or at least it would if she'd let it.

Sam would be home tonight. He'd left a message on the answering machine while she was at work this morning, telling her he'd be getting in late. Don't wait up.

She'd still be awake, though, when he did get home. She always was.

Although, wouldn't he be surprised as hell if he got home and she wasn't there?

Yeah, sure. Chances are, he wouldn't miss her for a moment.

Back to normal. Right.

All she'd ever wanted was normal, but normal constantly eluded her. It was always just out of reach, always being disrupted by some pain in the ass problem or situation or stupid phone call, like

340

the one she'd gotten just a few months ago from her sister, Janine, saying she and Clyde were moving all the way across the fucking country to Sarasota, Florida.

First Janine left town, and now Rene was moving, too. Lord, did Mary Lou wear a sign around her neck saying, ABANDON ME?

How could she achieve normal when ugly surprises just kept popping up?

Surprises like waking up in the night to hear Sam call out for another woman while he was fast asleep.

Like finding out that that woman was gorgeous and brilliant — college educated — a former naval officer herself, and some kind of crack FBI sharpshooter to boot.

Mary Lou would bet big money that if she died in a tragic car accident at noon, Sam would be on the phone to that woman — Alyssa Locke — by 2:30 that same afternoon.

But until she did get hit by a bus, Sam would just keep on coming home to pay the bills, to fling Haley around a little bit if she wasn't already asleep, to fall into bed exhausted, and then get up and out of the house, usually before dawn, to do it all again.

Was that really the *normal* she wanted to live with?

Mary Lou wanted to cry.

Ihbraham's truck was parked down the street, and she walked toward it, suddenly desperately wanting to see his smile. She made sure she could still hear the gurgle of the white-noise machine in Haley's room through the baby monitor's little speaker as she moved farther from her house.

He saw her and came to meet her, wiping his face and hands with a ragged towel he took from the back of his truck.

"I'm glad to see you today, Mary Lou," he said, his lilting accent making her name sound like the lyrics to a pop song. "Is everything all right?"

She forced a smile. "What, can you read my mind now, too?"

He laughed. "It would be a handy skill to have, but no. You're usually home in the afternoons, but you weren't yesterday, and then you weren't at your usual meeting last night. I must admit I was a little worried."

Ihbraham came to her usual meeting last night, looking for her. That was so sweet.

"Afraid I went on a binge?" she asked.

"No," he said. "No, no. I knew you would call me before you did something like that. I was afraid someone was sick, or that there'd been a death in your family. You told me your mother's health is failing. I thought . . ."

"That I rushed to Georgia to sit at her deathbed and hold her hand?" Would she go if her mother was dying? Maybe she would. Definitely, if asked. But her mother wouldn't ask. She'd be far more interested in holding hands with a bottle of gin. "No, I spent the morning picking up my car from the body shop with . . . a friend."

She knew he'd noticed her hesitation. He noticed everything.

"He took me and Haley to lunch after that," she

told him, wanting to tell him all of it. "It's this guy, Bob, I met at the library. He's really nice. He's . . ." She shook her head, rolled her eyes. "Who am I kidding? He's definitely hitting on me. He asked me to have dinner with him tonight. Lunch is one thing. I mean, Haley was with us. But dinner . . . ? Don't you think he's hitting on me?"

"It sounds as if he is." Ihbraham sat down on the curb. "He knows you're married, this Bob?"

"Yeah, he does." Mary Lou sat next to him.

"Then maybe he's not so nice, after all."

"Maybe he's just really lonely." She knew what that was like.

He nodded. "Maybe. Still. A good, honest man knows that he shouldn't have dinner with another man's wife."

"Part of me really wanted to say yes," Mary Lou admitted. "Sam's not going to be home until late tonight and . . . Do you think I'm awful?"

He shook his head. "No."

"I used to be really pretty," she told him, wanting him to understand. "Men used to ask me to dinner all the time."

Ihbraham looked at her. "Motherhood has taken away mere pretty. It has made you truly beautiful. It has revealed your generous nature."

Mary Lou had to look away from him. Lord, she was actually blushing. It was the weirdest thing. There was nothing even remotely — what was that word he'd used with her before? — *salacious* in his eyes, and yet she'd never felt so completely over-whelmed before just from gazing back at a man. It was as if he could see inside of her, clear through to her soul.

She wondered what it would feel like to kiss a man with a beard like Ihbraham's. What would it be like to make love to a man with such warm, all-seeing, yet gentle eyes?

Not that *that* would ever happen.

"Maybe you should go to a meeting tonight instead," he suggested. "Especially if you didn't get to one last night."

"I did," she said. "After lunch, I called Rene. My AA sponsor." Desperate to talk to someone after spending all that time with Bob, she'd actually called Ihbraham first, but he wasn't at home. "Haley and I went over to her place — she asked us to come out, so we did. We had dinner with her, and then went to a meeting together."

"That's good," he said.

"No, actually it's bad. She wanted me to come over so that she could tell me she's moving to San Francisco next month," Mary Lou told him. "It's too far away for her to be my sponsor anymore. I mean, maybe we could do it with long-distance phone calls, but . . . that would be pretty expensive. And Rene thinks I need to find someone right here in San Diego. She thinks I'm not ready yet for a long-distance sponsor."

"And what do you think?"

"Well, I guess I think she's right," Mary Lou said. "I'm just . . . I'm real sad to see her go. I don't have a whole lot of friends. Not since I stopped drinking." She looked at him. "In fact, it's down to you and crazy Don, now. And slimy ol' Bob, who probably has his radar set for pathetic, sex-starved married women who just want someone to want to be with them. I'm not having dinner with him. Not ever. He's no kind of real friend. Unless he seriously wants to be with me. In that case, he's looking pretty good."

Ihbraham just looked at her.

"I'm pathetic," she said. "I'm just completely pathetic. Someone should just kill me now."

"Don't say that."

"Yeah," Mary Lou said. "I know. I didn't mean it. If I wasn't here, who would take care of Haley? Not Sam, that's for damn sure." She stood up, brushing off the seat of her jeans. "I'll let you get back to work. I've got to wake up Haley — we've got an errand to run. They put a new trunk lid on my car, and it actually locks now, but there was only one key. I figure I better get it copied before I do something stupid and lose it." She paused. "You wouldn't happen to know if there's any place around here that copies keys?"

Ihbraham stood up, too. "There's a gardening center with a hardware section about four miles from here. Near my apartment. I have to go there this afternoon to pick up some grass seed. If you wish, I can take your key — copy it for you."

"Would you really?" Hope flared, but then quickly died. No, that wouldn't work. "But then you'd have to come all the way back."

"Are you going to a meeting tonight?" he asked. "We could plan to meet there."

"I guess I am," she said. "Over at the Catholic church."

"Good then," he said. "This way you don't have to wake Haley."

"Are you sure you don't mind?" she asked.

"It will be no trouble, I assure you. In fact, I'll

look forward to seeing you and Haley later."

Mary Lou nodded as she took her set of keys from her pocket and pulled the trunk key off the chain. She would look forward to seeing him, too. Way more than she would've looked forward to dinner with Bob Schwegel.

As he took the key from her, his fingers were warm against her hand. Warm, and very dark brown.

"Oh," she said. "I should give you the money to pay for it. Let me run inside."

He waved her off as he pocketed the key. "You can give it to me later. I'll bring you the receipt. One key won't cost very much."

"Thank you," she told him. "You're a good friend."

Who would have ever thought in a million years that she would become such good friends with a nearly black-skinned Arab man?

Who, for that matter, would have guessed that she could marry the man of her dreams — a real-life hero — and get exactly what she'd always wanted in terms of a home and financial security, and *still* be dissatisfied?

Life could be pretty damn weird.

SIXTEEN

It was 1748 that night before Muldoon found Joan.

Upon his arrival at the Hotel del Coronado, he was escorted up to a spacious suite that was, he was told, his room. He was told to please wait here.

Despite the fact that he didn't particularly want or need a room at the hotel since he lived only a few minutes away, it was nice enough. It had a third-story view of the ocean through sliders that led to a balcony.

But with the windows closed, the sound of the crashing surf was muted.

Ten minutes of waiting in that hushed, thickly carpeted, don't-put-your-feet-on-the-furniture silence was all he could stand, and after calling Joan's cell phone and repeatedly getting pushed over to her voice mail, he opened the door, intending to wander out into the corridor.

A man about his own height and build and dressed in a dark business suit was standing right outside the door. He had an earphone in one ear, the cord disappearing under his jacket collar, and a bulge under his left arm from a shoulder holster. "May I help you, sir?" he asked Muldoon.

He was Secret Service — no doubt about it. But

was he there to keep the unwanted, potentially dangerous riffraff out?

Or in?

"I need to speak with Joan DaCosta," Muldoon said. "She doesn't seem to be coming to me, so I thought I'd go looking for her. I know she's around here somewhere."

"I'm sorry, sir. You've been asked to stay here, in your room."

"Actually, I haven't been asked anything," Muldoon said, just as pleasantly. "I've only been told." He was running very low on patience — particularly after seeing his picture all over CNN and finding out that certain White House staff members were planning his wedding to a woman he'd never even met.

"I'm sorry, sir." The agent sounded anything but sorry. "But I can't let you out into the hall without authorization."

It was absurd. In fact, it was positively ridiculous. Was it possible that this whole thing was Joan's idea of a bad joke?

From down the corridor, possibly even from the next room over, he could hear the unmistakable sound of her laughter.

"Look," he told the agent, trying his best to sound not even remotely pissed off, "she's just down that way. I can hear her. I'd like to —"

"I'm sure she'll be here soon then," the agent said. "I'm going to have to ask you to step back into the room and wait for her there. There's a room service menu on the table, sir."

Oh, food made it all better. Right.

As much as he longed to put his fist in this guy's

smug face, Muldoon knew that that would be a mistake. If he really wanted to get into a brawl to blow off a little steam, he could do it easily enough later, in the parking lot of the Ladybug with Sam and Cosmo.

For the first time in a long time, he actually itched to get into a fight.

Not a good sign.

Maybe if he could talk to Joan and find out what in God's name was going on, everything would make sense and he'd start to feel better.

He closed the door on Smugly and, looking across at that still brightly sunlit balcony, he bolted the locks from the inside. Maybe he couldn't go out into the hall, but now Smugly couldn't come in, either.

The slider to the balcony unlocked easily. He slid the door open and was hit by a breezy gust of fresh air that made the filmy white curtains billow. He brushed past them and stepped outside.

And, sure enough, a child could get from his balcony to the next room's.

Well, okay, an athletic child.

Of course, timing was essential, considering that both balconies were in direct view of the windows of the function room where the admiral's party was due to start in just a short time.

In fact, Muldoon could see what had to be several more Secret Service agents through those windows. He could pick them out just from the way they stood.

He waited until he could see the backs of their heads and then quickly swung himself up onto the rail and . . .

Then there he was, standing nonchalantly on his immediate neighbor's balcony, as if he'd come out to look at the ocean view. He wasn't even breathing hard.

The first of two sliders was closed, the filmy curtain drawn. It was the bedroom, and he moved past it quickly, aware that about five people were in there, one of them sitting on the king-sized bed.

The second slider — the door leading into the suite's sitting room — was open. Muldoon stood there, listening, as he looked inside.

This suite was even bigger than his, and there were at least another half dozen people in various places around the room. The TV was on and tuned to CNN, but the volume was muted — no doubt because nearly everyone in there was talking on their cell phone.

Including Joan, who was over by the bedroom door.

He stepped into the room, and no one so much as gave him a second glance.

"I'm sure time will open up in several weeks," Joan was saying into her phone as Muldoon took a seat not far from her on a cushy sofa with a floral pattern. "Yes." Pause. "Yes, I understand the story's hot now, but there are only twenty-four hours in a day. I'm afraid even you can't —" Pause. "And we appreciate it. We do. And I'm sure you can appreciate Brooke's desire not to schedule television appearances while Lieutenant Muldoon is stateside."

Well, that pretty much took care of any of his lingering doubts. He'd been hoping that Joan had had nothing whatsoever to do with the news stories about his so-called relationship with Brooke Bryant. Yet here she was, spinning it like a pro, making it sound as if he were doing far more with Brooke than merely escorting her to one single party.

"Thank you," she said into the telephone. "I will definitely get back to you before the end of the day, but please don't be offended if . . ." Pause. "That's right. Thank you. *Thank* you." She hung up her phone with a snap. "Jee-zus!" She leaned farther into the bedroom. "Myra. We don't want to do *Larry King Live* tomorrow night, do we?"

"No!" came a shout back.

Joan had her cell phone open and was dialing again. "Yeah, Meredith. Joan. I need a huge-large. In about an hour, call Matt over at *Larry King* and tell him we can't do tomorrow's show. Apologize, send flowers, make sure they know we love them, and that if Brooke were doing any TV appearances, they'd be high on our list." Pause. "Bad," she said. "And, God, I still haven't talked to Mike — we've been playing telephone tag all afternoon." Pause. "Wouldn't *you* be mad? He's here at the hotel, right next door, in fact. I just can't bring myself to go over there." Pause. Laughter. "Yeah. Avoid. Always a good policy. Except I'm going to have to talk to him sooner or later. Right. Later, babe."

Snap.

There was a counter separating a kitchen area from the rest of the room, and Joan put her cell phone down on it and climbed up on one of the stools. "Give me a scotch and soda on the rocks — make it a double," she said to one of the men who was in the kitchen.

"Sorry, this is for Brooke," he said. "You have to wait until you're downstairs for yours."

"I have to wait until tonight is over," she countered. She pointed to the drink. "That's watered down, right? She's already had a few."

He took a sip, testing. "If it's too watery, she'll come out here and add more scotch herself. We definitely don't want that."

"Good point. Grab me a coffee mug while you're back there, will you, Dave?"

"Just what you need — more caffeine," he said, but he took a mug down from the cabinet and slid it along the counter to her.

"Thanks." There was a coffee machine set up right there, the pot half full, and she poured herself a cup. "So she's agreed to go downstairs?"

Dave nodded as she took a sip. "Yeah. She'll do it. But she's pretty upset. Do you trust your guy? Should we let him into the loop?"

"I haven't talked to him yet." Joan put the mug and then her head down on the counter. "Oh, God. I've been putting it off. As of right now, Myra says no. The fewer people who know the real deal, the better." She lifted her head. "I just wish I had been let in a little sooner."

"Welcome to the White House." The man named Dave carried the drink into the bedroom.

As Muldoon watched, Joan sat there, forehead in hand, dressed to the nines in a black evening gown, staring into her coffee. She looked gorgeous. And exhausted.

He refused to feel badly for her. There was no doubt about it now. She'd used him.

With one finger, she made her cell phone spin on the counter.

Muldoon took out his own phone and dialed her number.

Across the room, Joan's phone shrilled, and she sat up. She opened it up, looked at the number on its screen — his — and made a face. "Shit."

Not too happy to hear from him, apparently.

She didn't blow him off, though. She braced herself, took a deep breath, exhaled hard, then punched the talk button and brought the phone to her ear. "Hey, Mike." She managed to sound practically cheerful.

"Hey, Joan. Am I just going to sit here in suspense all night or are you going to bother to explain to me what the hell is going on?"

Across the room, her head was in her hands again. "Oh, Mike, I am so sorry. I had no idea it would get out of hand like this. And then that picture of you appeared and —"

"It appeared," he said. "You didn't go searching for it?"

"Absolutely not."

"And I should believe you because . . . ?"

"Because I value your friendship. And because I have no reason to lie to you."

"Ah," he said. "But when you *do* have reason to lie, that's when I should look out, huh? Like when you want to set me up so you can send out a press release announcing that Brooke and I have been exchanging email? Or maybe you don't think writing and sending email in someone else's name is lying."

Joan's back stiffened. "You knew?"

"Yeah," he told her. "How about that? I'm not as dumb as I look."

"I never thought you were dumb." Joan slipped off the stool and moved across the room, right past him, literally inches from his white shoes, over to the sliders and out onto the balcony. Clearly, she wanted a little privacy. "I just . . . Brooke didn't want to write to you. She's . . . I can't tell you the details about what's going on here. I wish I could. I can only tell you that she's been distracted lately. I'm sorry, I know that's not enough, but . . . She asked me to send you a reply, to use her email address and sign her name, so I did. I should have sent a stock message, 'Looking forward to seeing you, blah, blah, blah.' I didn't, and you wrote back and I . . . It was a mistake and I'm sorry, but I swear to you that I wasn't trying to set you up for this current media circus. I know that's what you're thinking, but it's just not what happened."

As she spoke, he got to his feet and moved to the balcony door. She was standing out there, all by herself.

"Okay," he said into his telephone as he stepped outside, too. "I'm listening. What *did* happen?"

Joan did a double take as he leaned against the railing right next to her. "Who let you . . ." She realized she was still talking into her telephone, and she snapped it shut. "Who let you into Brooke's room?" she asked him directly.

Muldoon closed his phone, too, and put it into his pocket as he gazed at her. "I let myself in. I got tired of waiting. Good thing I did. Obviously you weren't in any rush to come talk to me."

"It wasn't supposed to happen this way," she said, looking him squarely in the eye. "None of this. My boss called me yesterday and said, 'Tell me about this Lt. Michael Muldoon who's listed on our sheet as Brooke's escort to tomorrow night's party in Coronado.'

"So I told her that you were a really great guy who'd volunteered to walk into the room with Brooke on your arm and to stand there, next to her, looking gorgeous and heroic while everyone stared.

"And *she* goes, 'Did you know she's been exchanging email with him?'

"And I said, 'Oops, boss, that wasn't Brooke, that was me.'

"And she said, 'Don't tell me that — I don't want to know. As far as I'm concerned, Brooke and the lieutenant have been corresponding and they're an item. It will be to everyone's advantage — particularly the President's — if we leak the story that she's dating a hero.'

"And I said, 'Don't use his name. Call him an officer in the Navy SEALs, if you must. And whatever you do, don't mention that he spent any time in Afghanistan — we don't know for a fact that he was there.'

"The story went out," Joan continued, "and all the major news organizations wanted a piece of it. We didn't give them any more information, but someone apparently leaked a copy of Brooke's schedule and your name was on it. Like I said, I honestly had no idea —"

"Oh, come on," Muldoon said. She made a convincing argument, particularly when she looked up

355

at him with those big brown eyes, but he wasn't that naive. "You work with the media. You expect me to believe you didn't know they'd jump on this story? That they wouldn't be satisfied until they IDed that 'unnamed SEAL officer'?"

Joan looked out at the water. "Yeah, that was stupid of me, wasn't it?"

"A little too stupid," he agreed.

She turned to face him. "Whether you believe me or not doesn't matter right now. What matters is whether you'll help us out — help the President — and put in an appearance with Brooke at this party tonight."

"I'm here," Muldoon said. "Aren't I?"

She nodded. "Yes, you are. And you look fabulous." She forced a smile. "Are you sure you're not going to fall over from the weight of all those medals?"

Muldoon didn't crack a smile. He didn't even blink as he gazed back at her. "I'd like to get this over with, if possible. I'm meeting some of the guys for a beer and a game of pool as soon as I'm done here."

"Okay. You're still pissed. I get it. But are you sure that's smart?" she asked. "Shouldn't you keep a low profile, at least for a while? You know, I've made arrangements for you to have a room here at the hotel for as long as you need it. You're on the same floor as Brooke, and you'll have Secret Service protection as well, any time you're off the naval base. I mean, if you want it."

"Why would I want it?" he asked.

"Because of that picture of you running down the side of a mountain with — God — a broken kneecap," Joan said. "Because your name is all over the news. Because it's now common knowledge that you're a SEAL and that you spent time in Afghanistan."

He realized exactly what she was thinking. He might have been pleased at her concern for him — if she hadn't used him so completely.

"You think now I'm going to be a terrorist target or something?" He made a rude noise. "Just let them try. Come and get me, Osama."

"But —"

"I don't need it," he told her. "I don't need the hotel room, I don't need the Secret Service getting in my way, thanks but no thanks."

"But you said . . . When I wanted to set up a photo op with Kelly and Meg and some of the other wives . . .''

"That's a different deal entirely," Muldoon said. "We don't take any chances with our families. But as for us — believe me, we can take care of ourselves. Now, do you mind if we get this show on the road? I've got things to do."

Charlotte stayed in the car again as Vince checked in on Donny before they went out to a movie.

Tonight was some big important event over at the Del, something that Joanie had been worried about. She hadn't said as much, but Charlie knew her granddaughter quite well.

And then that news story broke — the one about Brooke Bryant dating that young man of Joan's.

After seeing Lieutenant Muldoon with Joan the other day, and knowing that it was Joan's job to

357

help keep Brooke's mischief — if you could call it that — from the public eye, Charlie thought the whole thing smelled like a decoy story. It smelled like something made up to draw the reporters away from the real story, which — whatever it was — probably put the President's daughter in a far less positive light.

And if that was the case, poor Lieutenant Muldoon. He was probably going in circles right about now, trying to figure out which way was up.

Joan, poor dear, was probably still in intense denial. No doubt she wasn't being very much help.

Charlotte could relate. She'd spent quite a long time in denial herself.

Yes, she had been kidding herself completely that night that she'd put on her nightgown — not her best one, but rather the cotton one that James had always loved most. It looked innocent and sweet in its simplicity. But if the light was shining from behind her, the outline of her body was clearly visible.

Her heart had pounded as she brushed out her hair, letting it fall loose and gleaming around her shoulders. Her hands and feet tingled with a mixture of fear and anticipation as she dabbed the tiniest amount of perfume behind her ears and between her breasts.

She wanted to be touched so very badly. But that wasn't why she was doing this, she'd told herself. Ah, denial! She'd convinced herself that this wasn't for her.

This was for Vince. To save Vince. To keep him from going back to that fighting and death.

Upstairs, Sally still hadn't returned to her habit

358

of sharing her bed with the entire First Infantry or 101st Airborne or whoever was passing through D.C. at the moment. Still, Charlie had waited until after midnight. It was going to be hard enough to do this without having the bedspring serenade squeaking in the background. But when she heard Sally turn off her radio and go — alone — into her bedroom, there was no longer a reason to delay.

With a last silent and heartfelt apology to James, Charlie took a deep breath and went into the hall, turning on the light switch with a click.

Vince's door was closed.

She knocked on it softly even as she opened it. "Vince, are you still awake?"

He sat up in bed. "Is something . . ." He saw her standing there. "Uh, is, um, something wrong?"

Charlotte felt herself blush, knowing that from where he sat, with the hall light streaming in from behind her, it was almost as if she were standing there naked.

At least he didn't seem to be too horrified. In fact, the expression on his face was a mixture of awe and disbelief and hope.

It gave her the strength she needed not to run away. This was going to work. She almost wept with relief.

"I need to talk to you," she told him instead. "May I come in?"

She didn't wait for him to answer. She crossed to the dresser and turned on the lamp that sat there before she went back and closed the door. Still strategically lit from behind, she moved toward him and sat down beside him on the bed.

He was trying to be polite, to keep his eyes on her face, but he couldn't keep his gaze from dropping down to her breasts. He didn't say a word as he looked at her. He just waited for her to speak.

There was no need to do anything other than get directly to the point. "Do you still want to marry me?"

"Charlotte, what are you doing?" he asked quietly, the muscles jumping in his jaw.

She put her hand lightly on the lump beneath the covers that was his leg. "I'm making you an offer that I hope you can't refuse. Marry me, Vince."

She was being shockingly bold, and she felt another rush of heat to her face.

He took her hand from his leg — his hand was warm, his fingers big and square and roughened from work. It was a man's hand. He may have been younger than she was, but his hands were that of a grown man.

"You're cold," he said, still in that same quiet, gentle voice. "Maybe you should get a robe. Then we can talk."

This wasn't happening the way she'd imagined. He wanted to talk. When she'd run this scenario in her head, he was already kissing her by now.

But he was definitely keeping his distance. And she *was* cold.

She pulled back the covers and slipped into bed beside him, shocking them both.

"Charlotte —"

"Please don't tell me to leave!" She reached for Vince and found the warm flannel of James's pajamas covering his hard, lean body. She fit against him perfectly, and his arms — as they went around her — felt so warm and solid, so familiar, just from the few times he'd held her in the past weeks. It shouldn't have been, but it was like coming home.

He was so different, physically, from James. James, whose memory had started to blur around the edges. It was all she could do not to cry.

Vince held her tightly. "God, Charlie, I won't. I'm not that strong, I'm sorry to admit. I just . . . I really don't want you to do something that you're not ready for."

She may not have been ready, but he certainly was. At close proximity like this, his desire for her was undeniable.

"Do you really want to marry me?" he asked her.

"Yes," she told him. "I've thought about it, and yes, I really do." She might've sounded more convincing if her voice hadn't shook. "We can take the train up to Maryland and get married right away. Tomorrow."

He laughed. "You're serious." There was wonder in his voice, and he pulled back slightly from her so that he could look down into her eyes.

"I've never been more serious about anything in my life." Somehow she managed to hold his gaze.

"Ah, God, Charlie," he whispered.

And then he finally kissed her.

It was not the kiss that she'd imagined, however. Oh, it started that way — sweet and practically reverent. But she was the one who opened her mouth wide to him. She was the one who deepened that kiss, who came close to swallowing him whole. She was the one who took his hand and placed it upon her breast, who leaned into him, and who actually moaned aloud at the sensation.

For someone inexperienced in the ways of the flesh, Vince had her beneath him in a record amount of time. She could feel him, heavy against her leg, and knew that it wouldn't take much effort on his part for him to join them. God knows her body was willing even if her soul was stunned at the fact that this was actually happening.

She'd imagined this, but she hadn't dreamed she'd feel this way.

And if James were watching from somewhere in heaven, surely he understood that this wasn't about him, that she was doing this to keep Vince safe.

"God, I love you!" Vince kissed her face, her jaw, her throat. "I'll do everything in my power to make you happy, I swear I will. Tell me what to do. Tell me what you want. Tell me how to make love to you — how to make it last an hour."

He was dead serious and as he kissed her again, it was all she could do not to laugh. Or cry. Did she really want him to know what she liked? Did she really want him kissing her where only James had kissed her, touching her, stroking her where only James had touched and stroked?

Yes!

No.

"I don't know," she admitted. "It's different for women and men, and . . ." She touched his face, hoping he couldn't tell how close to tears she still was.

His love for her was so clearly written in his eyes. "I want this to be perfect."

She didn't. She didn't want it to be anything

362

close to perfect. She just wanted . . . relief. And the knowledge that Vince was going to be safe.

"It doesn't have to be perfect right away," she told him. "Really. We'll have a whole lifetime to get it right."

"I've only got a week."

"No," she said. "You see, that's just the thing. If you're my husband, you can still serve in the Marines, but the senator can pull some strings for us. I know he can. His influence, along with the fact that, well . . ." It was hard to choke out her husband's name while Vince lay between her legs. She rushed the words. "James won a Medal of Honor. We can keep you stationed here in Washington. It can be done. It's not talked about, but I know it's done."

But Vincent was shaking his head. "I can't do that."

"There are positions," she said, "*important* positions here in Washington, that need to be filled by *some*one. You'll still be serving your country, Vince."

"Sweetheart, I'm an experienced combat veteran."

"Yes," she said. "You are. It makes more sense for you to stay home then. You've done more than your share."

He sighed. "Charlie, come on. You know that's not how it works."

"Please." She kissed him, pressed herself up against him. "Please don't go back . . ."

But Vince rolled off of her to lie on his back beside her, his eyes closed. "Shit! Excuse me. I'm sorry. I'm . . . God, you don't know how sorry I am."

She reached for him, but he pulled himself out from under the covers. It was rather obvious just how sorry he was, and he quickly sat down on the far edge of the bed. "I guess the big question now is, do you really want to marry a guy who could end up just as dead as James?"

Her eyes flooded with tears that she could no longer blink back, and the overflow escaped. She brushed them fiercely away. "I thought I could make you want to stay."

He turned to look at her. "There's nothing in this world I want more than to spend the next eighty years right here with you. But I'm not the only man in the Marines who's in love with someone incredible."

Charlotte held out her hand to him. "Please, will you let me try to convince you?"

He looked at her fingers, saw her tears, but didn't reach to take her hand. His face was so serious. "Will you marry me after, even when I tell you that I still have to leave?"

She couldn't deceive him and she let her hand drop to the blanket below. "No."

Vince nodded. "Do you . . ." He cleared his throat. "Do you honestly love me, Charlie?"

She didn't want to answer that, but her silence was just as revealing.

"Ah," he said.

"I don't want you to die," she told him.

"That's what this is really about, isn't it?" he asked. He laughed softly. "Wow. You *really* don't want me to die, huh? My God."

"Is that so awful?" she said. "I care about you, Vince, I do —"

"But you still love James."

She couldn't deny that.

"And yet you're willing to . . . to give yourself to me as some kind of prize. Some kind of virgin sacrifice. You're the sacrifice and I'm the virgin — that's a nice twist, huh? But I'm supposed to be so grateful to you and so enthralled that I simply throw away everything I believe in because making love to you is so great?"

"You're twisting it all around."

"Am I?" he asked.

She climbed out of bed, wanting him to understand. "You don't know what it was like, waiting for news after Pearl Harbor was attacked. I can't do that again. I can't spend the next five years or however long this awful war lasts terrified that I'm going to get another of those telegrams. And I am *not* going to bury another husband."

"You're not going to *have* another husband," he told her, quiet again, "until you manage to bury your first. God, you're beautiful, but I want more than your body, Charlotte." He turned away from her. "I think you better go."

She went.

Back to her room where, knowing how thin the walls in this house were, she cried as quietly as she could.

"So you're my consolation prize."

Brooke Bryant was more than just a little bit drunk. Joan could see it in her eyes and in the looseness of her movements as she held out her hand to Muldoon in greeting.

Muldoon glanced at Joan before he answered

Brooke. "Yes, ma'am. That seems to be what I am."

"You're a little young," Brooke said.

The staff from the White House had discussed the Brooke-Muldoon age difference for several hours. Considering the alternatives, it was decided that it would be addressed in their press releases. They would call Brooke "young at heart," and Muldoon would be a "mature young officer accustomed to a great deal of responsibility." Whatever they did, though, the fifteen-year difference would be noticed and commented on. On late-night TV, Brooke would probably be the butt of more than one cradle-robbing joke because of it. But the positive press far outweighed the negative in this case.

"Although someone with all those medals on his chest can't be too young, can he?" Brooke continued. "So sure, why the hell not?"

"My thoughts exactly," Muldoon said, again with another look in Joan's direction. When he looked back at Brooke, he bestowed his best smile upon her. It wasn't as good as his genuine one, but it was pretty damn close. "You look beautiful tonight, ma'am."

Her gown was a deep shade of red that few women could wear. Brooke managed, as she always did, to look amazing. The gown was low cut and it seemed to be held on by a single tied bow in the back. When Joan first saw what Brooke was wearing, she'd started praying that the bow didn't accidentally come undone while she was greeting Admirals Tucker and Crowley.

There was a picture she didn't want on page one of *USA Today*.

"Thank you, darling," Brooke said. "So do you. Although, if we're going to fool anyone into thinking we've been fucking for weeks now, you might want to call me something other than *ma'am*. Unless we want the press to speculate on the intimate details of our so-called relationship. Of course, maybe we should drop them a few hints." She turned to look for Dick. "What do you think, Dick? How about if Lieutenant Muldoon mentions to the press that I'm particularly good at giving head? Because surely the idea of me going down on a hero would boost my father's popularity rating."

Okay.

Myra and Dick pulled Brooke aside, as Joan took Muldoon's arm and dragged him off a few feet.

"I'm so sorry," she said. "She's not usually like this. She's drunk."

"She's pissed at being manipulated. I can relate."

"Will you do me a favor? When you get downstairs, try to keep her from having another drink."

Muldoon laughed. "She's a grown-up. I can't make her do anything she doesn't want to do — including not drink."

"You can steer her away from the bar," Joan said. "Please?"

He didn't answer right away. He just stood there looking at her. "I don't think I owe you any favors right now," he finally said.

Oh, God. Joan closed her eyes briefly. She felt terrible. "I've apologized, Michael. I've tried to explain that I didn't mean for any of this to happen —"

"Except for the part where I escort Brooke to this party," he interrupted. "That *was* your idea, thanks so much."

"One you didn't seem to mind," she countered sharply. "Especially when you called me up and asked for advice on how to make sure Brooke went home with you tonight, because you thought she was so hot . . ." Because of her email. Which Joan had written. Which Muldoon had known that Joan had written, which really meant . . . that he'd thought *Joan* was hot?

She looked up at Muldoon and saw him watching her, waiting for her to figure it out.

"You lied to me, too," she said. It was not what she should have said, but unfortunately it was the first thing to fly out of her big mouth.

"No," he said. "Not really. I was just being stupid. I got it into my head that maybe you'd get jealous or, shoot, I don't know. Notice me at least. I was going to come back here and lay it on the line — tell you I'm crazy about you. Make it clear that I don't think of you as any kind of a sister." He laughed. "Yeah, I had it all figured out. I was going to tell you that I think you're a goddess and that I'd love to be your personal slave. That was how you put it, wasn't it? Except now that I've been handed off to Brooke as a *consolation prize* without a single word of protest from you, I'm not sure that I think so highly of you anymore."

Joan didn't know what to say. She didn't know what to think. She could barely even breathe. She'd received plenty of criticism and her fair share of reprimands throughout her life, but nothing had ever stabbed as deeply as Muldoon's quiet words.

And to have it come on top of the news that he was crazy about her . . . ?

"I'm good at carrying out orders," he continued. "Apparently tonight's involve making the world believe Brooke and I have a relationship. Okay. You got it. Can do. And who knows? Maybe by tomorrow morning, it'll be true. It can be a night of consolation prizes all around. Except for you. You get to win big, right?"

Brooke was done being lectured by Myra and Dick, and there was no time for Joan to defend herself or rebut or even say anything to Muldoon at all.

"I've been ordered to muzzle it," Brooke said as she took his arm. "Under pain of death, I suppose. Shall we face the gauntlet with our heads held high?"

"Brooke," Joan said. "Lieutenant Muldoon is not your consolation prize. He's not any kind of a prize. He's a . . . a friend of mine, and I'd appreciate it if you treated him with respect."

"Don't worry, darling," Brooke called over her shoulder. Muldoon didn't even glance back. "I'll take very good care of him."

"Brooke, I'm serious!"

"I am, too," she said.

Joan followed them to the elevators, but with all the Secret Service agents piling in behind them, she had to wait for the next one. As the doors closed, Muldoon didn't even look at her. He was busy smiling at something Brooke said.

He was wrong.

Joan wasn't the one who was winning big here. She wasn't even close.

SEVENTEEN

"And where exactly do you live?" Mary Lou asked.

Ihbraham pointed with the hand that wasn't holding Haley to one of a row of nondescript apartment buildings across the street from the church. "I have a studio apartment on the fifth floor. It's pretty small but it's economical. Right now I have more important things upon which to spend my money."

"I know what *that's* about," she told him.

They'd come down here to an AA meeting in Ihbraham's neighborhood, because when they arrived at the Catholic church up by her house, the meeting room was being painted. There was a sign directing them to another location across town, but Ihbraham shook his head. It was a part of the city he wasn't comfortable even driving through.

That was when they decided to come down here. This meeting started a full hour later than most in the city, and it was a larger, open meeting, with chairs set up in anonymous rows instead of a more intimate circle.

They'd sat in the back, near the door, in case Haley decided to go ballistic.

The meeting was crowded, and the message, although not at all new, was a good one. Don't drink tonight. Worry about tomorrow when tomorrow dawned.

Instead of fighting to the front of the room for some store-bought refreshments, and since Haley was still wide awake and at her charming best after having spent the meeting sitting on Ihbraham's lap and playing with his set of keys, they decided to go down the block to a little place that served ice cream.

As usual, many people in the meeting had lit up cigarettes immediately upon exiting the church.

"She could lose it any second," Mary Lou warned Ihbraham, pushing the stroller alongside of him as they navigated their way through the crowd. Even though it was night, the sidewalks in this part of the city were bright as day. "I can take her now, if you want."

"Haley and I have reached an understanding," Ihbraham said, giving Mary Lou one of what she had begun to think of as his nuclear-powered smiles. "If she won't pull my beard, I'll carry her — which we all know is more fun than riding in that stroller. Isn't that right, little one?"

He turned his smile on Haley, who laughed and clapped her hands, then reached out to hug Ihbraham tightly around the neck.

For a moment he actually looked rattled. But only for a moment. Then he laughed, too.

"She really likes you," Mary Lou said. "Don't you, jelly bean?"

"I like you, too, Haley," Ihbraham told her daughter. He spoke to her as if she were full grown and able to understand his every word. He didn't talk down to her the way Bob did. Of course what Bob did was better than Sam, who just plain didn't talk to her at all.

Sure, he tickled her and flew her through the air and made raspberry noises on her neck.

Of course, Mary Lou didn't know what Sam did when she wasn't around. It was possible he discussed physics with Haley then — but she wouldn't bet on it.

"Isn't that the best feeling in the world?" she asked Ihbraham. "To get a hug like that from someone so, I don't know, so . . . pure and perfect?"

"It is probably one of them," he agreed. "Yes."

"It's kind of like hugging God." Mary Lou laughed self-consciously. "Lordy, listen to me. I sound like I have a future writing sappy greeting cards. 'Course, I happen to love sappy greeting cards."

Not that she ever got more than one or two a year.

Still, she loved looking at them in the grocery store. *Thinking of you* . . . Damn, someday she wanted to get a card from someone that said *Thinking of you* . . . on the front. Problem was, no one ever was thinking of her.

"Do you ever think of me," she asked Ihbraham, "you know, when I'm not around?"

The look he shot her was indecipherable and he didn't answer her — at least not right away.

"I think of you at certain times, yes," he said.

"I'm sorry, that was actually a pretty dumb question," she apologized. "I shouldn't have asked, because what are you going to say? No, you never think of me at all? I mean, even if it's true . . ."

"It's not. At the very least, I remember you in my prayers," he told her.

Mary Lou stopped walking. "Well now, I think that that might be the nicest thing anyone's ever said to me."

"Mary Lou! Hey, it *is* you. I thought I saw you and Haley sitting in the back of the church."

She turned, blinking like mad to cover up the fact that her eyes had welled with tears, only to see Bob Schwegel, Insurance Sales, pushing his way out of the crowd in front of the church doors.

What was he doing here? And wasn't this awkward, considering she'd left a message on his machine telling him that she couldn't have dinner with him tonight — that something important had come up.

He was dressed down in blue jeans and the kind of shirt Sam swore he wouldn't be caught dead wearing — one of those nice short-sleeved polo shirts with a collar.

He'd already extended his hand to Ihbraham. "Bob Schwegel, Insurance Sales. You must be . . ." Bob looked from Haley's blond curls and blue eyes to Ihbraham's jet-black hair and mahogany-colored skin and frowned slightly. "Mr. Starrett . . . ?"

Mary Lou shrieked with laughter. "Oh, God, no! You thought he was my . . . ? No, no, this is Ihbraham Rahman. He's . . ."

And just then she realized just how it must look, with Ihbraham holding Haley like that, with the two of them strolling down the sidewalk, as if they were — Lord save her — a couple. If she called him her friend, Bob might well assume they were intimate friends — and wouldn't *that* be mortifying. Yet if she introduced him as the guy who did the neighbors' yard work, well, that wouldn't sound too good either — like she was getting it on with the pool boy.

"He's my AA sponsor," she flat-out lied, because everyone in the program knew that it was seriously frowned upon for a person to have a sexual relationship with her sponsor.

Ihbraham looked at her, and she felt her face heat in a blush. He didn't contradict her, though, thank goodness.

"Ah," Bob said. "Yeah, I was wondering what you were doing down here in my neck of the woods. My office is right around the corner. I attend this meeting pretty often because it starts at eight o'clock — I can work late if I have to."

"I didn't know you were in the program," she said.

"For just over a year now." He smiled at her. "It took the breakup of my marriage to get me in the door. Too little, too late, my ex says. I don't think I agree."

"It's never too late." Mary Lou reached over to keep Haley from grabbing Ihbraham's earring. "Sorry," she told him before turning back to Bob. "I got really tanked a few times when I was first pregnant with Haley. But then my downstairs neighbor gave me this article on FAS — fetal alcohol syndrome. She was like, 'Look what you've gone and done.'"

A car drove past, its horn blaring. It double-parked just around the corner up ahead. Ihbraham's eyes narrowed slightly as he watched it, and he handed Haley back to Mary Lou.

"That article scared the bejeezus out of me," she continued, telling her story to Bob as she settled Haley on her hip, "and you know, I could've assumed that the damage had already been done and just kept on drinking. But instead I thought, Lord, if I'm going to have a baby with all these problems, then she *really* better have a mother who's stone cold sober all the time."

"Excuse me," Ihbraham said. "I'll be right back."

"I went to my first meeting that very night," she told Bob as Ihbraham headed toward the double-parked car. It was brand-new, one of those enormous cars that was just one step down from a limo. A Town Car, she thought they were called.

What was Ihbraham doing?

Three men had gotten out and had come up onto the sidewalk. They were just as darkly complexioned as Ihbraham, but their hair was shorter and their clothes more expensive. Two of them wore suits; the third wore a shiny sweat suit. They all looked angry, but then again, Ihbraham always looked angry from a distance, too.

One of them pointed at Ihbraham and let loose a stream of gibberish. Well, of course it wasn't gibberish to him. And probably not to Ihbraham, either.

"I had a lot of tests done," she said to Bob, still watching Ihbraham and his friends with one eye. "Amnio and some other stuff that came back looking good — and I did a lot of praying. And I got lucky. Really lucky, thank you, Lord Jesus. Because Haley's fine. Your marriage might be over, Bob, but somewhere out there, there's good luck waiting to happen to you. I just know it."

Bob was watching Ihbraham, who was now surrounded by the three other men. "How well do you know this guy?" he asked. "I mean, you must know him pretty well if he's your sponsor, right?"

"Uh, yeah," she said. "I've known him for . . ." Had it really only been a few days since she threw her keys into the Robinsons' garden? It seemed as if she'd been friends with Ihbraham for close to forever. "A while."

"Where's he from? How did you meet him?"

On the corner, one of the men gave Ihbraham a solid push, causing him to step back a few feet toward a chain-link fence that cordoned off a construction zone. Ihbraham had his hands out in front of him in a gesture of peace. It was very clear that he didn't want to fight with these men, whoever they were.

"He's a landscaper in my neighborhood," she said. "He's very good with flowers."

Bob laughed. "I bet. So what, did he just show up one day? Where did he come from?"

"You make it sound as if he's a stalker or something."

"Yeah, well, maybe he is."

She rolled her eyes. "That's silly."

"Is it?"

"Yes," she said.

"You really trust him, huh? I'm not sure I would, with a name like Ihbraham Rahman. I mean, look at him. He could be the poster boy for al-Qaeda."

"Well, he's not, and you're being racist to assume —"

The man with the sweat suit shoved Ihbraham so hard that he fell back against the fence, making it rattle loudly. Dear Lord, they were going to beat him up.

"Hey!" Mary Lou started toward them. "Leave him alone!"

One of the men said something she couldn't understand, and the two others laughed.

Ihbraham launched himself at his attackers, managing to bloody one of the men's noses even as he sent another to the sidewalk with a kick to the knee and an elbow to the back of the head. It happened so fast, she would have missed it if she'd blinked. The third man quickly moved back out of range — no doubt terrified by the murderous look in Ihbraham's eyes.

He spoke to them then, in that same strange language, and they dragged themselves back to their car. But not without babbling back at him — getting in the last word, no doubt.

Ihbraham let them. But he stood there, silently glaring, as they drove away.

"Are you all right?" Mary Lou asked, hiking Haley farther up on her hip.

He was still breathing hard, and it took him a moment to pull his eyes away from the car's disappearing taillights, glowing red in the night. His face was hard, and his eyes were cold. But then he blinked, and the Ihbraham she knew was back. "I'm very sorry about that."

"Who were they?" she asked as Bob finally

caught up with her, pushing the stroller she'd left farther down the sidewalk.

Ihbraham ran his hands down his face. "They were my brothers."

"What did they want?" she asked.

He just shook his head, glancing at Bob.

Mary Lou turned to Bob, holding out her hand for him to shake. "It was nice seeing you. I'm sure we'll run into each other again before too long."

He took the hint, and although he squeezed her fingers meaningfully, he started backing away. "I'm sure we will, Mary Lou. Nice meeting you, Mr. Rahman."

And then he was gone and there she was. Standing on a city sidewalk, looking up at Ihbraham, who was ruefully examining a hole torn in his shirt.

"What did they want?" she asked again.

Haley, of course, picked that exact moment to start to fuss. She went almost instantly from mildly annoyed to completely inconsolable. A sniff test and a pat to the bottom revealed that her diaper was clean and not entirely soggy.

Mary Lou knew only one way to quiet Haley down fast. But where to go for a little semiprivacy? She looked around.

Back the way they had come was the church where the meeting had been held. It had a small side yard with a bench. She'd parked right next to it in the church lot. The entire area was lit with a floodlight, but at least she could sit with her back to the street.

"Grab the stroller, would you, hon?" she asked Ihbraham.

Haley was in full wail by the time Mary Lou hit the bench, and she pulled up both her shirt and bra without ceremony.

Then, oh, blissful silence. Of course, if she kept this up, this baby was never going to get weaned.

Friend.

After everything Muldoon had admitted, Joan still called him her friend.

As soon as they'd entered the ballroom, Brooke had been immediately approached by a waiter, who conjured up two scotch and sodas in record time, despite Muldoon's attempts to signal him otherwise.

"Gee, that's not really my drink," Muldoon admitted as Brooke handed him one of the glasses. Apparently keeping her from the bar was not going to be easy.

"Good," she said. "You can hold it for me, darling."

Yes, the evening was off to a roaring start.

"You should probably slow down," he cautioned her, annoyed with himself for being Joan's mouth-piece — or at least agreeing with her about this.

"Why would I want to do that?"

"Because your father's the most powerful and important man in the world, and you owe it to him not to get tanked while you're out acting as his representative," Muldoon suggested.

"You're awfully young to be such a stick-in-the-mud."

"There are a lot of people watching you to-night," he said.

"Everything I do, every breath I take," she told

379

him, "is watched. There is not one single moment in one single day that I can call my own. God forbid I should fart while out in public — it makes headlines. Do you know the reason it's so important that we're seen together tonight — that the White House pushed the story to the press that we've been an item for several weeks now?"

"Is there a reason?" he asked, as she finished her first drink and took her second from him.

"Don't tell," she said, "but about a month ago, I became involved with a senator who was being groomed to step into the vice president's role in about five years, after Daddy's final term is up — assuming Daddy wins a second term, of course. Anyway, this senator, John — I think it's okay if I call him that — he's a former aide of my father's whom I've known close to forever, if you'll believe that. He's even more conservative than you are, but I've been in love with him since I was, oh, I don't know. Twelve?"

Her eyes became suspiciously moist, which she tried to hide by draining her second drink. "His wife's a total bitch. They've been separated for several months but she won't give him a quiet divorce. And now Vice President Walker is about to announce that he'll be stepping down next year — he's got cancer. *There's* a story that's going to break big in a few days, huh? So John gets a call from the party saying he's their new man. He'll be VP on the ticket with Daddy for this next election, but he's got to patch things up with Lisa the bitch so he's got that good family values image. And they tell him that he's got to lose me.

"We were *so* discreet," she told him with the earnest righteousness of inebriation. "We didn't see each other half as much as we wanted to, and it was always completely clandestine. But apparently someone in the party knew. And suddenly I'm touring *Texas*, of all the godforsaken places, so that he'll have time to think without me around distracting him. They won't let me see him, won't let me talk to him, and then today I get a note from him. He's glad — *glad* — I've found someone new — like he doesn't know the news stories about me and you are total bullshit. He wishes me the best. The bastard *wishes* me the fucking *best*. It's about as personal as the note he sent me for my graduation from high school."

Muldoon didn't know what to say. "I'm sorry."

Brooke laughed. "Yeah. Me, too. I actually thought he loved me. What a farce." She held out her empty glass, and that same waiter was right there, ready to take it from her. "Two more."

Again, Muldoon tried to signal the man, but he couldn't even get eye contact.

"Yes, ma'am," the waiter said, bowing slightly.

"Thanks, Tim."

"Tim?" Muldoon asked Brooke as the waiter headed for the bar.

"I've stayed at this hotel before," she explained. "I've found that if I make friends with the staff — and tip well — I can find one or two brave souls who will actually bring me drinks that aren't completely watered down. I'm always getting cut off, which can be annoying on a night like tonight when I'm trying my best to get good and drunk."

"Is getting drunk really going to help?" Muldoon asked.

"I was thinking more along the lines of getting drunk and then screwing your brains out," she said. "And that sure as hell can't hurt, darling."

"Vince. *Vincent.*"

Vince opened his eyes to find Charlie giving him her best exasperated look.

"What?" he said.

Up on the movie screen, two very young, very beautiful people cavorted through an open-air market. No, wait. That wasn't a smile on the man's face — it was a grimace of anger or maybe concentration. It was hard to tell, exactly. Ah, yes. It *was* supposed to be anger. They were running from someone with a gun, who apparently wanted to kill them, hence all the bared teeth.

And yet throughout their ordeal, everyone's hair looked perfect.

"You paid five dollars; you might as well stay awake and actually *watch* the movie," Charlie scolded him.

"I'm awake," he whispered back.

On the screen, the scene changed. It was now night and the beautiful people with perfect hair had taken refuge in the basement of a dilapidated building. Their words to each other were snippety and sometimes even downright mean. But it was pitifully obvious that these two characters were about to explode with passion in what was to be this movie's obligatory love scene.

He snorted, winning another look and a whispered, "Hush, you!" from Charlie.

She'd be just as scornful of the bad acting in this movie after the damn thing was over. But he knew not to ask her to duck out early. No, not unless he wanted to get the "We paid good money for those tickets, so of course we're going to stay to the bitter end — besides, what if it actually had gotten better?" speech on the way home.

He reached for her hand, and she squeezed his fingers, flashing him a look of amusement that let him know that *she* knew exactly what he was thinking.

Although, as he stared up at the screen where two blatantly talentless, uninterested people pretended — rather badly — to give in to carnal longings, he suspected that she didn't know *exactly* what he was thinking.

He'd yet to see a love scene in a Hollywood movie that held a candle to his own memories of the first time Charlie came into his room and — what was that new expression? — got busy with him.

No, it wasn't the first time. The first time she came looking for a little play — another very nice euphemism; he approved of it completely — he'd actually sent her away.

It was the next night, the last night he'd planned to spend under the Fletchers' roof, that his defenses were totally overrun.

She awakened him that night from a deep sleep. An uneasy sleep.

He'd been dreaming again. About Ray. About Tarawa. They were in the water, under heavy enemy fire, working together to help move the Marines who were struggling with their heavy loads to shore.

He was disoriented at first as he stared up at her face, but she helped.

"It's me. Charlotte," she said. "Charlie Fletcher, remember?"

Oh, yeah. But what was she doing in . . . ? Where the hell was he?

"You're in my apartment, Vince, in Washington, D.C. You came here because you were sick, but you're much better now. No one's attacking, everyone's safe, but there *is* a storm approaching."

As if on cue, thunder rumbled. It was very much in the distance, yet still the sound — so much like the shelling he'd lived through — had permeated his sleep and invaded his dreams.

Even awake and knowing that it was merely thunder, he felt his palms start to sweat and his heart rate quicken.

"I thought it might be better to wake you up before it got worse," she explained. "I think the storm's coming in this direction, and I thought it might be easier for you if you were awake."

She was wearing her thick flannel robe tonight, and it was fastened clear up to her neck. She was blushing, too, no doubt remembering last night's visit. *Let me try to convince you.*

"Thank you," he said, pushing himself back so that he was sitting up in bed.

She looked as if she were about to return to her own room, when thunder rolled again. It was a little bit closer now, and although he managed to keep from diving underneath the bed, he couldn't stop himself from jumping, which in turn startled her.

"Sorry," he said. His palms weren't the only parts of him that were sweating now. He wiped his upper lip with the back of one hand, hoping she didn't notice.

Of course, she did.

"I'll stay with you until the storm passes," she decided, going around the room and turning on all the lights. "I better get some candles from downstairs, in case we lose power again."

"I'm okay," he lied. God, being alone with her like this was killing him. He should have left this morning, but he'd let himself get talked into staying another night. This was nobody's fault but his own. "Really, Charlie. I don't need —"

"Find the playing cards," she ordered. "We can play a few hands of gin rummy."

Gin rummy.

It was pretty surreal.

Vince, clad in her dead husband's pajamas, sat on the bed with Charlie, holding a handful of cards while the room blazed with light both electric and candle-powered.

She'd pulled up the bedspread to make it lie flat so they could use the bed as a table — the way they'd played cards all those days when he was recovering from being ill.

Neither of them mentioned the fact that just last night, she'd climbed beneath those very covers with him and begged him to . . .

Ah, God, he still wanted her. He loved her.

But the sad truth was, she didn't love him.

Maybe it would be enough — his loving her.

Thunder boomed, closer now, and she surely couldn't help but notice the droplet of sweat that slid down past his right ear. At least his hands didn't shake. Too much. He fumbled only a card or two.

"Who's Ray?" she asked as she discarded the seven of hearts.

When he didn't answer right away, she glanced up at him. "You called me Ray when I was trying to wake you up. You've mentioned him before."

"He was a friend of mine," Vince told her, drawing the nine of spades and discarding it immediately. "A good friend. He died at Tarawa."

"How did he die?" she asked.

"You don't want to know." Thunder. Shit, this time he dropped his entire hand.

She covered her eyes because some of the cards had fallen faceup. "Maybe you should let me decide that for myself," she countered tartly. "You think you're doing me favors by keeping things from me, Vince, but you're not. How can I begin to understand why you want to go back, if you tell me these polite, censored versions of what it was like?"

The thunder was moving closer, and outside of the house the wind picked up, rattling the windows nearly as much as he was rattled by her presence.

"Okay," he said, giving up on his attempt to rearrange his cards. He threw them down onto the bed. "Okay, you want to know how Ray died? His head was blown off, okay? It was ripped from his neck. One second I was shouting instructions to him — he was helping a bunch of men from our unit get to shore — and the next thing I knew I was covered with his blood and his brains and pieces of his skull. And you know what the really stupid thing was?"

Her face was pale and her eyes were enormous, and he knew he shouldn't be telling her any of this, but now that he'd started, he couldn't stop.

"I started screaming for the medics — like they were going to be able to patch him back up. Like they were going to help. But even if they could have, all of our unit's medics were already dead. None of them even made it to shore. Two of them stepped out of the Higgins boats and drowned. There's something that I left out of the *polite* version. The water out by that reef was too goddamn deep," he told her. "Hundreds of men waded through both chest-deep water and Japanese machine-gun fire, and the water proved to be the deadliest. They goddamn walked right into an underwater trough, is that what you want to hear? With eighty pounds of gear, those men sank. Even the strongest swimmers didn't stand a chance in water that was well over their heads, with all that gear on their backs, with all those other men struggling around them, pulling them down. And most of those farm boys couldn't swim a single stroke to save their lives."

Charlie looked as if she were going to burst into tears. "My God, they *drowned?*"

"Do you know why *we* didn't drown?" Vince's voice shook. "Me and Ray?" He didn't wait for her to answer. "Because those dead Marines finally filled in that trough enough to keep the rest of us from going under. We were far enough back in the line, and we walked over them. We *walked* over their bodies, Charles."

He was the one who started to cry.

"Oh, God, Vince." She crawled across the bed to him.

"Please," he said, damn near shaking her as she came close enough to grab hold of. "You've got to

387

help me talk to Senator Howard, or, Jesus, *some-one*, so this doesn't ever happen again. You said you could get him to pull strings . . ."

She was crying, too, as she clung to him, as he clung to her. "I don't want you to go. Don't go back! Please don't go back to that!"

"I don't want to," he confessed. "But, Jesus God, I have to. Don't you see?"

"I know," she wept. "I know. I just . . . I don't want to lose you, too."

"You'll never lose me," he told her, pushing her hair back from her face, away from his face, too. "I love you too much, Charlotte — I'll come back to you, I swear I *will* come back."

"When you say it like that," she said as she looked up at him, "I can almost believe you. But I know that's not something you can promise." Her eyes welled with a fresh rush of tears.

And then she kissed him.

The thunderstorm didn't move any closer that night. It never came near enough to distract him completely.

Which was his ultimate downfall.

Yeah, blame it on the weather rather than the fact that Charlie looked and moved like a movie star, that her smile was the definition of glorious, and — most important of all — that beneath her brisk, no-nonsense attitude resided a truly kind woman with infinite patience and a bone-deep sweetness of spirit.

Vince had replayed their first night together tens of thousands of times over the years — particularly the war years — that followed. And no matter how often he ran that memory, he couldn't for the life of him figure out how Charlotte had gotten out of that robe and nightgown so quickly. All he knew was that she was kissing him and he was kissing her, and then, holy God, there was all that incredible smooth skin beneath his hands, pressed against his own miraculously naked body.

It happened so quickly. In a heartbeat, she was touching him, guiding him, and then . . .

Every cliché ever written was true. Every overused description, every tired line of poetry that waxed rhapsodic about making love, was right on the money.

There was nothing on earth that compared — even remotely — to doing this act with this one incredible woman who totally owned his heart.

And who loved him, too, despite everything she'd said the night before. This proved that she loved him — the fact that she would do this with him. She wouldn't do this if she didn't intend to marry him, would she?

His heart felt as swollen and as ready to burst as the part of him that was buried so deeply inside of her, so much so that he felt compelled to speak.

It was a miracle his voice worked, although he definitely sounded hoarse and very unlike himself. "Charlotte, are you sure?"

A little late for that question, actually. Because what was he going to do if she said no?

But, "Yes," she told him. "Oh, please, oh yes!"

And then, just as he was convinced beyond a shadow of a doubt that there could be no better pleasure than this, he discovered, all in a rapid sequence, the true wonder of her release, his own release, and then the intense, drifting sweetness of an aftermath filled with the bone-melting satisfaction of knowing that he'd sent his seed deep inside of her.

He'd heard men talking about the fear of getting their girlfriends pregnant, about breaking into a cold sweat after the heat of the moment had passed.

But Vince wasn't afraid. In fact, he wanted — he *prayed* — that he'd made her pregnant. Imagine that! Charlie carrying his child. He couldn't think of anything he wanted more.

It was wonderful, lying there with her, imagining their lives together.

At least it was until he opened his big mouth. "We'll take the train to Maryland tomorrow, right after you get off from work."

She seemed to wake up, to realize that they were lying naked, bodies intertwined amid the remains of their card game on top of his bed — *her* bed — in a room that was blazing with light.

"I'm not going to marry you, Vince," she told him, pushing him off of her.

"But . . ." He propped himself up onto one elbow as she scrambled to find her nightgown on the bedroom floor. She had to turn it inside out and while she did, she stood with her back to him as if to try to hide her nakedness.

"Nothing's changed," she said. "You're not going to stay. I know that. It was wrong of me to ask it of you. I know that, too." She slipped her robe back on, and when she finally turned to face him, he saw that she was working very hard not to cry.

He sat up. "Charlotte —"

She backed toward the door. "Forgive me,

please, for my lack of restraint tonight. It was lovely. *You're* lovely. I hope you know just how lovely it was to . . . But I can't . . . I —"

Vince stood up, and she bumped into the door with her back and reached for the knob. "Whoa," he said. "Slow down, okay? Let's sit down and —"

"There's nothing to say," she interrupted. "I knew you had expectations, but I wanted . . . I wanted . . . I was selfish and I'm sorry. I'm so, so sorry, Vince."

Charlie slipped out the door and was gone.

"Wait!" He searched for his pajamas so that he could follow her, but of course they were tangled. He cursed as he tried to jam his legs into them and nearly fell onto his face on the floor.

On the movie screen, all those years later, the actor and actress — obviously hired because of how good they looked naked rather than for their ability to recite dialogue convincingly — put their clothes back on effortlessly.

They were completely clean, too, after making sweaty, steamy love in that grimy, rat-infested basement. Their hair remained perfectly styled.

The magic of Hollywood definitely wasn't with Vince that first night he'd made love to Charlotte, that was for sure.

Before he could get dressed and go after her, he'd had to peel the jack of hearts and three of clubs off his naked butt.

"I was thinking more along the lines of getting drunk and then screwing your brains out," Joan had heard Brooke say to Muldoon. "And that sure as hell can't hurt, darling."

"Well," he'd said in response. "That's, um . . . quite an idea."

"Let's get out of here and go back upstairs as soon as possible," Brooke suggested.

How did this happen? And how could she fix it?

As Muldoon escorted Brooke across the room to introduce her to Admiral Crowley and the other military VIPs, Joan seriously considered the possibility of running after him, of tackling him around the knees if necessary.

But then what, after she got him onto the floor? What would she say?

Don't go upstairs with Brooke, because she'd just be using you. But God, look at Brooke in that dress. If Joan were Muldoon, she probably wouldn't be too upset about being used.

She could say, *I was wrong.*

Hey, story of her life. Sometimes it seemed as if she spent more time wrong than right. And in this case, she wasn't even completely sure what she'd been wrong about.

She was still convinced that any kind of relationship — anything public, that is — with Muldoon would be looked at askance in terms of her career. But maybe something temporary, something short term with a very definite end date, something that went on privately, behind closed and locked doors . . .

Yes, that was definitely what she wanted. And it sure seemed to be what he'd wanted, too — up to three hours ago.

The night wore on, interminably long, each minute seeming like a millennium, with absolutely no chance for her to pull Muldoon aside and beg his forgiveness.

While Muldoon and Brooke were out on the dance floor, Myra sent Joan to go talk to the reporter from Fox. An entire camera crew was there, hoping to get an interview with the "happy couple."

Every time the reporter called them that, Joan's teeth hurt.

It was impossible to talk without screaming while the music was playing, so they stepped out onto the patio, where Joan gave her four thousandth apology of the day. Brooke had no time right now. This was a pleasant social event for her — a chance to reunite with her *friend*, Lieutenant Muldoon.

She gave the reporter a top-ten list of reasons why she couldn't talk to Brooke right now, careful to leave off reason number one — that her married lover had just chosen the vice presidential candidacy over his relationship with her, and in an attempt to deal with the pain of his rejection, Brooke was totally shit-faced drunk.

Halfway through, Joan's cell phone rang. She checked the number — Myra.

"Excuse me," she told the news crew. "I've got to take this."

Myra sounded stressed. "Please tell me Brooke's with you."

Uh-oh. "She's not."

Myra's response was blisteringly succinct.

"Darlings! Up here!"

The reporter spotted Brooke the same moment Joan did.

"I found her," Joan told Myra. "She's up on the balcony outside of her room."

Brooke was actually waving to get their attention. Muldoon was with her, and as Joan watched, he tried to talk to her, tried to tug her back into the hotel suite.

The video camera started rolling.

"Excuse me," Joan said loudly. "No one's given you permission to —"

"Who's your affiliate?" Brooke called down to the reporter.

"We're with Fox News, Ms. Bryant," the reporter called back. "May we ask you some questions?"

"I think you better get over here," Joan told Myra as she tried to step in front of the camera. "I'm sorry," she said to the cameraman, "you'll have to turn that off and go back inside."

"Is your camera on?" Brooke asked.

"Yes, it is," the reporter replied.

Joan tried talking directly to Brooke. "If you want to give an interview, Ms. Bryant, please let me set —"

"Good." Brooke ignored her. "Because I have a message I'd like to broadcast to my good friend John."

Oh, no. Oh, no, no. Joan tried to get in front of the lens, but the cameraman was too quick for her.

And then the reporter and some bruiser of an equipment-lugging guy was there, blocking her way.

"John, darling, I appreciate your note wishing me the very best." Brooke projected nicely with her stage voice.

"Don't make me go through you," Joan said to the three-hundred-pound man. "Because I will."

"You don't have to be concerned, sweetheart — my new friend, Mike, has that covered." Brooke was doing her best Evita from the balcony. "He's a SEAL and SEAL teams accept only the best."

"What's the harm in letting her talk?" the big guy said in a remarkably high-pitched voice.

Joan could see Muldoon, purposely standing with his back to the camera, talking to Brooke, trying to talk her down from the ledge, so to speak.

That was when she realized that she had her cell phone, and Muldoon had his cell phone. She quickly dialed his number.

Shit, she could hear it ringing, but he was ignoring it. "Come on, Michael, pick up!" Or read my mind and grab Brooke and get her the hell inside. Although, if she resisted him, that wouldn't look too good on camera . . .

Whatever he was saying to her, it served to distract Brooke only temporarily.

"I seem to remember you telling me once that you tried to get into the SEAL program while you were in the Navy," Brooke continued for the cameras, for John, poor bastard, whose political career was going to be in jeopardy if she mentioned his last name. "But, golly, you just weren't good enough, were you?"

A crowd was starting to gather, some people watching from inside the ballroom and others from out here on the patio. Joan redialed Muldoon's number.

"I'm going to ask you again to get out of my way," she told the giant squeaky-toy man.

"You're going to have to try to go through me," he responded, managing somehow to sound both apologetic and bored — as if this sort of thing happened to him more than once a day. "But if you *do* lay a hand on me, there will be a lawsuit, plus a whole lot more bad press for the current administration."

"I hate you," Joan told him.

"That doesn't particularly break me up."

Brooke continued orating. "I suppose I should end this by being gracious and wishing you the best, too."

End this. She was going to end this. Thank you, Lord, have her end this fast. Joan saw both Myra and Dick picking their way through the crowd, trying to move quickly without revealing how completely panicked they were.

"Except — whoops! — you've already had the best, but you threw it away, didn't you?" Brooke said. "Have a nice evening, darling."

"Okay," Joan said loudly. "That's all. Thank you. We don't have time for any questions. Lieutenant, will you please take Ms. Bryant inside?"

But wait. Brooke shook Muldoon off, because, like the chef selling Ginsu knives on that late-night TV infomercial, there apparently was still more.

"God knows I'll enjoy *my* evening." Brooke got even louder and more dramatic, if that was possible. "Think of me, darling. Tonight I'll be doing it Navy SEAL style."

Oh, dear Lord in heaven.

"Well, *there's* the Brooke Bryant sound bite of the year," the giant squeaked.

No freaking kidding. "Thank you," Joan said again. "That's all we have time for."

But Brooke had a different finale in mind. "And in case you want a reminder of what you've been missing . . ."

Oh, shit, shit, triple shit!

"Whoa!" The bruiser's eyes opened more than halfway as Brooke pulled her gown up and over her head.

It was a smooth move that a stripper would have had to train for years to pull off. It left her standing there in only her fancy underpants for the entire world to see.

But alas, the visuals were not yet over. As Muldoon grabbed her to pull her inside — enough was apparently enough for him and he took her over his shoulder in a fireman's hold — Brooke threw her gown off the balcony. The shiny red fabric caught the light as it fell to the ground.

Joan turned away from the sight of the heavy curtains closing in Brooke's room to find Myra bearing down on her.

"I'm prepared to take full responsibility for this," Joan said. "I should have been able to stop it. I should have done *some*thing." Jesus, maybe she should have taken off *her* dress.

"She did the best she could," the giant told Joan's boss.

"Shut up, you nasty man." Joan startled herself with her own ferocity. She turned back to Myra. "Will you please fire me and get it over with, because I really need to get out of here right now."

What she wanted to do was get in her rental car and drive far, far away from this hotel where, in one of the grand suites, the one man she liked better than any other man she'd ever met in her life — yes, it was true, and she'd completely and foolishly blown any chance at all with him because she was an *idiot* — and the President's daughter were doing it, Navy SEAL style.

But Myra had other plans. "Meeting. My suite. Ten minutes."

Well, gee, wasn't *this* going to be fun — figuring out how to take this outburst of Brooke's and spin it into something positive. Well, barring that, they'd try to spin it into something less destructive.

Less destructive to the President, that is. Brooke and Muldoon and Joan were all just pawns in this game.

Joan knew that if she opened up to Myra and confessed that she had a personal interest in Muldoon, that damn it, she really liked this guy, the response would be "So what?"

Of course, it didn't really matter, because that would probably be Muldoon's response right now as well.

Ihbraham looked stunned, and Mary Lou modestly pulled her shirt down slightly, attempting to cover herself while still providing Haley with some air. Haley, of course, immediately grabbed her shirt and yanked it up.

"There's room for you to sit," she said, shifting over so that there indeed was room on the bench.

"Uh," he said. "Yes. Thank you." As he sat, he glanced at her, then looked away. "It doesn't bother you to do that out here? Where anyone can see?"

She looked around. The little churchyard was deserted. And her back was to the street. The only person who could see her was Ihbraham.

"It would bother me more to drive home with a screaming kid," she said. "I used to carry a scarf to cover us, but these days she just pulls it off. I could sit in my car, if you want. I mean, if it bothers you . . ."

He laughed. "No. I just thought I could no longer be surprised by American ways and —" He looked at her, looked at Haley, who was slowing down, her eyes drifting shut. "You're beautiful and she's beautiful and . . . it's beautiful to watch. I don't know why most of the world insists on hiding such a beautiful thing."

"Because most men can't seem to grasp the idea that breasts were put on this earth for something other than their own personal pleasure," she said. "They can't walk past a woman breast-feeding a baby without getting a woody. So we have to keep ourselves covered up because of *their* problem. Oh, shoot, I'm leaking on the other side." Dammit, she'd ruined another shirt. By the time she got home, the milk would have stained.

"A woody," he said. He laughed. "I think I know what that means. I've never heard it called that, but . . ." He laughed again. "And this is something you're comfortable talking about with a man who's not your husband?"

"I think of you as a friend," she told him. "Friends say whatever they want to each other, don't they? If you want, I'll watch what I say. I just thought —"

"No," he said. "I don't want you to watch what

you say. I'm just . . . aware of how differently we were raised by our parents, you and I."

"Yeah, well, my mother was too busy fucking anyone who brought home a bottle of gin to raise me. My sister raised me." She didn't want to talk about that again. "What's with your brothers? They're not very nice."

Ihbraham sighed. "It's ugly. It's . . . We inherited my father's business — a car dealership — when he died. I don't want to work with them, but they want me to come back because the business is jointly owned with our uncle and cousins. If I come back, we'll have control. It's foolish and petty and they shouldn't have come looking for me." He muttered something in that funny language. "But I guess they're angry, and now I am, too. A perfect situation, huh?"

"They said something about me, didn't they?"

He glanced at her. "Yes, they did. It was not kind and I will not repeat it. They're fools."

Haley had definitely crashed. Mary Lou gently pulled her nipple free from the baby's mouth, and put her on her shoulder. The trick now was to get her to burp without waking her up. She rubbed Haley's back. Come on, baby . . .

"So that was this guy Bob, huh?" Ihbraham asked, clearly wanting to change the subject.

"That was Bob." A burp. And Haley slept on. Alleluia! "Cute, huh?"

"Cute?"

"Handsome, I mean."

"Ah. Is that what you think?"

"Definitely. What do you think?"

"I think he's up to no good," Ihbraham told her.

"I think you should be careful. His being here was no coincidence. I think he is . . . what is it called? Stalking you."

She had to laugh. "You know, he said the exact same thing about you. Here, would you . . . ?"

She held Haley out so that he could take the baby from her. It wasn't easy to do, but the alternative was to sit there with her boob hanging out.

"How could I be stalking you when you are the one who comes outside to see me?" he asked. His hands were so dark against Haley's fair skin.

Mary Lou pulled down her bra, and then examined the damage done to the other side of her shirt. It looked as if she'd dipped the tip of her breast into a cup of water. So much for getting ice cream. She wasn't going anywhere looking like that.

"Maybe you're just such a good stalker that you're able to lure me to you without me knowing it," she said.

He laughed. "Ah. Of course."

"Or maybe I'm stalking you."

"Feel free to continue," he said. "I'm enjoying it very much."

If anyone else had said it, it would have been creepy. Or heavy with innuendo. But combined with Ihbraham's wide smile and warm eyes, it was simply nice.

He was terribly nice — much nicer than she was. "I'm sorry I lied, you know, about you being my sponsor. I just . . . I . . ."

"I know why you said it," he said quietly. "There's no need to explain."

"You could be, you know. My sponsor, I mean.

401

You're already doing everything that Rene used to do. More, actually."

But he was shaking his head. "I can't."

"Sure you can." She loved the idea — it was brilliant. Why hadn't she thought of it earlier? "It would be perfect —"

"No," he said, his voice almost as sharp as it had been when he spoke to his brothers. Haley jumped and he spoke more softly so as not to wake her. "I'm sorry. But it's not possible. Not at all."

Embarrassed, Mary Lou stood up, scooping Haley from his arms. "Well, I have to go. I won't trouble you anymore tonight then."

He sighed. "You're no trouble to me, Mary Lou. I would like very much to help you but . . ."

She waited for him to finish, but he just shook his head.

"Just think about it, okay? Don't say no right now," she said, stopping him from speaking. "Sleep on it for a day or two, please?"

He was shaking his head again, but he didn't say a word.

"I do have to go. Sam'll be home soon." Maybe. "And I really should get Haley into bed."

Ihbraham stood up and walked her the few feet to her car, folding the stroller as she put Haley into the car seat.

She used her new key to unlock the trunk. "Thanks for copying this for me," she told him, holding up the key.

"It was no trouble," he said.

"See you tomorrow," she said as she got into her car and headed for home.

EIGHTEEN

The call on his cell phone came a full forty minutes after Muldoon had expected it.

It was Joan. "Are you decent?" she asked without even saying hello.

"Uh, *yeah*." God, what did she think he was doing in here with Brooke?

"Good," she said, "because there are about fifteen people standing in the hallway outside the door."

"Well, what are you waiting for? Come on in."

"The night lock's been thrown."

Brooke must've done that when they first came back to her room. "Sorry," he said. "I'll unlock it." He closed his phone as he pulled the door open and . . .

Joan hadn't been kidding. A busload of people filed past him and into the suite's sitting room.

"Where's Brooke?" Joan's boss Myra asked.

"She's in the bedroom," he told her. "She, uh, well, she passed out, I guess."

"I don't guess it, I know it." Myra vanished into the other room.

Joan was one of the last inside, and she looked at him and laughed, shaking her head in what sure looked a hell of a lot like derision. "Good job keeping Brooke from drinking too much."

"I tried to keep her away from the bar," he said as evenly as he could, considering how angry he was. How dare she look at him like that after throwing him to the wolves the way she had? "But she had a way of getting the bar to come to her. Besides, she was drunk before we even went downstairs. You can't even remotely blame that on me."

"I'm not blaming you," she said. "I'm just . . . disappointed. I hope you had fun, Lieutenant, because welcome to the part of the evening that's not going to be so enjoyable."

He honestly doubted that it could get much worse.

She joined the others in the sitting room, and Muldoon closed the door. And caught sight of himself in the entryway mirror.

His hair looked as if he'd spent most of the past hour in that bed with Brooke. His uniform wasn't just rumpled. He'd actually rebuttoned his jacket one button off all the way down. And — oh, shit! — there were actually lipstick stains in some extremely risqué places.

"Lieutenant Muldoon, will you please join us?" Myra was back in the sitting room, having dispatched some of the others into the bedroom with Brooke.

He smoothed down his hair and hurriedly rebuttoned his jacket. There was nothing he could do about the lipstick, except stand with his hands clasped in front of him and pray that they invited him to sit down quickly.

"Please have a seat," Myra commanded, thank God, and he did.

Joan was on the other side of the room, on the same sofa he'd sat on just a few hours ago. She had a legal pad with her, and her full attention was focused on whatever it was that she was jotting down.

"We'd like to issue a statement to the press," Myra told him, "about your relationship with Brooke. We'd like to make public the fact that you and the President's daughter are in the middle of a long-term, committed relationship."

"But we're not."

"Actually, what we'd like to do is announce your engagement," Myra said.

Muldoon laughed. "Yeah, right." But holy shit, she wasn't kidding. And Joan . . . Joan still wasn't looking at him. "You guys want me to *marry* Brooke? I mean, I know what it probably looked like, but I didn't . . . I mean, I stayed because I didn't want to leave her alone after she . . . But honestly, we didn't even —"

"Relax, Lieutenant," Myra said. "Of course we don't expect you to marry her. We just want to announce that you intend to get married — let the public know that the dress off the balcony was Brooke's way of celebrating her powerful feelings for you."

"Except there's a videotape of her speech to that senator —"

"Apparently the audio track didn't record until the very end," Myra told him. "All they have of the first part is video, and you better believe that the part of that video they're going to show on the news — over and over as many times as they possibly can — is Brooke taking off her dress and you throwing her over your shoulder like a caveman, carrying her into her hotel room."

"First of all, it was a fireman's hold and . . ." Muldoon shook his head. They weren't interested in what happened after he'd pulled the curtains, only what was to come, because in their book, they all assumed they knew what had happened here tonight. Still . . . "This is crazy." He needed to state it at least once for the record. "I didn't sleep with her. I didn't have any sexual contact with her at all." He looked at Joan. Surely she'd believe him.

But when Joan looked back at him, her eyes were decidedly cool. "Myra, Lieutenant Muldoon is going to need a clean pair of pants before he leaves tonight. Shall I see about getting that for him?"

"Please do," Myra said.

Joan rose from her seat and, dialing her cell phone, she headed out of the room.

"Our plan is to announce the engagement, then have you appear in public with Brooke regularly over the next few months," Myra continued. "We've already started preliminary arrangements for you to be transferred to the East Coast, to a SEAL team out of Little Creek."

"What?"

"And in a few months, after things die down a bit, we'll announce that the engagement's off."

No way, no how, absolutely not. But Muldoon didn't have to put it in those terms, because he could not for the life of him imagine Brooke ever agreeing to this farce. "I think you might want to run this idea past Brooke," he said as evenly as he possibly could.

Joan came back in. "Pants in ten," she reported as she sat back down.

"Dick is with Brooke right now, talking to her," Myra told Muldoon.

"Dick is done talking to her," the man said, coming out into the sitting room. "She's too out of it to reason with. We're going to have to wait until the morning, see what she says in the sober light of day."

"But as of right now, it's a no, right?" Muldoon persisted. "I've got to tell you, it's still going to be a no in the morning. I don't think she likes me very much."

"It's not just a no, it's a hell no," Dick agreed.

"What exactly did she say?" Myra asked.

Dick shook his head. "She's drunk. She's incoherent."

A female aide stepped forward. "I believe her exact words were, 'There's no way in hell I'm going to spend two hours let alone two months with a man who can't even get it up.'"

Dick winced. "Thank you, Deb. That was probably not necessary to repeat."

Muldoon laughed, but no one in the room was looking at him. Everyone was suddenly intensely preoccupied with a spot on the rug or on the wall. They didn't actually *believe* that he was . . . Did they?

God, even Joan was staring at her shoe.

"Just in case you were wondering, that's not true," Muldoon said.

"Of course it's not," Myra said much too quickly. It was transparently obvious that she was humoring him.

This was a lose-lose situation — the more he protested, the less they would believe him.

Joan stood up. "I think we've abused Lieutenant Muldoon enough for one night."

"All right," Myra decided. "We'll meet in the morning."

"No," Muldoon said. "I'm done here. I'm not transferring anywhere. And I'm not lying to the American public for two months. I'm sorry, I'm as big a supporter of President Bryant as anyone, but I'm not going to do that. Brooke is one messed up, incredibly unhappy woman, and playing games like this, covering up her embarrassments — that's not helping her at all."

"He's right," Joan said. "A lot of people heard what Brooke said on that balcony tonight. Just because we don't have audio doesn't mean the real story won't break —"

"God!" Muldoon couldn't stand it. "Tell the truth because it's the truth — not because you know you'll be caught in a lie." He looked directly at Joan right before he went out the door, lipstick stains be damned. "You should be ashamed of yourselves."

The Ladybug Lounge was quiet for a Saturday night. Sam sat at the bar, watching Cosmo play pool with a pair of college girls who weren't much older than Mary Lou had been when he'd first laid eyes on her. Laid eyes on her and laid her — all within the span of a few short hours. All in an attempt to exorcise the ghost of the woman he really wanted to be with.

Sam nursed his beer, knowing he was going to

have to go home when he finished it, knowing he was going to have to bring up this most unpleasant subject. *Hey, I've been thinking, and this marriage thing really isn't working out.*

Mary Lou would start to cry.

Jesus.

He'd done some impossibly hard things in his life, including becoming a SEAL and then making the leap from enlisted to officer. Fuck, that had been a battle all the way. Forget about the fact that his job was filled with kill-or-be-killed scenarios that he'd faced without blinking. Yet here he was, nearly shitting in his pants at the thought of going home and telling a five-foot-three-inch woman the bitter, unhappy truth.

He didn't love her. He'd never loved her. He was never going to love her.

He should have married her purely to provide prenatal care for her from his health plan. He should have made it clear right from the start that they were not going to live together as husband and wife, and that they were going to divorce right after the baby was born. Yes, he'd pay both alimony and child support, but the fact was that he couldn't marry her for real because he didn't love her.

He loved someone else.

Christ, he was a stupid fool to think that love didn't matter, that it was a luxury that a man could learn to live without. That it was an extra — a bonus if you found it, a double plus if you actually managed to make it work.

He'd fucked up royally, assuming that he could actually make his marriage to Mary Lou into

something real even though there was no love between them. He'd hurt Mary Lou; he'd hurt Haley
who, although she was still tiny, no doubt felt the
tension in the house; he'd hurt himself; and,
maybe worst of all, he'd hurt Alyssa.

And he had hurt Alyssa. He knew that was true,
despite her rapid rebound and her current per-
fect-seeming love affair with that perfect fucker
Max. The look on her face as Sam had told her he
was marrying Mary Lou was one he'd carry with
him to his grave.

Sam sighed.

Muldoon — who was sitting several seats down
the bar — sighed, too. What a misery fest. He sat
with his head in his hands, drinking beer cut with
lemonade — a habit he'd picked up during time
spent in Germany.

He'd said nothing when he'd arrived, even
though Sam and Cosmo had been playing pool at
the time. He waved off their offer for him to take
on the winner and sat down at the bar, where he
still sat.

"If you're looking to get drunk, that's not going
to do it," Sam had said to Muldoon two beers ago,
after the coeds attacked and he'd retreated back to
the bar himself.

"Believe me, sir," Muldoon had replied, "I'm
not looking to get drunk."

"Didn't go too well tonight, huh?" Sam had sat
down about four stools away from Muldoon,
careful not to get too close. Sometimes misery
needed a whole lot of elbow room.

Muldoon looked up at him. "It was a total goatfuck."

That had been the first time Sam had ever heard little Mikey use the F-word, even in that context. He'd worked hard not to react — to drop his beer bottle or fall to the floor in a dead faint. Instead he'd cleared his throat, wishing he was better at this. want to talk about —"

"No."

Sam knew when to shut the fuck up, and that had been definitely one of those times.

Over at the pool table now, Cosmo was staunchly ignoring some pretty obvious body language that those two girls were giving him. If he wanted to, he wasn't going to go home alone tonight. But it sure as hell seemed as if he didn't want to. Although, really, who knew what went on inside of Cosmo's head. Maybe he was purposely playing hard to get.

Across the room, the main entrance opened and . . .

"Mike," Sam said. "Heads up."

Muldoon looked over his shoulder and saw Joan DaCosta picking her way through the little tables that dotted the floor, heading directly toward him. Shaking his head, he turned back around. "Shit," he said on a sigh, closing his eyes briefly.

Muldoon's giving her his back didn't slow down Joan. In fact, she slid onto the barstool next to him and ordered a glass of white wine from the bartender.

She waited until it was delivered, until after she took a sip, to speak.

"Are you okay?" she asked Muldoon.

"Me? Yeah, I'm just great. Thanks."

Whoa, sarcasm coming from the King of Polite.

This was a night full of firsts. Sam knew he shouldn't be listening and he tried to focus his attention on the pool table.

"I'm really sorry," Joan said to Muldoon, loudly enough so that Sam couldn't help but overhear. "About everything."

"Fine," he said. "Apology accepted. Conversation over."

She was silent then, but only for a minute or two. "I'm pretty sure I owe you a bigger apology than that," she said. "At least an explanation. I really feel awful —"

"Yeah," he said. "That's great. Because that's what apologies are all about, right? Making the person who's giving the apology feel better — feel less guilty?"

"Ouch," she said.

"Sorry."

"No, you're right. I'm wrong. Again. I've been wrong about an awful lot lately. I was wrong about you and me. *Really* wrong."

Well, that caught Muldoon's full attention. He turned to look at her — a real, long look, not just a quick glance this time.

"So I guess what I need to know," Joan said quietly — almost too quietly for Sam to hear, but not quite, "is whether or not you now think so poorly of me that there's nothing I can do or say to bring us back to where we were before. Well, not *exactly* where we were before, but . . ."

"How could you even think I'd agree to going along with that crazy scheme — to actually announce my engagement to the President's daughter?"

412

What the fuck . . . ? It took everything Sam had in him not to turn and look at Joan and Muldoon. But if he looked, then they'd know he was listening. He stared at Cosmo, who was making an intricate bank shot, sinking not one but two balls in opposite corner pockets. It was a beauty, but Sam's real attention was on Joan.

"I don't know," she admitted. "I thought you might have slept with her and, I don't know. Become enthralled. I thought if that had happened, maybe you wouldn't mind spending the next two months with her. She's beautiful, and she's funny and brilliant — I mean, at least she is when she's sober."

"Yeah, well, she's too old for me," Muldoon said.

Joan laughed — a sharp burst of noise — but then got serious again, right away. "We had this meeting before we came into Brooke's room, and you can ask anyone who was there — I *was* opposed to the engagement announcement idea. And it wasn't because I was afraid of getting caught in a lie. I only said that because I was trying to present an alternate reason for them all to just leave you alone — a reason that Myra would understand. She's, um, pretty moral-free, I guess is one way of saying it." Her voice got soft. "Mike, I really hate the idea of you thinking poorly of me."

"I'm not so keen on the idea of you thinking I would tell you what I told you — that I was crazy about you — and then kind of randomly go and have sex with someone else," Muldoon countered.

"I thought you were angry with me," she said. "I thought you were going to try to make me jealous. Which worked."

"Yeah?" he asked.

She nodded. "Yeah."

They just sat there then, looking at each other for a long time.

"You were really jealous, huh?" Muldoon finally asked.

"I wanted to punch Brooke in the nose. You, too," Joan added. "God, I thought maybe you got her drunk on purpose."

"Yeah, right," he scoffed. "Nothing turns me on like a woman who's completely slobbering drunk."

They were both silent then, and it was a silence that was loaded with some cryptic meaning. Muldoon wasn't looking at Joan anymore, and she cleared her throat.

"Well, yeah," she said. "It's understandable that . . . I mean . . . it probably happens to a lot of guys, all the time. It's a common enough problem, right?"

Muldoon closed his eyes and laughed, then turned to face her. "Look, maybe I'm an old-fashioned guy, but pathetic, scotch-soaked, revenge-inspired groping doesn't do a thing to rev me up. There's no problem. I don't have any kind of a problem."

"Okay," she said. "I hear you. Absolutely. I believe you."

"Jesus, you're humoring me."

"No, I'm not."

"You don't think I know when I'm being hu-

414

mored? Do you really think I have some kind of a problem?"

"It's not that big a deal to me," Joan said. "I mean, in this day and age, with a little Viagra . . ."

Sam nearly choked on his beer. Oh, this was just too good.

Muldoon stood up.

"Where are you going?" Joan asked, but he wasn't going anywhere. He took her hand and pulled her out of her seat, too.

And then, right there, at the bar in the Ladybug Lounge, Muldoon put his arms around Joan DaCosta and kissed the living shit out of her.

It was like something out of a movie. Sweeping music with lots of violins should have swelled. Instead Travis Tritt wailed on the jukebox. *Hello, T-R-O-U-B-L-E* . . .

On the other hand, maybe old Travis was the perfect sound track to this moment.

That was no "I'm kissing you because it seems like a nice way to pass the time" kind of kiss. Instead it was a "If I don't kiss you right fucking now, I just might die" kind of kiss.

And Jesus, if that wasn't trouble . . . Sam could remember kissing Alyssa like that, and look where it got him.

He scanned the room for any senior officers, watching Muldoon's six. An officer in dress uniform wasn't supposed to suck face like this in public, and Jesus Lord, Mikey still had the woman in a lip lock.

And as for Joan, well, she was very definitely kissing him back.

Unless Sam was very much mistaken, someone

in this room was going to get some tonight.

Finally Muldoon lifted his head. But the way he was looking down at the woman in his arms, he might as well still have been kissing her. It was a look that sizzled, a look that was more palpable and possibly even more intimate than a touch.

Joan was definitely hypnotized, staring back up at him.

Muldoon tugged her even closer, his hands on her backside, her hips tight against his, and she laughed breathlessly.

"Okay," she said. "Point taken. I think we're both in agreement that you don't have any kind of a problem."

"Damn right I don't."

"I knew you didn't," she said. "I was really just jerking your chain. It was too good an opportunity to pass up."

"The big irony is that I've been walking around like this all week," he told her. "I think you're sexy as hell, Joan. I don't need Viagra. I just need to think about you."

This time, she kissed him.

And oh, yeah. Muldoon was definitely on his way to GetItOnVille.

Kiss number two lasted even longer than kiss number one.

And when they finally came up for air, Joan managed to ask, "Do you —"

"Yes," Muldoon said.

He threw a twenty on the bar, took her by the hand and they were gone.

Sam, on the other hand, didn't have such a good reason to leave.

He watched Cosmo line up another perfect shot, hoping to hell that Muldoon and Joan had better luck with their birth control than he and Mary Lou had had.

"Okay," Joan said to Muldoon via their cell phones, as she peered out from her hotel room doorway. "There's no one in the hall. Get your butt down here, fast."

And then there he was, coming out of the stairwell and moving swiftly down the corridor. She opened the door a little bit farther, and he was inside without anyone seeing him.

"That fast enough for you?" he said, still talking to her on his phone.

"Good-bye," she said into her phone, loving the way he was looking at her, remembering those incredible kisses back in the bar. "I can't talk right now."

Muldoon hung up his phone, too, his eyes never leaving hers.

But he didn't move. He just stood there, watching her. What was he waiting for?

"Kiss me," she finally had to say.

But he shook his head. "Nah," he said.

She laughed. What?

"I'm going to," he said. "But I want to look at you first and . . . think about you some more. I do want to talk. Do you mind?" he added.

"No," Joan said. "Of course I don't." He'd told her how he'd always watched for cues when he was with a woman, how he'd learned to pick up subtle hints as to what that woman wanted him to do to fulfill her fantasies.

But tonight was different, she realized with something of a jolt. She was his fantasy.

It was a rather large turn-on knowing that. But, God, the pressure was suddenly a bit intense.

"Come on in," she said, leading the way into the hotel room. "Can I get you something to drink? Are you hungry? We could order room service if you want. This hotel has a really terrific fish chowder that I for one would love to lick off your body."

Muldoon laughed as he sat down on the sofa.

"I'm not entirely kidding," she told him.

"Yeah, I know," he countered, smiling at her. "That's what makes it so nice to hear."

"I'm not sure what you want," she admitted. "I want to do this right, but you're going to have to give me a little direction."

"Just talk to me," he said. "I just . . . I love to talk to you, Joan, and I just want to do it knowing that in a little while I'm going to get a chance to kiss you again."

Oh, honey, that's not all you're going to do . . .

He was adorable. He honestly didn't realize that saying *I love to talk to you* made her heart pound even harder.

"It sounds kind of dumb, doesn't it?" he added sheepishly.

"No," she said quite firmly. "It doesn't."

"I've never been very good at talking to women, and . . . you make it so easy." His earnestness wasn't an act. It was amazing. Somehow she'd found the last truly earnest and sincere man on earth. "You make me feel comfortable, and . . . I don't know. Eloquent almost. In control. And out of control at the same time." He laughed at himself, rolling his eyes. "Jeez, I'm not making any sense, am I?"

He was making significantly more sense than all of the other men whom Joan had ever invited back to her room with the intention of beginning a hot romantic fling.

Not that there had been that many of them.

"You *are* making sense." Her voice sounded breathless. "That's what worries me."

He laughed, and oh, God, he was good-looking, sitting there on the sofa in his gleaming white uniform. He'd changed his pants sometime between Brooke's suite and the Ladybug Lounge. He'd once told her that he carried a spare pair in his truck.

"What do you want to talk about?" she asked. This was one of the few times in her life that she wasn't sure what to say.

"Whatever you want. Whatever you're thinking."

Joan sat down on the other end of the sofa. "Well. I'm thinking pretty much nonstop about making love to you."

He nodded.

"You want that drink?" she asked.

"No."

"Yeah, me neither," she said.

"Will you say that again?"

"You want that drink?"

He just looked at her.

"I'm thinking about you, inside of me," she whispered. "I'm thinking that simply kissing you was better than the best sex I've ever had. I want you, Michael. If you want, I'll talk the entire time, but please, please, *please* kiss me now."

He moved toward her before the last words had left her lips, taking her mouth in a hungry kiss.

It was enough to knock her over, but she went willingly, pulling him back with her onto the couch, her fingers in the softness of his hair.

Joan had thought those kisses back in the bar were powerful, but this was unbelievable. He didn't hold back this time, because, hey, this time there was no one watching them.

He was a man who knew what women liked, and that was more than evident — he kissed like a pro. He kissed her with the same self-confidence that had impressed her so completely when he took command of a team of men. Long, slow, sexy, soul-deep kisses designed to light her on fire — as if she weren't already in flames.

She'd always known Muldoon was a big man, but it never quite occurred to her just how big he was — until he was on top of her like this. He almost made her feel tiny.

He stopped kissing her, pulling back to look down at her, amusement in his pretty blue eyes. "You're not talking."

"Yes, I am. I'm having a long internal dialogue chastising myself about how utterly stupid I was not to jump your bones that first day we met."

Muldoon laughed.

"Kiss me again," Joan demanded. "That's enough talking for the rest of this decade."

He kissed her, and then — God, she didn't know how he did it — somehow he got to his feet and scooped her off the sofa.

He actually picked her up in his arms and carried her to the bed. It was incredibly romantic — particularly since he didn't gasp or wheeze or stagger or even break a sweat.

If she hadn't already decided that she was going to sleep with him, his macho act would have clinched the deal.

And if it hadn't, the way he pulled back to look at her with such heat in his eyes after he gently placed her on the bed would have done the trick. Particularly when he said, "You don't know how many times I've dreamed about this."

She had managed to unbutton more than half of the buttons on his jacket during those nuclear kisses on the sofa, desperate to feel his skin beneath her palms. She sat up now, eager to finish the job.

He helped — so to speak — by unzipping the back of her dress and peeling her top down from her shoulders and lazily — worshipfully — kissing her neck, her throat, her collarbone.

She had his tailored jacket almost off one of his muscular arms — no easy trick — when he pulled her dress down even farther, exposing her breasts clad only in the barely there lace of her bra.

"Oh, yeah," he said. "Oh, yeah," and nothing he did was lazy anymore.

He managed to shake his jacket off his arms even as he unfastened the back clasp of her bra and pulled her on top of him, so that he was on his back and her unrestrained breasts were right in his face.

She was straddling him, her dress pushed down to her waist, and she heard herself moan aloud as he touched and kissed and licked her. Or maybe that moan was because she finally pushed his shirt up and got her hands onto his smooth, bare, beautiful skin.

His belt buckle was digging into her, and he pushed her back a few inches. And then his erection was pressing up against the silk crotch of her panties instead.

She had to laugh. Yeah, this man needed Viagra about as much as he needed someone to hold his hand when he crossed the street.

"What?" He stopped his onslaught of her breasts long enough to ask, pushing her back so that he could look at her sitting up above him. "God, you're amazingly beautiful."

It was then that Joan realized all the lights in the room were blazing. It was just slightly less well lit in there than noon on the surface of the sun.

Thank the Lord that her dress covered her hips. Her hips may have been amazing, but they very definitely were not beautiful.

However, her breasts — although unfashionably large — weren't too hideous. In fact, from the way Muldoon was looking at her, she didn't feel hideous at all. Except, "My right breast is bigger than my left," she felt compelled to point out.

"That's incredibly sexy," he said. "You're the sexiest woman I've ever been with. Ever."

"Well, that's nice," she said, "but I really kind of doubt —"

"Don't," he said. "Don't doubt it. I want you naked, right now. I want to see your tattoo."

He pulled her back down to kiss her, his hands busy again with the zipper at the back of her dress, checking to see if he could push it even farther down.

As far as naked went, her panties could go, along with his clothes. But Joan wanted to keep her dress right where it was, covering her thighs — and the tiny rose she'd had tattooed on her left hip in a moment of drunken madness. Of course he'd remembered that from her so-called file. Didn't it figure?

As she kissed him, she slipped her fingers inside the waistband of his pants in an attempt to distract him.

It worked, particularly when she slid her hand all the way down, inside his boxers, and wrapped her fingers around him.

He made a noise, deep in his throat, and he stopped fooling with her zipper long enough to hastily unfasten his pants. She helped, and his penis sprang free. It burst onto the scene in such a happy, joyful way that she had to laugh.

And then, because even with her somewhat limited experience she knew that laughing at the very first sight of a lover's equipment was not necessarily the most romantic thing to do, she took him into her mouth.

From the sounds he made, all was forgiven.

But damn, that belt buckle was still jabbing her. His pants had to go.

"I'll be back," she said in her best Ah-nold imitation as she smiled up at him, giving him one last lick for good measure. He looked pretty damn happy and joyful about that himself.

She pulled both his pants and his boxers down his legs as he kicked off his shoes and yanked his shirt over his head.

And then, except for his socks, he was a naked, naked, *naked* man.

And why a man like this ever wore clothes was a mystery.

He sat up, still trying to pull off her dress, but she moved her backside out of range of his hands, taking off his socks to make the picture perfect.

And perfect, he was.

Suntanned skin, with springy golden hair on his arms and legs and chest. Muscles, muscles, and more muscles. Tousled wavy hair, hot blue eyes, square jaw, movie star worthy cheekbones, and that little smile that played about his perfect lips and lit his face with genuine and unabashed amusement and pleasure. And then, to top it all off, an Empire State Building of an erection that confirmed the desire that burned in his eyes.

Even his toes were lovely.

"Come here," he said.

"I was going to get a condom," she said. And on the way back in from the bathroom, she was going to turn off the bedroom light.

"I put some in my jacket pocket," he said, holding one of the little wrapped squares out on his palm. "Hope springs eternal and all that."

He reached for her, grabbing her wrist and pulling her back onto the bed with him, kissing her mouth, long and sweet and hard. Her bare breasts were against his naked chest.

"This is what I want," he whispered. "I want to be skin to skin with you."

"I do, too, but I want to turn off the light first," she admitted. "I'm not as perfect as you. My ass is big. And my hips —"

He laughed. "Your ass is sexy and I love every

inch of your hips, baby. I've been dying to get my hands on you for days now."

"Careful," she warned. "If you call me baby, I just might have to call you Junior." She looked down between them. "Or maybe not."

He laughed, tickling her, and she shrieked, pulling away from him, leaping off the bed.

He followed, and she backed away.

"Aha," he said. He was trying to keep a straight face and failing rather miserably. "So you *do* want to play bad cop and naughty nun — I knew you were secretly kinky, DaCosta."

She laughed. "Naughty nun?"

Muldoon laughed, too.

Dear God, was it really possible that a man who looked like Muldoon was actually capable of not taking himself seriously, of having some completely silly fun?

Yes, apparently it was. If she were smart, she'd start figuring out some way to keep him around for longer than the next few weeks. Oh, and wasn't it a complete mistake to start thinking about that? They lived about as far apart as two people could and both still be Americans. They were both completely devoted to their careers.

And that wasn't even taking into consideration the fact that Michael Muldoon was not a long-term man. He couldn't possibly be. If she weren't careful, she was going to get emotionally pulverized. If she didn't stay in control . . .

But, God, look at him, smiling at her like that. His laughter had turned once more into heat as he gazed at her bare breasts and . . .

She realized that her dress was hanging down

around her hips, and she hiked it up to cover her stomach. She didn't have the same kind of belly button action that Britney Spears had going.

"Wait," Muldoon said. "I want to show you something, okay?"

He gently pulled her across the room and turned her around. She was now facing the nearly full-length mirror that hung over the low dresser on the opposite wall from the bed. And, God, there she was, naked breasts and messy hair and all.

Muldoon moved so that he was directly behind her, his arms around her.

"Look how sexy you are," he said. He touched her breasts, her throat, her torso, his big hands sweeping across her body.

Yes, her hair was messy, but it was a sexy kind of messy. And when he touched her like that, his hands warm and his fingers slightly rough, her mouth opened slightly, and eyes half closed and . . .

"You're incredibly beautiful," he whispered. "If you really want the light off, we can turn it off. But I'd prefer to see this. To see you. Is that okay?"

"Yeah," she breathed. At that point, anything he asked would have been okay with her.

"Let it go," he murmured, tugging at her dress. She opened her fingers, hypnotized by both the sight and sensation of his hands moving across her skin, down the soft curve of her stomach, across her hips. Across that tiny rose tattoo. And lower.

As she watched in the mirror, he dipped one hand beneath the edge of her dress, beneath the edge of her panties and . . .

"Oh, yeah," he breathed into her ear, pressing himself against her rear end as he filled her with his fingers. "You make me crazy, Joan. You're so hot."

And what do you know? She actually was. Tummy and hips and all, when Muldoon touched her, when he looked at her like that, she was steaming hot.

"I love your legs," he said as he pushed her dress down her thighs, and the silky fabric pooled at her feet. He trailed his fingers along the insides of her thighs, stopping just short of touching her intimately again. She was leaning back against him slightly, breathing hard, her nipples taut and at attention. She watched herself in the mirror as she opened her legs slightly for him, in a silent invitation.

He met her eyes in the mirror and smiled — and pushed her panties down her legs. "Do it again," he whispered.

She did. Oh, my.

And then . . . oh, my. She felt him against her, behind her, hot and thick, as he slid his hand down her stomach and touched her. He kept going, reaching between her legs to guide himself to her, even as he tipped her slightly forward.

Slowly, so slowly, he moved, filling her a little bit farther with each stroke, as he kept touching her.

"Condom," she remembered, even though she wasn't quite sure that she knew her own name.

"It's on." His voice sounded funny, too. "God, you're tight."

He kept moving, slowly, slowly, his fingers creating the friction that their position made impossible.

But she wanted more, and she was ready for

him, reaching behind her to pull him more closely to her, to fill her completely.

"Oh, yeah," he breathed, his eyes locked on hers in the mirror. "Oh, baby. Oh, man, that's a little too nice. Hang on a sec, Joan, will you?"

She wouldn't. She didn't want to. She was about to explode, and she wanted him exploding with her.

"Don't stop," she said, moving against him. "Oh, please . . ."

And there, in the mirror, Joan could have watched herself fly apart. Instead she watched Muldoon as he watched her come, and the look on his face — satisfaction and desire and pure, hot, raw male admiration — was one she knew she'd remember for the rest of her life.

And when he met her gaze, he came, too. Even if she hadn't felt the tightening and sudden surge of his body, she would have known just from looking into his eyes.

Then there they were, breathing hard, eyes and body still locked together.

Muldoon smiled at her. "I hope I broke you of your irrational fear of mirrors and bright lights."

Joan laughed. "Was that what that was? A selfless humanitarian act for the good of mankind?"

He laughed, too. "No, it was entirely selfish. I happen to enjoy an occasional mirror or two." He pulled her back with him to collapse on the bed. "God, my knees. You just aren't quite tall enough." He turned his head to look at her. "For that, I mean. Not that I'm complaining." He smiled and reached over to touch her cheek.

This was where, if her life were like one of the romance novels she loved to read, he would confess that he loved her.

His smile was so sweet, and his eyes were so warm and filled with emotion.

He moistened his lips slightly before he spoke. Cleared his throat. Here it came . . .

"I'm starving. Want to get room service?"

Joan had to laugh at herself. It had been more than twenty years since she was a ten-year-old, and she still struggled with her Snow White complex. Some day her prince might come, indeed, but if he did, honey, the truth was, he was going to have to run to keep up with her. He was going to have to hunt her down, because she wasn't sitting at home waiting for him to show. *And* he was going to have to be willing to abdicate the crown to be with her.

Muldoon was a prince, for sure, but she just couldn't see him doing that. As much as she might want him to.

Oh, but don't do this, Joan. Don't make this into something that it's not. Don't start making any plans that include Mike Muldoon.

"I hear they have a mean fish chowder here," he told her, a devilish light in his eyes.

Enjoy this for what it was. Enjoy *him*. "Kiss me first," she said.

"With pleasure," he whispered, pulling her more completely into his arms.

He kissed her slowly and quite thoroughly, his mouth hot and sweet.

Just like the man himself.

NINETEEN

Sam was hungover.

Mary Lou knew from just one glance when he walked into the kitchen. She'd seen more than her share of hangovers starting back when she was Haley's age.

"When did you get home?" she asked.

He winced — she was talking too loudly. Well, screw him. He had no right to go out and get drunk with God knows who and then come crawling back home at some ungodly hour, after last call, no doubt.

"A little after two," he said.

Last call, indeed.

Sam Starrett was a very good-looking man — tall and lean with blue eyes and brown hair that streaked golden when he spent a lot of time out in the sun. His face wasn't pretty-boy handsome like a movie star's, though. Instead, he had prominent features that were going to be called craggy when he got a lot older. But regardless of that, he was one of those men who was going to be just as attractive at sixty as he was at thirty-something.

Because no matter how old he got, he was still going to have that smile.

It was a killer — a combination of genuine

amusement with life and a sly awareness that he was, indeed, the King of the World. It had slayed her completely the first time he'd aimed it in her direction.

But he wasn't smiling right now.

"You stink," she told him sharply. "Go take a shower and brush your teeth. And shave while you're at it. I'm getting Haley up in a few minutes and I don't want her seeing you looking like human garbage."

Well, that surprised the shit out of him. Just a few days ago, she would've quietly gotten him some painkillers and a big glass of water, and tippy-toed around, talking in hushed tones, treating him like royalty. She would have ignored the fact that she'd already made a pot of oatmeal. She would have woken up Haley and then taken her out of the house for some high-calorie fast-food crappola breakfast so her little girl wouldn't have to see her father at his worst.

But that wasn't fair — why should she and Haley be the ones always to accommodate him?

What was he going to do? Move out? Tell her he wanted a divorce?

And so what if he did? She loaded dirty dishes into the dishwasher with a rattle and bang that made him wince again. She'd be better off without him.

"What time do you have to be at work?" he asked, opening the cabinet where they kept the aspirin and shaking more than he should be taking into his hand. He swallowed all of the pills at once, without any water.

"Same time that I always have to be there," she

told him. "I always work the same hours." It felt good to allow herself to be pissed at him. "I'm mad at you, in case you haven't noticed."

Sam nodded, so serious. "Yeah, you have a right to be. I've been . . . I don't know. Phoning it in, I guess, for a long time." He took a deep breath. "I know you've been really unhappy, Mary Lou, and I have been, too. We need to find some time to sit down and talk."

Mary Lou felt faint. Oh, shit. He wanted a divorce. He was going to ask her for a divorce. What had she done?

"I'm not unhappy," she said. "I'm very happy. I shouldn't have spoken to you that way. That was wrong of me and I apologize. Do you want some oatmeal? Why don't you sit down and I'll get you a bowl?"

He caught her arm as she was reaching up into the cabinet. "Stop," he said. "I'm the one who should be apologizing, not you. I'm going to go shower, like you said. I have to be on base in just a few minutes — I don't have time to talk right now. In fact, the next few days are going to be hectic. I just thought that maybe after this President's thing is over, we can sit down and be honest with each other."

"We don't need to do that," she said. "Really, Sam, I'll try harder —"

"Jesus, Mary Lou . . ." He rubbed his forehead, rubbed his entire face. "Will you just do me one little favor, please?"

"Of course. You know all you ever have to do is ask. I'd do anything for you, Sam. Anything," she stressed. "I know it must bother you not to have beer in the house, and well, I've been thinking, I've been doing so well that I'd be fine if —"

"Stop," he said. "Christ, just stop and listen."

She shut her mouth, trying to hide the fact that her lower lip was trembling. He was going to leave her. She just knew it. And she *wouldn't* be better off without him. She'd be alone, just like her mother had been, with a baby and bills she wouldn't be able to pay and —

"I don't want alcohol in this house. Under no circumstances whatsoever. Is that clear?"

She nodded.

"Now. All I'm asking you to do is to spend some time over the next few days thinking. Think about what you want out of life. Think about what makes you happy — truly happy. I know it has a lot to do with Haley — I think you're a wonderful mother, I really do. But look beyond her, if you can, and try to think about what *you* want. Can you try to do that?"

Mary Lou couldn't keep her mouth shut any longer. "This is about Alyssa Locke, isn't it?"

He sighed. "No, it isn't. I'm taking a shower."

"She doesn't want you — she's with someone else now. You told me that yourself!" She followed him out of the kitchen and into the hall. Her voice was shrill but she couldn't seem to make herself shut up.

From the other end of the house, Haley woke up and started to cry.

"Yeah, see, but you don't want me, either," Sam said, his voice surprisingly gentle, his eyes not unkind. "Not really."

"You are so wrong!"

433

"Am I?" Sam asked as he went into the bathroom. "Maybe you should think some about that,
as well. I'm going to be late and you are, too, if you
don't get going."

He shut the door.

Heart racing, Mary Lou went in to Haley. She
had to stop and sit down, putting her head between her knees to regain her equilibrium, before
she got the little girl out of the crib.

She hadn't been this panicked, this uncertain
about her future since those unsettling weeks before her wedding day.

Husaam slid down in the driver's seat so that
Mary Lou wouldn't see him as she loaded the kid
into her car.

She looked upset.

Of course, she looked upset most mornings —
who wouldn't, with that asshole Sam Starrett for a
husband?

And yet Mary Lou was no prize. He'd thought
she might be — he'd actually started to genuinely
like her. She was pretty and stacked and none too
bright. He didn't like women who were rocket sci-
entists. But then . . .

He still couldn't get over the way she'd so casually pulled up her shirt and fed Haley out in the
churchyard, where anyone could see.

That was no way for a married woman to be-
have. If she were his wife, he'd have her beaten for
indecency. She had no right to go and flash the
world. No right at all.

And what was with this man who was following
her around? This wasn't the first time he'd seen

this loser with Mary Lou. Clearly, he was after something.

He'd had him checked out, but background checks could be falsified. He himself knew that quite well.

Still, the information he'd found seemed to be real.

Ihbraham Rahman, born in Saudi Arabia — not too far from the city where Husaam had spent much of his childhood — had become an American citizen in 1990. He owned a share in a Lincoln dealership in Anaheim with three younger brothers, two cousins, and an uncle — none of whom were even remotely tied to any terrorist activity. And why should they be? They'd embraced the American Dream and were making it pay off.

Not that there wasn't strife in their lives. Apparently Ihbraham had quit his job at the dealership a few years back, ditched a fiancée who was the only daughter of the ailing owner of a nearby BMW dealer, and ran off to reinvent himself as a landscaper, courtesy of the twelve-step program.

The fiancée was still carrying a torch and the brothers still had hopes of turning Rahman Lincoln Mercury into Rahman Lincoln Mercury BMW.

So what was Ihbraham doing with Mary Lou?

Obviously, he was sniffing out an easy target — looking for an easy lay. And there was no doubt about it. Mary Lou Starrett was ripe and ready for the picking, thanks to her husband's neglect.

She got into her car, and Husaam followed her along the same route she always took to her baby-sitter's house, letting her get way ahead of him. There was no chance she'd see him. None at all.

He was going to have to make it clear that if Mary Lou wanted some extramarital sex, she wouldn't have to look to the hired help. *He* was willing to do whatever he needed to do — even sleep with her, what a hardship — to make sure Rahman didn't mess up this operation.

It was bad enough when Mary Lou had sent her car in to have the trunk lid replaced. His clients had been ready to bolt after she'd discovered one of the weapons he'd put in the trunk of her car.

But Husaam doubted she was bright enough to put two and two together and come up with a plan to assassinate the U.S. President. Still, if she told someone else what she had seen . . .

But she hadn't told anyone. He was willing to bet his reputation and his very life on that — and even use her and her car as a delivery vehicle one last time, even though her trunk now locked.

A lock wasn't much of a problem in the first place, and it was less of a problem because he now had a key.

No doubt about it, this was going to be some of the sweetest, easiest money he'd ever earned.

Muldoon woke up alone in Joan's bed.

He could hear the sound of the shower running. Light was coming in through a crack in the curtains, and when he turned to look, the clock on the bedside table read 5:24 A.M.

Hello, morning after.

He briefly closed his eyes. Please, God, let this time be different.

436

He'd woken up shortly after 0200 to find Joan sprawled bonelessly on the bed beside him, her head on his shoulder, her hand resting almost possessively over his heart.

That was the time — were she just some random woman he'd met in a bar — that he would have slipped out of the bed, put on his clothes, and left, leaving his phone number if she'd mentioned she'd be in town for a few days, or just a note — *It was fun* — if she'd made it clear right from the start that there would be no tomorrow.

Only rarely did he stay until dawn. He'd learned the hard way that the morning after could be fraught with all kinds of peril and pain.

The morning after was the part where he either had to leave or be left. It was the time in which there would be a slight change in the voice of last night's warm lover. There might be a second or two of uncomfortable silence before she cleared her throat and spoke just a shade too politely, or maybe a tad too cheerfully.

Either way, he'd learned that it meant that the night — and their brief relationship — was over.

Was it any wonder that he'd made it his MO to leave before being shown the door?

At 0210, he'd gotten up to go to the bathroom, careful not to wake Joan. Or so he'd thought. When he came back into the bedroom and climbed into bed — no way was he leaving her until he absolutely had to — she'd snuggled up against him, resuming her same position with her head on his shoulder.

Only her hand had slipped down to his stomach and then lower and . . .

Muldoon lay there now, tangled in the sheets, smiling up at the ceiling. He should be tired after a night with so little sleep, but really, he couldn't remember the last time he'd felt better.

He had two immediate options. Stay here in bed until Joan got out of the bathroom, or go in there, maybe join her in the shower.

Getting it on in the shower would put an entirely new spin on the concept of a morning after. It would be the Energizer Bunny version of the morning after — where the night before just kept on going and going.

He got out of bed, aware that he'd run out of condoms. He'd tucked only a small handful into his jacket pocket before leaving his apartment, but they'd used them all.

Yes, *all*. Give me an A, give me an L, give me another L, what does that spell? A night filled with a mind-blowing amount of laughter and heart-stopping pleasure.

If there was any getting it on to be done yet this morning, they were going to have to improvise. Unless Joan had some . . .

When he got to the bathroom, the shower had gone off, but he knocked on the door anyway, trying the knob.

Unlocked. He pushed the door open.

Joan was drying herself with one of those over-sized hotel towels, and when she saw him looking in, she quickly wrapped it around herself. "You're awake."

Modesty. In the time-tested language of the typical bummer morning after, rediscovered modesty was never a positive sign.

438

Still, Joan had spent one night with Muldoon, and thirty years' worth of nights thinking that she was a whole lot less than perfect. It made sense that it might take her some time to adjust to his more accurate reality.

He pointed to the toilet. "Mind if I . . . ?"

"Oh," she said. "No. Not at all." She took her hairbrush and, still wrapped in her towel, left him alone in the bathroom.

Also not a good sign. Nor was the fact that she completely failed to comment on his body's rather obvious good morning message.

He flushed the toilet.

To shower or not to shower?

If he showered, she might expect him to put his clothes on and shuffle on out the door. As long as he had bed head and was buck naked, she couldn't kick him out so easily.

Could she?

Oh, screw this trying to second-guess every little last thing Joan was thinking. Muldoon went out into the bedroom where she'd turned on the TV to Fox's cable news. He turned it off.

"Hey, I was listening to that." She was wearing her robe and was putting a pair of panty hose on her killer legs.

"Am I going to get to see you again tonight?" he asked, point-blank.

She sighed. Oh, damn. Sighs were definitely bad signs.

But then she laughed, thank God. At least he hoped it was the right kind of laughter. Sure enough, though, she finally seemed to be looking directly at him, and even noting his physical condition, which although having waned significantly was still pretty obviously revved up.

"You can see me all day if you want to come along to this meeting that starts in thirty minutes," she said. "But somehow I think, from rather obvious clues, that *see* is a euphemism for something that involves body parts other than eyeballs."

"I want to see you tonight," he said. "And yes, not only do I want to see you with my eyes, I want to taste you and touch you and make you come at least three different ways."

That caught her attention. And so much for his waning physical condition.

"You're making this really hard for me." Joan didn't look happy. "Mike, I already decided . . ."

Oh, shit. Decisions had been made. "You decided what?"

Another sigh. "That we cool it until after the President's visit. I mean, come on. I'm sleeping with the President's daughter's boyfriend," she said. "This is not a smart career move."

"I'm not anyone's boyfriend," he said, aware that his words were pathetically true. He'd hoped, after last night, that he and Joan . . .

But no. What was wrong with him? This was old news. He'd seen it plenty of times before. He was drawn to women like Joan. Strong women. Career women. Women who saw him as a temporary diversion, a short-term plaything instead of a legitimate boyfriend.

Legitimate boyfriends were corporate CEOs or the attorney general or a vice president at Microsoft. Legitimate boyfriends were not Navy SEALs.

Not once in his life had he ever been taken home to meet his lover's parents. Not once.

So, yeah. Cooling it for the next week for the sake of Joan's career was nothing new. In fact, any shrink worth his fee would tell Muldoon that he sought out this type of women. He was only attracted to the kind of women who would beat the crap out of him emotionally, if he were dumb enough to wait around for it.

"Today the entire world is going to watch that video clip of you and Brooke from last night," she told him. "They're already showing it. I'm really lucky they don't have additional footage of you and me in the Ladybug Lounge. Sweet God above, what was I thinking? Not that I'm regretting last night," she hastily added. "But making out in a bar isn't appropriate behavior for a member of the President's staff — never mind the fact that you're —"

"Okay," he interrupted. "Okay. Say we cool it for a week. Then what?"

"Then I'm on vacation," she said, as if that answered everything.

"For two weeks," he clarified.

"That's right."

He shook his head. "There's no guarantee I'll be around for those two weeks." In fact, he knew Operation Black Lagoon would be happening shortly after the President's visit. He could very well be gone for most of that time. But he couldn't tell Joan that. He couldn't mention the op at all. "If I *do* have to leave town, I probably won't have time to call you to tell you about it. So if I suddenly disappear, you need to know that I'm not just blowing you off, okay?"

Her eyes had widened. "Are you telling me that you're going to Afghanistan?"

"No. Joan. God. I'm not telling you anything. I *can't* tell you anything. I'm . . . Look, what if we see each other this week, but we're really discreet? You know, careful that no one sees us together and —"

"That's a given," she said. "No matter if it's now or a week from now. I have to think about what it looks like, and it's going to look like I'm sleeping with the President's daughter's boyfriend."

"Who cares what it looks like? It's not the truth —"

"*I* care," Joan told him. "I would care what it looks like even if Brooke weren't in the picture. Even if her senator friend announced he wasn't going to be Bryant's running mate, that he wasn't running for reelection, that he was divorcing his bitchy wife and marrying Brooke. Even then, I'd be extremely careful about our relationship. Have you looked into a mirror lately, Michael? If we showed up in public with our hands all over each other, people are going to wonder what the hell a beautiful young man like you is doing with me."

He shook his head. "That's ridiculous —"

"No, it's not. To be frank and to the point, I don't want them thinking about me like that — wondering if I'm that good in bed, or if I pay you, or if there's some other kind of favor that I'm —"

"Maybe they'll think that you're fun to be with," he said. "Maybe they'll think —"

"Look, Michael, I'm sorry about this, but I honestly don't know what to do about us. It's freaking me out. Yes, I want to see you again. I really do. But I don't think it can be until —"

"Next week," he finished for her. "Okay. Yeah. I hear you. I don't like it, but I'll respect your decision. You know, call me if you change your mind and all that, but . . ."

"Please don't be angry. Last night was —"

"Great. I know. I thought so, too." He started pulling on his clothes, bed head be damned. He didn't want to hear this. He'd heard this kind of speech before. Next week would come, and she wouldn't call him. Or, shoot, maybe she would. And maybe he'd be in town for a few days during her vacation and he'd get laid again. But eventually she'd have to go back to Washington, and that would be that.

End of story.

He should have left at 0200.

"I have to get over to the base," he told her as he jammed his feet into his shoes and raked his hair down with his fingers, looking into the same mirror that they'd both looked into just last night and . . . "Good luck with your meeting." Good luck with your life. Thanks for sharing a night of it. Too bad it wasn't more.

"It's just a week," she said. She actually looked genuinely upset. Or maybe she was just a good actress.

"Yeah," he said. "Sure. I'll, um, wait for your call." And he would. Like the fool that he was.

"I'll see you later this afternoon," she said. "There's a meeting about the President's visit. I'll be there."

"Oh," he said. "Yeah. I'm . . . Steve's taking care of that."

"Why?"

Because Muldoon was going to ask him to. "I don't know. I guess he's more knowledgeable."

"Mike —"

"Look, I really have to go." He headed for the door.

She followed, and clearly her anxiety about whether or not anyone saw him coming out of her room took priority over whatever it was she had been about to say. "Don't let anyone see you leave."

"I'm a SEAL," he said. He wanted to kiss her good-bye, but he was afraid if he did he might start to cry — which would embarrass him to death as well as take some of the punch out of his exit line. "I think I can probably handle it."

The phone rang just a little after noon, and Charlie picked it up, knowing it was Joan.

"I don't have long to talk," her granddaughter said, "but I didn't want you to think I've been ignoring you."

"We know you've been busy — we've been watching the news."

"Yeah." Joan changed the subject. "How's Donny?"

"Much better," Charlie said. "Vince is still checking in on him every day. Did you know your father's been sending him email?"

"No, I didn't," Joan said. "Whoa, that's a surprise. I mean, Tony-the-bonehead's emailed me a few times this month. He even left a message on my answering machine last week. But I never in a million years would have expected him to get in touch with Don."

"I wish you wouldn't call him that," Charlie said mildly. "He's your father. It's disrespectful."

"Walking out on Mommy didn't exactly make him worthy of my respect," Joan countered. "Oh, and getting angry at Donny the way he used to? That really helped. Shout at him louder, Dad. Maybe *that'll* cure his mental illness."

"Cut him a little slack," Charlie said. "It wasn't easy being Donny's parent — you have to admit that."

"Mom managed."

"Some people are simply better equipped to deal with tragedy than others."

"I'm sorry. I didn't call you up to argue about Tony," Joan said. "I am in *one* snarling bad mood so I should probably just tell you that I love you and get off the phone."

"What happened?" Charlie asked. "Other than what's been on the news, that is."

"Isn't that enough?"

"Not that I believe any of the things that have been reported. I'm waiting with baited breath for this press conference that's going to be held this afternoon."

"Yes," Joan told her. "Me, too. It's nice to know that something good has come out of this mess. Brooke recognized how badly she screwed up last night, and she's actually going to make a public apology. She's announcing that she's leaving immediately to check in to the Betty Ford Center. This is her choice, Gram. No one's

445

sending her away. This is really, *finally* what she wants to do."

"Alleluia," Charlie said. "One would think from *that* news your mood wouldn't include any snarling at all."

"Yeah, well . . ."

"So what else happened last night?"

"Nothing," Joan said.

"You slept with him," Charlie guessed. "Your lieutenant."

"Oh, God, *Gramma . . . !*"

"I'm not supposed to talk to you about things that matter?"

"Well, yeah, but not about *that*. You're supposed to think, I don't know . . . that I'm still a virgin because, well, because I'm not married."

Charlie snorted with laughter. "I happen to know, my dearest, that you haven't been a virgin since you were a teenager. I believe his name was Nathan? You brought him to your aunt Wendy's birthday party."

"Oh, my God! You *knew?*"

"Who do you think put that box of condoms in the top drawer of your dresser?" Charlie asked. "Old people aren't necessarily idiots."

"I know that, but I thought . . . I don't know what I thought. That Nate bought them and put them there? Like, hint, hint. I just . . . I mean, I knew it wasn't Mom. She was clueless — she had no idea what was going on with me. She was, you know, dealing with Donny."

They were both silent for a moment, then Charlie said, "I never talked to my mother about anything that mattered. I wish I had, but she died when I was quite young, too. Before I was married. And then after I was married . . . Do you remember your great-grandmother Edna? She died when you were five."

"Yeah," Joan said. "But . . . wait a minute. Now I'm confused. I thought she was your mother, not Gramps's."

"She was my first husband James's mother," Charlie told her. "Edna Fletcher."

Joan laughed. "I had no idea."

"I used to talk to her all the time," Charlie admitted. She still missed Edna. To this day. "We talked about all sorts of things. In fact, the first time Vince and I . . . well, long story short, we made love before we were married — shame on us — and we did it in the same bed James and I had slept in, just down the hall from my mother-in-law's bedroom. The walls were so thin in that apartment, she had to know what we were up to."

"Oh, God, you're kidding."

"Nope. Afterward I had something of a . . . break-down, I guess you'd call it nowadays," she continued. "Vince thought — of course, because he was an honorable man — that since we'd done what we'd done, we'd rush right out and get married immediately. He loved me very much, I knew that — but I couldn't deal with anything I was feeling about him and about James . . . And I was so sure that Vince was going to go back to the war and die and . . . I knew I couldn't bear that."

Joan made a sound that might've been agreement or might've been pain, Charlie couldn't quite tell.

"I don't really know what I was planning to do,"

she told her granddaughter. "I packed my suitcase and threw my coat on right over my robe and I marched downstairs with Vince on my heels. He was begging me to slow down and take a deep breath and not do anything crazy. And there was Mother Edna in the kitchen, making us all a pot of tea.

"I burst into tears when I saw her. I told her that I had to leave this house because I didn't deserve to stay there any longer. I'd betrayed James and I'd betrayed her, and . . . Poor Vince. I know that must've hurt him so much to hear that, but I was a terrible mess.

"She asked him to go back upstairs and give us some privacy, and he went. And then your great-grandma Edna just grabbed hold of me and held on to me and let me cry my heart out. She told me that I hadn't betrayed anyone, especially not her, and that she was glad — so glad — that I'd taken this step back to the world of the living. She knew just what to say to calm me down. She knew not to push me, too. She told me if I wanted to marry Vince — if *I* wanted to — then she couldn't wait to throw rice at my wedding.

"And she knew what to say to Vince, too — I heard her talking to him in the hall after she'd tucked me into bed. She told him, 'James would have liked you.' " Charlie laughed, remembering. "That was — as Vince would say — one hell of a night. And it didn't end there. I had a lot of figuring out to do before I really came to know what exactly it was that I wanted."

Joan was quiet on the other end of the phone.

But she finally spoke. "Both of your husbands fought in the war."

"Yes, they did."

More silence, then, "How did you stand it?"

Figures that would be the question she asked. Charlie laughed softly. There was only one answer. "You pray a lot, and you never take the time you spend together for granted."

Joan was silent again for a few moments. Then she laughed. "I have absolutely no idea what I'm doing, Gramma," she said. "I have no idea what I really want. I thought I did, but . . . God, this man is going to mess up my life. I just know it. I don't think I can see him again. I don't think I can bear it. He's . . . wonderful. If I'm not careful, I'm going to do something really stupid like fall in love with him and . . . God, he's a SEAL and he's a *child* and there's no way it would *ever* work. If I don't end this now . . . I have to end this now. I *have* to."

"Vince and I are supposed to come out to the base tomorrow," Charlie reminded her. "Your Lieutenant Muldoon was going to give us a tour. Maybe we should postpone it."

"No," Joan said. "That's not why I called. That's . . . No, I want you to come out. And . . . oh, God, Gramma, I want to see him again. I'm such a loser. But with you guys there, it'll be safe. Safer. I'll meet you at the gate at . . . We said ten, right?"

"We'll be there," Charlie promised. "And you're not a loser."

"I've already really hurt his feelings," Joan confessed. "I get scared and then I turn into such a bitch."

"So apologize," Charlie told her. "I'm sure you

can think of ways to apologize that will make him forgive you."

Joan laughed. "Gramma, you're shocking me." But then she sighed. "Maybe it's better if he stays mad at me."

"Better for whom?"

"I don't know," Joan admitted. "Both of us. Look, I've got to go. I'll see you and Gramps tomorrow."

TWENTY

Mary Lou drove around for almost an hour before she found Ihbraham.

He was working over in Commander Paoletti and Kelly Ashton's neighborhood today, raking out the overgrown garden of a run-down little house that had a FOR SALE sign out in front.

He saw her immediately as she pulled up and came toward the street to meet her, concern in his eyes.

She was not going to cry. She was not going to cry.

"Got a sec?" she called over the top of her car, trying to sound cheery and breezy and not at all as if her life were falling apart around her.

He glanced back at the garden he'd been working on, and then looked back at her. She forced a smile. It wasn't that hard — she'd been doing it all morning at work.

As he got closer, he leaned over, trying to look into the windows of the car, checking to see if she had Haley with her.

"She's still at the sitter's," Mary Lou told him. "She'll take her nap over there today. Can I talk you into taking a break?"

"Do you mind if I work while we talk?" he countered. "This is a big job and I must get it finished today."

"I don't mind," she said.

"How did you know where to find me?" he asked as they walked back across the lawn.

"I didn't," she admitted as he started raking again. Some of the plants in there were still alive, and he was as careful of them as he was of every living thing he encountered. "I guessed. I hoped. I . . . I think my husband wants a divorce." Her voice wobbled, but somehow she kept herself from actually sobbing. "He told me this morning that we have to sit down and talk after President Bryant's visit is over."

She may not have been crying, but she sounded as if she was going to start any second.

Ihbraham sighed and leaned his rake against the side of the house. Taking her hand, he led her the few steps to the front stoop and together they sat down.

"I am sorry to hear that," he said. "But I think it's good that you're finally going to talk with him."

"You said you need to work," she said, staring down at her hand still engulfed in his. Her fingers were so pale against his dark skin.

"Not as much, I think, as you need me to listen." His smile was a mixture of sad and kind. She had to look away and blink hard to keep her tears from escaping. "Tell me why you think that your husband is so set on divorce. Sam, right?"

She nodded. "His real name's Roger, but everyone calls him Sam." Who cared what everyone called him? Her entire world was crumbling. "He

452

told me he was unhappy. He said he knew I was unhappy, too."

"Are you?"

"Yes," she admitted. "I'm miserable. You know that better than anyone."

"And do you want to divorce him?" Ihbraham asked.

"No!"

He gently released her hand. "Why is it then, that you can be unhappy and yet not wish for a divorce, yet be so certain that this is what he wants?"

"Because I'm not screwing around on the side the way he is." Even as she said the words, she knew they weren't really true. She believed Sam when he'd said he hadn't been with Alyssa since they were married.

But the fact remained that he still wanted Alyssa. He dreamed about her. He thought about her. He closed his eyes when he was with Mary Lou — back in the days when they were still having sex — and pretended he was with Alyssa. She knew it.

"He hasn't touched me in months," Mary Lou confessed. "If he's not cheating on me, that means he'd rather go without sex than be with me." And wasn't that a terrible thought? This time she couldn't do anything to stop the tears that rolled down her cheeks. "Am I really that fat and ugly?"

Ihbraham shook his head. "Maybe he refrains from touching you because he knows you don't love him."

"But I do." Although even as she said the words, she knew they weren't true. "I did. I thought I did. Lord, he's so different than he was when we first met. I guess that's not a huge surprise since all we did together was get drunk and have sex. Now we do neither. Is it really any wonder we don't have anything in common? I hate all the movies and books that he loves. His eyes glaze over when I want to talk about fixing up the house. Okay, we both like country music, but I can't go out to a bar without fear of falling off the wagon — so much for dancing. As if I even could get him to do something like dance anymore. He's so tense and angry and . . . *dark*. When we first met he was such a party boy. Everything was a joke, a good laugh. Mercy, that smile . . . But he's not like that at all. Not really. He scares me to death sometimes."

Ihbraham looked at her sharply. "Does he beat you?"

"*No!* I think he'd rather die before hitting a woman," Mary Lou said. "I just . . . I think he's seen and done some really terrible things. You know, in this war. And he's been fighting it for a long time — long before September eleventh. I don't want to hear about it, which is good because he's not allowed to tell me much. But when he *can* talk about it, I just don't want to know. I want him to be that man who smiles and laughs all the time, the man I met back in the bar. I don't want to see him start to cry."

"You married more than a smile and some laughter," Ihbraham said gently. "You married an entire man. Laughter is just a very small part of any person."

"No kidding." She hugged her knees in to her chest, resting her chin on top of them. "I think I always knew there was more to Sam than he let on.

454

He always scared me a little. But back then I liked that, too. SEALs always came into the bar, and everyone was in such total awe of them. *Every*one. The guys, too. I thought if I could get a man like that, then I'd be special. I thought, oh, my Lord, what it would be like to spend the rest of my life with someone like that . . . I thought, if I could get Sam to marry me, I'd work my ass off to make sure that he'd never leave me. And then I'd always be special, and I'd always have someone to take care of me. I'd never have to worry about *any*thing again and . . ."

Mary Lou wiped her nose with her soggy sleeve. "I'm good in bed. I am." She laughed ruefully. "Or at least I was. I was sure once I got Sam into bed he wouldn't want to leave, but then he started making noises like he was going to break it off with me, and I just . . . I got so scared."

Dear Jesus Lord, she was actually going to tell Ihbraham this, wasn't she?

"My sister, Janine, she lives in Florida now, she told me . . ." Mary Lou took a deep breath and said it. She had to say it — she had to tell someone and she trusted Ihbraham as much as she'd ever trusted anybody. "She told me that if I got pregnant, Sam would marry me — he was that kind of guy — and then I'd have him forever. He'd never leave. And then she gave me this box of condoms to use next time he came over. She didn't say anything, and I didn't ask, but I knew. I pretended I didn't, but I did. She must've done something to them, so that they wouldn't work right. And sure enough, I got pregnant. And sure enough, he married me, and I'm so ashamed, because I knew. I

455

knew. And this is my punishment now, it must be, catching up with me. I'm completely miserable. I hate my life. I'm married to a man who doesn't love me, who *never* loved me. I tricked him into marrying me and now he's going to leave me anyway."

Ihbraham was silent, and she closed her eyes, afraid to look at him, afraid that he hated her now. He had every right to — she was despicable. She prayed for him to say *some*thing.

"It is my thinking that this kind of man, a man who would take responsibility for his actions, wouldn't simply desert you," he said. "If you really want my opinion —"

"I do." She risked a look at him. He wasn't smiling, but his eyes weren't cold and angry, the way he'd looked at his brothers. His eyes were filled with sympathy and sadness.

"You've made a mess," Ihbraham told her, not unkindly. "And now Haley is caught in the middle of it, too. It's not just you and Sam anymore."

"I know that."

"Sam deserves to know this difficult truth which you have told me."

Oh, shit. Sam was the *last* person she was going to tell. "If he finds out, he's going to be *so* mad — at me and at Janine, too. I can't —"

"Maybe Janine deserves some of that anger. It was not her place to play God."

"She did it because she loves me," Mary Lou defended her sister. "She might be the only one on this planet besides Haley who does!"

"Yet she made it impossible for you to have an honest relationship with your husband. Do you really wonder why you've been so unhappy? Burdened with the weight of your deceit?"

His words twisted her insides and made her too upset even to cry. Deceit! "You think I'm awful, don't you? Oh, Lord, you're right."

"I think you are human," he told her in his gentle, musical voice. "Everyone who is human makes mistakes. But not everyone attempts to repair them. Not everyone fights to stay sober the way you have fought. Not everyone loves their children as much as you do. Not everyone would take the time to give friendship to a mentally ill neighbor. Not everyone stops to see another person beneath the color of skin or an Arabic name in these difficult times."

He was listing her virtues, but Lord help her, didn't he have that last one completely wrong?

"Alyssa's black," she told him, needing him to know just how awful she truly was. "Did I ever tell you that?"

He frowned slightly. "Alyssa . . . ?"

"The woman Sam's hot for. After I met her, I said some things that weren't very nice. She was so beautiful and thin and I'm so fat. And he's more than hot for her," she corrected herself. "He actually wanted to marry her, which is completely insane."

Ihbraham thought about that. "Because he's white and she's not?" he asked.

"Don't you think that would be cruel to their children? Which world would they belong to?"

"The last time I checked there was only one world," he countered mildly.

"That's not true," she argued. "And you know it.

You wouldn't go to that meeting because it was in a part of town where you don't feel safe. And I'm sure there are parts of this city you could go where *I* wouldn't feel safe."

"And for that — because of that — you'd throw away a chance for love, for real happiness?"

"What if they had a son?" Mary Lou said. "How is Sam supposed to raise a son who's black? How is that black child going to feel being shut out of his father's world? It's way harder for a young black man to succeed in America than a young white man. You can't deny that."

"So you think it's better simply not to have a life filled with love and sweet children like Haley than it is to try to change these different angry worlds and make them one good place where everyone is welcome?"

"Change it, yeah," Mary Lou said. "Like that's going to happen in *this* lifetime."

"So should all non-white men and women in America therefore stop having children simply because life will be harder for them than it will be for your white children? And what about Haley?" he asked. "Haven't you given her her own burden? Alcoholism can be hereditary — I'm sure this is something you know. And this is your potential gift to her, just as my son — were I to have one — would be born with his own struggles to endure."

Mary Lou started crying again. That was no fair. This wasn't about Haley. He shouldn't have brought her into it. And yet she knew he was right.

"I should never have had her," she sobbed. "I know it."

"But you did." Ihbraham stood up and started

raking again, his movements almost jerky. "So take full responsibility. Be honest — both with yourself and Sam. See what happens. Maybe you will be able to start over with him. Maybe if you try to understand and accept him as a complete man things will be better between you. Maybe you'll fall in love with him and he'll fall in love with you. The honest you. The one whom you show to me all the time. Not this deceitful person who lives in his house, cowering with all her fear and shame."

Oh, Lord, he was right again. She *had* been cowering.

"What if he kicks me out?" she asked.

"What if he doesn't?"

"Yeah, but what if he *does?* Or what if he moves out?" She had to know. "Will you help me? I need to know that you'll help me. Ihbraham, please, I really need you to be my sponsor right now. I need to know that I have someone to go to, someone to trust, if things get really bad. *Please.*"

He stopped raking. Opened his mouth. Shut his mouth. Shook his head. Started raking again. "I can't be your sponsor. No. I'm sorry."

"Why not?"

He just shook his head.

Her voice came out sounding very small. "Is it because you hate me now after hearing all of this?"

He laughed at that. "No, I don't hate you."

"Then why?" She didn't believe him.

Ihbraham looked at her and sighed. "You really must know?"

"Yes," she said.

He put down his rake and held out his hand to her. "Come here."

Mary Lou didn't hesitate. She stood up and went to him willingly. Took his hand.

"Don't be so sad," he told her. "Today is a good day to start fresh, to change all that you don't like about your life, so don't cry anymore, little one, okay?"

He pulled her close, into an embrace, and she held him just as tightly as he held her, her face against his shoulder, against the soft, sweet-smelling cotton of his T-shirt. She could feel his cheek against the top of her head.

"I'm so glad you don't hate me," she whispered, finally lifting her head to look up at him. "But I don't understand —"

He kissed her.

She saw it coming, saw his gaze flicker down to her mouth, saw him slowly lower his head and . . .

His lips were unbelievably soft and he tasted just as exotic as he always smelled. His beard and mustache were raspy against her cheeks and chin, but not as rough as Sam's perpetual two-day-old stubble.

His kiss was so much like Ihbraham himself — gentle but in complete command. He knew exactly where he was going and how to get there as he kissed her deeper, longer, his hands sliding down and across her back, pulling her in to him.

It was meltingly lovely. It was heart-stoppingly perfect. It was completely, shockingly exactly what she so desperately wanted.

A man she really liked — who wanted her the way she longed to be wanted.

Except he was black. Or brown. Certainly non-white.

Although who the hell could tell what color either of them were while her eyes were closed, while she was kissing him?

Of course, anyone watching could certainly see.

Mary Lou jerked back away from him and he instantly let her go. And there she stood, staring up at him in shock.

He'd kissed her. And she'd kissed him back.

And she wanted to kiss him again.

She couldn't look at him. She had to turn away. Her head was spinning.

"This is why I must not be your sponsor," he said in his same musical, gentle voice, as if whatever had been left of her uncertain world hadn't just collapsed into rubble and dust. "My friendship for you is no longer just a friendship. So you see, it would be inappropriate for me to offer you guidance or counseling of any kind. I could not trust myself not to take advantage of your trust. You need a sponsor with no ulterior motives, Mary Lou."

She didn't know what to say, what to do.

"Go home," he commanded her. "Go and talk to Sam. Tell him the truth and then figure out a way you both can be happy. If you truly let him know you, I'm certain that he'll come to love you, too."

She turned, and ran for her car.

"So," Vince said. "Hawaii, 2003."

Charlie looked up from the kitchen table, where piles of papers were spread out around her. She was, quite possibly, the only person in America who did her taxes in early November, because once the holiday season started, "things got too hectic."

Hello! January, anyone?

But no. That tax return had to be sent as close to January the first as possible, in order to properly conclude the previous year. And if she did most of the work now, then all that was left to do during the busy holiday months was just wait for the bank's and other documents to arrive.

And hope to hell that if they finally *did* win the lottery, they'd earn enough to be able to afford to pay an accountant to fill out those forms all over again.

But really, how could he complain? All he had to do was sign his name on the line that Charlie pointed to. God bless her for doing all the work, for taking care of the details of their lives, for doing the things that would have made him pull out all of his remaining hair.

"You really want to go to Hawaii next year?" she asked him, those little worry lines appearing on her forehead between her eyes.

"We've never been," Vince said. "Maybe it's time, huh?"

She was silent, just looking at him, and he felt a stab of doubt. Maybe she really didn't want to see Pearl Harbor, to see where James had died, to visit his grave. Maybe — even after all these years — that would be too hard for her.

Maybe he was the one who needed her to go there to see those things. Maybe he was the fool who needed to be sure James Fletcher truly had been laid to rest.

All these years, and he could read Charlie's mind. Except when it came to James.

Ignore him and maybe he'll go away. And if he

doesn't, well, just be glad that out of the three people in the room, you're one of the ones who's still alive. Vince had lived for years with that philosophy.

Don't mention him, don't talk about him, don't think about him if you can help it.

There had actually been weeks — months, even — during which Vince hadn't had a single thought about Charlie's first husband.

But James had always come back.

James had been there, in spirit at least, at every crucial, important moment in Vince and Charlie's lives.

It was James who had finally gotten him in to talk to someone important about Tarawa, about his hopes that a special team of swimmers could be formed to keep such disasters from happening again.

He'd woken up that morning — the one after that night with Charlotte that had been such a mixture of sheer pleasure and pain — to find she'd slipped a note under his door.

He'd reached for it with dread, praying it wasn't another apology.

Vincent, it said in Charlie's no-nonsense handwriting. *Please get dressed today in your uniform. We have an appointment at eleven o'clock.*

He was probably the only man on earth who'd walked into a meeting with FDR, disappointed to be at the White House.

He'd hoped, right up to the minute that he and Charlotte had climbed into the taxi, that they were going to Maryland, where a marriage could be performed without any delay.

But Charlie had had something else in mind.

Apparently when James had won that posthumous Medal of Honor, there was a big ceremony at the White House honoring all of the heroes of that terrible day. Charlie had been supposed to attend, but she'd had the flu. President Roosevelt had extended an invitation to her to visit him at the White House at her convenience — provided his schedule allowed.

And that January morning in 1944, his schedule apparently allowed.

"Be concise and to the point," Charlotte instructed Vince quietly as they were escorted to the Oval Office.

"Thank you for doing this," he said. He knew his words were inadequate. She was giving him a chance — a slim chance, but a chance nonetheless — to participate in this war in a way that could make a difference.

And probably get him killed.

He saw that in her eyes, loud and clear, despite the fact that her face was a calm mask. "Yes," she said. "Well. No doubt I'll regret it."

And then there they were. Face-to-face with the President.

Vince could remember reaching across the huge desk to shake FDR's hand. He had no idea what he'd said.

Tarawa. He told President Roosevelt about what it had been like at Tarawa. He told him about growing up the son of a Cape Cod lobsterman, and about his idea — to use his strength as a swimmer to provide information for island invasions.

464

He remembered the glint of light against the president's glasses, the smell of his cigarette smoke, the aide who stepped forward to rush him and Charlotte out of the room when they'd overstayed their allotted time, the slight gesture from Roosevelt that made the man stop and back away.

He remembered being offered a seat on a sofa, as Roosevelt pushed himself out from behind his desk and joined him at a small sitting area. The president told him about a team of men already formed and training in Fort Pierce, Florida. Underwater Demolition Teams or Combat Demolition Units, they were called. It was Vince's idea almost exactly, already set into motion.

Somewhere during the conversation, after FDR asked him if he'd be interested in joining this team of men, after Vince had told him a heartfelt "Yes, sir," Charlotte quietly excused herself from the conversation and left the room.

It was a victory, but it was bittersweet. He was to leave for Florida almost immediately.

He'd gotten what he thought he'd wanted.

Except the one thing he wanted most of all, more than anything, was a woman who didn't want him.

At least not until fate intervened.

"Yes," Vince said to Charlotte now. "I really want to go to Hawaii. Will you think about it?"

"Why is it so important to you?" she asked.

And suddenly he knew.

It was because he'd lived James's life.

Vince had lived the life that should have been James Fletcher's. He needed to make this pilgrimage to pay his respects to the man whose death had made Vince's happiness possible.

"Just think about it," he said. He grabbed his car keys from the box by the door. "We're out of milk. I'm going to go pick some up."

She put down her pencil. "Vincent —"

He fled.

And he realized, as he pulled out of the garage, that for all these years, it hadn't been Charlotte who didn't want to talk about James.

It had been *him*.

TWENTY-ONE

"Do you have a minute, Lieutenant?"

Muldoon looked up to find Joan standing in the open doorway of Sam Starrett's office.

It was clear, however, that the lieutenant she wanted a minute from was not Sam.

"Hey, Joan." Sam couldn't have missed her frosty tone, but he pretended not to have noticed. "Come on in. I'm on my way out." Yeah, right. He had just told Muldoon his plan to spend the next few hours tackling some paperwork. "Make yourselves at home."

He closed the door behind him as he made a hasty exit.

And there they were, Muldoon pulling himself to his feet.

He should have been the one who had bolted. Just looking at her made him angry all over again — angry enough to say things he definitely shouldn't say, neither aloud nor in mixed company.

"I really only have a minute," he lied. "So if this is going to take longer —"

"Oh, my God," she said. "You are hiding from me, aren't you? At first I was worried when you didn't show up, because you promised me you'd give my grandparents this tour —"

"Was there some kind of problem with Steve?" he asked. "He's the one who usually gives our VIP tours. I didn't think you'd have a problem with having someone more knowledgeable on hand."

"He was fine," Joan said. "But . . . well, you know, I was kind of looking forward to seeing you. I mean, hey, I didn't spend the night with Steve."

It was supposed to be a joke, meant to lighten the mood, but he didn't laugh. "I'm sure we could arrange that for you if you like."

Joan probably wouldn't have looked more shocked if he'd reached out and slapped her across the face. And after the shock came anger. Her eyes actually flashed as she glared at him.

"What is *wrong* with you?" she asked hotly. "What an awful thing to say!"

It was. But goddamn it, he was angry and frustrated. And hurt. *Really* hurt. "If you were looking forward to seeing me, you could've called me, Joan. Like last night, for example. Like *hours* after Brooke had her press conference and told the world that there was nothing going on between the two of us. Like after there was no longer any reason on earth why you and I couldn't be seen together — except maybe your own insecurity about your career."

He'd waited hours for Joan to call, assuming she was in meetings or up to her ears in making arrangements for Brooke's admission to that rehab center. But no. She'd been in the hotel bar, kicking back with some of her White House friends.

Pathetic asshole that he was, he'd gone looking for her, like some kind of creepy stalker, desperate for just a glimpse of her smile.

Joan's silence last night had been a very clear message to him, letting him know that their night together had meant far more to him than it had to her.

Jesus Christ, you'd think he'd learn. What a loser.

Oh, yeah, he was feeling really good about himself today. . . .

"You're the one who stood me up — in front of my grandparents, no less — and *you're* mad at *me* for not calling you?" she clarified. "What's that about? You couldn't call me?"

"I told you very specifically that the next move was yours," Muldoon told her tightly. "You want to see me again, you call me. That's how it works."

"Well, excuse me for not knowing the rules! I've never dated a gigolo before!"

Silence.

She didn't meet his gaze. Or maybe he was the one who couldn't bring himself to look at her, because, God, it was hard to maintain eye contact with a knife in the gut.

"Well," he finally managed to say. "At least we now know what you think of me."

"I didn't mean that."

"I think you did."

"Look, I should have called you," Joan admitted. "I'm sorry. I was scared. I'm confused about this." She gestured between the two of them. "About us. I don't know how we can make this work, Mike, and it's *completely* freaking me out."

"Yeah, well, we can't make it work," he told her, looking out of Sam's window. "It won't work. I mean, yeah, we can see each other as often as we possibly can for the next few weeks, and, sure, it'll

469

be fun. We'll talk and laugh a lot and make love for hours." He sighed. "And then you'll go back to D.C. You'll tell me you'll call me, that we'll get together soon, and you'll get on a plane and . . . that'll be it. That's the last I'll hear from you."

"That's not true."

"Yes, it is." He turned to look at her, angry at her all over again for not admitting it. "I'll call you, and your assistant or secretary or someone in your office will tell me you're busy and take a message. They'll even take my name and phone number — at least they will the first few times I call. But you won't call me back. And then, when I call again and again, they won't even bother taking my number, and eventually I'll stop calling. Eventually I'll stop bothering you. I'll become a distant memory — part of the good time you had on your last vacation. I'll be just another barely remembered name on your 'guys I had fun fucking' list."

Color was spreading across her cheeks, and her lips got tighter and tighter with each word he spoke. He'd offended her with his language, there was no doubt about that. But damn it, she'd offended him, too.

"Well, I guess we now know what *you* think of *me*," she said. "You know, this kind of insecurity and . . . and . . . *cowardice* is pretty unappealing in a grown man. But wait, I forgot. You're only twenty-five."

He felt his own face flush at her particularly low blow. "I thought women liked honesty. Because, hey, I'm just being honest here — call it whatever you want. And you know what? Right now I'd just rather skip it all. Maybe if we can both manage to be honest, we can cut out that entire month of me pitifully hoping you will call back. We can just skip ahead to the part where the lightbulb comes on and — God, I'm a fool — I realize too little too late that you were just another lousy mistake in a long string of lousy, god-awful, goddamned mistakes."

Joan didn't slam the door on her way out. She closed it gently behind her, with a tiny but entirely too final sounding click.

Mary Lou was in such a fog, she almost didn't recognize Bob Schwegel, Insurance Sales, when she saw him.

"Hey," he said, his blond hair and white teeth gleaming in the sunlight. "Wow, that's good timing. I was just coming in to see you. Are you on break?"

He was standing there in the parking lot of Mc-Donald's, and he followed her back to the Dumpster, to her car.

"I just took my break," she told him. Which was a relief. She would have hated spending her entire fifteen minutes with Insurance Bob breathing down her neck. She was already too rattled by yesterday's conversations with both Sam and . . .

Ihbraham.

Whom she hadn't been able to stop thinking about. Not for one minute in the past eighteen hours.

She'd actually gathered up her nerve and called him, just a few minutes ago, from the pay phone back by the bathrooms.

She'd pretended that everything was normal.

That nothing had happened. That he hadn't kissed her, that she hadn't kissed him back.

"I'm going to a meeting tonight," she'd said, leaving a message on his machine. "Give me a call if you want to go, too."

It was a friendly enough message, without a hint of sexual invitation. Because what she really wanted was to go back to that place where they'd been friends and only friends.

Anything else was too frightening to think about.

Even though she'd been able to think about nothing else.

"I guess my timing's bad then." Bob watched as she unlocked the front door of her car and put her book bag onto the seat.

"Sorry," she said, not sorry at all as she relocked her car and slipped her keys into her pants pocket.

He blocked her way back to the restaurant. She hadn't realized he was quite so tall and broad. Or maybe he'd just never stood that close to her before. "You can make it up to me. Have dinner with me tonight."

"I'm sorry, I'm busy tonight."

"Tomorrow night, then."

"Why?" she asked.

Her frank question caught him off guard, and he blinked at her.

"What could you possibly see in me?" she persisted.

A few more blinks and then he laughed. But then he got serious. Really serious.

"I see someone who's been neglected for too long," he said quietly. "Someone who's as lonely as I am." He backed off. "I'm sorry if I came on too strong. I didn't mean to scare you or upset you or . . . I just . . . I haven't met a woman I've liked as much as you in a long time."

"I'm married," she said. And completely unable to stop thinking about someone else.

"I don't care," he told her, still with that same disarmingly quiet sincerity. "Maybe that makes me a bad person, but I think if you meet someone you're meant to be with, you should do whatever it takes to wind up together."

"You think you're meant to be with . . ." Me. Mary Lou looked at him again, focusing this time on his face, his shoulders, his legs in the suit he was wearing. He was even more beautiful than Sam, and he thought . . .

"I think I'd like to get to know you better," he said. "So what do you say? Just dinner. No pressure. We can take it slow, see where it goes."

Mary Lou shook her head. "I don't think —"

"Don't think," he said. "Just say yes. Do something crazy for a change, Mary Lou."

She laughed. "Bob, I —"

"Okay, do think about it," he said. "Think hard, sleep on it, and I'll call you tomorrow." He lifted her hand to his lips and kissed her.

She watched as he got into his car — it was parked right next to hers — and pulled out onto the main road that went through the base.

It was only then that she wondered.

What was he doing here?

Vince had been oddly quiet all day. Even Joanie had commented on it, during their tour of the Navy base this morning.

473

"Is everything all right with Gramps?" she'd pulled Charlie aside to ask. "His health's okay, isn't it?"

Charlie sure hoped so. He was turning eighty this year. That was something to celebrate, considering many men in America didn't live to see that particular milestone of life.

She watched him now from the bedroom window. He was in the garden, just sitting and watching the wind move through the trees.

After sixty years of marriage, she'd learned that sometimes he sat and watched the leaves move in the wind because he had something on his mind. But sometimes he just liked to sit and watch the wind and the sky.

His silence, however, was a little bit harder to explain away.

But she'd learned as well that he'd talk to her when he was good and ready.

And if he couldn't bring himself to speak, he'd eventually write to her.

For a man who swore he was a walking disaster when it came to writing letters, Vince had written her quite a few doozies down through the years.

And he'd started with one heck of a letter back just weeks after they'd first met. He wrote to her the day he boarded the train for Fort Pierce, Florida. He left it for her to find, on the pillow of her bed.

Dear Charlotte,

I love you. I've never said those words to anyone before, let alone written them down on paper, but it's true.

I love you and I continue to hope that

someday you will marry me. In fact, I'll ask you again. Will you be my wife?

Charlotte had gone with him to the train. It seemed impolite not to, especially after having slept with him the night before.

She was still a mess — angry with him for leaving, angry at herself for her vast list of sins. And there were so many. Or so she'd believed.

He was silent in the taxi, silent as they walked into the station.

She wanted to tell him to be careful, to stay safe, but really, what was the point? He was going off to war and she probably wasn't going to see him alive again.

Somehow she managed not to cry.

And then there they were. Standing by the train. Moments from parting, perhaps forever.

Vince was in his uniform. It made him look even younger than he was — as if twenty-one wasn't young enough to die — because it hung on him a little too loosely. He still hadn't regained all the weight he'd lost from being injured and ill.

I don't need an answer right away. I hope you'll take a good long time to think about it — all the way to the end of the war. And this war will end, my sweet Charlie, and we will win. I can promise you that.

"Well," he said, setting his duffel bag down on the platform next to him.

"I just want you to know that I don't regret last night," she told him, all in a burst.

Vince nodded, looking searchingly into her eyes. If he wanted answers, he wasn't going to find them there. She didn't know anything right now. She could barely remember to keep breathing.

"I don't, either," he said, and smiled. "And *there's* the understatement of the century. Charlotte, last night —"

"Don't," she said. "I don't regret it, but it didn't . . . It wasn't real."

"It was very real to me. I'm going to come back, and we *are* going to make love again. Believe it."

"I can't," she whispered. "I wish I could, but . . ."

I know I've promised you that I'll return, and you're right. That is a promise I cannot truly make. I will try my best though, and God willing, you will *see me again.*

But I've been to war before, and I know — as you know — all too well what it's like. I've made arrangements with my sister to send a letter to you and Mrs. Fletcher if I should be killed, so that you aren't left wondering.

"I'm not waiting for you," she told him. As the words left her lips she couldn't believe she could be that cruel.

But he just laughed. "I know," he said. "I'm waiting for you. Just let me know when you're ready, okay?"

She refused to cry. She'd cried when James had left for the last time. He'd gotten on a train, too. Heading out to California, heading to a ship that was to be deployed from San Diego. She could have gone with him for that train ride, but they'd decided to save the money for the future — a future that never happened, because, halfway around the world from her, he'd died.

But I need you to know, my dearest, that if I am to die, I will not die alone. You are part of me now. You are in my heart. I know that you love me. I know this is true — whether you know it yourself or not. And that knowledge will be with me always. Your love for me will be my constant companion, along with my memories of the beautiful night we shared. It will keep me warm from now until the day I die — whether that day is tomorrow or a hundred years from tomorrow.

"All aboard!"

Vince glanced over his shoulder at the train, his mouth tightening and his eyes dark with worry. He was leaving to fight in a war, and *he* was worried about *her.* "If you need me, I'll be in Fort Pierce for a few months at least. The training is —"

She didn't want to hear about the training he was going to undertake. She didn't want to know. She didn't want to mark her calendar and think of him. She couldn't bear it. "You better go."

He nodded and put his arms around her, but she didn't respond. She couldn't. He kissed her, but she turned her face and he only kissed her cheek.

He picked up his bag and, touching her cheek one last time, he turned and climbed up the steps. She turned, too, and hurried away.

"Hey!" he shouted after her. "Charlie!"

She stopped but she didn't turn back. She couldn't bear to look at him again.

"I love you!" he shouted over the din as the train began to move. "And I know you love me, too!"

She ran for the stairs as she started to cry, wishing with all her heart that she hadn't been such a coward, wishing that she had kissed him, too.

Out in the grinder, Sam stretched his legs, waiting for the rest of Team Sixteen to gather for a late-afternoon run.

In just a few hours, the team's officers and chiefs would be locked inside in a meeting, putting the final details on this demo they were supposed to be doing during the presidential dog and pony show.

Final details — that was pretty funny, considering they didn't even have much more than preliminary details. Previous meetings about this event usually started with someone — usually Sam — saying, "Why the fuck can't the Leap Frogs put on this PR show so we can get our asses back to Afghanistan and do something worthwhile?" and then deteriorated into a discussion of security measures on base.

Muldoon was the next officer to arrive, looking grim. Whatever had gone down with Joan in his office earlier hadn't been good. Of that, Sam was certain.

"Everything okay?" Sam asked.

"Everything's great." Muldoon turned his attention to his knee brace.

"Hey, Lieutenant Muldoon. You're my new hero. I used to think you were too polite, but not anymore." Izzy joined them, with Gilligan and Cosmo trailing along behind him. "You had a rough assignment night before last — doing it Navy SEAL style! Hoo-yah! I laughed my ass off when I heard that. And man, that newsclip of that dress coming off! What a pair of h—"

"She was drunk," Muldoon said shortly. "The only thing I did that night was get Ms. Bryant away from the news camera. After we went inside she passed out. Didn't you see the press conference she gave yesterday? She's going into rehab. The woman is not well. Show a little respect."

"I must've missed that," Izzy said. "But rewind a sec. She passed out after you went inside, you said. Would that be *right* after?" The petty officer was determined to keep his big mouth flapping for as long as he possibly could. Sam suspected that he'd picked up on Muldoon's tension and was determined to get a rise out of the usually easygoing lieutenant. "Because I read somewhere — in *Penthouse*, I think — that Brooke Bryant is a real hummer. Kind of hard to turn *that* down, huh, sir? I mean, there's that face and that smile you've seen in a *lot* of magazines and newspapers, and she's going to work —"

"Don't you know what respect means, Zanella?" Muldoon asked, his voice a little too soft, a little too dangerous.

"Oh, I do, sir." Izzy was a son of a bitch. "And were it me, sir, I would have respected her *fully*."

"At that press conference today," Cosmo told Izzy, "she apologized and called Lieutenant Muldoon 'an officer and a gentleman.' "

"Okay." Sam straightened up. "Gossip hour is

479

over." Izzy opened his mouth to comment, but they were all spared his further pearls of wisdom by WildCard, who had hit the yard already at a dead run, dragging Jenk behind him.

"You guys hear this latest shit?" the Card asked, skidding to the kind of stop that would have made a cartoon character proud. Except the look on his face was almost as grim as Muldoon's. He was gazing directly at Sam, and when he got no response other than a headshake no, he pushed Mark Jenkins forward. "Tell 'em what you told me."

"I wasn't supposed to tell even you, Chief," Jenk protested.

"An FBI team went head-to-head in a firefight with an al-Qaeda cell right here in San Diego today," WildCard announced.

"Shit," Izzy said, Brooke Bryant finally forgotten. "Where?"

"Apartment complex on the edge of town. The TV news has released some kind of story about gang violence — someone wants to keep the real story hushed." WildCard turned to Sam and dropped an even bigger bomb. "There's a body count, Sam, and rumor has it the casualties are not all terrorists."

Alyssa.

Jesus, he'd know — somehow — if she were dead. Wouldn't he?

"Who was involved?" Sam asked, looking from WildCard to Jenk.

The look on his face must've been fucking fierce, because Jenkins stopped hesitating.

"I don't know for sure, sir," he told Sam, "but

Max Bhagat's entire unit has been in this area for a while, working on something. It's hard to believe they wouldn't be in the middle of this."

And Max's best agents — including Alyssa and, shit, even Jules, too — would have been front and center when those bullets had started flying.

Sam grabbed on to the fact that part of being the best also meant that they had both the skill and the guts to survive.

Of course, being the best didn't help when you were in the dead wrong place at the dead wrong time. Chief Frank O'Leary, may he rest in peace, was proof of that. He'd had the bad luck of being in a hotel lobby when an AK-47–wielding terrorist had opened fire.

O'Leary's death had come as a complete surprise to Sam, too.

Fear tightened its grip on him. Please, God, let Alyssa be safe. And Jules. And, Christ, even Max, too, the motherfucker. Whatever animosity Sam felt toward Max Bhagat, he didn't want the man to die.

"It's only a rumor — about the body count, right?" Muldoon had come to stand right next to Sam, a solid tower of support. "So how do we get verified information?"

"We don't," Jenk said. "I'm sorry, sir —"

"How did you hear about this?" Gilligan asked.

"We almost got sent out as support," Jenkins reported. "I was in Admiral Crowley's office when the call came in. The situation never even reached Commander Paoletti's desk, though, because apparently the firefight happened quickly, and then it was over. There was a second call, almost right away, ordering us to stand down. The good news is that everyone in this particular cell was apprehended or killed."

Muldoon took out his cell phone. "You're friends with Alyssa's partner," he said to Sam. "Right? What's his name?"

"Jules Cassidy," WildCard volunteered.

"Let's call him," Muldoon said to Sam. "Do you have his number?"

"It's in my office," Sam said.

"Come on," Muldoon said. "Let's take care of this. We'll make a phone call and then you'll know for sure what the situation is."

"I'll find Commander Paoletti," WildCard decided. "He'll be able to get in touch with Max Bhagat."

"I'm going back to Admiral Crowley's office," Jenk said. "See if I can dig up where Bhagat's team is being billeted. Sometimes the phone isn't the best way to get in touch with people after something like this goes down. Sometimes it's easier just to go and camp out where they're staying and wait for them to return."

"Is there anything we can do?" Izzy asked.

"Go find the senior chief," Muldoon ordered. "He always knows everything that's going on. See what he can tell us about this."

"Aye, aye, sir."

"Come on," Muldoon said again to Sam as they all went in different directions.

They walked toward the Team Sixteen building in silence. This was unreal. This was . . .

"She's not dead," Sam said, but as he said the words aloud, he knew he could be wrong. People

482

died fighting terrorism, and these days they didn't have to be sent over to Afghanistan to do it. Alyssa's job here in the States was no less dangerous than his.

"What do I do if she is?" he asked, knowing that Muldoon couldn't possibly answer that. No one could.

But Muldoon glanced at him. "Maybe the question you really should consider, sir, is what are you going to do if she's alive?"

TWENTY-TWO

Joan knew the very instant Mike Muldoon came out onto the deck.

She was wearing about three sweaters, just sitting out there with Dave and Angela and Liz, having a drink, looking up at the night sky, listening to the crash of the surf, and arguing about who made the better starship captain — Kirk, Picard, Janeway, or Archer.

They were all still recuperating from Brooke's latest "event." Even though the President's daughter had been safely locked down in rehab for more than twenty-four hours now, they'd spent most of the day scrambling to handle the increased news coverage, trying to steer the focus of all the attention toward the hope of recovery, rather than the dirt of past mistakes.

Joan had spent her day recuperating from Mike Muldoon, as well.

But here he was. Coming back for round two, apparently. God help her, she didn't have the emotional energy for this now. She was terrified that if she so much as met his gaze, she would start to cry.

The things he'd said to her . . . And the things she'd said in return . . . Joan felt sick just thinking about it. Obviously she'd really hurt him by not calling last night. And the stupid thing was that she'd *wanted* to call. She'd forced herself *not* to call him. And when she finally went to bed, she had lain awake for hours, dying to call, wondering what he'd say if she woke him up, if he'd come right over, if he'd . . .

And the next morning, she'd faced the terrifying fact that she was impatient and eager to see him again. Only, he didn't show.

Her first thought had been panic — he'd been sent to Afghanistan, where he'd instantly be killed.

"Excuse me," he said now. "I'm sorry if I'm interrupting, but . . ." He'd dressed for the occasion in a uniform that wasn't quite as formal as his white choker suit, but he still looked extremely sharp. And he'd shaved recently, too. Not that the man had to go to much effort to look good. He looked directly at Joan, his handsome face somber. "May I speak to you privately, please?"

Protocol demanded that she make introductions, or at least make sure everyone knew everyone else. But tonight protocol could go to hell.

"I don't think that's a good idea, Lieutenant," she told him, and dismissed him — or at least tried to — by turning back to Liz. "I think the best answer to the question of who do you want on your team in a pinch has to be Spock. And since Spock comes with Kirk . . ."

But Muldoon didn't go away. In fact, he did the opposite. He pulled a chair over next to hers and sat down in it. When she looked at him, he said, "I'm sorry. It's important."

Liz and Angela and Dave were looking at one another sideways, and Muldoon reached across

485

her to hold out his hand to them. "Lt. Mike Muldoon. I think we all met the other night."

They shook hands and introduced themselves, Liz looking at Muldoon with quite a bit of curiosity and interest in her eyes, but then Dave stood up. "Sorry to greet and run, but Liz and Angie and I really have to —"

Joan grabbed the edge of his jacket and pulled him back down into his chair. "No, you don't."

"No, we don't," Liz echoed.

Muldoon was embarrassed. Even though the light out on the hotel's deck was shadowy, she could see the heightened color in his cheeks.

"I don't want to chase you away," he told her co-workers. "But I do have to apologize to Joan. If she's not going to let me do it privately, then I'm going to have to do it in front of you because it needs to be said." He looked at her. "I'm really sorry that I got upset this afternoon. I'm . . ." He glanced at Dave, Liz, and Angie, but then focused his attention on her. "I'm scared, too, because I thought I was playing it safe. I thought I'd learned how to do that, how to protect myself, and I still got hurt — way worse than I anticipated."

God in heaven, the man was serious. He was going to have this entire conversation in front of Dave and Angela and Liz. Dave was squirming, but Angie and Liz looked like they'd settled in for the show, all but ready to order popcorn from the waitress.

And Liz was a bitch and a half. Everything Muldoon said was going to be public knowledge by tomorrow morning, and he'd already said quite enough.

Joan stood up. "Excuse us," she said to them, smiling extra sweetly at Liz. "Let's take a walk," she told Muldoon.

He was blessedly silent, thank you, Jesus God, as they went down the stairs to the beach.

"Well, that was nifty," she said as they hit the soft sand. The wind was stronger down here, and she wrapped her arms around herself in an attempt not to freeze. "But I guess you couldn't have hired a skywriter and made it even more public, huh? That doesn't work too well at night."

"You're not going to get me to apologize for that," he told her. He was wearing far fewer layers than she was, but it was as if he didn't even notice the cold as they headed down the beach. "I am sorry about everything else, though." He shook his head, laughing softly. "I'm even sorry we slept together. I knew that would be a mistake from the first moment I saw you."

Joan stopped walking. "If that's supposed to be your idea of an apology, I'm not sure I want to —"

"I'm sorry, because even though I knew I'd end up hurt, what I didn't figure was that I'd end up hurting you, too. That's what I'm sorry about. That's the last thing I wanted, please believe me. Those things I said to you were . . ." He shook his head. "I've never spoken to a woman like that before in my life. I've always just . . . I don't know. Crawled away to lick my wounds, I guess."

Spotlights from the hotel lit the beach for only a short distance. After that, it was entirely up to the moonlight.

Joan pulled a strand of her hair out of her mouth as they started walking again. "The things you said

487

to me were honest," she told him quietly. *"I'm* the one who should be apologizing to *you."*

"No. You came and found me this afternoon," he told her. "According to the gigolo handbook, I was supposed to lie and tell you that something came up this morning, and of course I would never have sent Steve in my place if it wasn't vitally important. I was supposed to sweet-talk you and kiss you and tell you everything you wanted to hear until you agreed to see me again tonight. But I was angry and frustrated and . . . Jesus, I'm just going to say it, okay? My heart was breaking. All because you were sixteen hours late."

And okay. That bit about the breaking heart made her fail to comment about his "gigolo handbook" crack. In fact, she couldn't think of anything to say at all.

"Talk about being scared to death," he continued, the wind sweeping his hair into his eyes and then back out again. "I knew I was being irrational. I knew it was because of . . . some intense thing I've got going here for you. And I couldn't play by the rules. When we first made love, Joan, I swear, I went into it the way I always go into a short-term relationship. Thinking what will be, will be. Don't think about tomorrow. Just, you know, get laid. As often as possible. Have a good time. I was completely intending to let it just play out all the way to the end, all the way to the point where you got on that plane and went home. But I couldn't do it." He struggled to find the words, to explain. "See, getting over you after just one night was . . . really hard. I mean, I haven't managed to do it yet. I'm still . . . But all I could think about was how much worse it was going to feel after a couple of weeks. I just . . . it'll be bad."

He laughed in disgust. "But this is bad, too. I want to be with you while you're here. Life is too short not to take chances — I was reminded of that today in a major way. So here I am. You want to give me part of your next three weeks, I'll take it. We can even do this one day at a time, if you want. It's your call."

It's your call. Joan kept on walking, afraid to look at him, afraid to speak. He honestly saw himself as insignificant and disposable. Someone — or a lot of someones — had taught him that he wasn't worth keeping. How sad was that?

He was living what was usually a woman's nightmare — his relationships were defined by his image as a sexual object. She had been wrong this afternoon when she called him a coward. He'd been trying to maintain some self-respect, and from a person whose sense of self-esteem as an equal partner in a relationship was close to zero, he had, in fact, been valiantly strong.

But here he was. Ready to surrender and take whatever she was willing to give him. Ready to give up total control.

What would he do if she said, *Okay, bucko. Let's try ten years.*

Oh, God — and wasn't *that* a scary thought? There was no way she was going to say that. She sympathized, sure. And she cared for him. Deeply. Far more than she wanted to. But she couldn't be the woman who would show him that he was wrong, that he was the least disposable man she'd ever met. She just couldn't do it.

"Michael," she finally said.

He grabbed her and swung her around, pulling her hard into his arms, and kissed her.

And, oh my God. The man could kiss.

"Don't say it," he said, between attacks on her mouth with his. "Whatever it was you were going to say. Let's just go back to your room. God, I want you. I want to be inside you again. Let's just have it be completely about sex for right now, okay? We don't have to talk, we don't have to think. Let's just get it on all night long and all tomorrow night and —"

"Michael . . ."

When he kissed her like that, she was ready to agree with anything he said. She was ready to tell him anything, promise him everything else.

"Mike . . ."

But none of it would be the truth.

"Michael, stop!"

He stopped kissing her, but he didn't let her go. He closed his eyes and rested his forehead against hers.

"I'm sorry, too," she said. "I'm really sorry. I'm going to be completely honest with you and please don't hate me —"

"I won't," he said. "I couldn't."

"You were mostly right," she admitted. "What you said this afternoon. I'm ashamed to say it, but you were going to be just part of what I did on my summer vacation. And when I went home . . . I *would've* called you back, absolutely I would have tried, but we probably would have just played phone tag. And even if we did connect, I wouldn't have time to talk for very long. You probably wouldn't either and . . . God, I don't have time for a relationship with a man who lives down the street from me. There's no way I could sustain something long distance. We'd end up hating each other."

"Okay," he said, opening his eyes and pulling back slightly to look at her. "So, okay. We let it end after a few weeks. At least we get these weeks, right?"

Joan shook her head. "I don't think that's such a good idea anymore. And you really don't want that, either. I mean, it's one thing to pretend that there's a chance of a future, but actually to know that the relationship is doomed from the start . . . ?"

He let go of her. Forced a smile. Pretended he was joking. "Ah, Joan, you're going to make me beg, aren't you?"

"Don't," she said. "Please. Unless . . ."

"Unless what?"

"Unless you plan to quit being a SEAL or to transfer east —" Joan laughed, rubbing her forehead. Where had this terrible headache come from? She needed a warm, dark room and at least four hours of uninterrupted sleep. "I can't believe the words that are coming out of my mouth." She turned and started walking rapidly back to the hotel. "Forget I said that, all right?"

"Maybe we should talk about it," Muldoon said. She was practically running, and all he had to do was lengthen his stride a little to keep up. "I mean, you're not going to work at the White House forever, are you?"

"I might. God — and the American voters — willing. I love my job, Mike."

491

"Well, I do, too, but I can tell you right now that there's no way I'm going to be a SEAL forever," he said. "My knee's already screwed up — I took at least three years off of my career with that one. I have maybe ten years left before I can't hold my own anymore. And the day I start slowing down the team is the day I leave."

"Perfect then," she said starting up the stairs to the deck of the hotel. "You want to see me again? I'll meet you right here on the beach ten years from tonight. I'll be the one who's approaching *fifty*. I'll wear a carnation in my lapel so you can recognize me beneath my wrinkles."

He laughed. "You'll be forty-two. That's not — What am I saying? I don't want to wait ten years to see you again!"

She turned on the stairs to face him, and for once she was taller. "I don't want to do this," she said. "I do not. And you're scaring me because if I'm not careful, I'll start thinking we might actually have a chance. But we don't. There are too many obstacles for me to handle — including our age difference, which *completely* freaks me out. I can't do it. I'm just . . . I'm not going to play this game with you. We had one night of sex — great sex — but you know what that means? *Nothing*. It means you're good in bed. Terrific. Thank you very much, it was wonderful, I loved every minute of it. You're a very sweet guy and you kiss like a dream and you know just where to touch me to make me crazy and I like you *so* much, I do, but I can't do this to you and most of all I can't do this to myself."

"Joan —"

492

"This conversation is over," she told him, praying he would leave before she started to cry. "Please. Just let it go."

He opened his mouth as if he were going to speak, but then he closed it. And he nodded. "Can we still be friends?"

She laughed. "Yeah, right. Good friends, right? The kind of friends who have sex? God, Muldoon, sometimes you are such a guy."

He followed her up the stairs. "Well, yes, okay, that would obviously be my preference, I won't lie about that, but that's not what I meant. I meant *friends* friends. As in no sex. As in 'Hi, Joan, it's me, Mike. Are you free to meet in a crowded well-lit room where we can sit and have lunch and talk while we keep all of our clothes on?' "

The deck was empty. Dave and Liz and Angie had gone inside. Where it was warm. Where sane people went when the wind was blowing hard off the Pacific. "I don't think —"

"I like talking to you," he said softly. "Please don't take that away from me, too."

And what could she say to that? "All bets are off if you try to talk me into sleeping with you again."

"Fair enough."

Shit. She wasn't sure she could be his friend after being his lover.

"Please," he said.

"All right. God."

"All right." He smiled — much more widely and happily than she would have thought possible. "All right. We've got a walk-through of the dog and pony show — the demo for the president — in the morning. You'll be there, right?"

"Yes," she said. "It's on my schedule."

"Okay," he said. "I'll see you tomorrow then."

And with that he walked away, leaving her to wonder why on earth he seemed so pleased with this arrangement. Friendship and no sex.

No sex, provided, of course, that she could keep *her* hands off of *him*.

God, he probably thought that she wouldn't be able to resist him.

"I'm not sleeping with you again," she called after him. "Really. I'm very strong when it comes to temptation."

He just waved and kept on walking.

What are you going to do if she's alive . . .

Sam stood in the hallway outside of Alyssa's hotel room for twenty minutes before he even got close enough to the door to knock.

He shouldn't be here. He knew that. But he just wanted to see her. To look into her eyes and know that she really was okay.

She'd had five stitches after being cut by flying glass — little more than a scratch compared to Jules who, last time Sam checked, was finally out of ICU.

Even Jules's injuries — getting plugged in the shoulder and the thigh — were nothing compared to those of FBI agent Carla Ramirez. Ramirez had been shot in the head and pronounced DOA at Mission Bay Memorial Hospital.

The news had trickled to Sam maddeningly slowly. The first thing he'd heard was that two FBI agents had been shot, one fatally.

Then, that the fatally wounded agent was a female who'd been part of Max's team off and on over the past few years. Just like Alyssa.

The fatally wounded agent was a woman of color. Just like Alyssa.

When Sam had heard that, he'd thrown up. He'd been in that meeting finalizing the details of the dog and pony show, and Jenk had slunk in and handed him a message that was really supposed to go to Commander Paoletti. The note said that the name of the deceased agent wasn't being released yet, but the agent in the hospital was definitely Jules Cassidy. Sam passed it over to the CO, excused himself, and went into the nearest head and puked until his stomach was empty.

He'd been *that* certain Alyssa was dead.

But it was while he was in there, sitting on the bathroom floor and wondering how he was going to pick himself up and walk back into that other room, that Jazz came in.

"Her name's Ramirez," he told Sam. "The DOA is FBI agent Carla Ramirez."

And so it was someone else who was grieving tonight. More than one someone, actually. Ramirez had a husband and a couple of kids. Sam had met the woman only a few times when Team Sixteen had worked with the FBI counter terrorist team. He didn't know her very well at all, but the one time they'd talked, she'd mentioned her kids.

He didn't know her well, but he knew Max Bhagat's reputation. If she was on his team, she was one of the agency's best.

And Sam knew that if Carla Ramirez could die on this op, then Alyssa could be blown away on the next.

And all the thoughts he'd had while he was sitting on that bathroom floor — things that he knew he should have told Alyssa before she died — kept echoing in his head.

Which brought him here.

To the hallway outside her hotel room.

So what was it going to be?

To knock or not to knock?

Okay, work this through. Say he knocks. She answers the door and he says . . . ?

What?

"Are you okay?"

It was simple, it got right to the point. It conveyed his concern without giving away the fact that he'd been frantic about her just a few hours ago.

But there she would be. Standing there in front of him. Of course she was okay. It was simple and to the point, sure, but it was also stupid as shit. "Are you okay?" Well, *yeah* . . .

Unless, of course, she realized that he wasn't talking about her physical okay-ness, but instead her emotional well-being.

So, okay. Take that a little bit further. How about, "I heard about Jules. The hospital wouldn't let me see him, but the word is he's going to be all right. Have you heard anything? That must've been tough to go through, thinking your partner might die. Are *you* okay?"

Uh, *no*. Way too long and complicated. And, Jesus, it sounded like he was in love with Jules and had rushed to see him upon receiving word that he was injured. Not quite the message Sam wanted to send, even if he *had* stopped at the hospital on his way over here.

How about, "I was sure you were dead for about ten minutes tonight, and I puked my guts out because I couldn't bear the thought of a world without you in it. Even though we're not sharing our lives, Lys, I know you're out there and I think about you and miss you every fucking day."

Make that "every *single* day." He had to keep the fucking out of everything here. Out of his language and out of his head as well. He couldn't even think about her that way right now. That's not why he was here. He didn't want her opening up this door and knowing that one of the first thoughts that came into his mind whenever he saw her had to do with him licking every inch of her body.

Which he actually had done. A million years and another lifetime ago.

Sam took a deep breath and cracked his neck. Okay. He was going to do it. He didn't know exactly what he was going to say, but he'd think of something. He always did better anyway, thinking on his feet. He raised his hand and knocked on the door.

Nothing. No movement — at least none that he could hear.

He knocked again, louder.

And there it was. Stirring from within. Then the sound of feet against the carpeting, coming closer to the door.

Now she'd look out the security viewer. He squared his shoulders and looked directly back at the little hole in the door.

One lock clicked and then another, and the door swung open.

And holy fuck.

It wasn't Alyssa, it was Max Bhagat who was standing there, in a T-shirt and jeans that he'd probably just thrown on to answer the door, his usually neatly combed dark hair a total mess. He looked as if he'd spent the past hour or so with it pressed against a pillow. He was squinting slightly, and his chin was covered with stubble, which probably only meant that it had been four or five hours since he'd last shaved, instead of his usual meticulous two to three.

And here was a scenario Sam stupidly hadn't considered. Jesus, he was an idiot. Of course Max would be there.

When he stopped to think about it, the only truly shocking thing about this moment was Sam's realization that Max actually owned a pair of blue jeans.

He'd known Max and Alyssa had been seeing each other — okay, skip the euphemisms. They'd been *fucking* each other for months now.

He'd just never expected Alyssa would allow Max to be so indiscreet as to share her hotel room while they were on assignment.

"She's okay," Max told him quietly. "She's sleeping now. It's been hell for the past twenty-four hours, though. She was with Carla Ramirez and Jules Cassidy when . . ." He shook his head. "It was pretty touch and go for a while, but Cassidy's going to be fine. I can't say the same for Carla, I'm afraid."

"Yeah, I heard," Sam said. This was unreal. Was he really standing here having a conversation with Max in the doorway of Alyssa's hotel room? Just two guys shooting the shit. "What happened?"

Max shook his head. There was no doubt about it, the man was fucking exhausted. He was completely drained. Sam recognized that look in Max's eyes. He'd seen it more than once in his own bathroom mirror.

"We stopped something very bad from happening today," Max said quietly. "You know I can't tell you more than that. I'm lucky we lost only one agent. The body count could've been much higher. Although try talking about that kind of luck with Darren Ramirez."

Sam was taller than Max, and he could look over the man's shoulder into the hotel room. A dim light was on and he could see Alyssa tightly curled up beneath the covers of one of the two double beds, like a little kid. He could see her face, sweetly relaxed in sleep.

There was a chair next to the bed, as if Max had been sitting beside her, instead of lying with her under the covers.

Yeah, wishful thinking, Starrett. Max and Alyssa had been in that bed together, making love, not too long ago. Count on it. Maybe even just moments before he'd arrived. Maybe while he'd been standing out in the hall.

Sex was God's best medicine for hours of fatigue and anger. It started the healing process. And it sure as hell took care of any extra adrenaline that might keep you from being able to fall asleep.

"She's really okay?" he asked, trying not to wonder if Max had ever kissed and licked his way across the curve of her waist. "I heard she needed stitches."

"In her hand," Max said. He ran his own hand

499

through his hair as if just suddenly aware of how disheveled he looked. "Why the hell are you here, Starrett?"

"I don't know," Sam said. "I just . . . I heard about it, and I thought . . . I had to see her. I'm glad she's okay."

Max nodded. He had eyes that were so dark brown, you couldn't tell the difference between the iris and the pupil. Sam had always thought of Max as calculating. Manipulative. Brilliant. Cold. But right now his eyes were warm and filled with empathy and understanding.

And Sam could imagine it. For the first time, he could actually picture Alyssa falling in love with Max Bhagat. Up to this moment, it had seemed impossible and absurd. How could *she* be with *him?* How could she be happy with someone like Max?

But now he could see that they were alike, Alyssa and Max. They were both a curious mix of hot and cool, of hidden emotions and carefully built facades.

Shit, Max probably understood her in ways that Sam never would have, not if they'd stayed together for a hundred years.

And a hundred-year relationship hadn't exactly been part of Alyssa's agenda, had it now? What was it she'd said to him last time they'd sat down to talk? Even if they'd stayed together, if life and Mary Lou hadn't intervened, their love affair wouldn't have lasted more than a month or two. Yeah, she'd said, *I definitely would have gotten sick of you.*

Not so Max, apparently.

"How's your wife?" Max asked. "And it's a daughter you've got, right? What is she now, twelve months old?"

Sam nodded. "Yeah," he said. "I know. I shouldn't have come."

Max nodded, too, and started to close the door. "I won't tell her you were here."

TWENTY-THREE

It was late in the morning before Ihbraham's truck pulled up in front of the Robinsons' house — hours later than he usually arrived to start work.

By the time he came, Mary Lou had already brought Donny his mail. She'd gone back and forth to his house about three different times, finding as many excuses as she could, bringing him a book she'd picked up at the library's yearly sale, bringing him the bag of burgers she'd brought home for him from work . . .

How many days ago had that been? It was back when he wasn't answering his door at all. But she'd put the sack in the refrigerator. Surely it had kept. And hell, finally giving it to him was a reason to go over there — to go back outside and be there when Ihbraham finally showed.

Eventually she ran out of reasons to keep bugging Donny, and she gave up and just brought Haley's playpen out into the front yard.

Maybe it wouldn't seem too obvious that she was waiting for Ihbraham to appear.

Yeah, and maybe Sam would come home from work tonight and announce that he was leaving the SEALs to join the San Diego Ballet.

Mary Lou sat up as Ihbraham got out of the cab of his truck. He looked at her — he definitely saw her sitting there on her front steps — but he didn't even wave. He just went to the back of his truck and lifted a large potted shrubbery — some kind of pretty flowering plant in an ornate clay container — from the bed. He carried it effortlessly to the Robinsons' front stoop and set it down.

As she watched, he went around to the hose that was attached at the side of the house, turned on the water, brought the hose to the front, watered the plant, brought the hose back, turned off the water, re-coiled the hose.

And then he returned to his truck without another glance in her direction and climbed back behind the wheel.

The engine turned over with a roar, and he drove away.

Mary Lou was up on her feet, heading out to the street before she could stop herself. *"Hey!"*

He must've been watching her in his rearview mirror, because his brake lights went on, and the truck stopped.

He just sat there for a moment, absolutely still.

And Mary Lou stood there, watching him, her heart in her throat.

His back-up lights came on as he put the truck into reverse. The engine whined as he pulled all the way back, until he was alongside of her.

Mary Lou checked to make sure Haley was still happily engaged with her pile of toys before she moved closer to Ihbraham's open window.

"I made some iced tea," she told him. "I don't

suppose I could talk you into taking a break and having a glass?"

He shook his head. "Thank you, but no. I can't."

Can't. "Wow," she said. "So that's it, huh? I don't put out, and you don't want to be my friend anymore? Is that what's going on here, Ihbraham?"

Ihbraham looked out the front windshield of his truck and sighed, no doubt wishing that he hadn't bothered to stop. "You know in your heart that that's not true."

"Well, what am I supposed to think?" She struggled not to cry. "You didn't call me back yesterday. I mean, you completely went off the map. And today, it's like you don't even know me. I don't know about you, but I don't have enough friends to be able to take it lightly — you know, just go, 'Oh, well' — when I lose one of them."

"You will never lose me as a friend," he said quietly. He turned and looked at her, his dark eyes intense. "That I can promise you."

"Will you come to a meeting with me tonight, then?" she asked.

"I can't," he said.

"Can't or won't?"

He sighed. "I've agreed to meet with my brothers. At five o'clock. I won't be back in San Diego until late."

"Tomorrow night, then."

Another sigh. "Tomorrow night I can't, either." He paused. "I mean, tomorrow night, I won't."

"Well, there we go," she said. "I won't ever lose you as a friend, except it sure as hell seems like you're already gone. Thanks a bunch. Have a nice life." She turned and started walking back toward Haley.

"My feelings for you continue to be inappropriate." He spoke in a low voice, but it was loud enough to carry to her. "I'm struggling to do what I know is right instead of that which I all too humanly want."

Of all the egotistical . . . "And, of course, *I'm* such a pushover that all you have to do is snap your fingers and I'll fall into bed with you. Is that really what you think of me?" She moved back to his truck, aware that she wasn't good at keeping her voice down when she was angry, and afraid of being overheard. "It takes two to tango, babycakes. I want to go to a meeting with you, period, the end. I assure you, I have no intention of making any side trips to the Sunny Daze hourly rate motel to fuck you blind."

Ihbraham just looked at her with those eyes that reminded her so much of pictures she'd seen of Jesus. "You misunderstand," he said. "I know you have no intention of . . ." He shook his head, with that strange little smile that was both sad and amused curling his lips. "The struggle is mine; I know this to be true. It's a struggle of spirit as well as of flesh. I see you, and I want . . ." He sighed. "I believe it is wrong to want something so much — something that doesn't belong to me, something that belongs to someone else."

"This is America," Mary Lou said. "Women don't belong to men in America."

"Yes," he said, "they do."

"Well, Lord," she said. "If that's what you think,

505

then good riddance to you. You're not someone I want as a friend anyway."

"Are you not *Sam's* wife?"

"Well, yes, but he's *my* husband, too."

"That's different," Ihbraham said.

"No, it is not," she argued.

"Yes, it is," he said. "Even here in America, the land of the free. Sam is a little more free than you are. And you are both more free than I am."

He glanced at his wristwatch, and Mary Lou knew it was really just a matter of seconds before he left. Lord help her, mad as she was at him, she didn't want him to leave.

"Why don't you come inside and have some iced tea and we can argue about this out of the heat?" she said. "Please?"

He sat there silently for several long moments, just looking at her. "You would invite me into your house?" he finally said.

"Is there a reason I shouldn't?" she countered.

"In some countries, such an offer would be considered an invitation to have sexual relations," he told her. "An offer to enter a woman's home, to be there alone with her —"

"Yeah, and in some countries the penalty for a woman who has sex with a man she's not married to is death. The man gets a rap on the knuckles and the woman is beheaded. I don't live in some countries, thank you very much," she said. "And neither do you. My invitation was for iced tea. Don't get weird on me now, Ihbraham."

"You have never invited me inside your home before," he pointed out.

"Okay," she said. "You're right. You're absolutely right. I'm dying to have sex with you. Right on the living room rug. In front of my baby daughter, no less." She rolled her eyes in exasperation. "You know, I'd almost forgotten that you were a man. But apparently you're just as stupid and hormone-crazed as the rest of them. And you've got some really dumb foreign ideas to boot. I thought you were an American."

"I am."

"Then act like one!" She marched away from his truck, to Haley's playpen, scooping up her daughter before she turned back to look at him. "Just out of curiosity, is that really what it would take?" she asked. "For you to be friends with me again? A quickie while my husband's at work and my daughter's down for a nap?"

He shook his head. "Mary Lou —"

"Why don't you come back in a couple of hours," she said, "and see just how desperate I am for *some*one to stick around."

He was looking at her as if he couldn't tell whether or not she was kidding.

Trouble was, Mary Lou wasn't quite sure herself.

"I'm sorry I upset you so much," he said, and put his truck into gear.

She watched as he drove away.

The phone rang, and Mary Lou hurried inside the house out of force of habit.

Except, really, the only person she wanted to talk to had just rolled out of her life. Probably for good.

She would not cry. She would not cry. At least not until Haley took her nap.

Still, she had to take a deep breath before she

picked up the phone. She tucked it between her shoulder and ear so she could use her hands to keep Haley from grabbing her earrings. "Hello?"

"Hey there, Mary Lou."

God damn it. It was Insurance Bob. His timing stank, as usual. He was the last person she wanted to talk to right now.

"So am I going to be able to talk you into dinner tonight?" he asked. His voice got softer, sweeter. "I'd really love to see you, honey. I can't stop thinking about you."

Dinner with Insurance Bob. Well, why the hell not? Mrs. U. was always willing to watch Haley in the evenings. Sam wouldn't be back until late again and even if he did get home before her, he wouldn't give a flying fuck. And as for Ihbraham . . .

Shoot, she might as well be with someone who liked her enough to actually *do* something about it. "Tell me where and when and I'll meet you over there," she told Bob.

"Oh, baby," he said. "You just made my year."

Commander Paoletti had looked hard at Muldoon when he'd first made his request to stand on the dais with the President and other VIPs during the SEAL demo.

Two Seahawks, each carrying a squad of men, were going to kick off the presentation. Those men, dressed in BDUs and combat vests, carrying a full arsenal of weapons, were going to fast-rope down to the parade ground. In a matter of seconds, they would rig an ancient antiaircraft launcher with enough explosives to create a controlled blast that would "put it out of commission."

They would then be pulled back off the parade grounds via helo and SPIE rigging.

It would all take place inside of a few short minutes. And that was just to get the show — which included plenty of colored smoke and other whizbang insertion and extraction techniques — started.

They did a dry run of the President's arrival, with the teams of Secret Service men and additional security under the command of Admiral Tucker all swarming the area. Also milling around were the members of the President's staff who would be on hand. Commander Paoletti came and stood next to Muldoon and shook his head at the chaos.

Joan had just walked about a dozen yards away to get a little privacy for a call coming in on her cell, and the CO looked at her pointedly and then looked back at Muldoon.

"You know, when you first asked to be kept out of the helos for this thing, I thought your knee was bothering you again," Paoletti said quietly. "I thought you were trying to avoid the fast-roping."

Sliding forty feet down a rope from a helo and going immediately into a dead run had been tough on Muldoon's knees *before* he'd been injured.

"No, sir," Muldoon said. "I'm fine. I still have twinges, and I'm still using the brace, but I'm fully up to speed. I wouldn't lie to you about that."

"I didn't think you were lying, Lieutenant," the CO said easily. "I thought you just conveniently forgot to tell me."

"No, sir," Muldoon said again.

"Yeah, I realize that now," he said, glancing at Joan again. "I'm curious though. Most guys would've leapt at the chance to play hero. Show off a little."

"I'm not going to impress anyone by jumping out of helicopters," Muldoon told the commander. "I'm not exactly sure how I am going to impress . . ." Jeez, who was he kidding here? Just use her name. ". . . Joan, but believe me, sir, I'm working on it."

He had decided to approach his entire relationship with Joan as if it were a mission with a "Do not fail" order. His plan so far was to spend the next few days as close to her as possible.

But no sex. That gigolo crack still stung. He had to make it clear to her that, in his eyes at least, their relationship was about way more than sex.

He'd realized last night, after he'd begged her to take him back to her room, that sex would only serve to make things even more complicated.

He'd realized a lot of things last night.

It had occurred to him then that as much as he wanted to spend all of the next three weeks in bed with Joan, that wasn't going to get him what he really wanted.

And what he really wanted was a long-distance relationship. If that really was the only way they could make a relationship with two high-octane careers work, then dammit, he wanted to try. He wanted a chance at having something real with this incredible woman.

"If that's the case, if you're really determined,

Muldoon, then she doesn't stand a chance," Paoletti said. "I'll definitely be dancing at your wedding, kid."

Wedding?

"Uh," Muldoon said. "Well . . ."

Jeez, the CO actually thought that he and Joan . . . ?

"Thanks," Muldoon said. "Sir. I'll be, um, sure to invite you."

To his wedding. To Joan. God, what a thought. What an incredible thought.

Muldoon and Joan — married. He started to laugh. *Married*. But, hey, why not? He was crazy out of his mind about her. The thought of never seeing her again scared him to death. For days now, he'd been alternating between deep depression and giddy euphoria.

He loved her.

Hopelessly. Endlessly. Totally.

He wanted to wake up every morning knowing that she was in his life.

The CO — as usual — was as right about this as he was about most things. Muldoon simply hadn't been thinking on a grand enough scale.

He could imagine their wedding — a simple ceremony where they'd put rings on each other's fingers and seal the promises they made with a kiss. God, he wanted that so badly he had to remind himself to keep breathing.

He'd never pursued a woman before, not like this. He'd never had to. He'd never *wanted* to. But like the CO had said, if he was determined . . .

What would she say if he asked her to marry him?

There are too many obstacles.

Yeah? As Sam Starrett would say, so the fuck what? What obstacle ever stopped a fuckin' SEAL?

What Muldoon had to do was find out exactly what her perceived obstacles were and . . .

He had to talk to her. He had to get inside her head. Find out what she was thinking. Let her know what he was thinking, too. God, he had to let her know what he was *feeling.*

Okay, that one wasn't going to be either easy or fun, but neither was BUD/S training, and he'd made it through that. You do what you have to do to get the job done. And if that's what it would take . . .

He had to make Joan see that it was worth it, that what they shared was well worth the hard work that came with a long-distance love affair. The sparks that they made together, and the sheer comfort of the fit that he felt when they were together — and he knew she felt it, too — was worth keeping. Forever.

He was not — *was not* — just going to let this one go. He wasn't just going to let her slip away from him. Not this time. Not Joan.

And he had to make her realize that he was worth keeping, too.

Paoletti glanced at Joan again. "You know, she made quite an impression on Kelly. Funny and really smart, Kel said. Really sharp, really together."

"Yeah," Muldoon said. "She's fabulous, sir."

"What is it about smart women?" Paoletti asked. "Don't try to answer that, Lieutenant. It was a rhetorical question. Although maybe someone as intelligent as you could actually figure it out. If you come up with anything, let me know, okay?"

Muldoon laughed. "Aye, aye, sir."

It was good to see the commander looking a little more relaxed. Or was he?

As Paoletti watched the Secret Service and other security personnel at work, his eyes narrowed slightly and his mouth got tight.

Muldoon had the feeling that the CO wished nothing more than for this *honor* to be over with.

"Joan seems to be under the impression that all threats have been diminished," Muldoon said. "The information she's received implies that when the FBI took out that terrorist cell yesterday, they completely eliminated any potential danger to the President. I tried to tell her that wasn't necessarily the case."

Paoletti shook his head and laughed his disgust. "Apparently there's only one al-Qaeda cell operating in this part of California, right? Yeah." He laughed again. "I've made my opinion as clear again today as I did yesterday and the day before, but no one wants to hear it — especially not since the current threat has been downgraded. And God knows it's time to start campaigning." He rolled his eyes. "I thank God I don't have to be reelected as Team Sixteen's CO every few years."

Muldoon did, too. Passionately, in fact. Tom Paoletti was a major part of the reason Sixteen was the best team in the Navy. "Twenty-four hours, and it'll all be over, sir."

"Twenty-one hours and twenty-eight minutes, Lieutenant. I'm practically counting seconds

513

here." Paoletti sighed, his easygoing smile fading. "I've actually got a love-hate thing happening with this assignment, if you know what I mean."

"I do, sir." Muldoon watched Joan as whoever was on the other end of her cell phone made her laugh. "The team hasn't had many assignments as easy as this one in a long time. Everyone's benefiting from having extra time to spend with their families." He thought about Sam. "Well, almost everyone."

"I'm glad to be home with Kelly every night," the CO admitted. "Very glad. But I think we're asking for trouble if we all assume there's no chance of any danger while we're here on base."

"I agree completely, sir. If I were a player on Osama's team . . ." Muldoon trailed off. This was probably not what the CO wanted to hear right now.

But Paoletti was looking at him with that thought-penetrating gaze. "Go on, Lieutenant. This should be interesting."

"Okay. I'd look to hit the United States in a place like this. A naval base or military compound. Maybe a federal government building. Someplace believed to be invincible. Do you remember your World War Two history, sir? How after Pearl Harbor we made a point to bomb Tokyo? It was just short of a suicide mission. Jimmy Doolittle and his Raiders took off in bombers from aircraft carriers — it was the first time in history that was done successfully. The pilots had to ditch over enemy territory because there wasn't enough fuel to get back to the ships. It was a logistical nightmare. But we did it. And we succeeded. Why? Be-

514

cause the Japanese government told the world that their island was untouchable. Invincible. Attack-proof. Safe. We intentionally went in there and rubbed their faces in the fact that they were dead wrong. They were not safe, and we demoralized the hell out of them.

"If I were a terrorist, that's what I'd try to do to the U.S."

"They're not going to demoralize us," Paoletti countered. "No matter what they do."

"No, it wouldn't work," Muldoon agreed. "It would be 9/11 all over again. But I think they don't get that. They don't understand the way we think. Same way we don't understand them."

"And with that, you have neatly summed up the reason why guys like you and me won't be out of a job for a good long time."

"And why it pays to be ready for anything," Muldoon said.

"That's my plan." The commander smiled. "I've been making so much noise about potential danger I've been a little afraid I'm going to be asked to go in for another series of psych evals. But when that demo starts, I'll be fully in command, and I'll be damned if any bad shit is going to go down on my watch. We'll both have radio headsets tomorrow — along with the rest of the team. While you're on that dais, Muldoon, I want your eyes open at all times. No staring at Joan's ass, do you hear me?"

"Aye, aye, sir."

"Not that you would — you're too polite. We'll be running through our part of the show again this afternoon," Commander Paoletti continued, "and we'll actually use real smoke bombs. I want the Secret Service to see what the colored smoke is going to look like. Hopefully, they'll request we don't use any smoke at all after they see how completely it's going to obscure the spectator stands. But that run-through's not scheduled until 1400. After lunch. Admiral Tucker set up some kind of fancy buffet for the President's staff. Any brilliant ideas as to how I can get out of that?"

Lunch . . . Muldoon looked over at Joan, who was still talking on her phone. Earlier, he'd asked her to have lunch with him, and although she hadn't given him a definite answer, he suspected he was going to get a no.

Which was a major problem if his goal was to talk to her. Although maybe what he should do was call her. She sure spent a lot of time talking on her phone.

"You never managed to have lunch with Joan," Muldoon told his CO now. "And you did promise her that you would."

"God bless you, I certainly did. Jenkins!" the commander shouted.

"Yes, sir?" Jenk appeared out of nowhere. He was dressed in cammy gear, with black and green greasepaint streaking his boyish face.

"Send my regrets to Admiral Tucker. I won't be able to join his party for lunch."

"I'll tell him you're real broken up about it, sir."

"And after you do that, call Joan DaCosta on her cell phone and ask if she'd like to join me for lunch at 1200 hours at that Greek place — what's it called?"

"You mean the Falafel Shack?"

"No, Jenk. The one that has chairs that aren't attached to the plastic tables, and plates that aren't paper. What is it, Alexi's?"

"Actually, Joan would probably prefer the Shack," Muldoon said.

The CO's face lit up. "Really?"

"Yes, sir. And they do have real tables and chairs. Outside. There's a nice little garden. If you call ahead, Nick will actually reserve a table for you. He pretty much gets his kid to sit there and color until you show up."

"Call Nick at the Shack and tell him to break out the Crayolas a few minutes before noon," Paoletti told Jenk.

"Aye, aye, sir."

"Don't forget to talk to Tucker's office first," Paoletti reminded him.

"You got it, boss." Jenkins vanished.

"That's a trick you might want to remember when you're CO of a team and want to avoid lunch with the base commander," Paoletti told Muldoon. "Send your regrets first. That way if your escape plan falls through, well, gee, you've already cancelled, right?"

"I'll keep it in mind, sir."

"You *will* be able to join us for lunch, won't you, Lieutenant?"

Alleluia. "Permission to kiss you, Commander?"

Commander Paoletti laughed as he headed toward some kind of problem the senior chief appeared to be having with three of the Secret Service agents. "Not a chance, Muldoon. You're smart enough, but other than that, you're not my type. You're much too polite."

★ ★ ★

"What are you doing out here?" Charlie asked.

Vince glanced up at her from his seat on the patio. "Sitting."

"I can see that."

"Do you remember when we moved to San Diego we thought it would be so great because we'd be able to spend all that time on the beach?" Vince asked her. "When was the last time we went to the beach? I mean with any regularity?"

"I don't know."

"It was at least thirty years ago." He shook his head. "You loved the beach. Maybe we should have bought that place right on the water. Remember that place?"

She sat down next to him. "Only very vaguely. It was damp and the playroom had all that awful dark paneling."

"It didn't have a playroom. You're mixing it up with that house we looked at that had the swimming pool."

Charlie gave him a look. "How can you possibly remember that?"

"I remember everything important," he said. "Finding the perfect house was always up there in importance. I wanted . . ." He cleared his throat. He'd wanted to make her happy. Why was it so hard to say these things aloud?

Because if he said it, then *she'd* say, "You made me very happy." It was an expected response like, "I love you, too." But happiness, like love, couldn't be measured. Vince *knew* Charlie loved him. Of course she loved him. She loved him — enough. Enough to marry him and spend sixty years with him, which was a whole hell of a lot of *enough*. And yes, she'd been happy — happy *enough*. But what did that mean, really? He'd never truly know if she'd really been happy, or if she'd simply been content.

"Remember that day you showed up in Fort Pierce?" he asked her.

"Yes, that one I remember, thank you very much," she said tartly. "Just because *I* don't have a superhuman, freakish ability to remember houses that we went inside of once a million years ago, doesn't mean I can't remember days like that one."

He'd been exhausted that day, down to his very bones. Training around the clock, swimming miles every day, and spending hours and hours learning about explosives and detonators and wires and the best way to rig an obstacle to blow while standing in the pounding surf.

But it wouldn't be any easier on the beach, under enemy fire. So each day they pushed themselves to the limit and beyond.

Each night, he fell into bed and dreamed about sweet Charlie Fletcher.

And then one day there she was. Standing by the barracks as if she were waiting for him.

He was cross-eyed from fatigue and over-exposure. The Atlantic ocean was cold this time of year and he'd been shivering for hours. His teeth felt as if they were about to rattle right out of his head.

"I had to ask Jerry Parks if he saw you standing there, too," Vince told Charlie now. "I thought maybe I was hallucinating."

"I was terrified," she said. "Traveling all that way

on the train. Not writing to tell you I was coming was quite possibly the stupidest thing I've ever done. And then you looked at me as if you were horrified to see me there. I almost turned and ran."

"I thought I was cracking up."

But Jerry had seen her, too. And it was all Vince could do not to cry. "What are you doing here?" he asked, hardly daring to hope.

"I came to see you," she whispered. "Do you mind?"

Vince started to laugh. At least he thought he was laughing. It was hard to tell because he had to keep wiping his eyes. "No," he said. "No, I don't mind."

He pulled her into his arms, and she came willingly, eagerly even. Her mouth was warm and sweet and God, he kissed her for about twelve minutes straight and for that entire time, she kissed him back and ran her fingers through his hair and pressed herself against him and damn near heated his formerly frozen body to a boiling point.

"Marry me," he said at his first opportunity.

"Yes," she said, and he kissed her again. "Except," she said, and he stopped kissing her. There was a catch.

"Except what?"

"Don't look so worried," she said, smiling up at him. "I just . . . I told your commanding officer that I was already your wife. I got his permission to, well, to take you back to my hotel room with me." She suddenly got shy. "That is, if you don't mind."

"You *are* going to marry me." He tried to make it

into a joke. "You're not going to just use me for sex and ditch me, are you?"

"I'm definitely going to marry you," she said. "But since we can't do it tonight . . ."

They got a ride into town with a truckload of Marines, one of whom gave up his seat so Vince could sit and hold "his wife" on his lap.

It was the sweetest night of his life. He learned a heck of a lot. He learned that there were vast amounts of information he'd yet to learn about lovemaking — so much so that he could probably spend his entire life doing it and still get surprised on a regular basis. He learned that nice women like Charlie Fletcher — Charlie DaCosta, in a matter of hours — liked sex as much as men did.

And he learned possibly more than he'd wanted to know when he woke up in the night to find Charlie crying.

She was in the bathroom and the door was closed. It was a long, long time before she came out. And when she did, she slipped back into bed, telling him, "Shhh. I'm all right. Go back to sleep."

"I can't believe you lied to my CO," he told her, almost sixty years later.

"It wasn't a lie," Charlie said, the way she always did when they reminisced. "It was a pre-truth. I was going to marry you. It seemed crazy not to grab every second together that we possibly could."

"Yeah," Vince said. "And it wasn't as if I could get you pregnant. Again."

No, he'd done that quite effectively the very first time they'd made love.

Finding out about it had been something of a shock. And a disappointment.

And suddenly it all made sense. Charlie's swift and sudden change of heart. Her tears at night.

She was marrying him because she had to. Fate had forced her hand.

Vince tried not to care. So what — she was marrying him and that was what mattered. From here on in, their lives would be joined. He could — and would — make this work. He'd do everything in his power to make her happy.

And he had, hadn't he?

He looked at her now, sitting with him in the yard behind this home they'd made together, and he knew that he'd made her happy — *enough*.

James Fletcher's spirit brushed past him. Or maybe it was just the afternoon breeze.

TWENTY-FOUR

"Do you think I'm too polite?"

Joan glanced up from her Greek salad and over at Tom Paoletti before looking at Muldoon.

He was looking at her as if he were remembering — in detail — the third time they'd made love the other night. When she'd . . . Oh, God. She had to look away.

This wasn't fair!

"Do you?" he asked again. "Because recently two different people referred to me as *too polite* and I don't think it was intended as a compliment."

"I think there are times when you're too polite," Tom told Muldoon. He looked at Joan. "Don't you?"

"Uh," she said. Not when Muldoon was looking at her like he wanted to take off her clothes. Oh, crap. This was what it was going to be like for him to be "friends" with her. He wouldn't touch her. He wouldn't say a word about sex. But every time he looked at her, she'd be in danger of going up in flames.

"You were one of the people who called me that, sir," Muldoon told his CO.

"Yeah. I remember. It was right after I didn't

grant you permission to kiss me. Who else?"

"What?" Joan said.

"Izzy Zanella."

Tom laughed. "Compared to Zanella, WildCard Karmody is too polite."

"Wait a minute," Joan said. "I think I missed something."

Tom looked at her over the top of his sunglasses. His face was perfectly straight, but his eyes were laughing. "Just making sure you're listening. You're awfully quiet over there."

She was. She risked another glance at Muldoon, who'd stopped smoldering at her, thank God, and was instead frowning slightly.

"Is it because I don't say *fuck* every fifth word, like Lieutenant Starrett?" Muldoon asked. "Because I fuckin' suppose I could fuckin' start."

"Oh, God, please don't," Joan said, laughing.

"I'm sorry," he said. "That was rude. I won't."

"I think it's a uniform thing," Tom said between bites of his gyro. "I've noticed that you don't take any crap while you're wearing BDUs. It's only when you're wearing the ice-cream suit that you start saying 'sir' too much." He turned to Joan. "Do you remember what I said when we first got here?"

"Try the stuffed grape leaves?"

"Before that. I said, 'Please, call me Tom.' " He gestured to Muldoon with his head. "How many times since we sat down have you heard him call me Tom?"

She didn't have to think about it. "None."

"None. Although he does get points for asking if you think he's too polite — initiating conversation

524

by volunteering information about himself. Ding, ding, ding. Good job, Mike."

Muldoon laughed. "I didn't bring it up to —"

"You know, all I really know about you is that your father was a college professor, you lived in Maine for a while as a kid, and you spent some time at MIT in Cambridge. New England stuff, because I'm from New England. That's what you talk about with me."

Joan looked at Muldoon. "You went to MIT?"

He shrugged it off. "Only briefly. My father got sick, and I had to leave."

"That must've sucked."

"No, it was —" He caught himself. "Well, yeah. It did really suck. For him most of all, I think. He had to stop teaching — and that was his passion."

Tom gestured at him with his fork. "Did you notice what he just did?"

"Yup," Joan said.

"What?" Muldoon asked.

"We were talking about you," she said. " 'Didn't it suck for *you* to have had to leave MIT?' And all of a sudden the focus of the conversation is on your father." She turned to Tom. "Maybe he's not too polite. Maybe he's really just shy. Shy people hate being the center of attention."

"Oh, come on," Muldoon said.

"You're probably right about the uniform thing," she continued. "When he puts on the super-sexy dress uniform, he knows he's going to draw attention. That makes him self-conscious so he gets *extra* uptight."

"Now, *that's* interesting," Tom said. "I think you might be on to something there."

"Hello," Muldoon said. He was actually blushing. The man who'd just spent the entire first half of lunch boldly looking at her as if he were trying to figure out the best way to pull her under the table and have his way with her was *blushing*. "I'm sitting right here."

"What were you like as a kid?" Tom asked.

"Fat."

"No kidding."

"No, sir. Tom."

"Were you shy?" Joan asked.

"Yeah. Aren't most kids shy?" he countered.

"I wasn't," she said.

"Most fat kids," Muldoon corrected himself. "You try to make yourself invisible, which of course you can't be, because you're the fat kid."

"So how did the fat kid become one of the most promising young officers in all of the SEAL teams?" Tom asked.

"Is he really?" Joan asked.

"Oh, yeah. He'll make admiral some day, if he wants to. And I think he wants to."

"Really?" Joan said. Muldoon had led her to believe otherwise — that he was planning to leave the Navy within the next ten years. Was it possible that he was willing to put a promising career backseat to their relationship? How dare he be so willing to give up his dreams? "Well, God. That's . . . quite an impressive future to look forward to."

She looked over to find him watching her again. He was no longer looking at her as if he were thinking about sliding deep inside of her. Now he was looking at her the way he'd looked at her after

526

they'd made love, with a tenderness that was even harder to bear.

She pushed her salad aside. She had to get out of here.

God, she had to get out of *California*.

"There's more to life than being in the Navy," Muldoon said quietly. "I love being a SEAL — it's what I always wanted to do — but I'm not sure I want to stay in after my knees give out for good."

"Ah," Tom said. "I'm sorry. I didn't realize . . ."

Joan pushed back her chair. "Thank you so much for lunch, Commander. But I really have to go."

"Not before you try the baklava. It's unbelievable." Tom stood up before she could. "Sit." It was an order. "I'll get us some coffee, too."

He didn't wait for an answer. Of course, he hadn't asked a question.

It was now her big chance to lambaste Muldoon for looking at her the way he had. But what was she supposed to say? *Stop thinking about having sex with me!*

"You don't really think I'm shy, do you?" he asked.

"Well, you sure don't like to talk about yourself."

"I told you I was a math geek. A *fat* math geek."

"Yeah," Joan said. "You went into such depths about it, too."

"What's there to say?" he countered. "Kids used to make fun of me. I'm sure you remember what it was like back in school."

"I do, which is why I find it hard to believe you can boil it all down to a single sentence."

"It doesn't do me any good to talk about all the

527

different ways I was tormented as a kid," Muldoon said. "I mean, what? Is that going to make you like me more? I don't think so. It sucked, all right? I got over it. Next page."

"Okay," she said, leaning forward to rest her chin in her hand as she gazed at him. Next page indeed. "Why did the fat math geek join the Navy?"

"To become a SEAL," he answered without hesitation. "I wanted that from the time I was in seventh grade."

Really? "So what happened in seventh grade?"

"I almost drowned," he told her. "That was the year we moved to Maine from Ohio. Not much of a need to learn to swim in Ohio. At least not where we lived. I mean I knew the basics, sure, but I really couldn't do more than doggy paddle."

"So you took one look at the ocean and fell in and . . . ?"

He shot her an exasperated look.

"Tell me the story. I'm dying of curiosity."

"A couple of kids from school took me out on their father's sailboat," Muldoon said. "And we capsized. I almost drowned, but I didn't."

"Whoa," she said. "Whoa, whoa, whoa. This is you, right? Fat math geek? And on top of that you're the new kid. I remember the new kids in middle school. They were the lowest of low scum in the pecking order. And suddenly you're getting invited out onto someone's yacht?"

He laughed, and now she was the one who was having a hard time not thinking about him naked. They'd spent much of their night together laughing.

"Sailboat, not yacht," he said. "It was a dinghy

528

with a mast — which is *way* not a yacht. And I wasn't invited. I was dared to go out one afternoon when the winds were pretty high — there was a storm coming. It was crazy."

Oh, God. "And you were stupid enough not to say no. I thought math geeks were smarter than that."

"I was stupid enough to hope I could gain their respect and maybe actually make a friend. And I wasn't used to the Maine weather patterns yet. I didn't realize it would be that dangerous; it just seemed really windy. So yes. We went out. And, man oh man, Joan, that puppy flew. I mean it soared." He grinned at her, remembering. Even now, all these years later, that boat ride still turned him on. "It was amazing. I loved it — I didn't ever want to stop.

"Of course, right about then we capsized, and the waves were so high, the dinghy just filled up and sank. They're not supposed to do that, they're designed to turn over and float, but this one went down like a rock. And Wayne was flipping out because Randy got knocked on the head by the boom and he was throwing up, right there in the water. It was all Wayne could do to keep them both afloat. And he was going, 'We're going to die! We're gonna die!' and I thought about this book I'd read about Navy frogmen and SEALs, and it was all about how they didn't panic in the water, about how they didn't fight the currents and waves, but used them to get where they wanted to go.

"So I grabbed Wayne by the back of his jeans and, well, we made it to shore." He looked up and pushed himself halfway out of his chair as Tom carried three mugs of coffee toward the table. "Let me help you, sir."

"Sit," Tom ordered. "I've got it."

"Thank you, sir."

Tom went back for the dessert.

"So then what?" Joan asked.

Muldoon took a sip of coffee and she did, too. It was hot and black with a hint of cinnamon.

"I ran for the nearest house and pounded on the door. They called 911 and we all went to the hospital. Randy stayed in for a few days. He actually had a hairline fracture of his skull. I remember sitting with Wayne in the waiting room, wrapped in blankets, waiting for our parents to come pick us up."

"Don't tell me," Joan said. "After that, Wayne and Randy wanted to be your best friends, but you kept your distance, because not only were they cruel, they were stupid. And you were smart enough to not want to be friends with them. And you always just smiled whenever you saw them because you knew that without you, they would have drowned."

Muldoon smiled and shook his head very slightly. He started to say something, but then Tom was there, carrying three plates with enormous slices of baklava.

"I'm going to have to toss this at you and run," he told Joan. "I just got a call from Chip Crowley. I'm needed in his office." He turned to Muldoon. "We're going to get a chance to talk to Max Bhagat. I need you to go over to that restaurant that Larry Tucker likes so much — it's right down here somewhere by the water —"

"I know where it is," Muldoon said, getting to his feet. "It's that French place where cell phone service doesn't work. You walk in, and you might as well be on the moon."

"Yeah, and the staff speaks with such strong French accents, you have no idea if they get your message straight if you call on the land line. Although you speak French, don't you, Mike?"

"I'll go over there, sir. It's just around the corner."

"Good. Find the senior chief and Jacquette," Tom ordered. "I want them to join me at Crowley's, ASAP. Thank you. And I'm sorry," he added to Joan. He grabbed one of the pieces of baklava before he dashed away.

"I'll be back in a few minutes," Muldoon said to her. "Can you wait?"

"I can't," she lied.

"I guess I'll see you later then," he said.

"Mike, this friend thing isn't working," she said, but he, too, was already gone.

Mary Lou knew this was a terrible mistake long before the salads were served.

Bob looked incredible. He wore a suit with his tie neatly fastened, and his golden hair was slicked back from his face, a style that accentuated his male modelesque cheekbones.

He kept touching her. Her arm, her hand, her shoulder. And she knew he expected more than an opportunity to share a meal. She was married, but she'd said yes, and he'd thought she'd meant the Big Yes.

And when he'd called this morning, when she'd

said it, maybe she had. It was more than obvious that she had no future with Sam. And it had been her MO in the past to hook up with a new lover before her old one was even out of her bed.

She'd always thought of it as finding a relationship parachute. The new man might not be perfect, but he'd keep her from spending even a single day alone.

The thought of being alone scared the shit out of her. And now she had Haley to take care of, too.

So here she was, and there was no doubt about it any longer. Bob Schwegel, Insurance Sales, wanted to fuck her. He was handsome, he was smart, he had money and a nice car.

He was, without a doubt, the perfect parachute.

But all she could think about was Ihbraham. Who loved her. Enough to keep his distance so that he *didn't* fuck her.

And wasn't *that* the oddest thing?

Bob was talking about his work, about selling insurance — which was just about as interesting to her as shoveling cow manure from a barn — and she let her mind wander.

Back to Ihbraham.

Who loved her.

Ihbraham, who, with his quiet gentleness, simply by sitting beside her and breathing, made her happier than she'd ever been in her entire life.

Even though he wasn't a SEAL. Even though he wasn't white. Even though he was only a gardener.

Bob put down his salad fork. "You're not really interested in Mrs. Wilke's policy changes, are you?"

She shook her head. "I'm sorry."

"Have I told you that you look incredible to-night?" he asked.

He had. "Thank you," she said again. The dress she was wearing was too tight across her chest, but Bob sure didn't seem to mind. He kept scraping his eyes across her body, making her more and more uncomfortable by the minute.

Which was strange. Since when did it bother her to have a man check out her boobs with a look in his eye that broadcast his intent to have her naked within moments of leaving this table? She'd been entering — and winning — wet T-shirt contests since she was seventeen. She'd grown up on wolf whistles and catcalls, and had wondered what she was doing wrong when she walked down a silent street.

"I have to be honest, Mary Lou," Bob told her now. "I want more than dinner from you. I've wanted you from the first time we met."

And she knew part of what her problem was. She'd seen herself in her mirror before she left the house, and she knew she didn't look hot. She looked pathetic and fat. Which meant that Bob was either blind or lying.

Ihbraham, however, loved her.

All she wanted was to pick up Haley from Mrs. U.'s and go home.

Mary Lou used her napkin to wipe her mouth and set it beside her plate. "I'm sorry, Bob. I really am, but I —"

"Hear me out, okay? I know what you're think-ing, and yes, I want you to come home with me, but not tonight."

Well, wasn't that . . . different.

"When you come to me," he told her, "I want it to be permanent." He leaned across the table, his eyes intense as he took her hand. "Leave your husband, Mary Lou. He doesn't treat you the way you deserve to be treated, the way *I'll* treat you. Run away with me."

She pulled her hand free. "That's crazy. I can't run away, I have a daughter."

"You didn't think I meant . . ." He laughed. "God, no. I meant we should all run away. Haley, too, of course. Remember that trip I'm taking to New York?"

She nodded.

"I'm leaving tomorrow, and I want you and Haley to come with me. Pack a suitcase, bring what you need — bring it with you to work. I'll meet you, we'll go pick up Haley from day care and leave right then and there. You told me you always wanted to go to New York. Come on, let's do it. What do you say?"

She said nothing for a moment. She just sat there, looking at Bob across the table, and she knew that she was going to leave Sam. She was going to jump. And she did have a parachute.

But it wasn't Bob.

No, she was going to leave Sam for Ihbraham.

Who loved her.

Bob was handsome and gleaming and perfect in so many ways. Mary Lou would bet her entire savings account that he was great in bed, too.

And if it weren't for Ihbraham, she might be tempted to find out just how great he was.

But while she could've used Bob to cheat on

Sam, she didn't want to cheat on Ihbraham.

Who *loved* her. Who loved *her.*

She pushed her chair back from the table. "I'm so sorry. I can't do this."

"Sure you can. Sam treats you like shit, Mary Lou. We can really screw him while we're at it — empty his bank accounts, use his credit cards — have fun while he pays for it."

And it became very clear what Bob was after.

"I'm sorry," she told him as she stood up to leave. "But I can't go with you. I don't love you and I honestly don't believe that you love me."

"You busy?" Muldoon said quietly into his cell phone.

Joan was sitting on the other side of the crowded room, and she turned to look at him, shaking her head slightly. "What do you think?"

It was the so-called final meeting before tomorrow's presidential extravaganza, and Admiral Tucker was standing up at the front of the room, giving a long-winded speech about . . . well, Muldoon wasn't sure exactly what Tucker was talking about, but the man's public speaking skills were legendarily bad, and as usual, he'd gone into repeat mode.

Everything of importance had already been said by the men who were truly in charge of the SEAL demonstration. Lieutenant Commander Paoletti had given a few last-minute instructions and talked about some changes. He was still feeling unhappy about releasing smoke into the crowd and had announced that he was taking it upon himself to play it by ear tomorrow. If he had any sense that there might be trouble, he was reserving the right not to use the smoke.

Muldoon had had a chance to talk to the CO after his meeting with FBI team leader Max Bhagat. Apparently whatever Bhagat said hadn't reassured him.

Bhagat was here now, with a small group of agents from his counterterrorist team, including the infamous Alyssa Locke and a man Muldoon had met in Indonesia last year — George Faulkner. Good guy. Solid sense of humor considering he spent all that time each day in a suit.

"I'm thinking about getting something to eat — maybe a slice of pizza — and having a beer after this endurance test is over," Muldoon whispered into his cell phone.

"Wow, one whole slice of pizza," Joan said. "Go crazy." As he watched, she got to her feet and quietly slipped out of the room, standing just outside the half-opened doorway to the corridor. This way she could talk quietly without disturbing anyone.

Good idea.

But to get over to where she was now standing, Muldoon would have to cross directly in front of Admiral Tucker — not a smart career move. Instead he went out the open doors on the other side of the room. He could see Joan from where he stood, and even though he was standing in shadows, he knew she could see him, too.

"I still watch my weight," he told her quietly. "Force of habit. I'm aware of how many calories I burn each day, and I eat accordingly. Today was a one-slice day. Believe me, there are days when I just start eating from the moment I get up to the moment I go to sleep and I'll still lose weight — which is not something I'm looking to do, because when I lose weight these days, I lose muscle mass. BUD/S training was like that — you eat to refuel, and you need lots of fuel. Some guys come home after a particularly strenuous op, and they keep eating huge amounts, but they're not burning the calories anymore and . . . that's when you can run into trouble."

"And yet you encourage me to have dessert."

"Yeah, you don't have to run eight-minute miles. I think women should have curves. I think there are too many people these days who confuse being skinny with being physically fit. Starving yourself down to skin and bones doesn't make you healthy. On the contrary."

"I know that," she said. "It's just hard to stand next to a woman who's scary-thin and not feel . . . large. I feel large most of the time," she admitted.

"Maybe you should spend more time standing next to me," he suggested. And maybe that was a little too friendly, because across the room, over in the other hallway, he saw her sigh.

Okay, don't let her talk. Don't let her start that same old "I don't think this friends thing is working" speech that she'd tried to deliver all the other times he'd called her on her cell phone this afternoon.

Calling her was, without a doubt, the only way he could talk to her. Their afternoon was filled with downtime, but they both had to be in range of their superiors — ready to leap into action if necessary.

"You're in excellent shape, by the way. You're

the perfect weight for a woman of your height," he told her in an attempt to hold on to the conversational ball. "I couldn't help but, you know, notice when, uh . . ." When she was naked and in his arms. Damn, that was not the way to go, either. This platonic friendship thing was much harder than he'd dreamed it would be.

He wanted to make love to her again so desperately that it was all he could do not to lie down right there in the hall and howl in frustration.

"So. Pizza?" he said instead.

"I've got more meetings to go to," she said. "This might be it for you, but I've still got Brooke duty to take care of tonight."

"How's she doing?" Muldoon asked.

"She's still in the detox part of the treatment," Joan told him. "I think it's harder than she thought. But she's hanging in." She sighed again. "Look, Michael. I think we probably do need to talk — face-to-face, I mean. How about tomorrow evening, after this thing is over?"

"I'm not sure," he said. "We can plan for it, but don't forget there's a chance I'll have to leave right away. And I may not be able to call you to tell you, so . . . Just remember that it's not intentional if I suddenly don't show up."

She was silent for several long moments, but then she asked, "Why do you do it? What's the appeal of going out there and risking your life? I just . . . I don't get it. Why do *you* have to do it?"

"Someone's got to," he said. "We've talked about this before — you know how I feel."

"And you've wanted to do this — be a SEAL — since seventh grade," she said. "I don't get that, either. Was it surviving that sailing accident that made you want to be a SEAL? Or was it . . . ? I don't know, I've been thinking all day about that story you told me, and I just keep wondering, when you were in the water and you were swimming with those two other boys, pulling them along, trying to make it to shore . . . how on earth did you do it?"

"First of all," Muldoon said, "I didn't *try*. There was no *trying* going on. I had to do it, so I did it. I wasn't ready to die, and I refused to accept that option as a real possibility. Wayne kept screaming, 'We're going to die, oh, my God, we're going to die,' and maybe that's what kept me going, because every time he said that, I thought, *Not me*. I'd read about Hell Week — you know, the part of BUD/S training where you get no sleep, and they run you around like lunatics — it's a physical and mental endurance test. I'd read some accounts of guys who'd been through it, who'd succeeded, and they all seemed to break that week down into much smaller moments. Heartbeats, if you will. Boom. You take one step forward. Boom. You take another. Boom. Breathe in. Boom. Exhale. You don't set your eyes on the end of the week because that's too far away. That's an impossible goal to achieve. You keep it doable. You don't look beyond that very next step that you're going to take.

"That's what I did when I was in the water," he told her. "I swam for one heartbeat and then one heartbeat more. And then another, and another. I think luck had a lot to do with us hitting shore when we did. We were in a harbor, there was land on three sides, so our chances of reaching solid ground at some point were pretty good. As it was, we didn't take the shortest route. As it was, we swam for a quarter of a mile." He laughed. "That doesn't seem like a lot to me anymore, but believe me, at the time it was a major deal."

"Was that what it was?" she asked. "You tasted what it was like to be a hero, so . . . ?"

He had to laugh. "Hero, huh?" Yeah, that's right — she'd made up a nifty end to his story, complete with a virtual ticker tape parade through the center of town. "I was grounded for three weeks after that. And Wayne told everyone that I'd capsized the boat on purpose."

"No way!" Joan said. "The little piece of *shit!* No wonder you didn't want to be friends with him."

"Yeah, it didn't happen quite the way you imagined," he said. "Wayne didn't even thank me for saving his life."

"You've *got* to be kidding."

Muldoon loved the fact that she could get so indignant about injustices that had happened to him so long ago.

"So what did he say to you?" she asked. "You said you both sat in the hospital, waiting for your parents. He must've said *some*thing."

"He said . . ." Muldoon laughed softly. "You're going to hate this."

"I know," she said. "I can feel it. I'm going to want to track this little bastard down and kick him in the balls for you. Just like, *wham.* 'That's for Mike Muldoon, you little jerk,' and then I'd vanish."

"With the police hot on your heels shouting your Miranda rights and charging you with assault and battery."

"Okay," she said. "I'm feeling more in control. What'd that fucker — excuse me, I know you don't like that language, but I have only so much control over being in control. What did he say to you?"

"At this point, it feels a little anticlimactic," Muldoon admitted. "And I love the fact that you called him what you called him because, well, part of me is still that fat kid that nobody cared about and everyone made fun of, and here you are standing up for him — me — him. You know what I mean, don't you? I'm still him, but I'm not. And it's like, because you're so upset about this now, there's some kind of weird warp in time. And the fat kid who's grounded for three weeks for doing something incredible knows that fifteen years later there's going to be someone who cares enough to get pissed about the injustice of it all, and he actually feels better." He laughed. "Yeah, and now you think I'm totally schizoid."

"I don't," Joan said. The meeting was over, and everyone was filing out of the room, making it harder for him to see her. "God, Michael, you are one dangerous man."

"What?" he said. "Why?" He started toward her, moving slowly along with the crowd of people.

"Just tell me what the you-know-what said. I've got five minutes before my next meeting starts. As it is, I'm going to have to run to get there."

"He said the reason we didn't drown was because I was so fat. He said, 'Blubber floats.' "

He saw her again — she was pacing in a part of the hall that wasn't so crowded.

"I'm going to do it," Joan said. "I'm going to find him and I'm going to . . . No, you know what I'm going to do? What's his last name, because I know a woman who works for the IRS. I'm going to have the little prick audited."

Muldoon laughed as he broke free from the throng and walked those last few steps to her. "You can't do that. You wouldn't. That's an abuse of power."

"Oh, my God," she said, snapping her cell phone shut and finally talking directly to him. "How did you survive, Mike? How could you have lived through that and grown up to be so freaking nice?"

"Well, thanks," he said. "I'm glad you think that —"

"I'm late," she said, and bolted.

Mary Lou had surprised him.

Husaam Abdul-Fataah sat in his car and watched the lights go on in her house as she moved from room to room, putting the baby to bed.

The husband was already home. He could only guess what kind of excuse she gave him when she went inside, obviously overdressed for an AA meeting.

If the husband hadn't been home, Husaam would have been tempted to go inside and convince Mary Lou — at gunpoint — to write a farewell note. *Dear Sam, Things aren't working out. Take care of the baby. Love, Mary Lou.*

Not that he had any problem in taking and disposing of the kid, too. But it was his experience that while unwanted wives could disappear without anyone hardly noticing they were gone, people tended to get a little upset when their children went missing, too. Even if they didn't particularly pay much attention to those children when they were around.

But forcing Mary Lou to go with him, with or without the baby, was a moot point, since the husband was home. There was no way he was breaking into the house of a Navy SEAL the night before a job was set to go down.

Husaam had no doubt of his own ability to get inside and pump Starrett full of bullets before he even got out of his TV chair. He would, in fact, enjoy it — it had been a while since he'd taken a hands-on assignment. But the minute Starrett failed to show up at the base tomorrow morning, an alarm would be raised. And with the discovery of his body in his TV room, well, President Bryant wouldn't even disembark from Air Force One.

And wouldn't *that* be a shame, after five brave al-Qaeda fighters did their version of a suicide squeeze — setting up evidence of a "plot" to bomb the airport so that the FBI could find them and kill them and make San Diego seem secure. The terrorist plot's been handled, the Western world is safe, everyone relax. Of course, the real plan — all along — was to gun down the American President during his visit to the U.S. Naval Base.

Husaam had hoped to get out of town in the morning, before the action started. He'd hoped Mary Lou would have agreed to go with him willingly. Baby or not, her disappearance was critical.

He'd woken up in the night with the realization that her fingerprints were on one of the weapons that were going to be used tomorrow. The FBI would find those prints, and if Mary Lou had a police record, they would ID her.

And wouldn't *that* be sweet? The wife of a Navy SEAL involved in terrorist activity. The fallout from that was going to immobilize Team Sixteen for months, possibly even years.

Husaam was going to get a neat little bonus for that.

But Mary Lou had to disappear. She couldn't be around to defend herself, or to cast any doubt on her obvious guilt.

Ihbraham would have to disappear, too. While Sam Starrett probably wouldn't care if Mary Lou vanished without a trace, Ihbraham Rahman might actually try to find her.

As the lights went off in the Starrett house, Husaam settled back in his seat.

The night was still young, and filled with possibilities. Sam Starrett got called down to the base in the middle of the night pretty frequently — leaving Mary Lou and Haley home all alone.

TWENTY-FIVE

"Joan, it's Mike."

"Are you insane?" Joan rolled over to look at the clock on the hotel bedside table. It was 1:44. "I was finally asleep, you jerk!"

She hung up the phone with a crash.

It rang again, almost immediately.

"What?"

"Don't hang up," Muldoon said.

"Don't you sleep?" she asked. "Normal people don't call at 1:44 unless it's an emergency!"

"It is an emergency," he said. "It's your brother."

Joan sat up. "Oh, my God. Donny? What's wrong?"

"I don't know, exactly," Muldoon said as she fumbled for the light. "I got a call from Sam Starrett about two minutes ago. He said it might be Don's appendix, but Sam's not a corpsman — a medic — so he's just guessing. He and his wife are over there with your brother right now. An ambulance is on its way."

Joan was already out of bed and throwing on her clothes. "Donny's not going to go for that. He's not going to want to leave the house."

"Yeah, Sam's a little worried about that. He thinks Don definitely needs to go to the hospital.

He thought maybe if you came —"

"I'm already dressed." She gathered up her handbag and her room and rental car keys. "What's the fastest way over there?"

"With me," he said. "I'm already on my way — I'm about four minutes from you."

Mike was already on his way. He was going to drive her over there. "I'm sorry I called you a jerk."

"Do you often have trouble falling asleep?" he asked. "I could help you with that, you know."

"Hey," she said.

"I figured I'd earned enough points tonight to toss in a mildly suggestive comment. But that's it. I'm done. I won't mention it again. I'll meet you out front in a few."

Crazy Donny the Nutjob was in some serious pain.

Mary Lou was kneeling beside him, on the closet floor, trying to teach him the Lamaze breathing techniques she'd learned when she was pregnant with Haley.

It would have been almost funny if Don hadn't been so upset. He was convinced aliens were inside of him and that it was only a matter of time before they came bursting out, like they did in that movie with Sigourney Weaver.

Sam had been on the phone pretty much non-stop since Mary Lou got that first call from Donny. He'd called 911 shortly after coming over here and seeing the Nutjob writhing on the floor. That got an ambulance on its way. He'd called Muldoon, who had Joan's number. And then he'd called Jay Lopez, the team's corpsman, who recommended

Sam check Don's abdomen for rigidity — something that would suggest a ruptured appendix.

In theory it was a good idea. In practice it was something else entirely.

"I'm just going to touch you very gently, Don," Sam said.

"No," Donny sobbed. "No! Don't touch me!"

Sam did it anyway, but since he didn't really know what appendicitis felt like, all it served to do was get the Nutjob more upset. He sat back on his heels. "We should probably get him out of here," he said to Mary Lou. "It's going to be real close quarters when the EMTs come in."

"Let them worry about that," she said. "You don't need to save the world, Sam. We just need to keep Donny as quiet and comfortable as possible until they get here. And I happen to know he's most comfortable right here in this closet. There's no point in freaking him out." She leaned closer to Don, who was trying to speak. "Hush, hon. Just breathe the way I showed you. Through your teeth now. Little short exhales. That's right." She looked up at Sam again. "If it's too close in here for you, you could wait outside the house — guard against attack from, you know."

Aliens. He knew.

"Donny says he's seen 'em around lately — in our driveway, no less."

Way to go, Don. "I'll go stand guard," Sam said loudly enough for the Nutjob to hear, but he rolled his eyes when his back was turned.

"First could you run back home, check on Haley, and grab the baby monitor? And while you're there, there's a phone number pinned to the bulletin board in the kitchen. It's for Vincent and Charlotte DaCosta — Donny's grandparents. I think they'd probably appreciate a call."

And wasn't this a change of pace? Sam following Mary Lou's orders instead of the other way around. He went out the front, the screen door banging closed behind him.

The neighborhood was silent, lights off, shades down, sidewalks all but rolled up for the night. Everyone was sleeping.

Well, maybe not everyone. A car was parked out in front of the Bentons' house again. Sam had seen it there a few other times lately, when he'd come home late at night.

Kyle Benton traveled a lot — he was out of town right now, in Hong Kong, on business. And here was that car again. Shame on you, Mrs. Benton.

Sam stood there a moment, wondering almost idly if there was a car parked out in front of *his* house when *he* was away.

He doubted it, although he wished it were true. It would make life a whole hell of a lot easier if Mary Lou was unfaithful.

He went inside his house, went into Haley's room.

She was doing what he'd heard Mary Lou call her angel imitation. She was fast asleep, her eyes tightly shut with those golden curls around her face, a picture of innocent serenity.

Sam stood there for a long time, his heart in his throat, thinking about sitting down with Mary Lou tomorrow night and telling her that he'd tried his best, but he couldn't do this anymore.

Telling her that their marriage was over — that it had been before it even started.

Things would be radically different when he moved out. Or maybe Mary Lou would move out. He hoped not. If Mary Lou left San Diego, he didn't have a prayer of seeing Haley more than a few times a year.

And he wouldn't put it past Mary Lou to do that, to leave town out of spite. And to make Sam out as the villain of the piece for the rest of their lives. Haley'd probably grow up hating him. Or at least disdainful of that loser who'd quit on her mom.

Maybe someday she'd understand that he *had* been tough enough to stick it out, but smart enough to realize that that wouldn't be best for any of them.

Especially Haley, who deserved to grow up surrounded by love, not obligation.

"I suck at being a father," he told her as she slept. "You'll be better off without me."

Well, hell, that sounded like something a pathetic loser would say.

Sam tiptoed out of the room, feeling like shit and knowing there were no easy outs, no easy answers.

Tomorrow night was going to be the pits.

The DaCostas' phone number was right on the board in the kitchen, in Mary Lou's loopy handwriting, just where she'd said it would be.

He dialed his cell phone as he headed back across their two yards, letting it ring and ring and ring.

Muldoon's truck pulled up, and Joan DaCosta came flying out. Her T-shirt was on inside out.

Funny, that was usually Sam's MO when getting dressed in a hurry.

"Where is he?"

"In the closet." He followed her inside. "Are your grandparents hard of hearing, because they're not picking up." Of course, it *was* fricking late.

"They're already on their way," Joan told him before disappearing into the closet.

Muldoon was right behind her. "Thanks for calling me," he told Sam.

"No problem. Thanks for getting here so quickly."

Outside the house, the ambulance pulled up. And then, yes, there *were* six adults in Donny's walk-in closet.

Sam stayed out in the bedroom.

The conversation going on in there was like something from a science fiction movie, with Donny wailing about the aliens in his stomach and Joan trying to reason with him.

"Well, Don, if there were aliens in *my* stomach, I'd *want* to be taken to the hospital as soon as possible."

"No!" he cried. "No!"

Joan came out then, with the two EMTs trailing behind. Together, they discussed the pros and cons of sedating Donny. Mary Lou came out, too, and joined in the fray. She was on Joan's side — she thought the shock of waking up in the hospital would be terribly hard for Donny to deal with. They should — and could, as long as his life wasn't immediately in danger — try to talk him into leaving willingly.

Mary Lou said she knew that would be very

hard to do. But wasn't it worth spending just a little more time? For Donny's sake . . . ?

She was in her pajamas — flannel boxers and a tank top with nothing underneath — and one of the EMTs was actually flirting with her. A breast man, apparently. She was giving them all quite an eyeful.

But that wasn't all it was that made those men look, Sam realized. She had color in her cheeks and life in her eyes and fire in her voice as she defended Donny with real passion.

Holy fuck, was it possible Mary Lou . . . ? And Donny the Nutjob . . . ?

No fucking way.

But God knows Mary Lou hadn't been getting any from Sam lately. And she looked . . .

Happy?

Or at least happier.

And Don was rumored to be some kind of stock market genius worth millions. He had hundreds of thousands in his chump change savings account. Maybe Mary Lou had discovered that the key to her happiness lay not in living with a Navy SEAL, but with a lunatic millionaire. Sam sure as hell wouldn't put it past her.

But Jesus. That meant Mary Lou could well be moving out of their house into this one. Haley, too. How weird would that be?

Sam flat-out didn't like the idea of Haley being raised with a freak for a stepfather. But on the other hand, she would be right next door . . .

Before he could speculate any further, Muldoon came to the door of the closet.

With Donny.

The Nutjob was bent over, clutching his gut, but he was on his feet.

"I'm going to ride with Don in the ambulance," Muldoon said as if he weren't aware he'd performed a major miracle. "We'd like to go to the hospital now, if that's all right."

Everyone stood there, staring with their mouths open for about two seconds. And then everyone moved at once.

Sam just stepped back and let 'em run.

"I'm going to the hospital, too," Mary Lou told him. "Will you stay with Haley?"

Sam nodded. "Better put some real clothes on."

"I will."

They were the last ones in the room, and he had to ask. "Are you actually screwing Donny DaCosta?"

She laughed — a loud whoop of surprise — as she turned back to him. But then incredulousness replaced the amusement on her face. "You're serious."

If it was an act, she deserved an Oscar. Especially when she shot him a look of pure disgust and headed out the door. "Fuck you, Sam. Would you even care if I was?"

No. Sam didn't say it aloud, but she glanced back at him again, and he knew she saw it written clearly on his face.

Vince watched Mike Muldoon as Mike watched Joanie pace.

The hospital waiting room was crowded, as was the actual ER.

Don had been given a bed right away in a ward

with four other patients. Charlie was with him, along with that nice little neighbor gal, Mary Lou.

Donny seemed to like holding her hand. And aside from her obvious physical attributes, Vince could relate. She had a sweetness to her, a child-like, almost angelic quality that contrasted sharply with that stripper's body.

The doctors were doing some kind of tests on Don to see if it was in fact his appendix that was giving him so much pain. Apparently they could tell enough from a relatively simple blood count to keep them from immediately diving in with explor-atory surgery, although that was always an option.

As Vince watched, Joanie paced her way back to Muldoon and stopped right in front of him. She was not, as Charlie would've said, a happy camper.

"How could you promise him something like that?" she said loudly enough so that Vince could overhear without straining. Which meant she was talking pretty loudly. "Something you couldn't possibly deliver?"

Mike made room for her on the bench. She didn't sit.

He sighed. "First of all, I didn't promise any-thing I couldn't deliver."

"So what are you going to do?" she asked. "You're really going to stay here all night?"

"Yes," he said. "If your father doesn't show —"

She rolled her eyes. "Not if. *When*. Tony's offi-cial title in life is No Show."

"Actually —" Vince leaned over to interject. "— your father's on his way. I spoke to him just a few minutes ago."

"Oh, my God." Joan pretended to push her hair

back from her forehead. It was obvious that her real intention was to hold on to her head so that it didn't explode from the shock. She sank down onto the bench, next to Mike. "Donny's right. Aliens are invading people's bodies. That's the only reason I can think of for why he'd come — because he's not really Tony anymore."

"Very funny," Vince said. "Give the kid a break. He's trying, okay?"

She got all self-righteous — something she was very good at. "He's not a kid, Gramps. And he's had *lots* of breaks."

"Well, give him one more," Vince recommended, and snapped open his newspaper, pretending to read. He didn't want to argue with Joan about Tony. Not right now, with Donny maybe headed for surgery.

From the corner of his eye, he saw her turn to Mike. "If my father's really coming, you don't have to stay."

He nodded, obviously going nowhere because he was settled back in his seat. "I'm not here for your brother, Joan. I'm here for you."

Ah, it was beautifully said. Perfectly delivered with complete, baldly honest sincerity. If she didn't melt at that, Don was right. Aliens were invading people's bodies and this young woman was no longer his sweet Joanie.

She didn't speak, which was a pretty good sign that she was melting. It was rare indeed when Joan didn't have a snappy comeback line.

And then Charlie was there with some good news. "It's not Donny's appendix," she announced. "The doctor thinks it might be some kind of food poisoning, but nothing too serious."

Joan stood up. "Can I go in and see him?"

"Of course," Charlie said.

Joan looked at Muldoon and opened her mouth to speak.

He didn't give her a chance. "I'll be right here," he said. "I'm not going anywhere."

"Did you know your T-shirt's on inside out?" Muldoon asked as he and Joan walked all the way back to hospital lot C, where his truck was parked.

Man, he wanted to put his arms around her and kiss the heck out of her. All night long, he'd been aware of every move she made. Every time she stretched out her legs, every time she started to pace, every time she so much as took a breath.

She looked down at her chest in the dim light. "Inside out *and* backward," she said. She laughed. "No wonder I spent the entire night feeling like I was choking. God, and I thought it was psychological."

"I know that was rough for you," he said. "Watching Donny hurting like that, and then seeing your father. I'm sorry, I can't even offer to take you out and buy you a stiff drink. Nothing's open."

"What time is it?" she asked. "And please God, let it be before three . . ."

He glanced at his watch. "Uh-oh."

"Don't tell me," she said. "I don't want to know."

She looked beat. Without any makeup, she looked almost sweet. She looked younger. Innocent, even.

She'd talked briefly to her father, who looked

555

quite a bit like a younger version of her granddad. She'd even hugged the guy. But Muldoon knew just from watching her that this was only a temporary truce, not a real peace settlement. Still, it was a start. Life was too short to carry grudges, but now was not the time to start preaching at her.

"I don't know how to thank you for this," she said as he unlocked the door to his truck and helped her up and inside.

"You don't have to thank me." He closed the door, then crossed around the front and climbed in.

"Let's just sleep here," she said. "It's so quiet and dark and perfect and I'm so exhausted . . ."

"The seat reclines," Muldoon told her. "Why don't you push it back as far as it goes? I'll wake you when we get to the hotel."

She reached out her hand, stopping him from putting the key in the ignition. "Don't you ever get tired of being so unbelievably nice?"

He laughed softly. "I didn't realize I was doing anything unbelievable."

He looked up to find her gazing at him, her expression such a mix of emotions he couldn't read her at all.

If it had been any other woman in the world looking at him like that, he would have taken a chance that all that emotion was a good thing, and he would have kissed her. But Joan didn't want him to kiss her.

Or did she?

He moistened his lips and her gaze dropped to his mouth.

And stayed there, for a good long time.

Okay.

When she looked back into his eyes, he knew he was completely unable to hide his desire for her.

"Aha," she whispered. "You're nice to me because you want to get laid, am I right?"

"No. I mean, yes, of course, I want us to . . . but . . ." He shook his head.

"What you said to me in the hospital was . . ." Joan cleared her throat. "It was very sweet. I haven't been very nice to you these past few days, and —"

He cut her off. "It's okay. Look, I've decided that I can wait until you figure some stuff out, you know, that you need to get figured out. Take as long as you want. I'm just . . . I'm just going to be here. But I'm not going to let us not be friends, Joan. I'm going to fight you for that. I'm not going to go away, even when you go back to D.C. I'm going to call, I'm going to write, and I'm going to visit. So you better get used to me hanging around."

She was silent for a long time, just gazing at him. Then she said, "We're going to make love again, aren't we?"

"Eventually," he said, his pulse kicking up a notch. He was beyond glad that she recognized that as a universal truth. "Yeah. We are."

"Tonight," she said. "I meant tonight."

And *that* was what that look on her face meant. She wanted . . .

"God," he said, "I hope so."

He kissed her. Hard. With absolutely no finesse. One minute they were talking, and the next he was on top of her, kissing her more deeply than he'd ever kissed anyone without a lengthy warm-up.

Except he wasn't really on top of her. She was as desperate for him as he was for her, and she had met him halfway.

He had her shirt pulled up, her bra unfastened, and her bare breasts in his hands within a few short seconds.

She laughed. "Whoa, Mike, we're in the parking —"

He stopped her from saying more by kissing her. Yes, they were in the parking lot. The very empty parking lot with nothing around them but empty parking slots. Anyone pulling in wouldn't come near them — they'd park much closer to the hospital entrance.

And, Jesus, he didn't want to wait to drive all the way back to the hotel.

And maybe have her change her mind.

Muldoon pushed his seat back as far as it would go, which was far enough — thank you, Mr. Ford — as he unfastened her jeans.

He had to stop kissing her to pull them off her legs, which was dangerous because that meant she could talk.

"Oh, my God," she gasped, even as she helped him by kicking off her sneakers. "You actually want to . . . Anyone walking past can see us!"

"No, they can't," he said.

She wasn't wearing any underpants, which would have been a really excellent discovery if he'd been taking his time. As it was, it only served to distract him.

"I happen to know that we're not invisible. At least I'm not —"

"No one's walking past," he told her, cupping her with his hand, quickly trying to calculate how, in their limited amount of space, he could kiss her there.

No, there was really only one way two people their size could make love in the front seat of a truck like this one.

He pulled her on top of him, so that she was straddling him.

"Mike —"

"No one's walking past."

"Easy for you to be blasé — I'm the one who's naked and you're not!"

"I noticed." He grinned at her as he dug a condom out of his wallet. He'd put it there just a few days ago, in a burst of hope. "I'm finding that to be quite an incredible turn on. Shades of slave girl and cruel master."

That completely cracked her up. "I think you just like the idea of getting caught," she said, but she pulled her T-shirt over her head and her bra off her arms so that she really was completely naked and waiting for him.

It almost seemed a shame to unfasten his pants. But he did it without hesitating, quickly covering himself with the condom. "Who's going to catch us, slave girl? It's after four A.M."

"It's after four?" Her voice rose in dismay.

He grabbed her hips and pulled her toward him and . . .

"God!"

He was inside of her, and she was laughing. He hoped it was because this felt as mind-blowingly wonderful to her as it did to him. He was in heaven with her breasts in his face and her body straining to get even closer to his.

"Suddenly four A.M. doesn't seem so awful anymore," she gasped, and he had to laugh, too. "In fact, it's my new favorite time of day. Oh, God, if you don't slow down, I'm going to come right away!"

He didn't. "Tell me," he demanded. "Tell me when. I'm going to come with you."

What he was doing to her was apparently really right. She was making a lot of wordless noise, deep, sexy sounds of intense pleasure, and it was pushing him hard against the edge of his own release.

Was she coming? He wasn't completely sure.

"Tell me," he ordered.

"I'm . . . yes!" she said. "Yes!"

He let go.

The crash of pleasure was so intense that he shook, that bright colors actually cartwheeled before his eyes.

And she was feeling that pleasure, too. Right at that exact same moment. Knowing that made it ten times better, and he started to laugh.

It was either that or cry.

Joan collapsed against him, and he held her close.

"Oh, man." He could feel her heart pounding, racing in time with his. "Oh, baby. That was amazing. Fast, but amazing."

She sighed, a bone-deep sigh of contentment that made his throat ache.

Please, God, let her realize that this was not just another mistake, that what they'd found together could truly make her happy.

She sighed again. "Can you really do that?" she asked. "Come on command?"

"It's just a control thing," he said. "You fight it, and you fight it, and then you stop fighting it. And bang."

"Bang?" she repeated, lifting her head to look down at him.

"Yeah." He smiled back at her. "That's pretty much how it happens."

She touched his face, the amusement in her eyes changing to something tender, something that had a hint of sadness. "What on earth am I going to do with you?"

He tried to make it into a joke. "Something really kinky I hope."

She opened her mouth, as if she were going to speak, but headlights swept across them.

A car was pulling into the parking lot.

Joan leapt down onto the floor on the passenger's side of the cab, scrambling for her clothes.

"They parked on the other end," he told her. "It's safe to come back."

But she didn't. She quickly pulled on her clothes before sitting back in her seat. "God," she said, as he refastened his own belt buckle. "I haven't had sex in a motor vehicle since college. That was . . . something of a novelty."

He didn't want to be a novelty. But he tried to keep things light. "Stick with me, babe. It'll be high class all the way. Tomorrow I'll take you out and we can get rockin' in my boat."

"Tomorrow we're both going to be a little busy," she said.

"Not tomorrow night." He started the truck

561

with a roar and pulled out of the hospital lot. "Can I see you tomorrow night?"

Joan glanced out of the window, as if gauging how fast they were moving and if it were possible for her to jump out of the truck and get away from him without injuring herself.

Not a good sign.

She gave him a smile that was forced, and his heart sank even further. "I don't know what I'm going to be up to, with Brooke, with Donny — God, now that Tony's visiting . . ."

"I know you have things to do," he said quietly, "but sooner or later you *will* be done for the night. I don't care if it's really late —"

She closed her eyes. "I know this is going to sound awful, but please, let's not do this right now."

Muldoon shut his mouth, and they drove the rest of the way back to Joan's hotel in silence.

Muldoon parked in the lot, over by the side entrance, instead of dropping her at the front of the hotel.

"Thank you," Joan said, hating herself for having been cruel to him — again. But if she was terrified before, now she was in a complete panic. What *was* she going to do? "And, Mike, I'm really sorry —"

"I want you again," he told her, his voice low. "Already. Can you believe that?" He looked over at her, and his expression was as serious as she'd ever seen it.

It was as if she were suddenly sitting in this truck with that man who'd run down a mountain with a broken kneecap instead of her good ol' buddy Mike.

"At the risk of being crude . . ." He took her hand and placed it over the zipper of his shorts.

Joan snatched her hand back. He wasn't exaggerating. "Wow. I guess that's one of the perks of having a younger boyfriend."

"Is that how you think of me?" He didn't so much as crack a smile. "As your boyfriend?"

Shit. "I shouldn't have said that. It was a lousy attempt to make a joke."

"Okay, so then I'm *not* your boyfriend. I'm just someone you had sex with twenty minutes ago . . . ?"

Joan sighed. "Mike. We're both exhausted —"

"I'm just looking for a little clarification," he said. "Don't misunderstand — I'm not accusing you of anything, honest. I'm just trying to figure out how to proceed from here. See, the pathetic thing is I had this plan to keep sex out of our relationship entirely, to show you there's more between us than this physical attraction thing. That worked real well, huh?"

"Yeah." She had to laugh at that, but her heart was in her throat. He had a *plan* . . .

"I don't know what to do now, because making love to you tonight was so incredible, I'm not sure I can go back to that friend place without going completely insane. I want you endlessly, Joan."

She looked up at him. God, that was such a romantic thing to say.

And he looked the part of the romantic hero, with the soft light from the hotel parking lot casting shadows on his beautiful face.

563

"I don't know *what* I'm doing," she admitted. "I can't seem to keep my hands off of you, and I love spending time with you, I really do . . ."

"Then spend time with me," he said. "Spend lots of time with me. Starting right now. Let's go back to your room."

"And have sex? Again?"

"No," he said, absolutely. "I want us to make love."

Okay, that was another really romantic thing to say. He was wearing her down, and he knew it.

He touched her lightly, pushing her hair back from her face with just one finger. "Invite me to your room."

Madness. It was total madness. The idea of any kind of relationship with this man scared her to death. There were so many reasons why she should get out of this truck and run like hell.

"There's not enough time to get any real sleep before we both need to be up and in the shower," he persisted. "Think of what we could do with this next hour."

Oh, she was thinking about that, all right.

Cheerful Muldoon was always hard to resist, but this decisive, determined Muldoon was impossible to turn down. He just sat there, watching her, waiting for her to speak.

Joan cleared her throat. "Please," she said. "Will you come up to my room?"

He kissed her. Oh, baby, the man could kiss.

"I'll come up on one condition," he said, as if she were the one talking *him* into going upstairs. "It's a little kinky — you might not want to do this."

Was he serious? God, he was.

"You have to promise to do whatever I want," he said. "We make love exactly the way I want to. You know, from my script."

His *script* . . . He'd told her that, in his experience, most women's sexual fantasies followed a script.

"You have a script?" she asked.

"Yeah," he said. She could tell from his slow smile that he knew she was completely intrigued. "It's kind of new. It's something I've kind of figured out over the past few days. And since you're the star in it, I thought . . . I might as well ask."

She was the star of his fantasy script. "Wow. Is it just you and me or are there any special guest stars?"

He laughed. "No barnyard animals, if that's what you mean."

"Do I, like, have lines?"

"A few," he said. "But they're pretty easy. You mostly say yes. You can improvise and embellish it if you want."

"This is a little weird," Joan admitted.

"If you get the least bit uncomfortable, we can stop. At any time, okay?" He was smiling at her as if he knew she wasn't going to say no.

Maybe she *was* a little bit kinky. She was the star of his fantasy script. "What's the first thing you're going to ask me to do?"

"Take off your clothes."

Muldoon watched as Joan followed his first order. T-shirt, sneakers, bra, and jeans. She actually folded her jeans before turning back to him, standing up straight, chin held high as she let him look at her.

"What next?" she asked. It was pretty warm in her hotel room, which meant . . . she was getting into this.

Good.

"Kiss me," he said.

She started toward him, but then stopped. "Where?" She was trying not to smile, but the edges of her lips kept twitching.

"You can start with my mouth," he told her.

She kissed him sweetly at first, then deeper, longer, as he pulled her into his arms and ran his hands over and across all that soft, bare skin.

"Help me get out of my clothes," he said.

In truth, she was more of a hindrance than a help — she couldn't quite get his belt to unbuckle. But it was fun to let her try.

And finally he was naked, too.

She was sitting on the floor, having just pulled off his sneakers and socks, and she smiled up at him, waiting for his next command.

Yeah, she was *definitely* getting into this.

"I think we better have a condom on hand," he told her. "Can you get one?"

"Just one?" she asked, on her way into the bathroom.

He laughed. "We've got only an hour."

"Forty-eight minutes now," she called back to him.

Yikes. He had to speed this up.

"Hurry," he said.

She did, which was incredible to watch.

"On the bed," he said.

She climbed onto the bed, and knelt there, looking at him questioningly. God, she was sexy.

"Time for you to say one of your lines," he said. "Okay?"

"Yes," she said. She held out her arms to him. *"Yes."*

"Okay," Muldoon admitted. "I lied a little bit about the lines. There's more to them than just yes. I want you to ask me, well . . ." He laughed. "To go down on you. You can say it however you want."

"But aren't I supposed to . . ."

"My script doesn't say, 'And then she argued,' " he countered.

She laughed as she shrugged. "Okay. I mean, if that's really what you want. I think I'm getting the better end of the deal, but it's *your* fantasy."

"Yes," he said. "It is."

She lay back on the bed, blushing slightly. "I don't know exactly what you want me to say . . . How about . . . Kiss me, baby, where the sun don't shine. I need you to kiss me. I'm *dying* for you to kiss me." She extended one foot toward him, let her other leg fall open. Oh, yeah. "Starting with my instep and then my ankle and so on and so on and just keep heading north until I tell you to stop."

"Perfect," he said, doing just that.

"Stop," she said. "I mean, *don't* stop . . ."

Oh, *yeah.*

She was soft, she was sweet, and he was setting her on fire.

"Please," she moaned. "Oh, *please!*"

It was close enough to what he'd wanted her to

say next, without any prompting at all. He covered himself with the condom, and buried himself deeply inside of her.

Joan made a sound that was identical to the way he was feeling. Somehow she opened her eyes and looked up at him, obviously struggling to keep this about him and what he wanted. "Do you want me to get on top?"

"No." He wanted to be in control. He wanted to be face-to-face with her, to look into her eyes. He moved slowly, setting a rhythm that made her eyelids close halfway.

"Mmmm," she said.

"You have another line," he said.

Her eyes opened a little wider. "Now?"

"Yeah. You say, 'Let's do it. Let's make this long-distance thing work.' "

She closed her eyes. "Oh, God, *Mike* . . ."

"Come on. It's my fantasy. My script. You promised you'd make it good for me."

"Okay," she said. "All right. I'll try. I'm willing to try to make this work."

"That's not the line. It's 'Let's do it,' " he repeated. " 'Let's make this long-distance thing work.' If you want something done, you *do* it," he reminded her. "You don't *try*."

"Let's do it," she gasped. "This is not fair. This is coercion . . . Let's make this long-distance thing work!"

He kissed her. "Thank you."

"That's it," she said. "There're no more lines except for the part where I scream *yes*, right?"

"Actually, there are a few more, but we can do it pretty quickly. You say, 'I understand that our age difference is inconsequential, that it doesn't matter to you, and it doesn't matter to me, either. Seven years is nothing in the grand scheme of things.' "

"Mike . . ."

"You promised."

Joan groaned and closed her eyes. "Seven years is nothing in the grand scheme of things and if you don't fuck me harder, I'm going to die."

"Close enough." He did as she asked. "Better?"

"Uhhhh," she said. "Oh, God!"

"My turn for a line." It was getting harder for him to think, let alone talk. "I say, 'If you're worried about what people will think when they see us together, don't be.' You say, 'Why not?' "

"Why . . . not . . . ?"

"Because people will think, 'Wow, he really loves her.' And they'll be right."

She opened her eyes and looked right up at him, shock on her face. "Did you just say . . . ?"

"I love you," he said. "Yeah, that's what I said."

He reached between them, knowing exactly where to touch her to push her over the edge.

"Oh, Michael," Joan gasped as she exploded.

He had to grit his teeth and think about differential equations to keep from joining her.

And when she finally lay beneath him, limp and exhausted, he was still hard inside of her.

Her eyelids fluttered open in surprise as he began moving again. "You didn't . . . ?"

He shook his head. "No. We have a little time left, and, well, I still have this one thing that I really want you to do. Something that'll completely get me off. Something that'll rock my world for a long, long time."

"Ask me," she said. "I'll do it. Just tell me what to do."

Muldoon nodded. "Promise?"

"Yes."

He took a deep breath and said it. "Marry me."

TWENTY-SIX

As Mary Lou drove to work, she saw Ihbraham walking along the road that led to the base.

What was he doing, walking?

She passed him, but then pulled over, out of the heavy stream of traffic, reaching to roll down the passenger's-side window as she waited for him to catch up.

"Where are you going?" she called.

He came and leaned in the window. "To see the President speak at the Navy base," he told her. "I knew there would be much traffic and trouble with parking, and it's a nice enough day to walk, so . . ."

"Hop in. I'll give you a lift."

"That's not necessary." He started backing away.

"But I wanted to talk to you. It's important. I had dinner with Bob Schwegel last night."

Ihbraham stopped moving, but he didn't lean back down so she could see his face. "And you are telling me this because . . . ?"

"You were right about him," she said to his blue T-shirt. "He's a creep. I think he's a con artist. He asked me to run away with him to New York — can you believe that? I was supposed to pack a bag and bring it to work today. He said he'd meet me here

571

and then we'd go pick up Haley and leave town. Of course, we'd make a quick stop and clear out all of Sam and my bank accounts before we hit the road. I called Medway Insurance — that's where he said he worked — and they never even heard of a Bob Schwegel. He was scamming me right from the start."

Ihbraham sighed, and then crouched down next to the car. "I'm sorry."

"Will you please get in?" she said.

"No," he said. "I don't think that's wise."

"Don't be a dope. I'm not going to jump you in the short amount of time it takes to drive to the base. I mean, while I'm driving? In busy traffic? I'm good, but I'm not that good."

He sighed again, then opened the door and climbed in.

Mary Lou put the car into gear and signaled her intent to move back into the line of cars. It was moving even more slowly now, looking to be stop-and-go all the way to the base. But that was okay. She was very early, and the more time she could spend with Ihbraham, the better.

"Did you call the police about this Bob?" he asked.

"No."

"You must."

"How'm I supposed to do that without everyone in the world finding out I had dinner with a scumball?" She sighed. "I don't know . . . maybe it doesn't matter who finds out. Sam asked me last night if I was screwing around with my next-door neighbor. You know, Crazy Donny? Can you believe that? He actually thought . . . But he wasn't

572

even angry or even the slightest bit jealous. Just kind of curious about it — which is pretty depressing, don't you think?" She glanced at Ihbraham. "So I went to see a lawyer this morning, about a divorce."

Well, now she had his attention.

"She said I'd get child support from Sam, and alimony, too. I had no idea it would be as much as this lawyer said — at least until I get married again. If I get married again." She sneaked another look at him.

He was silent as they rolled up another few car lengths. "Sam may not agree to give you this divorce."

"Yeah, he will," Mary Lou said. "I'm, like, 99.999 percent certain this is what he wants."

"You seem quite certain it's what you want, as well."

"I am," she told him. "I'm scared, sure, but, see, well . . . I'm not in love with Sam anymore. And I wasn't even remotely interested in Bob — I was just real mad. At you." She glanced at him again.

He was just silently watching her, a slight furrow in his brow as if he were struggling to understand what she was saying. She didn't really blame him for not getting it. She hadn't been particularly clear.

"I was mad because, well, you've been hiding from me, and . . . I've gotten kind of used to you being around." Come on, girl, just say it. "I'm kind of in love with you," she told him.

But he still didn't utter a sound, didn't move, didn't jump up and down or cheer.

So Mary Lou forced a laugh. "How'd that

happen, huh? I mean, we're so different from each other, and, well, *different*. In every way. But . . . if you maybe still have feelings for me, I thought . . . After Sam and I separate, which will probably be tonight or tomorrow . . . maybe you could come over sometime and I could cook you dinner. If you want."

She was actually blushing. She could feel her cheeks heat, remembering that conversation they'd had when she'd invited him in for iced tea. She wondered if he thought she was inviting him over for more than dinner — and if he would mind very much if she was.

But when she glanced at him again, he was shaking his head. "I was sure you would never leave him," he admitted. "I promised my brothers . . ."

"What?" she asked, but he just shook his head.

They were in a line of cars waiting to get into the base. The guards at the gate were doing full searches, both of the interior and the trunk. They were even checking under the hood.

Ihbraham opened his door. "I should get out here. They'll check your car more carefully and take twice as long if I'm riding with you."

"I don't care," she said, knowing that he was talking about more than just passing this checkpoint.

"My sons may have skin as dark as mine," he told her. "You said you don't want that. You said —"

"I wanted life to be easy," she said. "But there's no such thing. You're the best person I've ever met, Ihbraham. And if you want to be with me, then . . . But if you've changed your mind —"

"No, I didn't, but I also didn't expect you to

change yours," Ihbraham said. "I've agreed to help my brothers and . . . You must give me some time to figure out what to do. Will you do that, please?"

She nodded. "Help them how?"

"It has to do with a woman," he said, and her heart sank. "I'm supposed to take her to dinner tonight and then . . . But I'll get out of it — I'll get out of all of it." He climbed out of her car.

She leaned over so she could see him. "Will you call me tonight?"

"Yes — if I can."

"I love you," she said.

He smiled, and her morning got even brighter. "It is a day, I think, for miracles all around."

"How are you, Lieutenant?" Vince said as he greeted Mike Muldoon in front of the VIP dais that was set up catty-corner to the spectator stands. "Crazy night last night. Thanks for being there for Joanie."

He nodded. "It was my pleasure, sir."

Vince nodded, looking out onto the field where SEALs from Team Sixteen would fast-rope down from two helicopters and take out a large piece of artillery. He knew from his own experience that it wouldn't take much to prevent a gun like that from firing. Putting all of the various parts out of commission would take a little more effort. He suspected that was what they were going to be doing here today.

Either way, it was going to be so fast that most people would have no idea exactly what they had witnessed.

This entire shindig had a carnival-type atmosphere. Families with little kids and tourists of all shapes and sizes had come out in force on this gorgeous — but hot — day to see this show.

"Did you get any sleep at all last night?" he asked the kid.

Muldoon smiled and answered him honestly. "No, sir."

That was some smile. It must've been one hell of a night. "Ask her to marry you yet?"

The kid seemed surprised for only a second. But then nodded. "Yes, sir. She's, um, thinking about it."

Vince turned to face him. "Really?" Joanie, thinking about getting *married?* "I'm impressed."

Every now and then a chopper flew overhead, making it impossible to hear. Muldoon waited for this latest one to move off a bit before answering. "Yes, sir. I, uh, kind of put her in a position where she didn't want to, um, disappoint me by saying no right away. So she said maybe. I consider that to be something of a victory."

"I'd say so," Vince said. "How on earth did you . . . ?"

Muldoon was shaking his head. "Sorry, sir. I can't, uh . . ."

Oh ho, so it was like *that,* was it? Vince had to work to keep from laughing. Good for him. Good for Joanie, too. "Well, if you want some advice from an old man, persistence triumphs. Just keep coming back — whatever she throws at you. Don't quit. Just keep showing up."

"That's my plan," Muldoon said. "Do me a favor and don't tell her we talked about this, okay?"

"I wouldn't dream of it. No point making her go postal."

Muldoon laughed. Yeah, he knew Joanie pretty well. "Is there anything I can get for you today, sir? Do you have everything you need?"

Vince glanced over to where Charlie was talking to Joanie and several other ladies who were part of the White House staff. She had color in her cheeks — no doubt about it, she was enjoying this very much.

"I'm perfect," he said, giving the boy a smile. "Thanks."

Husaam Abdul-Fataah walked into the Navy base without being searched.

Sure, he walked through a metal detector, and he'd had to take off his shoes and get them checked, but other than that, he was just waved on through.

Despite claims that this country avoided racial profiling, there were far more places he could go with his fair skin and light-colored eyes and hair than could most people who had such an obviously Muslim name.

Of course, Husaam Abdul-Fataah was the name he took seven years ago, after his first meeting with al-Qaeda leaders, when it became obvious that embracing the Muslim faith would be a smart business move. He'd converted, enthusiastically. He'd worship zucchini squash if it would help him bring home the kind of money he was earning these days.

And as for his new name, it roughly translated into "sword and servant of the opener of the gates of sustenance."

And those gates were open, indeed. He was steadily and quite gainfully employed. And the work was laughably easy. It was amusing indeed that, after years of working as a hired gun, a shooter with an ability rivaled by few, his biggest "skill" now was his ability to blend in in America. His greatest asset was the genes he'd inherited from Glen and Irene Canton of Lenexa, Kansas.

As Husaam watched, an obviously Arabic-looking man was pulled from the line and swept with the metal detector wand, even though he hadn't set off the walk-through alarm. The man was patient and serene despite the obvious indignity of being singled out.

And look at that. It was Ihbraham Rahman. Wasn't that provident? Maybe there was something to this blessings from Allah thing after all.

Husaam hadn't been intending to stay here on the base for long. Once the bullets started flying, it was going to get very dangerous in this vicinity. In fact, he was expecting a call on his cell phone warning him when the President's motorcade crossed the causeway.

But Ihbraham's presence was too neat a gift from God to pass up. And Husaam knew where the martyrs were intending to stand. He could position himself well out of range of their weapons.

Husaam hung back and waited. And as Ihbraham finally was allowed into the area, he followed him.

Sam Starrett watched the crowd filtering in through the gates from his bird's-eye perspective in Seahawk One.

As the helicopter made another pass overhead, he could see the metal detectors and the security personnel hard at work, bomb-sniffing dogs nearby. Everyone's shoes had to come off and get sent through the X-ray machines. Bags and packages weren't allowed inside, but ladies' purses were. It was ridiculous — like women couldn't be as murderous as the next guy?

Obviously the policymakers didn't know the same women who Sam knew.

Mary Lou had gotten up and out early this morning, taking Haley with her, before he even woke up. And for the first time since they were married, she'd left the dishes in the sink.

Which, in Mary Lou's head, was probably a most heinous act of domestic terrorism — probably retaliation for him asking if she was getting it on with Donny the Nutjob.

She was a strange woman. Last night, when she'd told him to fuck himself, he'd gotten a glimpse of the girl he'd lusted after at the Ladybug Lounge all those months ago. It almost made him want her again.

Almost.

But he was smarter now — and determined to think things through before he took action. In other words, he was going to keep his pants zipped.

Yeah, *that* was one mistake he wasn't going to repeat. Sex for the sake of sex. It wasn't going to happen, not ever again.

He looked down at the metal detectors now, and watched as the guards ran a whole line of folded-up baby strollers through the X-ray machine.

Jesus, they were actually allowing baby strollers in. That was one big fucking mistake.

If he were a terrorist, he'd carry all his explosives in a baby stroller, right under junior's diaper-padded little butt.

Wheel his way to his destination with the greatest of ease, pick up junior, set the timer, and walk away.

And then, after the blast, he'd run away crying, "Someone help me get my darling baby to safety!"

But hey, that was just him.

Suicide bombers didn't bother with timers, either, so maybe the baby stroller thing wasn't a real threat.

"Starrett, Nilsson, do you read?"

"Got you loud and clear, Commander," Sam answered Paoletti, speaking into his lip mike.

"Ditto that, sir," Nils reported in from Seahawk Two. "What can we do to make your day a little easier?"

Commander Paoletti was freaking out about this op.

Okay, that was an overstatement, considering that Paoletti's version of freaking out meant that he ground his teeth slightly harder than usual.

All joking aside, the man *was* about as grim as Sam had ever seen him. It was almost as bad as that time they were pulling an ambassador's wife out of a country in which a coup had taken place. The new government had decided at the last minute that they really didn't want any of them to leave after all and started shooting. Their helo suffered a direct hit — a lucky shot. Those losers couldn't have done that kind of damage in a million years if they'd actually tried. The team managed to make a controlled crash landing, but the Seahawk — it — was a lot like this one, as a matter of fact — blew sky-high shortly after, and the force of the explosion had thrown Paoletti right on his head.

Kind of the way Sam's older sister Lainey used to throw his GI Joe dolls across the driveway during the great Barbie Wars of third and fourth grade.

Tom Paoletti had regained consciousness almost right away. But while the team was hustling to make it out of the country on foot, he recognized that the tunnel vision he was experiencing was a sign of a serious head injury. He knew it was just a matter of time before he went into a coma and became a very heavy addition to their already too heavy load.

He got pretty fucking grim that day.

A lot like he was today.

What disaster did he think was going to happen?

Something bad. Sam hoped to God he was wrong.

"Keep your eyes open while you're up there," Paoletti told them. "I want Jefferson, Jenkins, MacInnough, and Zanella in place. Starrett and Nilsson — you made the arrangements we discussed yesterday?"

"Yes, sir." He and Nils answered almost in unison.

They didn't use live ammunition during a demonstration like this one. But since Paoletti was afraid that there might be trouble, he'd ordered Sam and Nils to double check that there were magazines with real bullets on board both these helos. And sniper rifles, ready to be pulled out of the rack and tossed to Duke Jefferson and the other top-notch sharpshooters that Paoletti had ordered to be given special seating at the doors of the two Seahawks.

"I want eyes open at all times," the CO stressed again. "And no idle chatter on the radio. We still have about twenty minutes before the president arrives, and ten minutes after that before you do your fast-roping tricks. But as of right now, as far as we're concerned, this op has already started. The clock is running. I want all eyes on the crowd. Let's do what we do best."

Sam looked around the helo at his team of men. Jenk, WildCard, Cosmo, Gilligan, Duke, and Lopez.

If any of them thought the commander was worrying just a little too much, they didn't show it by so much as a blink. Truth was, they probably respected Paoletti's gut feelings and hunches as much as Sam did. They all returned his gaze steadily, giving him a short nod and a solid thumbs-up.

They were all good to go.

"Joan!"

Joan turned to see Kelly Ashton, Commander Paoletti's fiancée, waving to her from the crowd that was milling directly in front of the dais.

There was standing room only down there, although many people preferred it to the bleachers, since it was a chance to be up close and personal when the President gave his speech.

The crowd wasn't too thick yet, and Joan went down the front stairs and over to Kelly.

Anything to keep her from standing on the dais with Muldoon watching her.

Whenever she met his eyes, he smiled.

And she flashed hot and cold and hot again.

He loved her. He wanted to . . . She couldn't even think the M-word.

Except she was thinking about nothing *but* the M-word.

She glanced up at the dais where Mike was talking to Tom Paoletti, both of them looking incredible in their dress uniforms, weighed down by a ton of medals.

They'd be getting another one, a unit citation, from the President today.

"How are you? It's nice to see you again," Kelly greeted her. She was with an elderly man. "This is Tom's uncle, Joe Paoletti — he just got in from Boston. He actually caught an earlier flight, which is why we're here. We wouldn't have made it otherwise. Joe, this is Joan DaCosta. She works in the West Wing of the White House — isn't that cool?"

"Very. Pleased to meet you, Joan." Joe Paoletti shook her hand and smiled — the family resemblance was pretty amazing, despite the fact that Joe was in his eighties and somehow managed to have more hair than Tom.

"Joe!" Meg Nilsson came over and gave the old man a hug. She had a big-eyed baby with dark curly hair in a pack on her back. "How *are* you? How long will you be in town?"

Kelly pulled Joan aside. "I heard your brother was in the hospital. Is everything all right?"

"Yeah, it was something he ate — some kind of

food poisoning. We don't really know exactly what it was. He's not quite all there mentally."

"I'm sorry to hear that." With her freckles and her blond hair up in a ponytail, dressed down the way she was in shorts and a T-shirt and a baseball cap, Dr. Kelly Ashton looked about twenty-four years old today.

"May I ask you a personal question?" Joan said.

Kelly nodded. "Sure."

"Rumor has it —"

Kelly rolled her eyes. "Oh, jeez."

"Wait, hear me out," Joan said. "The urban legend I've heard says that when you and Tom first got together a few years ago, you moved to San Diego all the way from New England."

"Okay," Kelly said. "That much is true."

"But you're a doctor," Joan said. "Didn't you have a practice there?"

"In Boston," she said. "Yes, I did."

"And you just . . . walked away from it, from your whole life and career?"

"I'm still practicing medicine," Kelly said. "Doctors never lack patients. Trust me on that one."

"Did you and Tom even talk for one minute about him moving to Boston?"

"No," Kelly said. "That was never a serious option."

"That doesn't seem very fair."

Kelly smiled. "It's fair."

Joan laughed in disbelief. "How can you say that?"

"Because it *is* fair. Look, Tom is *the* most incredible man in the world. He does things that only a few people on this planet are capable of doing — and he does them for our country. He could make astronomical amounts of money in the private sector, but he chooses to serve. I figure I can do my share, too, by taking on the role of Navy spouse — although, okay, I haven't managed to marry him yet but I'm working on that. Marriage license or not, when you're the wife of a Navy SEAL, Joan, you do things like move when he gets reassigned. God, I'd fly halfway around the world for a chance to see him for fifteen minutes."

Whoa. "You really love him, don't you?"

"Yes, I do."

Joan sighed. "What if you loved him that much, but you had a career that you absolutely couldn't — didn't want to — give up. What if you were doing research at Harvard and you were only years away from, I don't know, say . . . curing childhood cancer?"

Kelly didn't laugh at her, even though it was clear she was trying not to smile. "Or what if you worked in the White House and really loved your job there?" she countered.

Joan rolled her eyes. "I'm that transparent, huh?"

"Mike Muldoon is the sweetest guy I've ever met on any of the teams."

Shit. "Obviously our attempts to be discreet have failed miserably. Does everyone know?"

"No. Tom told me about having lunch with you and Mike, and I put two and two together. Don't worry — I haven't told anyone else. Not even Meg. You didn't get a chance to meet Savannah, did you? Kenny's wife?"

"Kenny?"

"WildCard Karmody," Kelly explained. "No, I guess you didn't — she was out of town that evening you came over. Long story short, she and Ken have been married for close to six months now, and she still lives in New York — which doesn't mean she doesn't love him, because I know she does. She just has other things happening in her life, things that she couldn't just drop the way I could. They're making it work. It's not easy, but they meet in Dallas or Chicago as often as they can. It *is* possible."

"What are you doing here?"

They both turned to see Tom Paoletti standing behind them. He was looking at Kelly, and he didn't look happy.

Muldoon made sure his lip microphone was off before he dialed Joan's cell phone number.

As he watched, she excused herself from the CO and Kelly Ashton, and dug her cell out of her pocket, flipping it open.

"Hello?"

"Hey," he said. "It's the rescue squad. Need a good excuse not to be in the middle of a domestic squabble?"

"It's not exactly a squabble," she said. "He's just really worried about this event, and he's trying to get her to go home without flat-out ordering her to leave. Did you know Meg Nilsson's here, too?"

"Oh, crap." They'd made a point of suggesting — strongly — that wives and families stay home from this event. Paoletti went as far as setting up an alternate demo date for wives and families. "Is she alone?"

"No, she's got her baby with her." Joan paused. "Cute kid."

"I like kids," Muldoon said. "On the off chance that you were wondering . . ."

She laughed. *"Mike."*

"I love you," he said. "In case you were having trouble remembering that. Sleep deprivation can screw up your memory, you know, so I should also probably remind you that you promised to meet me in your hotel room right after this is over."

"No, I did not."

"See? Maybe I should be more explicit, so as to jog your brain cells," he said. "I was planning to come over, and we were going to order room service, and we were going to get very, *very* naked and take turns licking . . . Uh . . ."

Lt. Jazz Jacquette was standing right beside him, listening to every word he was saying, one eyebrow heading toward the sky.

"Gotta go," Muldoon said to Joan. He closed his cell phone with a snap.

"Were you actually making a booty call, Lieutenant?" Jacquette asked in his basso profundo.

"I know, sir," Muldoon said. "Wrong time and place. It won't happen again."

Jacquette looked at him. "Damn," he said. "I just lost my bet. I had twenty dollars riding on the fact that you were not entirely human. Stay focused, Lieutenant," he added as he walked away. "Who would've ever thought I'd have to say that to you?"

The President was coming.

The call had just come in on Husaam's cell

phone, letting him know that Bryant's entourage was almost here.

Ihbraham was standing pretty close to the stage. If Husaam had really been a religious man, he might've turned around and left — leaving Ihbraham's fate in God's hands.

But he hadn't made it this far in his career by letting someone else — even God — orchestrate the fate of a man who had to die.

He approached a group of bikers — three men dressed in leather jackets that declared them to be members of Hell's Angels. Good. They wouldn't be afraid to get into a fight.

"There's a man over there," he said to them in a low voice, pointing to Ihbraham. "An Arab man. He's acting really strange. I'm going to go find one of the Secret Service guys — I know they're around here somewhere. But will you keep an eye on him? You know, get close to him, make sure he doesn't go anywhere. And if he does anything, just, you know, beat the shit out of him."

"That guy in the blue T-shirt?" one of them asked.

"Yeah," Husaam said. "With the sandals. Don't let him out of your sight. I'll be as fast as I can, but I may have to go all the way back to the gate."

"You got it, chief."

They moved closer to Ihbraham, as Husaam, true to at least part of his word, moved back toward the gates, well out of range of all the weapons he'd helped smuggle onto the base.

"When the President climbs up the stairs," the woman named Myra — Joan's boss — told

Charlie and Vince for the umpteenth time, "he's going to stop and greet you and your husband. You'll already be on your feet — everyone will stand when his car pulls up. But if you need to sit down, don't be ashamed or afraid to do it. It's quite warm out today. No heroics, do you understand?"

"Absolutely," Charlie told her. "I'm not a hero — I'm only the wife of heroes. Did you know that my husband, Chief Vincent DaCosta, was a frogman during the Second World War?"

One of the officers with the fancy uniform — Admiral Crowley — turned to face them. "You were a frogman, sir? With the UDT — the Underwater Demolition Teams?" he asked Vince. He had a craggy face filled with character and lines, but for the briefest of instances, he looked like a wide-eyed little boy.

"I was," Vince replied.

"Where did you serve, Chief?"

"I was in the Pacific from March '44 to the end of the war, sir."

"He also served as a Marine at Tarawa, back in November 1943," Charlie added. "He never bothers to mention that. Or the fact that he was on the team assigned to scout and clear landing zones on mainland Japan. I thank God every day that the Japanese surrendered before that ever got off the ground."

Crowley was looking around at his staff members. "Why didn't we know any of this? Sir, it's an honor and a privilege to meet you." He snapped to attention and saluted.

Vince laughed as he returned Crowley's salute.

"That's really not necessary, Admiral. It's been a long time since I've been anything but Vince or Gramps. In fact, I'd prefer it if you called me that. Vince, I mean."

Crowley smiled as he shook Vince's hand. "Call me Chip. I'd love to sit down and talk to you sometime. Can I have my secretary call you and set up a time we can meet for lunch?"

"If you want war stories, Chip, it's best to meet in the afternoon or the evening, after dinner. It's not the kind of conversation that mixes well with food. For me, at least."

Crowley nodded. "Then we'll have to get together twice — once to share a meal and talk about our grandchildren."

"I'd like that," Vince said.

"Excuse me. The President's going to arrive soon. Since this is my party, I better get ready. I'll look forward to our lunch." Crowley went off to talk to several of the other officers.

Vince looked at Charlie and laughed. "He thinks I'm some kind of hero."

She shook her head in disbelief. "The thing that I don't understand, Vincent, is why you don't."

"We were just scared kids, doing what had to be done," he told her. "That's the way I think of it. The real heroes are the boys who didn't come home."

"My God," Charlie said. "Is that actually what you believe?"

But he didn't answer because now the other admiral was coming over to meet him and shake his hand.

Mary Lou cleaned the second french fry machine while Aaron the asshole flirted with Brandi, the new girl he was allegedly training to work the cash register.

Kevin was leaning back against the counter, taking a load off. "Lunch rush is going to be nonexistent today. Everyone's over watching the SEALs do their supermen thing."

"Either that or everyone's going to decide they're hungry and need a burger and descend on us all at once." Aaron laughed. "*We'll* be the ones needing Secret Service protection."

God, he was a fool. The congealed grease she was cleaning was ten times funnier than he was.

"The area they're in is fenced off from the rest of the base," Kevin said. "They can't get here from there."

"Some fence," Aaron said. "You could go through that thing with a pair of wire cutters in a matter of seconds."

"Yeah, well, look where it is," Kevin pointed out. "Inside a Navy base. Like there's a lot of dangerous terrorists here on base, looking to crash through the fence and assassinate the President."

"Good point," Aaron said. "Although some of the sailors I've seen around here are pretty terrifying."

Yuck, yuck, yuck. Like he was such a prize himself. What an asshole.

"Did you say that President Bryant was going to be here?" Brandi asked.

Get out much, new girl? Bryant's impending visit had been a big story on the evening news for the past two weeks. Lord, did only foolish and stupid people work here? Mary Lou had to find a new job.

Maybe she could help Ihbraham do yard work. She could bring along the travel playpen for Haley and work outside all day. She'd probably lose weight. But the cool thing was, if she didn't, Ihbraham wouldn't care.

"Yeah, didn't you see that security by the gate?" Kevin asked Brandi. "You think they would do that for just anyone?"

Mary Lou could become one of those women who went barefoot and wore flowing cotton dresses without a bra. She would help Ihbraham grow flowers in the most beautiful gardens in town. And every day, in the afternoon, when Haley was napping beneath the shade of a tree, they would take a break and make love right there on those wealthy people's patios.

She wondered what Ihbraham looked like naked. Was his skin that same rich color all over? *All* over?

"You know, this would be the perfect time and place to assassinate Bryant," Aaron said, interrupting her thoughts. Salacious thoughts, she realized. Who ever would have guessed? "Imagine the uproar it would cause."

"Yeah, but how would you do it?" Kevin asked.

"It would have to be a bomb," Aaron said — as if he had even the slightest clue what he was talking about. Brandi was looking at him all wide-eyed, like she was actually impressed and thinking about fucking him. Yeah, that would be a smart move. Sleep with the manager of a fast-food restaurant, and who knows what it'll do for your career. Maybe someday you'll get to work the drive-through window.

"There's no way you could smuggle a gun past that security," Aaron continued. "You couldn't even get a water pistol onto this base today. They checked my car so thoroughly, I was tempted to ask them to vacuum it out while they were at it."

Har har har.

"I guess it would be easier to smuggle a bomb in, but you'd have to do it in pieces," Kevin speculated. "Assemble it once you were inside — and that'd be hard to do. The place is crawling with those dudes from the Secret Service."

"Yeah," Aaron said. "That's the way to go — smuggle it in way in advance and hide the various pieces around the parade grounds until you're ready to use 'em."

Mary Lou dropped the fry basket with a clatter.

"I've got a man in the crowd with some kind of radio in his ear," Jenk said suddenly from his perch at the open door of Seahawk One. "I've been watching him for a while because he's got a baby stroller but no baby. Seemed kind of weird, like, where's his wife and kid? But he's definitely alone."

Sam ordered the helo pilot to take them back around as he moved to Jenk's position. "Where?"

He could see the president's limo pulling up to the dais, the Secret Service surrounding him in a V-pattern as he climbed out of the car and headed toward the back stairs.

"He's in the crowd that's standing — he's about ten people back, left side of the dais, farthest from where Bryant is right now. White shirt, dark complexion, beard. Stroller, no kid. I guess it's possible that his wife and kid are sitting in the stands."

Sam had him. "Jesus, you have good eyes. I see the stroller, but I can't even tell if this guy has ears, let alone a radio. Someone give me a pair of glasses."

"He was fussing with it a second ago, sir," Jenk reported as WildCard tossed Sam a pair of binoculars. " 'Course, it could be a hearing aid."

Through the glasses, the man in question leapt into sharp focus. Sure enough, he was wearing a wire that led from his right ear down into his collar.

"We've got him now, too," Nils reported from the other helo. "That's definitely not a hearing aid. But maybe he's listening to the game."

"What game?" Jenk — also known as Mr. ESPN — asked. "There's nothing scheduled until this afternoon."

"If he were listening to a Walkman, why conceal the wire inside his shirt?" Sam watched the guy closely, wishing that all terrorists had the words *Friend of Osama* tattooed on their foreheads. "It's possible he's one of us. Commander —"

"I'm on it," Paoletti's voice came through loud and clear. "There *are* plainclothes personnel in the crowd. If he's one of us, he's going to take off his hat — if he's wearing one — and scratch the top of his head. The Secret Service is sending that message now to everyone out there."

Sam kept the binoculars trained on the man. Who didn't so much as scratch his ass. "No movement from our man."

"I've got someone about twenty yards away

from him scratching away," Jenk reported.

"We need to get this guy checked out."

"President's on the dais," Muldoon's voice reported. "Should we get him back to his car?"

Something was going on.

Joan moved closer to Muldoon, to try to hear what he was saying.

Although it was hard to hear anything, because both helicopters were circling steadily now.

The crowd was applauding President Bryant's appearance, and the United States Navy Band had started to play "Hail to the Chief." The Secret Service agents who had led Bryant to the stage were still forming a half circle around him, one of them gesturing for him to hold up. So he chatted with her grandparents, leaning close to hear them over the din and shouting back into their ears.

That was nice for Gramps and Gramma, but something was definitely going on. She inched even closer to Muldoon.

The Secret Service agent who was in charge of the President's safety joined Paoletti, Muldoon, and the SEAL team's enormous XO, Lieutenant Jacquette.

"Get the weapons out of the racks," she heard Paoletti order. "Duke, I want this guy in your sights."

Weapons . . .

"You need to let us take care of this." The man in the dark suit didn't sound happy.

"Your snipers haven't located him yet," Paoletti said.

"We can't pick him out from the sniper towers

595

— the angle's wrong — but we're coming at him through the crowd. We'll find him."

"And until then," Paoletti said, "*we'll* be ready to take him down from the helos."

"He's probably no threat at all. Security here is tight, Commander. The only danger I see comes from putting live ammo into the hands of saltwater cowboys. I'd like to remind you that you have absolutely no authority here."

"You can give me that authority, Pete," Paoletti said.

"Dream on, Commander. This is *my* show. If there is trouble, we *will* take care of it."

Muldoon saw her standing there. "Get back," he said in a low voice. "Get back to the edge of the stage, Joan, as far from Bryant as possible. If there's trouble, you drop, do you hear me? Right to the ground. And you stay there."

She stared at him. My God, he seriously thought . . .

If there was going to be trouble, it was going to be focused on this stage — on the President.

Who was still talking to Vince and Charlie.

"Careful," Aaron chastised Mary Lou. "Those things cost money."

"Sorry." Her heart was pounding. The guards had checked her car when she'd pulled onto the base this morning. And she'd sat there thinking, Thank God Sam didn't leave an automatic weapon in the trunk today.

But what if that gun had never been Sam's? What if someone else had put it in her trunk? Someone who knew the lock was broken. Some-

596

one who knew that she worked here on base and regularly drove past the guards at the gate without ever being stopped and searched. Someone who wanted a weapon carried onto the base — to be used later.

Like on a day when the U.S. President was scheduled to appear.

What if Mary Lou hadn't brought just that one gun onto the base? What if she'd been used to carry a full arsenal of weapons?

How many times had she come out of work to find that her trunk had popped open? At least twice. She'd thought it was funny that it had done that all by itself, thought maybe it was the heat of the day that had made the metal expand or contract or whatever metal did when it got too hot.

She looked at her watch. Lord Jesus, the President was due to come to the base any second — if he hadn't already arrived.

"I have to make a phone call," Mary Lou told Aaron. She didn't wait for him to give her permission, she just pushed her way out of the kitchen into the little hall by the bathrooms.

Someone was using the pay phone there, so she went outside to the phone in the parking lot.

Boy, it sure must've put a crimp in someone's plans when she'd gotten her trunk lid replaced with a lock that worked. They couldn't use her as a mule anymore — not without a . . .

Key.

Ihbraham had made a copy of the new key for her. In fact, he'd been willing — even eager — to do it.

Dear Lord.

She could see him in her mind's eye, arguing with his brothers. All those Arabic faces and voices, dark with anger.

He'd said his brothers had wanted him to join them. He'd said he'd promised them . . . something.

Dear, dear Lord.

Was it possible . . . ?

Her hand shaking, Mary Lou picked up the receiver and dialed 911.

Muldoon scanned the crowd, looking for the man Jenk had spotted from the helicopter.

"I've got him." Duke Jefferson — the sniper in Sam Starrett's helo — sounded calm and almost detached. "Ready on your command, sir."

"Steady, Duke," Paoletti said. "We're just watching him here. Just an insurance policy. Sam, I want to know if he so much as moves an inch."

"Aye, sir. He's watching the dais, looking over toward Bryant, like he's waiting for the show to start."

There were a lot of men wearing white T-shirts today, and from Muldoon's viewpoint — because of the denseness of the crowd — he couldn't see who had a stroller and who didn't.

If this *were* an attack by a suicide bomber, chances were the man was acting alone.

But after 9/11, the entire world had learned to expect the unexpected.

"Okay," Sam said. "He's putting on a hat. Baseball cap — white — backward. Jesus, is that some kind of signal?"

And there he was.

Muldoon saw him. White cap on backward.

But there was someone else right down in front, over closer to the President, who was also just putting on a white baseball cap, backward.

"Our head scratcher is almost on top of our guy," Jenk reported from the helo. "And I see about four other suits closing in from all directions — and he does, too!"

"Gun!" Sam shouted.

"Duke, fire!" Paoletti shouted.

"Gun!" Muldoon echoed in unison with Jazz Jacquette, and chaos erupted.

Joan's first thought was *Where?*

"Get down!" someone was shouting. It was Muldoon, and he was shouting at *her,* a look of disbelief on his face that she should be over there, so close to where the President was being hustled away by the Secret Service.

What had he thought? That she would just ditch her grandparents when he'd told her that there might be trouble?

"Come on," she shouted to both Vince and Charlie, pulling them toward the stairs, following the President. This was just a false alarm — it had to be a false alarm. That really wasn't a gun that had been spotted — how could anyone get a gun in here?

But then shots exploded, a ragged burst of — God! — machine-gun fire.

Where was it coming from?

"Gun!" Sam shouted, and time clicked into slow motion. Through the binoculars, he could see their man pull a room broom — a 9mm submachine gun — from the baby stroller. He came up firing even as Tom Paoletti shouted, "Duke, fire!"

Duke Jefferson squeezed the trigger before the K of his name was out of Paoletti's mouth.

"Shooter down," he announced in his sniper's calm, and time clicked back to regular fast speed. It was over.

"Agent down!" Sam shouted.

But, Jesus, there were more shots being fired, the ripping sound audible even over the throb of the helos. Someone else down there was still shooting — and shooting into this crowd.

"Second shooter in the stands!" Cosmo shouted from Seahawk Two. "He's firing at us!"

And *that* would be one fucking disaster, if these fuckers brought one of these Seahawks down into this crowd.

"Take 'em out!" Paoletti's voice crackled over the radio.

"Third shooter out in front! White hat!" That was Muldoon's voice. Jesus, he was unarmed. Sam scrambled to see him.

"Second shooter down," Cosmo announced.

"Duke!" Sam shouted. "Do you see Muldoon's guy?"

The chaos was incredible. From where he was, Husaam could barely see Ihbraham. But he caught a flash of blue as his three biker friends brought him down to the ground. And then, as the crowd scattered, he could see one of them — the larger one — kick Ihbraham savagely in the head, hard enough to break his skull.

Husaam headed with the crush toward the gate.

★ ★ ★

Mary Lou heard the first of the gunshots as the emergency operator finally came on the line.

"Coronado security. This call is being recorded. What is the nature of your emergency?"

"They're trying to kill the President!"

"May I have your name and location, ma'am?"

"Terrorists are trying to kill the President over on the parade grounds!" she sobbed. There was more shooting, a tearing sound that echoed, contrasting hideously with the peaceful tranquility of this beautiful sunny day. Oh, Ihbraham, how could you have done this? "There are four of them. I think there are four of them — brothers — and their name is Rahman."

"What is your name, ma'am?"

"Who the hell cares what my name is! You need to send help! Now!"

Mary Lou hung up the phone and ran toward the parade grounds, praying that she was wrong.

Vince saw the gun.

It was a handgun, not one of those submachine guns he'd heard firing just seconds ago.

Still, a gun was a gun whether it fired dozens of rounds per second or only a few. It could still kill you and the people you loved just as dead.

The son of a bitch had it out and was pointing it where the President was being hustled off the stage and down the stairs. Where Joanie was trying to pull him and Charlie.

Vince did the only thing he could do. He tackled them both, pulling them down to the metal floor of the stage.

601

But before he got them down, he heard shots, felt one slap the back of his leg.

"Crawl!" he shouted to Joan, praying he was the only one who was hit. "Grab Gramma's arm and elbow crawl!"

Muldoon saw the shooter open fire, saw Vince get hit protecting Charlie and Joan.

The crowd was scattering in a panic, making it close to impossible for any of the Secret Service agents to reach the third man. And the shooter was running, moving with the crowd, trying to get even closer to the dais.

"I still don't see him," Jenk, the team's sharpest pair of eyes, reported from the helo overhead. If the man had stood still, they'd have no problem picking him out.

Muldoon was going to have to do the only thing he could do given these circumstances.

He was going to have to take this motherfucker out with his bare hands.

Joan saw Mike running, but unlike everyone who was sane, he was running *toward* the man with the gun.

He ran toward the edge of the stage, and when he got there he jumped and dove — kind of like Superman taking to the skies. Only Mike didn't go up, he went across and down.

The gunman turned and saw him and swung his gun around to fire.

Another shot rang out just as Mike hit him.

And Joan knew. If Mike Muldoon died here today, he'd die a hero.

And her life would never again be as bright, as sunny, as funny and wonderful as it had been these past few days.

If he lived, she was going to do it. She was going to marry the man. Life was too short to fool around. And if he died, she was going to rip the heart out of the bastard who killed him with her bare hands.

Muldoon connected hard with the last terrorist.

"Duke!" Sam ordered, and the sniper got ready in case the unthinkable happened and Muldoon got taken out before taking out the shooter.

Shit, there was blood on Mike's uniform, garishly red against the bright white.

But the kid was still kicking.

He had the shooter in a body lock and twisted hard. Sam could almost hear the crack from all the way up here.

"Shooter three down," Muldoon said, as he scrambled to claim the man's gun.

TWENTY-SEVEN

"Man down," Tom Paoletti said over the radio, and it wasn't until Muldoon stood up and saw the blood that he realized the man his CO was talking about was him. "Lopez, get your ass down here."

The bastard had shot him in the arm.

But that was the least of his worries.

"I'm okay," he said, looking around for Joan. The entire side of the dais where she'd been standing was empty. There was no one there at all. "It's just a scratch."

All of the SEALs in the helos were coming down the ropes — which was quite a show from this perspective — and they quickly secured the area.

As the Seahawks moved off, Muldoon could hear more ambulances approaching, people crying, the continuous chatter from the radio over his headset, and some kind of electronic ringing —

His cell phone.

He dug it out of his pocket and flipped it open. "Joan?"

"Michael, are you all right? I saw you jump on that man with the gun and —"

"I'm fine," he said. Shit, she'd seen that. She probably watched him break the bastard's neck, too. Way to convince the woman to marry him. "Are you okay? When I saw you over by the President —"

"I'm fine."

"Really? You're not wounded at all? Not even a little?"

"Oh, God," she said, smart enough to figure out that his concern came from his telling her that he was fine, when in fact he wasn't. "He shot you, didn't he? How bad is it?"

"It's just a scratch."

"What is it with stupidass macho he-men?" she ranted. "Gramps got shot in the leg, and he says he's fine, it's just a scratch. Let me give you a tip, okay, tough guy? When a bullet hits you — even if it just grazes you — it is not a *scratch*."

"Where are you?" Muldoon asked. He saw Tom's uncle with his arms around Meg Nilsson, helping shield her baby's eyes from the sight of the dead terrorists, who still lay where they'd fallen.

He caught sight of Kelly, too, hard at work over in a makeshift triage area that Lopez was helping her set up.

Tom Paoletti saw Kelly as well, and Muldoon could see some of the tension in the man's shoulders ease as he headed toward her.

There were far fewer casualties than Muldoon would have thought after hearing that first rip of machine-gun fire. Most of the wounded were able to walk.

"We're under the stage," Joan told him. "Gramma and I got everyone down here while you were doing your superhero imitation. Gramps isn't the only one wounded. There are two other men with *scratches*."

"Do you need help coming out?" he asked. He saw John Nilsson catch up with Meg, and with a nod from Tom Paoletti, Nils quickly led his wife and baby out of the area.

As Muldoon watched, Tom gave his elderly uncle a quick hug.

"No, we can do it," Joan said. "Gramps insists he can walk. I just wanted to make sure it was safe before we came out. Really, I wanted to make sure *you* were safe. That was, um, pretty goddamn scary, Mike. And you do this for a living, huh?"

"It's not usually like this," he told her. "This was what we call a goatfuck, if you'll excuse the expression. However, it could have been a lot worse. You can thank Commander Paoletti for the fact that the casualty count is so low. Two men with machine guns, a third with a handgun. It's a miracle we're not bringing in body bags by the dozens."

"God," she said. "What a thought."

He could see her now, leading a ramshackle band of VIPs and dignitaries out from behind the dais.

She faltered only slightly when she saw the blood on his jacket, hanging up her phone and pocketing it — as if she didn't trust herself to speak to him right at that moment. But by the time she reached him, she'd managed to smile.

"I think you need to go where we're going," she said. Her eyes were suspiciously bright. "To the hospital. I think your *scratch* needs stitches, babe."

He reached for her. "Joan —"

"Don't," she said, stepping away from him. "I'm just managing to keep it together."

"Sorry," he said. "I forgot we were still in hide-our-relationship mode."

"Whoa," she said. "Wait. We are?"

"Aren't we?" Muldoon asked.

"It's going to be kind of hard to have a wedding without telling anyone," she said. "I mean what kind of invitations would we send? I guess it could be like a surprise party in reverse."

Muldoon's chest felt tight and his throat filled, but instead of jumping or dancing or crying from happiness, he merely nodded, using one finger to push the hair back from her face. "I don't think you're allowed to say something like that to me without, you know, kissing me afterward."

"If I kiss you, I'm going to start to cry." She started anyway, her face scrunching up as if she were a little kid. "Who would shoot into a crowd like that? Who would do such a terrible thing?"

He pulled her into his arms and held her close, wishing he had answers for her. "I don't know," he said. "I don't get it, either. It's okay to cry, though, Joan. It is."

"Can we please just go and get you to the hospital? Because I'm so tired and I need you to get checked by a doctor, and I have to make sure Gramps is all right, and then, God, I really, *really* want to go home."

"Home?" he asked. "You mean to the hotel?"

"I don't care," Joan said. "The hotel will do. As long as I can have a bed to sleep in, and you. That's all I need to be home."

Muldoon kissed her.

As far as he was concerned, he didn't even need the bed.

Mary Lou made it past the guards by showing her ID and proving that she was, indeed, the wife of one of the SEALs in Team Sixteen. She'd had to run back to her car to get her purse, but once she got it, they let her in.

She could see where there was some kind of medical area set up to help the wounded, and she ran toward it as the first of the ambulances was pulling away.

There were seven bodies on the pavement — oh, God! — already neatly in a row, covered with tarps. They were being guarded by a stern-faced sailor, so she made a wide berth around them.

Please God, please God, please God, let her be wrong!

Kelly Ashton was there, her hands in surgical gloves and blood smeared down the front of her shirt.

"Kelly!"

"Sam's okay," Kelly told her as she took off her gloves and put on another pair. "All the guys are all right. Mike Muldoon needs a few stitches, but other than that . . ."

"Is the President . . . ?" She couldn't say it. If he was dead, she was an accomplice to a Presidential assassination. Even though it wasn't really her fault, she would be blamed. They were always looking for someone to blame when Presidents died.

"He's safe," Kelly said.

Mary Lou followed her over to a man who was holding his arm.

"I fell off the stands," he told Kelly. "I think it's broken."

"I think you're right," she said. "Sorry you had to wait so long."

"Hey, I'm not bleeding," he said. "I didn't mind the wait. How'd they get the guns in?"

"Your guess is as good as mine," Kelly said. "Although I'm sure there'll be an in-depth investigation. They'll figure it out and you can be darn sure it won't happen ever again."

Mary Lou had to sit down. An in-depth investigation . . .

"It looks to me like you've got a clean break," Kelly told the man. "Although you'll need X rays, of course. Is there a particular hospital you'd prefer to go to?"

He shook his head. "I'm from out of town."

Kelly showed him where to go to get a ride to the nearest medical facility. And once again the gloves came off with a snap. She noticed Mary Lou sitting there.

"Mary Lou, is there something else I can help you with?"

"Ihbraham Rahman," Mary Lou said, and Kelly sighed.

"Yeah, that's right, you knew him, too."

Knew. Past tense. Oh, God.

"He's hurt pretty badly," Kelly said. "I don't know if he's going to make it."

Mary Lou looked up at her. "He's still alive?"

"He was as of fifteen minutes ago. But he's got a serious head injury, and . . . these things can be tricky. I have to be honest, it doesn't look good."

"Is he . . . Was he involved?" Mary Lou couldn't help it. She started to cry. Kelly — a doctor — thought that Ihbraham was going to die. But,

Lord, maybe that was a good thing. If Ihbraham was a terrorist, he deserved to die. If he was a terrorist, then everything he'd said to her, everything he'd done, was a lie. She hoped that he died. She *prayed* that he died. And that way no one would ever know that he'd smuggled the weapons onto the base with her help. Her unwitting help — but no one would believe that.

"I don't know. The men with the guns were apparently all of Arabic descent," Kelly told her. "Does that automatically mean that Ihbraham was involved? *I* don't think so. I knew him pretty well, and I just don't believe . . . But everything happened so fast — no one who I've talked to really saw anything. I was near one of the gunmen myself, and I have to be honest — when I heard the shots, I didn't know who was shooting, I didn't know where it was coming from. All I know for sure is that after the shooting stopped, Ihbraham was one of the people on the ground, seriously injured. As of right now they've found only three weapons, so it doesn't look like he was armed. If you want my opinion, most of the people who were injured to that degree were the people who actually tried to disarm the three gunmen."

Mary Lou went even more numb. His brothers. He must have been trying to stop his three brothers. Maybe he wasn't a terrorist.

But what did it matter? He was going to die.

She stood up. She had to get out of here. She had to get Haley, to breathe in her sweet scent, to remind herself why it was important that she stay sober on a day when there were so many reasons to drown her pain in a drink.

Bob Schwegel, Insurance Scoundrel, had tried to steal her virtue and the money in her bank accounts.

Ihbraham had tried to steal her heart and soul.

The irony was that when she'd first met him, there'd been nothing for him to take. He'd nurtured her, grown her — like one of his flowers. He'd made her fall in love with him.

Now here she sat, even emptier than when she'd started.

"I'm sorry," she told Kelly. "I have to . . ."

Mary Lou ran for the gate, ran back to the restaurant. It took all of four seconds to give Aaron her resignation.

She went home before picking up Haley and quickly packed as much as she could fit into the set of matching luggage Sam had bought her from Sears on Mother's Day.

Gee, maybe his buying that for her had been a hint.

She loaded the car, packed a bag of food and snacks, wrote Sam a quick note.

Twenty minutes later, she and Haley were on the highway, heading east.

Charlie sat with Vince in the hospital, waiting for the doctor to give him a clean bill of health so they could go home.

Joan and her young officer had come to this hospital, too. Mike was getting his arm stitched, and Joan bounced back and forth between their two rooms.

"Well," Charlie said, "I think today answers the question of whether or not we're going to Hawaii

611

next year. I'd rather skip the VIP treatment next time, thank you very much."

Joan stuck her head in the door. "Gramma, there's a reporter outside who'd like to talk to you."

"Not interested," Charlie said. "Someone just shot my husband. How does it feel? It stinks, thank you very much. He could have died, so of course I'm very relieved, yet, funny, I'm also angry as hell that that bastard was shooting in the first place. No further comments."

"I'll tell him no, thank you." Joanie disappeared.

Vince was shaking his head. "I'm fine. This isn't that big a deal, and you know it. You've seen real bullet wounds, Charles."

She had. Still, she had the right to be good and mad.

"You saved Joanie's and my life," she said. "And you put yourself in the way of a bullet that could well have ricocheted off the metal of the stage and hit the President of the United States. And still it's me they want to talk to. When are they going to ask to interview you? You're the hero. You've always been my hero, Vince."

He actually looked embarrassed. "Well, thanks, Charlotte, but . . ." He shook his head and laughed.

"But what? You're so *annoyingly* easygoing. Everything's okay with you. Aren't you even the slightest bit mad that you were shot?"

"In the ass," he pointed out. "And sure. It's a . . . pain in the ass." He laughed, but then he got sober really fast. "I thought we were going to die,

Charlie. I thought I was going to watch you bleed to death in front of me like . . .”

“Ray?” she asked softly.

“Like Ray and a lot of other good men. *Brave* men.”

“And you think *they're* the heroes,” she said. “Like James. Because they didn't come home.”

“Yes,” he said quietly. “Like James.” He cleared his throat. “We've never really talked about him. All these years, and . . . I'm the one who didn't want to talk about him. Maybe you did, and I apologize for not letting you do that.”

“Vincent . . .”

“I think we should go to Hawaii,” he told her. “It doesn't have to be part of this ceremony next December. That's fine if you don't want to do that. In fact, I think we should go before then. Soon. I think it's important for you, and frankly, it's even more important for me.”

Charlie shook her head. “I don't understand.”

His smile was so sad it nearly made her start to cry as he said, “Don't you see, Charles, I've lived his life — the life that should have been his. I want to go there and visit him and . . . well, properly pay my respects.”

“Vincent, you didn't live his life. You lived *your* life. *Our* life. You don't really think —”

“Answer this for me,” he said. “Would you have married me if you hadn't been pregnant?”

“Yes!”

“Come on, Charlotte,” he said. “All those nights when we were first married — I heard you crying.”

“My God.” Charlie was shocked. “For all these years, you've actually believed . . . ?” She stood up

613

and went to the door and called down the hall. She could be good and loud when she put her mind to it. "Joan! Is that reporter still out there? I changed my mind — will you ask him if he'd like to come to our home for an interview? This evening, at seven?"

Mary Lou Starrett's car wasn't in the driveway of her little house on Westway Drive.

Husaam Abdul-Fataah sank down low in the driver's seat and waited for her to return, listening to the news on the radio.

Twenty-four people wounded, four killed — not counting the terrorists — two of them members of the Secret Service. It was a pathetic outcome, considering two of the three weapons he'd helped smuggle onto the base had been submachine guns.

President Bryant was, of course, untouched. Husaam had pretty much assumed that would be the case, although he hadn't attempted to correct his associates' hopes. Who was he to crush their pathetic little dreams of glory? He was just the man who helped them with their plan in exchange for a generous fee.

A briefing from the White House revealed that one man concealed his weapon in a baby stroller. Another carried a lady's purse. The third had a side arm hidden beneath his jacket.

They'd been identified as Jalaal Izz Udeen, Mamdouh Ihsaan, and Ghiyaath Abdullah. Two were from Saudi Arabia and one was from Syria. All had strong al-Qaeda connections.

What a surprise.

All three had come into the country on student visas that had long since expired.

All three of the terrorists had left this earth and gone on to their heavenly reward — although there were several others in critical condition in the hospital that the authorities were planning to question in terms of a possible connection to the attack.

And that was good news. Confusion always helped. In this case it was the United States with their "No, we don't do racial profiling" promises, even as they did just that, that were muddying the waters. He was willing to bet that all of the "several others" questioned would be of Arabic descent.

While Husaam Abdul-Fataah, formerly known as Warren Canton from Lenexa, Kansas, aka Bob Schwegel, or Luke Daniels, or John Manning, or Doug Fisk, was nowhere near the list of suspects.

And he was determined to stay that way.

As Husaam watched, Sam Starrett pulled into his driveway and went inside his house. The sun was starting to set, but there was still no sign of Mary Lou.

A few minutes later, the radio announcer said that a new Pentagon briefing revealed that holes had been cut in the fence surrounding the parade grounds. The gunmen and their weapons were believed to have entered the secure area that way, directly from the Navy base. Officials believed the three men had entered the base as part of a tour group, and remained in hiding there for four, possibly five days prior to the attack.

That was uncomfortably close to the truth, and Husaam started his car and pulled away.

It was time to get out of Dodge. To keep a low profile for a while.

Mary Lou would have to wait.

Vince had to sit with part of his buttocks centered on a plastic blow-up kiddie flotation ring, which, in his eyes, lacked a certain dignity for a gentleman of his years.

To make matters worse, Charlotte was holding a press conference right there in their living room with a reporter from the *San Diego Union-Tribune*.

Joan and Mike had come over, too, although they both looked about ready to drop. Over at the hospital, they'd made Charlie the happiest grandmother in the world by announcing their plans to get married.

They now sat on the couch, holding hands.

As they all gathered there in the living room, Charlie told their entire story — Vince's quest to talk to Senator Howard about Tarawa, his illness, their friendship that became something more. She'd even told the tale of Upstairs Sally.

She spoke at great length about the unsung bravery of the Underwater Demolition Teams — UDT men — throughout the war, about the important part they'd played clearing the beaches during the Normandy invasion and their vital roles in the Pacific island-hopping campaign.

She talked about James, about her unbearable grief after losing him, about her heartache as she thought of him dying so far from home and so terribly alone.

"I wasn't looking to fall in love again," she told them, told Vince, too. She looked right at him as she spoke. "But there he was. A young man who was so very special. My mother-in-law, Edna Fletcher, loved Vince, too, right from the first moment they met.

"Well, time came for him to go off to join the UDT training down in Florida. I'm ashamed to say that I took him to the train without so much as a kiss good-bye. I cried about that all the way home. And then I cried some more when I found out he'd left behind a letter asking me again to marry him. I have it here."

Charlie opened the notebook that was in front of her, and sure enough, there was his letter, carefully saved for all these years.

He knew she'd saved James's letters. He hadn't dared to hope she'd saved his.

"May I read some of it aloud?" she asked.

"Please," the reporter said.

"I was asking my husband," she told the young man gently.

Vince nodded. God, he'd labored over that letter, trying to get it just right.

Joanie sat forward as Charlotte cleared her throat.

"Dear Charlotte,

"I love you. I've never said those words to anyone before, let alone written them down on paper, but it's true.

"I love you and I continue to hope that someday you will marry me. In fact, I'll ask you again. Will you be my wife?"

She glanced up. "Skipping forward a little . . .

"I need you to know, my dearest, that if I am to die, I

will not die alone. You are part of me now. You are in my heart. I know that you love me. I know this is true — whether you know it yourself or not. And that knowledge will be with me always. Your love for me will be my constant companion, along with my memories of the beautiful night we shared." She looked up at him, glanced at Joan, too. "Guess the cat's out of the bag about that part of the story. *It will keep me warm from now until the day I die — whether that day is tomorrow or a hundred years from tomorrow."*

Over on the couch, Mike put his arm around Joan, and she rested her head against his shoulder.

"I go willingly to this fight. I go to keep my country — and you! — safe and free. If I die, it will not be in vain. I believe this completely. And like James before me, I know you will live on. I can picture you at forty, Charles. And at sixty and even eighty, and you will still be so beautiful to me. I hope I am there to see you, to share your life and to love you until we are both old and gray. But if I am not, I hope you will have the strength to live a good life, filled with love and hope and laughter, for me.

"Always yours, and always with you, too, Vince."

Charlotte put down his letter.

She cleared her throat. "Naturally, as I read that, I cried and cried. And then I cried even more because I knew without a doubt that I'd fallen in love with this young man.

"It was different than my love for James, but in its own way it was just as strong, just as powerful, and just as wonderful.

"But I was young and foolish and I had absolutely no idea on earth what to do.

"That night Edna came into my room. My dear

618

mother-in-law. And she sat down with me and do you know what she said?"

Vince shook his head, his heart in his throat. She'd never told him this before. They'd never talked about any of it, about his letter or her decision to come to Fort Pierce to find him. He'd just accepted her into his life, assuming that her pregnancy had been what had pushed her into their marriage.

"She gave me permission to let go of James," Charlie told him. She wasn't even pretending to talk to the reporter anymore. "She told me to put him — her beloved, precious son — into the past, to remember him with love, but now to move on. She gave me permission — she used those very words — to let myself love you."

There were tears in her eyes. "She told me that if James had lived, I would've had a good life — but it would have been a hard life. James wasn't easy to live with. Like his father before him, he was selfish and demanding and never satisfied — this a mother's view of her own son! She said that James had loved me with all his heart, but that our life would have been filled — like her own had been — with battles and uphill climbs. She told me, with the wisdom of her years, that most relationships were terribly hard work, but that every so often two people meet and click and it's obvious they're meant for each other. It's clear that their life together will be a gift, filled with joy."

Over on the couch, Joan gave Mike a kiss.

"Edna told me you would bring me that joy if only I'd let you." Charlie smiled at Vince. "So I decided to let you. With yours and Edna's help, I finally buried James. Your letter brought comfort to me because now when I thought of him, I no longer imagined him dying alone. Your letter made me believe that I *was* there, with him, in his heart, right to the very end."

She turned to the reporter. "So I made arrangements to travel to Fort Pierce. It took weeks to get a seat on a train going all the way to Florida, and while I was waiting for the opportunity, I discovered that Vince and I were going to be starting that family he'd said he'd always wanted a little bit sooner than I'd anticipated.

"We were married right away, and I lived there, in Florida, with him while he completed his training.

"It was the most emotional time of my life," Charlie admitted. "As our time together grew shorter and shorter, I cried every single night because I couldn't bear the thought of being apart from him. You see, I loved him so very much.

"That time when he left, I kissed him good-bye."

She certainly had.

Vince sat on his floaty toy as the reporter asked some questions, as they all pretended not to notice that he was pretty steadily wiping the corners of his eyes.

Charlie ended the interview like a queen, standing up and sweeping the reporter out of the room and out of the house.

Joan and Mike said good night, Mike shaking Vince's hand and Joanie giving him the fiercest of hugs. After promises to have dinner and lunch in the coming week, Charlie walked them to the door.

They were alone then. She came back into the living room and sat down beside him, taking his hand. "So now — finally — you know. I can't believe you spent nearly sixty years thinking —"

Vince brought her fingers to his lips. "I was happy to be your second choice for sixty years."

"You may have come second, my dearest, but you never were my second choice. I've had a wonderful, grand, *joyous* life — just as Edna predicted."

Vince nodded. Together they'd had more than their share of good times along with the bad.

"I wouldn't change a single moment," Charlie told him.

"I might change that one time I got that stomach flu," Vince said, and she laughed.

"Okay. And I would change your mind about getting those hearing aids," she said.

"Done," he said.

She kissed him. "Thank you."

"I'd still like to go to Hawaii," Vince told her. "If it's all right with you . . ."

Charlie kissed him again, longer this time. "As long as you're there, it's all right with me."

The sound of the doorbell woke Sam from a restless sleep.

What the fuck . . . ? It was barely 0600.

Mary Lou wasn't in bed beside him, and he sat up, remembering. She'd left a note on the kitchen table. He'd found it last night when he got home.

Gone to Janine's. That was all it said. She didn't sign it, didn't address it to him. Just, *Gone to Janine's.*

The doorbell rang again, and he swung his legs

out of bed and pulled on the shorts he'd dropped right on the floor before going to sleep last night.

First time he'd done that in well over a year. If he left his clothes on the floor, Mary Lou would pick them up and put them in the laundry. He would get a pair of shorts or jeans all comfortable and then she'd go and wash them and stiffen them up again.

The doorbell rang again and again and again. Whoever was out there was really leaning on it.

"Yeah, yeah, I'm coming! Hold on!" he shouted as he headed down the hall, combing his hair out of his face with his fingers.

It made sense that Mary Lou would escape and visit her sister now, when Sam had told her they had to sit down and talk. No doubt she hoped that that impending conversation would be forgotten while she was away.

He opened the front door to find a man standing out there who was broader, taller, and blacker than Jazz Jacquette. He was an enormous man with hands like boxing gloves and a gold front tooth.

"Lieutenant Roger Starrett?" he asked.

"Yeah," Sam said, scratching the stubble on his chin.

The man opened the screen and slapped an envelope into his hands. "You've been served."

"Served?" Shit. "Hey!" Sam caught the screen door before it bounced and went outside, but the man was already halfway to his car. "What's this about?"

He didn't even turn around. "Not my business, man."

As he got into his car and pulled away, Sam opened the envelope and . . .

Holy fuck. Mary Lou had filed for divorce.

He read the damn thing again. Yes, she most certainly had.

He sat down, right on his front steps, even more exhausted than he'd felt last night. It was the strangest thing. This was what he wanted for months — for nearly two years — wasn't it? So why wasn't he dancing? Why wasn't he doing handstands?

Because of that note on the kitchen table.

Because Mary Lou had moved — that was no short visit — to fucking Florida.

And Sam was going to be lucky if he saw his daughter once a year.

And he also wasn't dancing because all those last foolish hopes he'd had of being single again and calling Alyssa had been snuffed out when he'd gone to her room and come face-to-face with Max Bhagat.

Sam went inside the house and closed the door. These days even when he won, he lost.

Joan didn't wake up until late in the morning.

Mike was still sleeping, and she lay there for a long time watching the colors and lights from the sun on the ocean play across his face.

"What am I going to do with you?" she whispered.

It was barely loud enough for her to hear, yet he opened his eyes.

Just like that he was awake. One minute, sleeping, the next, alert.

"Are you a morning person?" she asked warily.

His smile was pure sin. "I'm an any time of the day person."

Joan laughed. "That's not what I meant."

He pulled her closer, nuzzling her throat. "Yeah, but it's what I meant."

She kissed him, then pulled back to look searchingly into his eyes. "Are you really all right?"

He released her, lying back on the bed with his hands up underneath his head. "Okay," he said. "Let's have this conversation."

What was he talking about? "Which conversation?"

He sighed. "The one where you tell me that you saw me eliminate that target yesterday."

"Eliminate that target," she repeated. "Yeah, Mike. I *did* see that."

"And here I am," he said. "No different than I was before. And you don't really understand how that could be, right?"

She sat up, cross-legged. "There's a lot I don't know or understand about you. I'm looking forward to finding out all the little details, but . . ."

"But . . . ?" He was watching her with such tenderness in his eyes.

"You told me it was okay to cry," she said. "I just want to make sure that you know those same rules apply to you. I'm here if you need me. Whenever you need me."

His eyes got even softer. "Thank you, baby," he said. "I *do* know that."

Joan nodded. "Good." Next tough topic. "How are we going to deal with a bicoastal marriage?"

she asked. "I mean, how are we *really* going to make this work?"

"Your grandparents did okay," Mike pointed out. "And they didn't even get to see each other for over a year."

"They were fighting a war," Joan said.

"So are we," he said quietly.

She looked at him and didn't try to hide what she was feeling. She knew he could see fear in her eyes. "I'm afraid that you're going to die."

Mike nodded. "I'm afraid that you're going to die, too," he said. "There's lots of danger in this world. Do you know it's safer to be a SEAL than it is to ride in a car on a highway? More people die each *day* in traffic accidents than the entire list of SEAL casualties starting with Vietnam."

She had to smile. "Did you, like, look that information up on the Internet because you knew I'd freak out about this?"

"Actually, I was guessing," he said. "But it's got to be true. The number of SEALs who have died in combat and in training combined is very small. We're hard to kill, Joan."

She traced the edge of his bandage with her finger. "I know for a fact that you're not bullet-proof."

"No," he said. "We're not. We're just really good."

"So how do we deal with this marriage thing? And don't say phone sex."

"I know you like things to be planned out," Mike told her, "but yesterday was a classic example of the way we're trained to think on our feet. I think we'll be able to do the same with our marriage. If it's working, keep doing it; if it doesn't, we stop and do something else." He reached for her, pulling her on top of him. "And the first thing we should do is make love as often as possible whenever we're together."

She laughed. "I'm serious."

He kissed her. "So am I. We can have all of our conversations on the telephone, so that when we're finally together we don't have to talk — we can just make love nonstop."

She smiled. "Yeah, like I could ever shut you up. You talk more during sex than any other man in the entire world."

"Really?"

"Yes."

"That's . . . a new one for me. Am I . . . Is it obnoxious?" He was actually worried.

Joan had to laugh. "Well, gee, let me think. You tell me how much you love me. You tell me how hot you think I am. You tell me how badly you want me. You ask me to marry you . . . Nah, it's not obnoxious."

He kissed her again, and she reached for a condom.

"Kind of puts a whole new spin on, 'Baby, we need to talk,' " she said as she handed it to him.

The smile Michael gave her was worth at least a thousand words.